Tales of Tibet

"Lo, the Serpent Gods and demons
Lurk behind me stern and mighty . . ."
—The sixth Dalai Lama, as
translated by Sir Charles Bell
(Photo by Fosco Maraini)

Tales of Tibet

*Sky Burials, Prayer Wheels,
and Wind Horses*

Edited and Translated by
Herbert J. Batt

Foreword by
Tsering Shakya

ROWMAN & LITTLEFIELD PUBLISHERS, INC.
Lanham · Boulder · New York · Oxford

ROWMAN & LITTLEFIELD PUBLISHERS, INC.

Published in the United States of America
by Rowman & Littlefield Publishers, Inc.
4720 Boston Way, Lanham, Maryland 20706
www.rowmanlittlefield.com

12 Hid's Copse Road
Cumnor Hill, Oxford OX2 9JJ, England

British Library Cataloguing in Publication Information Available

Library of Congress Cataloging-in-Publication Data

Tales of Tibet : sky burials, prayer wheels, and wind horses / Herbert J. Batt.
    p. cm.—(Asian voices)
  ISBN 0-7425-0052-7 (cloth : alk. paper)—ISBN 0-7425-0053-5 (paper : alk. paper)
    1. Tales—China—Tibet. I. Title: Sky burials, prayer wheels, and wind horses. II. Batt,
Herbert J., 1945– III. Series.

GR337 .T34 2001
398.2'0951'5—dc21

                                             2001016216

Printed in the United States of America

♾™ The paper used in this publication meets the minimum requirements of
American National Standard for Information Sciences—Permanence of Paper
for Printed Library Materials, ANSI/NISO Z39.48-1992.

To the Tibetan People

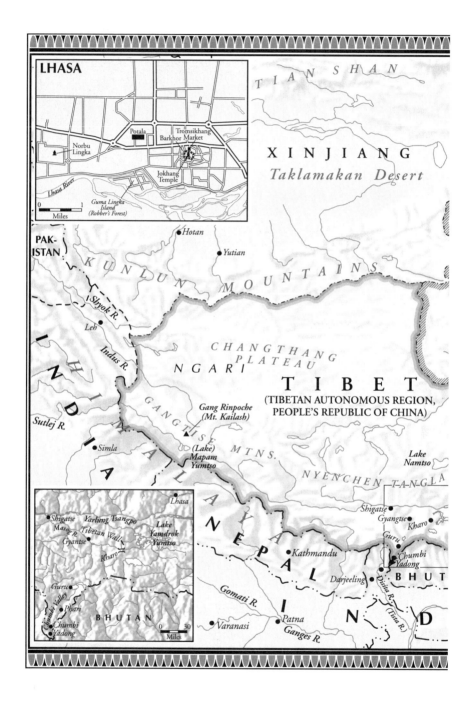

LHASA

Potala
Norbu Lingka
Tromsikhang
Barkhor Market
Jokhang Temple
Lhasa River
Guma Lingka Island
(Robber's Forest)
0   1
Miles

TIAN SHAN

XINJIANG
Taklamakan Desert

PAK-ISTAN

KUNLUN   MOUNTAINS

•Hotan
•Yutian

Shyok R.

Leh•

Indus R.

CHANGTHANG
PLATEAU

NGARI

TIBET
(TIBETAN AUTONOMOUS REGION,
PEOPLE'S REPUBLIC OF CHINA)

INDIA

GANGTISE

Gang Rinpoche
(Mt. Kailash)

MTNS.

Sutlej R.

•Simla

(Lake)
Mapam
Yumtso

Lake
Namtso

NYENCHEN TANGLA

Shigatse•
Gyangtse• •Kharo

Guru

•Lhasa

Shigatse• Yarlung Tsangpo
Masar R. Tibetan Wall
Gyantse•

Lake
Yamdrok
Yumtso

Kharo•

Guru•

Chumbi Valley

•Phari

Chumbi
Yadong

BHUTAN

0   30
Miles

HIMALAYA

NEPAL

•Kathmandu

Darjeeling•

Gomati R.

•Varanasi

•Patna

Ganges R.

Chumbi
Yadong

BHUT

Disita R.
(Tista R.)

N

D

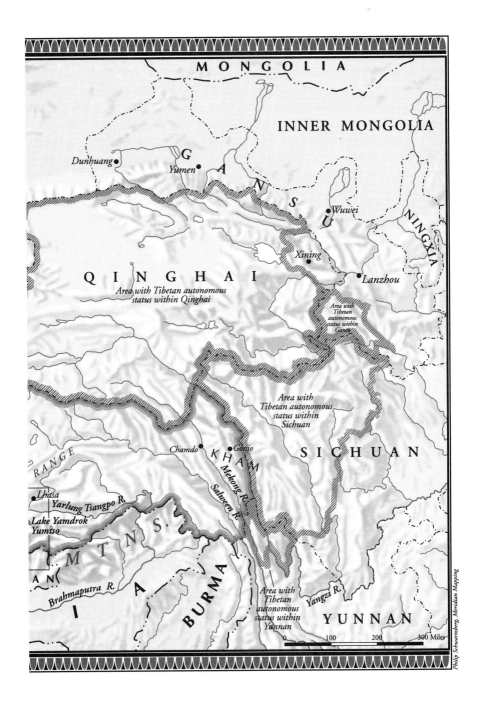

Philip Schwarzberg, Meridian Mapping

Contents

Foreword

~

Language, Literature, and Representation in Tibet

Tsering Shakya

The Politics of Language

There are two very important features to this collection of stories, a volume that has literary interest and signifies the shifting terrain of Chinese rule in Tibet. "Tibet" has become a literary inspiration among Chinese writers and intellectuals: this in itself is very significant. Despite the centuries of connection between China and Tibet, as far as I am aware, Tibetans were never featured as a subject in mainstream Chinese literature. This is not to say that there are no Chinese narrative texts on Tibet; in fact, a wealth of material exists. However, there is a clear distinction between the early narratives and the present construction of narrative texts about Tibet. Early works dealt with politics, religion, diplomacy, and history. There are numerous historical and religious texts from the earliest period of the Tang Dynasty to the Qing period. These imperial texts result from the political and historical intercourse between the two countries, while the present literature deals mainly with works of imagination grounded on very different premises. The incursion of Tibet as a subject into Chinese fiction is very recent, and has largely been brought about through the recent assertion of Chinese political rule and the introduction of Tibet into Chinese nationalist thought as integral to "the motherland." In recent years, the large-scale migration of Chinese into the Tibet Autonomous Region and other Tibetan-speaking areas in Kham and Amdo as administrators, teachers, cadres, technical experts, and traders has given a new grounding to China's presence there.

The Tibetans were aware of Chinese culture and literature from an early period. The Tang poets Bai Juyi, Li Bai, and Du Fu depict the Tibetans as a formidable adversary of the Tang. In the seventh century A.D., the Tibetan Emperor Srongtsan Gampo took the Tang Princess Wencheng as one of a number of queens. Both Tibetan and Chinese sources state that in 730 the princess requested Chinese classics such as the *Shi Jing, Zuo Zhuan*, and *Wen Xuan* to be sent to Tibet. The princess also encouraged Tibetan nobles to send their sons to study the Chinese classics. Chinese sources claim that in the early period, the Tibetan court used Chinese as the official language of correspondence. However, Tang records show that the Chinese were reluctant to give these classics to the Tibetans, their fierce enemies; the Tang envoy compared this to "giving weapons to brigands or one's possessions to thieves." The sources claim that Emperor Srongtsan dispatched four bright young Tibetans to study in Changan, the Tang Dynasty capital. Tibetans were also attracted and influenced by the Chan school of Buddhism, and a number of Chinese Buddhist texts were translated into Tibetan.

However, the Chinese language never achieved in Tibet the dominance that the Sanskrit language did. We have very little evidence of mass translation from Chinese into Tibetan being carried out, whereas much of the Buddhist canon was based on original Sanskrit works. Even if Chinese texts were translated, they remained on the periphery of Tibetan intellectual life during most centuries.

From the time of the introduction of Buddhism into Tibet from the early seventh to the tenth century, the only language of intellectuals was Sanskrit, which Tibetan scholars studied and knew well. As the vernacular language was established as a literary medium, the need to master Sanskrit seems to have slowly waned. Despite the establishment of a Buddhist stronghold in Tibet and the adoption of Buddhism as the state religion, Tibetans never replaced their native language. In fact, there seems to have been an instinctive desire to promote Tibetan both as a literary vehicle and as the language of religion. No attempt to promote Sanskrit as the only language of the sacred was made: there was never a perception that Sanskrit was the natural and only language capable of carrying the message. Although there was a deep reverence for Sanskrit, the Tibetans' attitude toward Sanskrit seems to have been driven by practical considerations: the need to translate Buddhist texts into their native language.

Even in Eastern Tibet, that is, Kham or Amdo, in the hinterland of the Chinese and Tibetan border, very few Tibetans spoke Chinese, and even fewer could read and write in Chinese. As late as the 1930s, only a tiny minority spoke Chinese, which was the practical language of commerce in the border areas. Most of the people spoke their regional dialects and wrote in standard Tibetan.

However, this monolingual situation was totally disrupted with the imposition of colonial rule in Tibet. The language of the Chinese colonizer was imposed as a language of control and domination. The development of the use of Chinese is comparable to the hegemony of English and other imperial languages of the West in colonized territories in Asia and Africa. Today, the colonial nature of the linguistic situation is glaringly obvious. Most educated Tibetans are bilingual, and the education system has ensured the dominance of Chinese as the language of knowledge and administration.

These two facts—the appropriation of the colonists' language by the Tibetans and the construct of Tibet in Chinese texts—pose interesting questions about the discursive practices emerging in Tibet. There is a clear parallel between the situation there and the formation of literature and language under Western colonial rule in Asia and Africa, where the ruler's language replaced and influenced native discursive practices. Given the social–political–military bases of Chinese rule in Tibet, the texts being produced can best be classed as "colonialist literature." In view of the emotive connotation of such a term, many would see this as political condemnation. However, it is necessary to detach the term from its pejorative connotations and see it as a description of a situation, where the matrix of sociolinguistic inequality is a reflection of the power relationships evident in Tibet. The material bases of colonial rule are undoubtedly founded on military, technological, and coercive power.

However, colonial imposition of Chinese as the language of power and administration has not eliminated native literature and language. In fact, there is a growing resurgence of literature, and all the evidence indicates that the Tibetan language has not been replaced. Tibetans show a deep emotional and practical concern for their native language, and texts produced in Chinese are in the minority, with most Tibetan writers continuing to produce works in their native language. The Tibetans' attitude to the colonizer's language is instrumental and practical: it is accepted that there are certain deficiencies in their native language, but this is not to imply that they believe that it is intrinsically inferior. This attitude is based on a pragmatic consideration, namely that in the field of social sciences, physical science, and other technical areas the Chinese have had a far longer period of development and modification, and therefore they are more advanced in dealing with technical subjects.

Another consideration is that many see acquisition of Chinese as a means of educational advancement and also as a window to the outside world. This is not only the case inside occupied Tibet: refugee groups living in India or in the West master English for the same purpose. This attitude is molded by objective factors and by the material conditions faced by all Tibetans. Today, most of the educated classes are bilingual, using Tibetan as a literary language and imbibing influences through Chinese. Contemporary Tibetan writers demonstrate considerable knowledge of Western literature, albeit read in Chinese translations. They are familiar with, and quote copiously, the works of great nineteenth-century French, Russian, and English realist writers such as Guy de Maupassant, Nikolai Gogol, and Charles Dickens. Much of the new Tibetan literature is influenced by the genre of realism, which is seen as suitable for apprehending the present reality in Tibet.

Chinese has become the second language of the new professional cadre class, doctors, engineers, banking officials, telecommunications personnel, and scientists, who use a mixture of their native language and Chinese, the language of power. However, they continue to use their native tongue as the language of home and community. In the lower levels of administration, Tibetan is used, and in rural areas administration is conducted entirely in the native language, while higher up the pyramid of power the Chinese language dominates. Similar situations exist in the education system.

The formation of linguistic disparities and the establishment of Chinese as the dominant language owe much to the education system that is emerging in Tibet today. While in most areas Tibetan still remains the primary language of education, at the lower levels of the education system, in fact, rural schools only have resources for teaching basic Tibetan writing and reading. Students soon realize that there are limits to their own, lived, language and that constraints are imposed by the colonial education system. The higher up the educational scale, the further the contradictions deepen, and the student finds that knowledge of the language of the colonizer is a prerequisite for attending colleges and universities. This issue, and the choice of the language of education, is the subject of hot debate among Tibetans, with no easy solution in sight. The privileging of Chinese is an inevitable result of the actual material condition of Tibet and its past failures in reform and innovation. This inherent condition has been compounded further by the assertion of hegemonic rule from Beijing, which has both destroyed the precapitalist peasant mode of production and replaced it with the state-centered economic structure. Today, there are new erasures in the socioeconomic fabric of Tibet as the state imposes a market capital-centered economy. In this process, the indigenous economy will be either obliterated or marginalized. The native economy is still essentially based on subsistence farming or nomadism, and it either does not allow for a means of exchange on the market-oriented economy or is limited by its inability to produce items of value for exchange in the wider market. As in any colonial situation, material power has been translated into moral and metaphysical superiority.

During the period between 1960 and 1976, Tibetan culture was assaulted on all levels, and the people experienced a profound sense of dislocation. It is beyond the scope of this short introduction to carry out an exegesis of this entire period. It is sufficient to say that the nature of cultural and literary production was altered, with literary engagement primarily serving the colonial strategy of containment, assimilation, and indoctrination. Indigenous literary production was destroyed, and language became merely an instrument carrying the colonizer's message; nothing else was permitted. However, after the death of Mao Zedong in 1976, the ascendancy of Deng Xiaoping in the late 1970s and early 1980s brought fundamental changes to China as a whole. Tibet was no exception. One of the most innovative results of the reforms was the limited freedom afforded to writers and artists.

Writing Back to the Motherland

Throughout China, the early 1980s saw a flowering of creative talent, and the intellectual community was swift to burst out in a "cultural fever." This surge of cultural innovation was also reflected in Tibet, which, however, took a divergent line. On the one hand, many older scholars, lamas, and rinpoches (incarnate lamas) felt that their newfound freedom should be utilized to recover and salvage what had been lost. The destruction and dislocation of the previous periods, particularly during the Cultural Revolution, had profoundly affected the body of Tibetan literature. The monastic and private libraries are now unrecoverable, and it is unlikely that we will ever know the extent of what has been lost or destroyed. However, the early 1980s saw the reprinting of old Tibetan texts. The publishing renaissance brought about a new impetus for publications in the Tibetan language and made many texts accessible to a larger audience.

For the first time, Tibetans were able to exploit new printing technology for dissemination of Tibetan texts.

Parallel to the growth of publications in Tibetan, an increasing number of younger Tibetan writers were working in Chinese. It is interesting to note that when the first Tibetan-language literary journal, *bod kyi rstom rig rgyu tsal* (Tibetan Literature and Arts), was established in the 1980s, the editor noted that they could not find a single Tibetan contributor, and more surprisingly, they were unable to locate any Tibetan text written in the previous ten years. The first issue of the journal was comprised of four short stories, "skal zang me tog" (Auspicious Flower), "dbyang chen" (Yangchen), "pha yul gyi sa" (Soil of the Native Land), and "sdi dbang gis gson pa'i mi" (An Honored Person), which all had been written in Chinese and then translated into Tibetan. These stories had been written several years before and already published in Chinese magazines. The primary aim of these early stories, written in Chinese about Tibet by Tibetans, was to move Chinese readers and to provide moral justification for the liberation of Tibet. Inevitably, the stories are about the "dark period" of feudal exploitation that prevailed in Tibet before the "liberation" of Tibet by the "People." These stories had been published widely in Chinese periodicals and also read in schools. The fact that they were written by Tibetans lent them authenticity: they were seen as the muted voice of the Tibetan serfs speaking against oppressive feudalism.

The texts of the early generation of Tibetan writers primarily focused on the crimes of the old and dark period of Tibetan "feudal" society and the miserable lives of the serfs. A typical example is Jamphel Gyatso's "gesang meiduo" (An Auspicious Flower) and Yeshi Tenzin's "xincun de ren" (The Defiant Ones). Both narratives rely on a dramatization of the colonizer's definition of Tibet. As noted before, the author's ethnic origin was seen as a confirmation of the correctness of the Chinese view of Tibet. These texts are written in a crude socialist-realist style, purporting to depict the "real lived experience" of the Tibetan self. The language and style merge in melodrama, with exaggerated characterization; the language is flowery and interspersed with party and socialist rhetoric. The narrative invokes powerful emotions and rage against feudal exploitation. In such texts, there is nothing positive in Tibet, and the reader is left with a sense of the legitimacy of the colonizer's civilizing mission and the benevolence of the Communist Party.

Here, literature's purpose is merely as a tool of Communist Party propaganda. The party's ideology and the usefulness of the literature in serving the party's goal determine the truth of the text. Tibetan readers, clearly aware of the ideological determinant of the text, read it as an official text with a certain detachment and degree of mirth. At the mass level, Tibetans see these texts as a product of those who have sold out to the Chinese, individual writers ingratiating themselves with all-powerful rulers. The dark and negative images of Tibet in the narrative are seen as a betrayal of one's own people and tradition.

If the earlier texts are overtly propagandistic, the later texts in this collection attest to a certain shift in style and content. The stories by the Tibetan authors Yangdon, Alai, and Sebo are free from overt party propaganda. This reflects the general relaxation in party policies toward minority groups and in particular toward art and literature. After the Third Plenum of its Eleventh Central Committee, the party allowed a degree of autonomy that freed writers from the militant ideological constraints of the past. Writers were allowed to explore more subjective issues, and there was no demand for an absolute fidelity to party norms.

This newfound freedom is evident in the subject matter and style of the writing that subsequently emerged in China and Tibet. The writings of Tibetan authors in this collection are interesting for a number of points. On the surface, one is immediately struck by the absence of the crude characterizations that dominated earlier writings. There are no clear-cut villainous serf owners and downtrodden serfs, and no obligatory references to the PLA as liberators.

Another important point is the time and location of the narrative. In earlier stories there is a clear delineation of past and present, with the past defined as "before liberation" and the present as the period of liberation. The past is portrayed as dark and negative, while the present is glorious and the future even brighter. It is clear that the younger generations of Tibetan writers in this collection have discarded the crude dyad of the brutish past and the happy present. Their texts reveal much in that they signify the rejection of the colonizer's linear view of history. In their understanding, the present is more meaningful, and their texts attempt to situate Tibet in the present.

More significantly, when we compare the chosen narrative style of the Chinese and Tibetan authors, there is a clear divide. Both Ma Jian and Ma Yuan write in a mythic style, while Tibetan writers in this collection write in a realist style. I would argue that the chosen style reflects the writer's ideological framing of Tibet and relates to differences in the discursive practices between colonizer and the colonized. The preference for realism among Tibetan authors is not accidental. If we take Georg

Lukács's definition of realism as a genre concerned with the present and showing the tension between the individual and the society, for the Tibetan authors it becomes a means of dealing with the present-day problems of man-in-society. Sebo's "The Circular Day" is a typical example. The surface narrative concerns the universal theme of the parent–child relationship—a young girl's demand for the latest fashion and the mother's wish to fulfill her child's desire. The mother labors to find the tracksuit for her child, only to find that it has been sold out. This story is repeated all over the world, with children demanding the latest astronomically priced Nike sneakers or Pokémon cards, sending parents scurrying into shopping malls and high streets, only to find that they cannot find the exact object desired by the child or that the shop has run out.

Yet, Sebo provides a twist to his story, with its narrative concerned with the current "socialist market economy" and the party-promoted get-rich-quick mentality. The avaricious desire for material wealth and commercialization is rebuked, and the narrator at the end incongruously places the object of desire on the body of a beggar. The ill-fitting suit is nothing more than an object of mockery. Sebo's story fits in well with Lukács's idea of critical realism. Here, the narrative becomes a social commentary on the present. The Tibetan writers chose to write in this manner as a means of apprehending present reality. The stories by Geyang and Yangdon employ a similar style and utilize similar subject matter, attempting to position Tibet within the realms of everyday or lived experience, a mundane world of family, individual desire, and the larger constraints of the social world.

Geyang's "An Old Nun Tells Her Story" is narrated in the first person, and the final paragraph contains these words: "As we tell each other the stories of our lives, everything we've suffered becomes something beautiful." The idea of telling stories is important for Tibetan writers; after all, they have lived through tremendous changes. The telling of tales becomes a means of articulating one's resistance. It may not be an overt voice of resistance, yet it is evident there is a line of resistance, as there is a calling for the recognition of the humanness of the Tibetan body. Walter Benjamin noted that the storyteller tells from his experience; by doing so, the teller "makes it the experience of those who are listening to his tale." The idea that a text entices the readers into the world of the narrator becomes problematic in the case of these Tibetan writers. We may ask, to whom are they writing? With the shift from a literary to a sociological question, the text becomes problematic. The deeper problem of ethics and the psychological impact of a text was best expressed by the great Indian writer Raja Rao, in the foreword to his novel English-language *Kan-thanpura* (1938): "One has to convey in a language that is not one's own the spirit that is one's own." Whether the Tibetan writers in this collection, writing in the Chinese language, are confronted with such a crisis of conscious or not, we cannot tell. However, the entwining of language and narrative has become a burning issue among Tibetan writers and critics. In 1987, two influential articles appeared in *bod ljongs zhib 'jug* (Tibetan Studies) arguing that the literature of Tibet could only be written in the Tibetan peoples' native language. The first article, by Sangya (sangs rgyas), appeared in issue number one of *Tibetan Studies*. The bold title of the paper itself is indicative of its content: "Creation of a Modern Tibetan Literature Must Be Based Definitely on Tibetan Language" (bod rigs kyi gsar rtsom byed na nges par du bod kyi skad dang yi ger brten dgos). In the next issue, an article appeared by Sonam (bsod nams), entitled "A Discussion of the Characteristics of a Nationality and Tibetan Literature" (rtsom rig gi mi rigs khyad chos dang bod rigs rtsom rig skor gleng ba). Both of these authors make a passionate appeal, arguing strongly that the psychology (sems kham) and consciousness ('du shis) of Tibetans cannot be rendered in Chinese and that to attempt to do so will result only in distortion. Sangya's article argues that language and culture are commensurate so that the representation of Tibet in a foreign text can only render Tibet incomprehensible. Sonam describes writing in Chinese as trying to attach a deer's antlers to the head of an ox (glang gi mgo la sha ba'i ra bzhin). Although both articles lack rigor and remain logically unconvincing, their sentiments highlight the nature of a growing debate among Tibetans.

I do not wish to go into the details of the complex arguments presented in the articles. It is sufficient to say that they object to the use of the Chinese language in writing Tibetan literature on a number of counts. On a pragmatic level, definition and classification present problems. The two articles reject the idea that texts written in Chinese are representative of Tibetan literature. In China, the official categories of "Nationalities' Literature" and "Tibetan Literature" are classifications expressed purely in ethnic terms. Much of this class of literature is in fact written in Chinese, while texts in the native language are often ignored and do not gain the same degree of attention. Tibetan authors who write in Chinese are often valorized and patronized by the state and promoted as the authentic voice of the people. In this, there is a strong element of the dominant group's condescension to the ruled group's success in assimilating the culture of the rulers. Tibetan-language writers are seldom known outside the small circle of Tibetan readers and thus are marginalized. For example, literary prizes given by the state so far have been awarded only to texts written in Chinese. It is right for Tibetans to feel that such categorizations erase and marginalize texts produced in their native language.

The Tibetans recognize that this concerns the community of readers. After all, Chinese texts have a much larger circulation, and also come to the attention of party leaders, while Tibetan texts have only a limited circulation within the confines of the Tibetan-speaking population. The illiteracy rate among Tibetans is extremely high; consequently, the reading public is tiny. However, it is not the material facts about circulation that anger the Tibetans. Critics such as Sangya and Sonam object to the assumptions about categorization and labels that lead to texts produced in Chinese being considered representative of Tibetan literature. The issue is certainly not unique to Tibet; similar debates take place in many other situations where a dominant language encroaches on the native language. Similar positions are raised by Indian critics, who object to the assumption that Indian literature is represented by texts written in English.

Sangya admits, however, that there may be some benefits in writing in Chinese: for example, the wider readership such a text receives. Making a concession to the official line, he couches this argument in party rhetoric, saying that these texts "serve the cause of the nationality" by providing an authentic image of Tibet. The idea that a text in the metropolitan language is able to speak to the dominant group has been prevalent in postcolonial discourse. The very act of construction of a text in an imposed language is seen as the recovery of agency and writing back to the center, with native writers ushering in a new discursive practice and disrupting the colonizer's narrative. Edward Said calls this the voyage in. It is a journey to wage a discourse against the dominant group and transform the discursive practices of the hegemonic power.

In this context of writing to the center, there is an appeal to the universality and humanity of the Tibetan self. In Geyang's story, the narrator speaks in the first person, in the end asserting "I'm a common, ordinary person" and going on to say "I've chosen an ordinary way to spend my remaining years." The texts by Tibetan authors in this collection strive to present an image of Tibet that is "ordinary." In Yangdon's "A God without Gender," the description of the immediate surroundings and the pace of the narrative emphasizes the slow unfolding of people's daily lives. The picture of lived experience and ordinariness is surely as powerful as Shylock's pathos.

It is interesting that in the stories by Geyang and Yangdon the depiction of religion and religious figures is almost positive: there is no attempt to show religion as a negative influence on Tibetan society. In Geyang's story, a nun, despite having become pregnant, is not presented as an example of the evils of religion. In old age, the protagonist returns to the nunnery and announces that she has "found serenity." There is a directness here, almost a moral narrative, which is quite refreshing. However, when we contrast the treatment of religion and clerical figures in Tibetan short stories and texts produced in Chinese by Tibetan writers today with those produced in Tibetan, we find that in the Tibetan-language texts, religion is invariably presented in a negative light and religious figures become the villains of the piece.

This is not really as perplexing as it appears on the surface. The party's control over texts produced in Tibetan is far greater than that over those produced in Chinese. The party still sees Tibetan texts as communicating with the masses and regards literature as a vehicle for propaganda. The authorities view Chinese texts as evidence of assimilation and acknowledgment of the superiority of the colonial language, and, as a result, a lesser degree of control is asserted. There are differences between the addresser and addressee: while texts constructed in Chinese address the metropolitan reader, texts in the native language are aimed at the Tibetan people. What the natives are saying to each other comes under greater surveillance.

In the early 1980s, the freeing of intellectuals and writers from absolute obedience to the party released writers and artists from the strictures of realism favored by the authorities. There was a new hunger among Chinese writers and artists to explore wider subject matter and styles, and a rush of artists turned to the minorities to fill their canvases. Prior to Deng's reforms the minorities were uniformly depicted as infants gratefully receiving the benevolence of the party; both in arts and in literature, Tibetans and other minorities were seen as innocent children, contented and happy in the embrace of the party. The "bosom of the motherland" became the metaphor for the containment of minorities within the scope and nourishment of the party.

There is a similarity between texts produced under Western imperialism and the texts that are being fashioned by the Chinese about Tibet.

The conquest of the colonized land is followed up by an ideology of containment that subsumes the texts of the subject people. In the texts produced by Chinese authors in this collection, Tibet is inscribed as the antithesis of the Chinese self. The binary opposition between Tibet and China is symbolized in Ma Yuan's "Vagrant Spirit" as a mold for a coin with a Tibetan inscription on one side and a Chinese inscription on the other. The search for a means to cement the two sides of the mold becomes an impossible task, and the two are never united. Even more telling is the narrator's comment in "A Fiction." As he is about to depart from the leper colony, he states, "Although we're contemporaries and live on the same planet, our worlds are cut off from each other. They are abandoned children. That's putting it cruelly, but it's true."

Ma Yuan's Machu village is an allegory for Tibet. In fact, we can go further and posit that Machu is a metonym for Tibet, in that Machu and Tibet are seen as one, and the two are inscribed in the same perceptual domain. The leper's diseased body is slowly decaying; there is no cure for the illness but the extinction of the group. For the narrator, Tibet is a putrid body, lacking vitality, degenerate, and slowly decaying in its own filth. As quoted earlier, as the narrator leaves Machu, he enunciates his final judgment that "They are abandoned children." Tibetans have been abandoned by time; they are children not in the sense of innocence, but as underdeveloped, irrational, and uneducated possessors of a child's mind.

The texts are the product of the colonizer's certainty of his mission. There is no questioning of the rightness of the colonizer's right to rule. It is only in Yan Geling's "A Blind Woman Selling Red Apples" that we see a hint of doubt. The story describes a hot spring, which is now under the control of the military, who have restricted the Tibetans' access to it. The narrator tells us that "the spring's had been theirs [the Tibetans'], and they'd soaked at it to their heart's content, and didn't have to wash in somebody else's bathwater." However, the narrator reverses this situation at the end, when the blind woman is shown washing in a filthy pond. The implication is that the natives are blind to the filth that immerses them and are incapable of recognizing the dirt that surrounds them. The story ends with the blind Tibetan woman being mocked by the Chinese driver as she rushes to get on the truck. The driver pulls away, and the blind woman is left falling to the ground. Are we meant to laugh at the driver's trick, or are we to raise our hands in horror? Sitting among the truck's Chinese passengers, the narrator writes, "We kept as silent as a load of freight." Does this show the indifference or the powerlessness of the narrator?

Since 1990, there have been fewer stories written about Tibet by Chinese authors. This is explained somewhat by the partial waning of the burst of creativity in Chinese literature and arts that had gripped China in the 1980s. Today, Ma Jian and Yan Geling live abroad and continue to write. Ma Yuan continues to live in China but has ceased writing. As for Tibetan writers, the situation is much more complicated. State control over what they can write is far greater than over what Chinese writers can produce, for various reasons. It must be pointed out that literary innovation in Tibet is still in its infancy. There is no doubt that Tibetan writers have much to write; they have had unique experiences and much to say about them. What is really interesting is that a growing number of Tibetans are experimenting and choosing to appropriate the imposed language as their medium of creative expression.

* * *

Tsering Shakya is a Fellow in Tibetan Studies at the School of Oriental and African Studies, University of London, and author of *The Dragon in the Land of Snows: A History of Modern Tibet Since 1947* (Columbia University Press, 1999).

Acknowledgments

This collection would never have come to be without the help of a great many people. I am indebted to those in China who assisted me with my translations, especially Zhao Gancheng and Zhu Guanya, and those who helped me in Canada, especially Fu Lijun and Cai Yongchun. Thanks to Yangdon Dhondup for the romanization of Tibetan words, to Henry Zhao, Cheng Yongxin, and Zhu Liyun for their recommendations of texts for translation, and to Tsering Shakya for his foreword. My gratitude to Arnie Achtman, Barry Fluxgold, Sylvia Warsh, Ian McKercher, Breandan O'Croinin, Sheldon Zitner, and Cecilia Kennedy for their many constructive suggestions; to Ann-Marie Gutierrez for help in selecting photos; to my editors, Mark Selden for his supportive criticisms and Susan McEachern for her listening ear; and to my mother Mary Batt and my cousin Catherine O'Donnell for their patient support. Finally, a great portion of thanks is due to one who is no longer here to receive it, my dear deceased friend Gertrude Roland. In 1985 Gertrude introduced me to Zhao Gancheng, who became my Chinese teacher. For our class one day Zhao gave me Ma Yuan's "Youshen," the story that enticed me into the fictional land the reader is about to enter.

Introduction

Herbert J. Batt

$\mathcal{T}$his landmark volume is the first collection of fiction on Tibet by Tibetan and Chinese writers published in the English-speaking world. Tibetan writers depict their ancient Buddhist culture threatened with extinction under the Chinese regime. Chinese writers portray this endangered Tibetan culture as a spiritual alternative to their own Chinese culture, overrun by rational materialism from the West. In translation from their original Chinese texts, these authors, men and women, lead us to a numinous land above the clouds.

In the opening scene of Ma Yuan's "Vagrant Spirit" a Tibetan beggar named Chimi pulls from his shirt a bag of twenty-seven antique silver coins and tells the narrator that ten years ago he sold his great mansion in return for these rare coins. Later the young woman who lives in the mansion tells the narrator that her husband "was born in this house. He says this house has been passed down in his family for nearly two centuries." Which story is true?

The stories in this collection abound with unresolved questions and paradoxes. Ma Yuan's "A Ballad of the Himalayas" ends with Norbu the guide telling the narrator the story of how the little hunter stabbed himself in the eyes. "You mean," Norbu asks the narrator, "you didn't notice he's blind?" But if he is blind, how could the little hunter have shot the snow cock? Ugyen in Tashi Dawa's "The Glory of a Wind Horse" spends his life trying to kill the son of his father's murderer . . . he hunts the man down and stabs him . . . the police catch him—he is tried and executed for murder . . . then he wakes up in his friend's tent . . . the phone (it's not hooked up) rings. . . . it's his victim, phoning him. . . . Tibetan author Tashi

1

Dawa likens his magic realism to the style of ancient Tibetan chronicles: realistic narrative intertwined with fantasy. At the end of "The Glory of a Wind Horse" the victim has not been killed . . . the executed murderer has not died . . . all the action is an illusion. . . . The story's time has gone round full circle, and nothing has happened. This, Tashi Dawa explains, is the vision of time in Tibetan Buddhism.

Chinese authors like Ma Yuan adopt this Tibetan circular time frame. Ma Yuan entitles the final chapter of his "Vagrant Spirit" "The End or the Beginning." At the close of the story Chimi the vagrant Tibetan beggar, spinning his prayer wheel, does not recognize his old friend—"It seems he doesn't recognize me anymore—just as if he never knew me," exclaims the surprised Chinese narrator. This Buddhist concept of circular time stands in contrast to the Western rationalist linear time. In the Tibetan author Sebo's "The Circular Day," the sun's movement across the sky delineates Buddhist time's circle. Mother and daughter go out shopping for a tracksuit in the morning, but return home empty-handed at night. The flight after new consumer goods is futile. Economic transformations come to naught, and the world never changes.

The artistic community of Lhasa in the 1980s was a place of fluid exchange between Chinese and Tibetan artists. During this decade—the high point of literary creativity in the People's Republic of China—Ma Yuan lived in Lhasa, where he knew the Tibetan authors Tashi Dawa and Sebo. Another Chinese writer, Ma Jian, trekked for three months through Tibet, like the narrator of his story "The Weevil." In the early 1970s, at the age of twelve, Yan Geling traveled through Tibet as a performer in a traveling army song and dance troupe, entertaining Chinese soldiers stationed there—as does the narrator of her story "A Blind Woman Selling Red Apples." Ge Fei wrote "Encounter" after a two-month visit to Lhasa in 1986. The Chinese writers in this collection introduce new subjects into Chinese literature with Tibetan motifs.

Ge Fei's "Encounter" is a fictionalized account of the British invasion of Tibet in 1904. The British commander Younghusband, a rationalist who commands modern Western military technology, defeats the medieval Tibetan army, and occupies Lhasa. But in the final scene he is ordered to withdraw, with the voice of the Tibetan abbot, who has fasted to death, ringing in his ears. The abbot has somehow mysteriously defeated Younghusband, who leaves Tibet, with the abbot's voice resounding in his ears: "The earth is not round. It is a triangle, like the shoulder bone of a sheep." Modern Western scientific rationalism meets with defeat at the hands of Tibet's premodern, religious nonrationalism.

Sometimes a particular theme epitomizes the concerns of an age, and inspires its greatest literature—as the theme of revenge in late Elizabethan and Jacobean England inspired *Hamlet*, *Othello*, and *The Duchess of Malfi*. The theme of Tibet crystallizes many of the most important issues that confronted China in the 1980s. The Chinese writers in this volume portray a mysterious, nonrational Tibet, a locus of alternative values, a philosophical counterpole of the Western techno-mercantile rationalism that has begun to flood China in the post-Mao era. Ge Fei and Ma Yuan present in their fictional portrayals of Tibet an alternative vision of the future of China, a view that rejects the rational materialist premise of today's Chinese neonationalists and espouses instead traditional Asian spiritual values.

The stories in this volume illuminate rich details of Tibetan life: incarnate lamas, prayer wheels, prayer flags, wind horses, tsampa, barley beer. Ma Yuan's "A Ballad of the Himalayas" ends with a sky burial, the traditional Tibetan funeral rite, in which the dead body is sliced to pieces and eaten by vultures. By exploring a Tibetan culture that many Chinese would consider barbaric, our Chinese narrators escape from the strict rationalism of post-Enlightenment Western culture; the setting of Tibet becomes a way of return to traditional religious views of the world, Daoist for Ma Yuan, Buddhist for Ge Fei. Their stories develop in modern literary forms their understanding of the spirituality of Tibetan Buddhism.

In their Chinese characters, Chinese authors in this volume reflect the contrast between a Westernizing, materialist China and a Tibet of Buddhist spirituality. In "Vagrant Spirit," Ma Yuan's narrator conceals from us the fact that he, the narrator, has bribed the Tibetan beggar to steal the coin-mold, a treasure of ancient Tibetan culture, but the Tibetan beggar spurns the crooked Chinese narrator's bribe. It is the Tibetan who is honest and preserves his integrity. In Ge Fei's "Encounter," the Chinese character is impotent to resist the West: Chinese official Master He makes friends with a Scottish missionary, a tainted friendship that leads to the Chinese official's destruction. The story's spiritual hero is the Tibetan abbot who defeats the modern technology of the invading British with the mysterious power of Buddhist spirituality. Ma Yuan and Ge Fei present in their work a conflict between Western rationalism and Tibetan nonrationalism; the moral stature of their Chinese characters declines as they reject the Tibetan Buddhist perspective that the stories develop.

In depicting Tibet as a fictional kingdom of the spirit, Chinese writers like Ma Yuan and Ge Fei are influenced by writers of Tibetan nationality like Tashi Dawa, Sebo, and Yangdon. Tibetan Buddhism is a central theme of Yangdon's "A God without Gender." The main character, a young girl, is described sometimes in first-person narration, sometimes in the third person; her story is interspersed with Buddhist legends, Buddhist prayers, and songs. She appears now in her mother's home, now in a nunnery, coming to us in so many different roles that the reader may have difficulty recognizing in all these kaleidoscopic personae the identical person. Just as she cannot at first even recognize her own mother, we readers cannot always recognize the heroine. The author calls into question the very notion of personality—as does Buddhism. Ultimately, "A God without Gender" conveys the Buddhist doctrine that all our perceptions of ourselves and of the cosmos are a dream. At the close of the story, the Chinese servant-man's song sounds in the mind of the young Tibetan heroine. The boundary between the two characters dissolves. The reverberation of the Chinese man's song within the Tibetan nun's mind shows us that she has attained the paramount Buddhist virtue, compassion—comprehending the Chinese man's view of life, embodied in his song.

In the Tibetan writers' work, Tibet emerges as a mysterious land of spirituality. The Chinese writers make of this nonrational Tibet an alternative model for a China in cultural turmoil. Traditional Chinese culture, after the ravages of the Cultural Revolution, faces a tidal wave of rationalist Western techno-mercantilism propelled by international capital. Chinese writers Ma Yuan and Ge Fei adapt the Tibetan motifs of their Tibetan colleagues, describing their Chinese characters who explore Tibet where the spirituality of the East endures.

· 1 ·

Vagrant Spirit

Ma Yuan

> He knew his task now was to dream. In the middle of the night
> he awoke with a start to a bird's mournful cry.
>
> —Jorge Luis Borges, "The Circular Ruins"

(i) Lord Chimi the Second

For my readers' sake, I'd like to shift the dates of this story from the Tibetan calendar to the international calendar. My story is short, but it covers a long period of time.

He's a character from the Barkhor in Lhasa.[1] He has no job, no notion of looking for one. He's the main character of my story. He's my friend. His name is Chimi. I don't exactly know his age, but I guess it's somewhere between twenty-seven and seventy-two.

How Chimi and I got to know each other—that's another story. I won't go into it here. It all happened by chance.

Chimi is poor, really poor, one of whom it can truly be said he has nothing—no wife, no family at all, not even the ability to work. He's a cripple. One side of his body is deformed: his mouth is twisted, his left eye looks askew, his left leg is lame, and his left hand is clutched in front of his chest like a chicken claw.

That a Tibetan like Chimi speaks Mandarin Chinese—that's nothing surprising. What's remarkable is that he speaks fluent English. He's one of the vast swarm of beggars on the Barkhor. But Chimi doesn't sit

---

1. See the inset of Lhasa on the map at the front of the book.

there intoning Buddhist sutras, or spinning a prayer wheel—doesn't seem like a Buddhist at all. He's the old Barkhor itself. He claims he's lived on Lhasa's main street for a hundred and ninety years, and that five generations of his ancestors lived there before him.

He took me into the second alley off the Barkhor's seventh corner. Twenty meters down we came to the great gate of a house with a big courtyard. He said it used to be his family's, that his great-great-great-grandfather bought it for twenty-seven silver Tibetan coins, that inside there's a two-story stone house, that ten years ago he sold it all for twenty-seven Tibetan silver coins.

"That was what my great-great-great-grandfather commanded in his will. His name was Chimi too, so, according to the English custom, you should call me—ha! ha!—"

Chimi is really cute when he laughs—his whole face becomes perfectly symmetrical.

"Lord Chimi the Second."

"Okay, Lord Chimi the Second." I didn't want to spoil his fun.

"Mine is a noble family—noble, you understand? Noble! Believe me? I'll give you proof—two proofs. Okay?"

"Okay, then, two proofs," I said.

"It's a deal. Let's not stick around here. Inside that courtyard there's a big watchdog, as big as a donkey, black. Let's go somewhere else."

"All right, let's go."

"Your place, okay? Your place? Is it far?"

"No, not far. Let's go to my place then. But I don't have any barley wine."

"Chinese white liquor? That'd be okay too."

"I have some grape wine—white grape wine."

He pondered this a minute, weighing the matter. "Okay," he decided, "let's go to your folks' place."

"My folks?"

"Oh . . . *your* place. *Your* place—okay?"

(ii) The Sixty-First Year of the Reign
of the Illustrious Emperor Qian Long

When we got to my place he solemnly undid the top button of his shirt, and to my surprise I saw a cat's-eye, long as your finger. I knew what the market value of such a treasure would be, but I'd never seen one so big before. Before I knew it, I was stammering, "Is it . . . is it real?"

"Sure it's real. Not every noble owns a treasure like this. Look at its quality—none finer."

I don't know anything about the quality of precious stones, but I enjoy admiring them, and stroking their ice-cold surfaces.

"How much is it worth?" I asked.

"Priceless," he said.

I stood facing the window, examining it carefully. It felt heavy, as if there was some connection between its weight and its value.

"Have you seen the Dalai Lama's palace at Norbu Lingka Garden?" he asked. "You've got to see it. The statue of Buddha is gold. The throne is gold too, with all kinds of jewels. It has cat's-eyes as big as this . . . not quite so big."

I'd been there. I'd seen the gold pedestal of the Buddha's statue in the main hall, all inlaid with precious stones. It was the epitome of wealth and power—what more can I say?

"So you believe me now?" he asked with a tinge of self-satisfaction.

"Believe you . . . about what?" I said, confused.

"I come from a noble family. Only a noble could own such a treasure!"

Then all at once I remembered. "Didn't you say you had two proofs? What's the second?"

Suddenly he became dejected. "Nothing."

"Nothing?" I got an inspiration. "Okay, forget it. I'm not going to believe all your sneaky talk. All the peddlers on the streets selling cat's-eyes, you trying to tell me they're all nobles?"

My disdain hurt his pride. Blood rushed to his face. "You're comparing me to them! Them, in their short robes?"

I knew Lhasa nobles wore robes below the knee. Only the common people wear short ones. I couldn't help laughing to myself. He'd fallen for my ploy.

"All right!" he said. "I'll show you. You'll meet my precious coins. They'll open your eyes, give you a scare, keep you awake at night, give you nightmares, send you a horrible death!"

He seemed to be cursing me in spite of himself. But what surprised me was that he'd said "coins." What's so special about a coin? All over the Barkhor, spread out on peddlers' carpets, all kinds of coins, a few yuan each. What's scary about coins?

He fumbled in his shirt and brought out a cloth bag, rolled up tight. As he undid it, his every movement displayed tremendous reverence. I confess that by the time he'd opened it, the coins in that bag held more than a tinge of mystery for me.

The head of Buddha Opame at Gyantse Kumbum. (Photo by Li Gotami Govinda)

Twenty-seven tiny silver coins, Tibetan script on one side, Chinese characters on the other. I could make out the Chinese: "Sixty-first year of Qian Long."

"So these are the coins you sold your house for?" I asked him.

(iii) An Indian Sari

The sixteenth year of the reign of Emperor Qian Long or the sixty-first year, what's the difference? An old Tibetan coin is an old Tibetan coin, that's all there is to it. To sell a house and courtyard for twenty-seven of these—old Chimi must have been out of his head.

He knocked back my grape wine the way they knock back their Tibetan barley wine, a whole glass in one gulp. Three glasses one after another, and all that was left of my Qingdao wine was the bottle.

"Good wine." He wiped his mouth. "Too bad the bottle's so small."

I was too embarrassed to tell him that the bottle cost me better than five yuan, and I usually make one bottle last me a couple of weeks. I thought maybe he'd just been shooting the bull, and never sold the house at all. Why would he do something so obviously stupid? He wasn't dumb, that's for sure.

From then on, whenever I strolled around the Barkhor, I paid special attention to the house Chimi had shown me. I asked a nearby shopkeeper who lived there. He said it belonged to a rich Tibetan merchant who'd moved back to Lhasa from India. He'd heard this merchant had a house in India, a car too. He said the master of the house often goes back to stay in India, and there's usually no one living here but one servant, who keeps an incredibly huge watchdog, really vicious, so outsiders never venture into the courtyard.

"And who's there now?" I asked.

"The young lady of the family is back from India. She wears an Indian sari and makeup. She has long, slender black eyebrows, a real beauty."

"And you?" I asked. "I see your shop's cloth and makeup are all imported too. Do you have any relatives in India?"

"No, we're Lhasa people. The trader who owns that house sells us all these goods wholesale. Lots of other shops buy from him too. He's a big importer. Me?"—he pointed to himself with his little finger—"I'm small fry."

I thought of sounding him out about something else. "Do you know Chimi?"

"Chimi? What Chimi?"

I mimed a cripple, half my body paralyzed. He laughed.

"Who on the Barkhor doesn't know *him?*"

"He says that house used to belong to his family, that he sold it to the merchant. Is that so?"

"Well, I couldn't say. I only moved here a few years ago. What happened before that, I don't know. Old Chimi hangs around this alley all the time, but I just don't know. . . ."

I'd already turned to go, when he was calling me in a low voice, "Hey! Hey!"

I looked back. He had turned the other way, up the alley. I followed his gaze and saw her.

It was the merchant's daughter, back from India. She was obviously long used to the admiring stares of strange men: myself, the shopkeeper, and several passersby were all gazing at her. She took no notice, eyes aloft, head high, walking aloof, a natural-born empress, as if everybody was beneath her and the whole world and everything in it existed just for her.

So this was the Indian sari the shopkeeper was telling me about, soft, elegant pink, embroidered with silver flowers. My eyes followed the slight heels of her leather boots. She was tall, half a head taller than the average man, almost as tall as me. She was absolutely fascinating. I smelled an exotic fragrance as she passed. Like other men's, my eyes followed her full hips, swaying slightly as she walked away.

The next time I saw her was a week later. I was on the Barkhor's third corner, talking to Lord Chimi the Second. This time I spotted her first. She was a long way off, coming out the gate of Jokhang Temple. She turned our way, her tall figure standing out above the crowd. I forgot what I'd been saying to Chimi.

He saw that my mind was wandering, and poked me in the ribs. "I don't have to look. I know what you're looking at. A woman. A tall woman. The woman who's back from India. Right?"

"How'd you know?"

"I've lived on the Barkhor for six generations. Is there anything I haven't seen, anything I don't know? Nothing on the Barkhor escapes Lord Chimi the Second. If I was blind and deaf I'd still know. Is it her?"

Abashed, I had to confess, "Yes, it is." Only as she neared us at a quick pace did I think to ask him, "Do you know her?"

Still, he didn't turn around. "She's *that* man's woman."

"His *woman?*" I didn't get it. Wasn't she the young lady of the house—the daughter? How could she be his woman . . . his wife?

He ignored her, his face a blank as he answered. If she understood Chinese, she must have heard him say, "She was still a filthy little brat when he took her to India, tall and skinny as a spring sheep. Not twenty years ago! In India he fed her up, so plump I didn't recognize her when she came back. Just look at those tits, so plump!"

She was walking by, her full breasts making the hearts of us staring men flutter like flags in a breeze.

Why was she staring at me?

Chimi sighed and lowered his crooked face. "Not twenty years ago!"

Now she was saying something to me in Tibetan.

"She's asking you what country you're from," Chimi said, not at all displeased.

And with that, Chimi turned back and jabbered with her in English. All Tibetans who go abroad come into contact with European culture, so I thought I'd try my German on her—I knew Chimi wouldn't be able to understand. I interrupted them in my shoddy pronunciation to ask, "Do you speak German?"

"Sure," she replied excitedly in German much better than mine. Not to be left out, Chimi put in that he'd told her I was from China. He said she hadn't even recognized him, said the little slut had earned a pile of money off him years ago, been selling her body since she was ten, a right little whore.

She begged my pardon in German, and said I didn't look Chinese to her, she'd taken me for a tourist. I explained what I was doing in Lhasa. When she said she'd like to invite me to her place for tea, I hesitated, then accepted . . . hesitated because I didn't know how to explain to Chimi. Then I realized there was nothing to explain.

I can't figure out why I found myself feeling guilty. It never occurred to me then that she might shut the door behind us and pull off her pants. I didn't have the least indecent thought—honest!

In a deliberately nonchalant voice I said good-bye to Chimi. I walked down the street beside this woman with an exhilarated feeling. We were attracting the crowd's attention, especially myself. Many men shot me envious looks. I felt superior, being taller than any of them.

I didn't stay long at her house, the same house Chimi said he'd sold. There wasn't so much as a risqué word between us. We drank coffee and she gave me some delicate little cakes. One thing struck my attention: a small door off the courtyard, sealed long ago, and locked. I took careful note of it. And I saw there was a big, black watchdog. And I noticed that only one room on the ground floor was occupied. Evidently it belonged to a dumb servant, who was about fifty. He'd planted flowers all over the courtyard. It's well known that the people of Lhasa love flowers, but the romantic atmosphere of all the fresh flowers in this courtyard was something unique. The yard was big, clean, and well swept—it all gave me a nice impression of the servant.

As I was leaving she invited me to come again.

(iv) His Ancestor's Legacy

I was still asleep when Chimi came to see me. It was that time of morning when the sun is still so soft. I didn't have any green tea to offer him, so I brewed up some milk-tea for him in my coffee pot—just put in powdered milk and black tea and boiled them together. Then I washed my face and gargled as I straightened up my room a little. By the time I sat down he'd sucked up half the pot.

Once again he pulled something from deep down in his shirt. This time it was a sheet of yellow paper. "A will—you understand?"

Of course I understood what a will was, but I didn't know that Tibetans pass on their property this way.

"I understand. . . . I think I understand."

"That's what this is. My great-great-great-grandfather left it. He was the one who bought that house. Whether to sell it, how to sell it, of course he decided all that. It says here . . . you understand Tibetan?"

"No. Not a word."

"Do you have any more of that sweet wine like last time?"

"No, I don't. Stop beating around the bush. What does your great-great-great-grandfather's will say?"

"It's in Tibetan. What a shame you don't read Tibetan. A real shame. Tibetan writing is the most wonderful writing in the world. You know why? Because it was invented by our great king, Srongtsan Gampo. King Srongtsan Gampo had a Chinese wife and a Nepalese wife. And you can't read a word of it? What a shame!"

"Not a word."

"This milk-tea's not so bad. I'll tell you, this will says. . ." And very seriously he read out the words on the old yellow paper, in Tibetan. "Now you understand."

"No," I said, "I don't."

"I forgot, you don't understand Tibetan. Make some more of that milk-tea. Your pot's too small."

"After the will."

"After the tea."

"After the will." I didn't bend a bit.

"Well, all right, if that's how you want it. It says here not to sell the house, whatever happens, never to sell it to anyone, unless. . . . Now the tea!"

"What do you mean tea? Finish the will. Unless what?"

"Unless someone offers twenty-seven silver coins of the sixty-first year of Emperor Qian Long. Then whoever they are, sell them the house."

"Twenty-seven—three times three times three?"

"Three times three times three. Twenty-seven coins. The sixty-first year."

"I still don't get it."

"You're Chinese, right? You know who Emperor Qian Long was, right? Don't you know how many years Qian Long reigned? It's a sad state of affairs when Lord Chimi the Second has to give the Chinese a lesson in their own history. Qian Long was the fourth emperor of the Qing Dynasty. The first three were Shun Zhi, Kang Xi, and Yong Zheng. Qian Long became emperor in 1736. In Chinese history, that's called the first year of Qian Long. Qian Long reigned a long time, sixty years. He died in 1795. So in Chinese history, there was no sixty-first year of Qian Long: 1796 was the first year of Jia Qing. Emperor Jia Qing took the throne that year. You understand now?"

I thought I understood now. "You mean the sixty-first year of Qian Long coins are counterfeit?"

"Counterfeit, my eye! You must be the world's number one dumb ass."

Now I may be dumb, I admit, but I'm not number one. When I went to see her again, I didn't forget to ask about the sixty-first year of Qian Long coins. What she told me was completely different. I didn't know who to believe.

I didn't leave that day, I stayed. A woman to make a man lose his soul!

By what she said, she was thirty years old, but she didn't look like a thirty-year-old woman. Her skin was smooth and firm. I thought she was deliberately giving herself out to be older than she was, but I don't see why. Maybe it was to help me relax. Not that I felt I was doing anything wrong. Not a bit. When the chance came, I tested her a little: she definitely didn't understand Tibetan.

(v) Another Way to Put It

I've translated the gist of what she said into Chinese and put it down here—just her general meaning, maybe not absolutely accurately. Reader, please excuse.

My man will be forty next year. He was born in this house. He says this house has been passed down in his family for nearly two centuries.

His ancestor was a prominent noble, administrator of the mint for the eighth Dalai Lama and the imperial Qing officials. He was even granted a title by the Beijing emperor—superintendent of the mint, you understand? He minted coins. First copper coins, later silver coins.

The ancient Tibetan coin was called the tranga. Most of them were copper. A few were silver, but there was no unified standard, so they were like the gold rings you buy in the market in Lhasa today. The weight depended on the amount of raw material the craftsman used to make them.

How do I know all this? I forgot to tell you, in India I studied old Tibetan coins. No, in a university. I specialized in the economy of the reign of the eighth Dalai Lama.

(I asked about the tranga, the Tibetan coin.)

After Qian Long's famous general Fu Kangan put down the Gurkha invasion of Tibet, he drew up an imperial protocol with the Dalai Lama's envoys. The third of its twenty-nine clauses provided for an official appointed by the Chinese imperial court to supervise the minting of Tibetan coins according to government standards, every coin to be uniformly minted from pure Chinese silver. The weight of each tranga coin was fixed at two and a half ounces. Three ounces of silver were allotted for the minting of each coin. The extra half ounce was to cover expenses. The words "Qian Long, Treasured Tibet" appeared in Chinese characters on one side of the coin, Tibetan script on the other side, and the year on the rim. The protocol was drawn up in the winter of 1792, the fifty-seventh year of Qian Long's reign. The first silver coins were minted the next spring, so all these coins are from the fifty-eighth year of Qian Long or later. The Beijing court appointed my man's ancestor as administrator of the mint. He was a trusted retainer of the Dalai Lama. They say he built this house then.

Those silver coins inscribed "Sixty-first year of Qian Long"? Sure I know them. There were strict quotas about how many coins could be minted each year. First the mint produced a steel mold, and every year they struck a few coins early to issue just after the New Year. Word of Emperor Qian Long's death didn't reach Tibet until the spring of 1796, so a few early coins marked "Sixty-first year" were already in circulation. The Dalai Lama's administration managed to recover some of them and melt them down. The few that are left have been the subject of thefts and squabbles among coin collectors ever since. Why do you want to know? Do you collect Tibetan coins? If you're really interested, next time I come back from India I'll bring the little sixty-first-year Qian Long coin from my collection to show you. But to be honest, I'd rather not. It's precious. There are only forty-odd left. The mint never made a mistake in minting silver coins again. Besides, it's made of fine Chinese silver, the softest kind. What else do you want to know?

(vi) A Story of the Telling of the Story

At this point I decided to turn all this into a story, but there were still a couple of facts I wanted to get straight. I had a consultant handy. One of my friends is an expert in these things: Bull. I'm not using that name to hide his identity, it's his nickname—because he's full of bull. But boasts and lies are just two of his sidelines. He's also the foremost collector of ancient Tibetan coins in the whole world. I've already devoted another of my works to telling his story, and spilled plenty of ink on his main lines and sidelines. Let's forget them.

(My other story about these coins involves me, Bull, and a few other friends. You can look it up in *Spring Wind Magazine*, 1986, number 4. Just remember the my name—Ma Yuan—it's my masterpiece!)

I should have thought of Bull long before. He didn't shed any new light on the mystery of the sixty-first-year Qian Long coins. But he told me their worth. He had all the collector's information about this little coin at his fingertips. He searched through coin catalogs from America, Japan, Taiwan, and Hong Kong, and even showed me pictures of it together with its market price—over a thousand U.S. dollars. There it was in black and white.

Bull didn't know Lord Chimi the Second. I could have introduced them. They both knew me. But I didn't want them to know each other. No special reason. Just looking after my own legitimate interests.

The number of coins Bull mentioned was precise—forty-three of these little coins in existence. That made me think of old Chimi's collection—twenty-seven coins—a startling number. He really was a remarkable person. Even if what he said was a hoax, if the house never was his and he never sold it for those twenty-seven coins, at least those coins proved one thing: even if he was no noble, he certainly was no ordinary person.

I asked about the mold for the Qian Long coins. Bull said, "All the original steel molds for Tibetan silver coins are preserved in a side temple of the Potala. I have a friend among the monks, and he took me to see them. They're registered as cultural relics. Dazzling. But when I saw there was no mold for the sixty-first-year Qian Long coin, my heart skipped a beat. I asked my friend as casually as I could, is every mold the government owns kept here. He said they're all there, absolutely certain. He'd taken part in the inventory of the Potala Temple's artifacts. It took more than seven years to complete. He had the whole Potala collection in his head. I thought maybe the mold for the sixty-first-year coin might still exist. I walked around the Barkhor a hundred times looking for it, went into every little shop asking for it, inquired at every stall, all in vain. If I found that mold, you know, I'd have it made."

That was one more reason I didn't want Bull to meet Chimi.

But like all men, I always let down my guard when I'm with a woman: I told the woman in the Indian sari the whole story—Chimi's coins, Bull's coins, Bull's search for the mold—didn't hold back a single thing. She said, "He likes you too." "He" meant the dumb servant. So I made friends with the servant and his big, black dog.

After that I often went to her courtyard to chat and drink tea. In a bit more than three months my range of expression in the German language improved amazingly. I don't know how she managed it, but she didn't get pregnant. It was a miracle.

She told me that she was going back to India soon.

The day she left, she said she'd come back, on account of me. When I told her I'd write a story for her, about the two of us, a hesitant look came over her lovely face. When she said, keeping her smile, that she looked forward to reading it, my heart suddenly felt as if it was tied in a knot.

After she departed I sometimes went to the house and sat with the dumb servant, drinking tea. There was a strange taste to the tea he made. I think he used coconut, because it tasted like Hainan Island coconut milk. The servant hardly ever sat down, he was so busy with the flowers. He'd only stop work just long enough to come over and take a sip of cold tea. But the black watchdog became my companion. He'd walk up without a sound, lie down by my knee, and gaze up at me with the relaxed look only a close friend can give you. I used to sit there for hours.

If it weren't for the following incident, my story would come to a prosaic end right here.

(vii) A Verbal Contract

It really surprised me. I couldn't figure out how Bull had hooked up with Chimi. I immediately suspected they'd been plotting together a long time behind my back. I have to admit I'd treated Bull badly, trying to keep him and Chimi apart. Though he was a sneak thief, a swindler, a cheat, capable of every kind of dishonesty, he'd always exercised some conscience in his dealings with me. I have to confess he's never deceived me. . . . but I'm going beyond the scope of my story.

They bumped into each other by chance one day in my room. What bothered me was that they acted like old buddies the moment they laid eyes on each other. They never mentioned where they'd got acquainted, but they didn't bother to hide that they not only knew each other, but were old friends. The term "daring daylight bandits" was made for these two. Right in front of my face, they started talking about the sixty-first-year of Qian Long coins. I noticed that old Chimi didn't tip his hand about his own twenty-seven silver treasures, but talked about the sixty-first-year coin as if he were some complete novice asking for news about the coin market. It looked like Bull was the one getting the wool pulled over his eyes.

Bull said, "Would you please look out for some sixty-first-year Qian Long coins for me? Price is negotiable. I need your help."

Chimi said, "When Lord Chimi the Second promises to look after something for you, your problem is solved." He paused a moment, then asked, "Anything else?"

"Nothing," said Bull decisively.

Chimi's not one to back away from trouble. He closed in on his prey. "Absolutely nothing else you want?"

This time Bull hesitated. "Well, maybe."

"What's on your mind? What are you after?" said Chimi.

"A steel mold. For the sixty-first-year of Qian Long coin."

"Is there such a thing!" said Chimi. "I've lived on the Barkhor for a hundred years and never heard of it."

"It exists. I'm sure of it. So look for it. I'll give you a hundred silver coins."

"Give me a hundred silver coins? What for? Lord Chimi the Second accepts no ill-gotten gains."

"We'll trade, then. A hundred silver coins for the mold."

"What's one of these molds look like? I've never seen one."

"Made of steel—this big." Bull sketched its shape with his hands. "Hollow, with the pattern of the sixty-first-year Qian Long coin inside. You never saw it?"

"I'll check around. So it's a deal? A hundred silver coins?"

"A hundred."

To bear witness to his promise, Bull expressly asked me to act as guarantor. I generously consented, and with a handshake the verbal contract was sealed.

After this I didn't see the two of them for quite a long while. Maybe they had both forgotten all about their deal, and I was the only one who couldn't get it off his mind. How had I gotten myself mixed up in this? Could it all have been the doing of spirits? If so, then it was all ordained. The will of heaven.

Not at all accidentally, I was staring at a small door next to the dumb servant's room. He was the only person who lived on the ground floor. The two other rooms had been made into a doghouse. Of all the doors on this floor, only this small one was locked, as tight as a drum, with an old copper padlock, of foreign make, corroded green. It was so low only a midget could have walked in without bending over. The door was sealed with strips of silk paper, stamped all over with someone's personal seal. The silk paper that sealed the door was covered in mildew, rotting, but still sealed the door tight. The seal bore the marks of the passage of time.

I didn't want to let the servant know how much the door fascinated me, so I went on casually drinking my tea. When, still casually, I strolled near it, I saw that the silk paper that sealed the door had turned the same shiny black as the door itself. The paper was beginning to rot away, but to my surprise I noticed that the seal marks were still intact, and you could read them if you looked carefully. As I leaned down to try to read the date, the big, black dog growled menacingly, so I immediately stood up straight and acted as naturally as I could. The dumb servant was far away, looking after the flowers, so absorbed in his work that he never turned around.

(viii) A Conspiracy beneath the Full Moon

"Lord Chimi the Second is completely trustworthy. Ask people on the Barkhor. If anybody says I'm a liar, Lord Buddha will send him a horrible death."

"Who's asking for an oath? I'm only asking if you know the layout of your ancestors' house."

"Sure I know it."

"Every room?"

"Every room."

"Then you know that downstairs room with the little low door?"

"It's locked. Locked by my ancestors. Dalai Lama the Eighth sealed it himself. No one must touch it. Why?"

So that's how it was!

"Why do you want to know?" Chimi persisted.

"No reason. I was just asking."

"No, no. Let me see, let me see." He patted his head, pondering. "The door. . . . Ah! You won't say, but I know what you're after. I know what you want me to do! There's nothing you can hide from Lord Chimi the Second."

I laughed warmheartedly.

And so we quickly reached a secret agreement. In three days it would be the Mid-Autumn Moon Festival. Before dusk I would take that big, black watchdog to the Lhasa River, cross the hanging bridge to the old haunt of robbers, Guma Lingka Island, there to wait with Bull at the appointed hour. So Chimi and I agreed.

On the night of the Mid-Autumn Moon Festival the clouds hide the moon. That's how it always is. It was so cloudy that the evening sky grew dark earlier than usual. Before taking out the black dog, I sat together with the servant for half an hour, drinking tea.

The dog rarely got out of the courtyard. The outside world was strange to him. He glared with hostility at everybody we encountered crossing the Barkhor. I kept a tight grip on the leash. I didn't want him to start any trouble in the still-crowded street.

He'd been shut in too long, and he wasn't used to crowds. His enormous size and his low growl scared people out of the way. I knew that what I was doing was crazy. This wicked dog was making me the object of attention of all the people who had come to spin their prayer wheels that evening.

When I got to the river, I realized I'd arrived early. Chimi probably wouldn't be there for a long while, and Bull probably wouldn't arrive soon either. I took the dog for a walk along the cool, refreshing riverbank, strolling westward.

The cowhide ferryboat that shuttles crowds across the river had stopped for the night. All that remained was the stone steps where passengers come ashore. The blankness of the scene started to play on my imagination—the so-called poetic fancy.

The dog was frisking on the gravel, racing off, stopping short, then madly racing off again. The moon had already risen, half-visible, half-hidden in clouds, never fully showing itself. Only a few remaining gaps in the heavy banks of clouds revealed the sky.

Bull came first. By his short stature I recognized him at once.

"When did you get here?" he said.

"What are you doing here?" I said.

"Didn't you say to come here at nightfall?"

"I haven't seen you the last couple of weeks."

"Chimi said you wanted me to come. He got you wrong, maybe?"

"For sure he got me wrong."

"That Chimi! What's he up to? I'll go on back then."

"No need to leave, now you're here. It's the Mid-Autumn Moon Festival. Stay a while and we'll enjoy the moonlight here by the river."

There was no moon. When Bull arrived the dog had already left my side. I didn't bother about him anyway. My mind was wandering. I realized I was only thinking of one thing—Chimi's arrival.

Bull knew how to handle the situation. He didn't make a sound. With hunched shoulders we walked out onto the hanging bridge. For some reason the dog didn't follow.

All the rest of that night, the moon only showed its round face once. This I swear: the moon took no part in our conspiracy. The moonlit night was pure.

(ix) The End or the Beginning

I've borrowed that title from a poem by my friend Bei Dao. If you've read the poem you recognize it right away.

As I said before, how I met Lord Chimi the Second is another story, and an intricate one at that. I got to know him through fictional fabrication, in my process of creation: the end is the beginning.

It would be difficult to narrate the rest of the events of that evening in order, so I think I'll just honestly tell you what happened, okay?

The night's single remaining beam of moonlight fell on an ecstatic Chimi. You could tell the mood he was in: the suspension bridge jumped with every step. He and I and Bull walked together to the southern tip of the moonlit island. Further south was the broad, swift

Lhasa River. The moon hid behind the clouds, and never came out again.

"Here it is! Where's my hundred silver coins?"

"You've got it? The mold?"

"A hundred! Here's our witness." Lord Chimi placed the steel mold in my hand. "No tricks."

I looked it over and passed it to Bull. "This is the one! This is it! For sure!"

"The hundred coins!"

"You'll get them. Don't worry, I won't cheat you." Bull checked it over, murmuring to himself. "This is it! A shame it's rusted . . . but not too badly." Suddenly, Bull looked up. "Where's the other part?"

"What other part?" Chimi didn't understand.

"The top. The part with Tibetan writing."

"You didn't say anything about a top. How was I supposed to know there was another part?"

"You didn't bring it? Everything's ruined! Just the bottom's no use!"

"No use for what?" Chimi still didn't get it.

"No use for anything, you dumb ass."

Chimi was despondent. "So that's the end of it. All for nothing."

"Think what to do next," Bull said. "Think!"

"There's nothing to think of. Nothing. All finished."

No matter what else Bull went on to say, Chimi never uttered another sound.

When I saw that Bull was still gripping the mold, I knew things were far from over. But not that far. I could already hear a low growl. The dog was racing our way at top speed, toward the end of the story.

It was Chimi who sensed what the dog had realized, and what it was after. With dexterity unimaginable for someone so ancient, he snatched the mold from Bull's hand and flung his arm. There was a splash. Chimi ran straight off into the night.

The great, black dog stopped, gazed where the splash had been, turned, and slowly started back home. Bull and I followed behind, like his bodyguards. In a low voice Bull said he remembered the exact place the mold went in, said he'd think of a way to bring it up.

I said the river was too cold, the current was too strong. It would be impossible unless you hired a diver.

"Then hire a diver." He said the cost didn't matter.

I knew he didn't have the money to hire anybody.

* * *

For the sake of my readers, I'd like to add a postscript. I never went back to the courtyard again. I found out she'd returned, but I didn't go back. Never again did I see the old servant, nearing death, or his great, black dog.

I often see old Chimi on the Barkhor, deep in concentration, spinning a prayer wheel, his clothes in rags. It seems he doesn't recognize me anymore—just as if he never knew me.

Bull still comes around to see me often, to bum a meal and show off his latest silver coins. About that Mid-Autumn Moon Festival evening, we never breathe a word.

• 2 •

A Fiction

Ma Yuan

Gods are all alike: blindly self-confident . . . whence their ego-centric faith in themselves. Each god believes himself extraordinary, unique. In reality they're all alike. In creation myths, for instance, their methods are similar as peas in a pod. Their method is perpetual refabrication.

—From an Apocryphal Sutra of the Legalist School

I

I'm Ma Yuan, that Chinese writer. My stories are all full of sensational material. I like to ride my celestial horse across the sky.[1]

Sounds like I'm implying I'm a great writer. Conceit? Who knows?

What a self-confident person says should express self-confidence. So he should never add a purple patch onto his work, and stubbornly force his readers to listen to him chatter about all his publications. If I tell you now about all I've written, it's out of a profound belief you haven't read any of it. No need for you to feel embarrassed. I'm perfectly at ease about the whole thing.

Some people say the reason I went to Tibet was for my writing. It's a fact I went to Tibet. It's also a fact that I've written hundreds of pages about Tibet. All written in Chinese characters: although it's a long time since I first arrived in Tibet, I still can't speak a word of the language. What I talk about is the people, the setting, and stories that might happen in the setting.

1. The author's family name, "Ma," is the character for "horse." He is literally Mr. Horse.

23

I wrote about a feminine deity, the Lhasa River Goddess. But I didn't write about how I'd racked my brains to decide that deity's gender. I've written about men, about women. I've written about what men and women do together. I've written about brown eagles, bald vultures, paper kites. I've written about bears, wolves, leopards, other dangerous animals. I've written about little animals, some dangerous (like scorpions), some docile (like lambs), some neither dangerous nor docile (like foxes and marmots). I've written about life and death among my own species, about ways of living, ways of dying. I've put it all down in my own extraordinary form. Maybe the reason I did all that was to prove I'm a unique writer. Who knows? I'm really not intrinsically different from other writers. I go observe something, then use the fruits of my observation as a basis to make something up. The celestial horse galloping across the sky always assumes a prerequisite horse . . . and a prerequisite sky.

To write this story I risked my life by spending seven days in Machu village. To make it clearer: this is a story about lepers, and Machu village is a forbidden zone quarantined by the government, a leper colony.

I wanted to employ this little village full of lepers as a setting. I used the fruits of those seven days' observation to compose this sensational story. Many writers (and even more would-be writers) who have a rough time finding knockout subjects might envy my luck. Is there any such person among my readers? Please write and let me know. My name's Ma Yuan . . . my real name. I've used pen names. But for this story I don't.

Other writers would rather abandon writing than take the risk I took. Don't take it! I'm now living in an institution called the Peace and Quiet Hospital. It's called a hospital just to reassure the public. People in the know understand it's a mental institution. That's where I live and write. The room is clean, about twenty square meters, with six beds. The maximum incubation period of leprosy is twelve years. I just left Machu village three months ago. I don't have any symptoms . . . yet.

I assumed a romantic pose. I believe in the extraordinary power of my imagination. I confidently proclaim that here and now I can create a masterpiece for all future generations.

I'm not like Hemingway, venting his melancholy with an "Isn't it nice to think so."[2] When I thought it, I had to do it, and I did it. That Hemingway was a Yank.

2. The closing line of Hemingway's *The Sun Also Rises*.

I can't boast I'm the only man who's dared to do it, because the first man I met there had done it before me. And he said he wasn't the first either.

II

I'd heard beforehand that there were two Tibetan doctors who looked after Machu village, one a woman; and I'd heard the man was quite handsome. The quarantine zone had no enclosure. Nothing prevented patients from going out, and nothing prevented outsiders from coming in. I hadn't been sure I would be able to obtain permission, so I slipped into this forbidden zone on the sly. I hadn't thought out exactly how many days I'd stay.

The road followed a river. The two little stone houses looked utterly desolate. The one to the west was for the road maintenance crew. Machu Hospital occupied the one to the east. But Machu village was still further on, at the foot of a mountain, separated from the road by ten kilometers of boulder-strewn ground. The little village lay ahead, plain and clear, linked to the outside world by a little path that wound back and forth like a tapeworm. There was nobody else living for fifty kilometers around.

I'd caught a ride on a delivery truck. In order not to alert the two doctors, I got off a long distance from their hospital and from the road crew's house, and trudged off straight north toward Machu village.

The mountain towered north of the village. The gullies down the mountainside had turned into flood runoffs, cutting through the rocky ground. Naturally, I meant to take care of my own meals and accommodation, so I'd brought a sleeping bag and some food. I decided to look for a place to sleep near the village, someplace with no sign of people. I found a bend in one of the deep, narrow gullies, buried my backpack and most of my food, and went into town carrying just a shoulder bag with my camera.

The afternoon sun shone down, parching. The village was absolutely quiet . . . no horses, cows, sheep, pigs, or chickens, just some dogs sleeping in the shade.

The houses were all stone, typical Tibetan peasant houses, flat-roofed and low, laid out just like in any other Tibetan village: unpaved mud streets, narrow, unused by wagons. I strolled about and saw no one in the courtyards. I'd decided I wasn't just going to walk right into people's courtyards. I walked around the whole village and didn't see a soul.

Not a single dog barked at me. I felt a profound sorrow. If I hadn't known about the village in advance, I'd have thought it was abandoned.

I knew it wasn't. There were over a hundred and twenty people living here. I also knew the inhabitants did no farming, kept no livestock. The government provided their food and necessities.

I'd walked to the end of the village. The first human sign came from the courtyard of the last building, the only two-story house. I heard the piercing wail of a child. Without the least hesitation I walked up the steps and pushed open the door.

I hadn't expected to see women. Three women leaning in a row against the wall, dozing. I'd be too embarrassed to describe how I felt; they were naked from the waist down, and from the waist up all they had on was worn-out Chinese blouses, unbuttoned to expose their breasts. A child lay on one woman's lap, nursing. Obviously, he'd been the source of the cry.

I knew I'd come in where I didn't belong. The three women seemed to pay me no mind. Their eyes were closed as they comfortably enjoyed sunbathing. The eyes of the little boy kept darting over to me. Like any susceptible young man, I took special note that the women had purposely spread their legs, as if deliberately to sun that place. Of course I couldn't go on staring at them, but I couldn't just turn around and run either.

The two-story building was no more than two little rooms built on top of a one-story building. Along the north side of the roof was a wall. Along the east side of the roof lay piles of brush for firewood. Apparently there were no men living here.

I deliberately hadn't looked at the women's faces. I stood at the entrance, uncertain whether to advance or withdraw. I was sure the little boy's mother was young. Just as I was turning to go, I heard a voice.

"I can speak Chinese."

I had no choice but to turn back again, and now I glanced at the face of the woman nursing the baby, the one who had spoken to me. I don't know if I trembled, but her face absolutely terrified me. Her nose was rotted away, and her whole face looked as if it was scarred with third-degree burns. The skin was shiny, cracked, split all over.

I said, "I can speak Chinese too."

Her expression was peculiar: her eyes stared askew, as if she was looking at me and not looking at me at the same time. She said, "You come from Lhasa. People who come from Lhasa speak Chinese."

I said, "Have you been to Lhasa?"

She said, "Lhasa's a big place."

"It's a big place. Where do you come from?"

"I have been to Chamdo.³ People say that Lhasa is even bigger than Chamdo."

"How come you can speak Chinese?"

"Where I come from everyone can speak Chinese."

I said, "And your man?"

"Which man do you mean? They live in their own houses. We are all women here . . . and the child."

I said, "Have you lived here long?"

"The mountain turned green once and turned green again." She patted the child's head. "He was born here. Come in."

"Does the doctor come to the village every day?"

She said, "I hear there are two new doctors, but I haven't seen them."

"Hmm . . . hmm . . . ." I murmured unconsciously. I didn't know what to say next. I turned around and went back down. When I reached the bottom of the stairs, I remembered I should have asked if there was anyone else in the village who spoke Chinese. When I turned to go back up again, I discovered all four of them clinging to the doorframe, looking at me.

III

She was the only one in the village who could speak Chinese.

I had no other choice. I told her to dress and have the others put on their clothes too. I could see that all three were young. She was more energetic than the other two, and her figure was much fuller. The other two were thin and weak, but the faces of all three were the same.

I followed her into the room. It was all hers—hers and her child's. Hesitantly, I sat down on a wooden chair.

She said, "The short one's retarded. The tall one's back is hurt. They can't have children."

The child turned around and looked at me as he toddled out the door. The sunlight on his naked body made him look almost transparent. There was a look of experience in his eyes that twisted my heart.

She said, "He understands everything. When someone comes, he goes outside."

The way we'd see it, there was an implication in what she said. I have to say we would be wrong. She wasn't any kind of woman we're familiar with. I reached this conclusion over the next several days.

---

3. See the map.

I told her I wanted to stay in the village.

She said, "No one from outside stays in the village. They come with the doctors, walk around, and go away with the doctors. They do not stay in the village. There is no place in the village for them to stay."

I firmly told her I wanted to stay in the village. I said, "I don't speak Tibetan, I only speak Chinese."

She said, "Then speak Chinese."

As I spoke with her, I was unconsciously observing the two holes where her nose had been. I'd completely forgotten my fear. I just felt those two holes in her face were absurdly funny.

I said, "If an outsider like me stays here, the villagers won't like it, will they?"

She said, "The people in the village will not notice you. What other people do is not important to them. They only notice the people who deliver food and the people who come to show movies. They do not notice other people who come from outside." What she said was always broken and disconnected. I only got used to it gradually. After a while, she spoke again, "You want to go to the village. People from outside all walk around the village. They all have the doctors go with them. Only you are alone. There is no one to go with you."

"I came alone. I don't want the doctors to go with me."

She said, "I will go with you to the village. You can ask me."

"Ask you what?"

"You can ask me what you want to ask. I know much more than those doctors. I live in the village."

Before we went out, I said, "Hold the child. I'll take a picture for you."

"I do not take pictures. I do not understand taking pictures."

From my shoulder bag I pulled out a little photo album that I'd brought with me, drew out a color photo of myself and pointed to it.

Without the least hesitation she said, "This is you."

I pressed my advantage by saying I could preserve her like this. She shook her head. "I understand. I do not take pictures. I do not understand taking pictures."

She was contradicting herself, but I guessed what she meant: she was saying she knew (understood) what taking a picture was, but she didn't know (understand) how taking a picture could preserve someone on a piece of paper. I remembered a story I'd read: people unfamiliar with modern culture saw a photograph and thought it was witchcraft to capture someone's soul, that after the picture was taken the person's soul was shut inside the little black box (the camera). Apparently she'd seen some cameras. I knew these details would appear in my subsequent masterpiece.

She didn't want to take a picture. I had to let it go at that. Events would prove I'd made the mistake of thinking I was right. I'd forgotten that people here had seen movies. Photography wasn't as difficult for them to comprehend as I'd imagined. In fact, she had another reason for saying she didn't understand, didn't want to take a picture. More of that later.

IV

South of the town's center was a big open space, with basketball hoops set up on either end. People arrived at dusk in twos and threes to gather around this space. This must have been the only public place in the village.

She and I stood a little distance from the crowd. Her expression was carefree and detached as she held the little toddler by the hand. I didn't take out my camera.

The people looked indifferent, apathetic. No one showed concern about anyone else. Just as she'd said, the residents of the village seemed to take no notice of one extra person, me. Gradually this discovery eased my anxiety. All this cracked skin wasn't nearly so frightening as it had been a while ago. The brilliant golden light of the setting sun changed their faces into fantastic color portraits.

The symptoms of the disease made all the many people look alike: collapsed noses, glistening faces, even their eyes were all the same, too wide apart. I noticed that many people's eyes stared askew.

I said, "They all take their time walking."

She said, "They do not need to walk fast."

"Some of them play basketball?"

She looked at me as if she found such a question odd. Immediately, a young man came out of a building opposite, dribbling a basketball. Others came out to meet him. They whistled and shouted with a vitality I'd never expected.

Some of the men on the court were no longer young. They divided into two sides. There was no referee, so the game was a chaotic mess, like American football. She acted as a sideline commentator: "Every evening all the men play basketball."

I let out a "Hmm."

Then she said, "Why don't you play? Men should play basketball."

I realized she was saying something, but at the moment I was too absentminded to reply. I'm a good basketball player, but I had no intention of taking this opportunity to show off for her.

Little by little we pressed toward the court, with the rest of the crowd. She held the child. I stood by her side.

One of the players was a short fellow, particularly agile, about forty. Of all the players he was the only one who knew the basics of dribbling and shooting. He made a few baskets, and each time he drew a roaring cheer.

Now he scored again. Just as everyone was cheering, she nudged me and patted her boy. "This is his son." Even if I'd been an idiot, I'd have caught the tone of pride in her voice.

She added, "Sometimes he comes over and sleeps with me." She didn't lower her voice when she said it, even with all the spectators crowded around us.

She didn't care, but I was blushing.

I didn't have time to think about what happened next. Attracted by who knows what, the basketball rolled to my feet. I gave it a flip with my toe, and it landed in my hands. With no time to give it a thought, already repenting my rashness, from the side of the court, ten steps from the basket, I concentrated. . . . I flicked my wrists. . . . You guessed it—with God's help my shot went in, never even touched the rim. Too bad there was no net for a swish.

At last I'd attracted the attention of Machu village . . . they were all cheering for me. The eyes of the masses were upon me.

Right away I regretted revealing myself. For in that instant, I discovered two people gazing at me, neither very friendly. One was the short basketball player. The other was elderly, tall, his skin gloomy and dark, with none of the obvious symptoms of a leper, terribly hunchbacked, with a dried-up, beardless face like a shriveled old walnut and alert eyes, evidently the only villager whose mind hadn't stagnated here.

The villagers immediately forgot me, and the game went on.

On an impulse, I'd momentarily forgotten where I was. I'd never imagined I could feel so free and easy in the middle of a crowd of lepers.

V

I quietly pushed my way out of the crowd.

Sometimes one's sixth sense is frighteningly accurate. I sensed the tall hunchback watching me from behind. As soon as he saw me look round at him, he hurriedly glanced away. I didn't know I'd be climbing the mountain with him the next morning.

I stopped and waited for him to look back again. He didn't disappoint me: with an agility unimaginable for someone so old he spun around, looked, then walked off into the crowd. The sun had already fallen to the ridge of the mountain. It was getting dark.

Just as I was trying to decide whether or not to say good-bye, she approached me with the child in her arms. With ponderous steps, feet thumping the ground, she walked up, then set the child down.

She said, "The deaf mute always stares at outsiders. Don't be afraid of him."

"Which one is the deaf mute?"

"The old hunchback. He never bothers anyone."

I said, "Is he alone? Does he have any relatives here with him?"

"He is the oldest one in the village. He lives in a little house in the southwest corner. He has nothing to do with other people. Every morning he goes alone to climb the north mountain."

"When?"

"In the morning when we are eating tsampa."

I said, "I'll come back tomorrow."

"It is cold outside at night. It is going to rain."

I didn't understand why she said this. I hadn't told her where I intended to sleep. Besides, there wasn't a cloud in the sky. The stars had come out.

"I'll be going."

She insisted, "It is going to rain. It is cold outside."

It wasn't cold outside. I was silently laughing at her: saying over and over, it's cold, it's going to rain. I lay in my sleeping bag, eyes open, looking up at the stars that filled the sky. Not cold at all. I didn't have a bad spot here in the runoff channel, quiet and out of the wind. . . . I don't know when I fell asleep.

But I remember that before I fell asleep I decided to go back behind the village early next morning to wait for the old deaf mute who climbed the mountain. . . .

I dreamed about Lhasa. I saw my Lhasa friends and the Khampa pilgrim women on the Barkhor.

A cold rain woke me. I climbed out of my sleeping bag all flustered and confused. The sky was dark as the bottom of a scorched pot, not a break in the clouds anywhere. The raindrops were big, but scattered. There were strong gusts of wind. I was cold. I couldn't stop shivering. I had to roll up my food inside the sleeping bag to protect it from the water running along the ground. I walked up and down in the gully to try to get warm. If the rain got heavier it would soak into my dried rations. I had nowhere to turn, I thought though I knew clearly enough that Machu village wasn't far away. Luckily, the wind quickly scattered the rain clouds. I checked the ground with my hand: to my surprise it wasn't even damp. But the temperature had dropped a good thirty degrees. I unrolled my sleeping bag and lay down, but I didn't really go to sleep again all night. I'd gotten a chill. I felt hot.

As soon as light flooded the sky, I got up. The morning was so cold that I almost forgot about going behind the village to wait for the old deaf mute. Maybe I should go into the village first, go to her little room and say hello. I buried my backpack again, but I didn't go to her place.

VI

"How old do you think I am? Give me your first impression. Don't humor me. Don't just tell me something to make me feel good.

"There are mirrors here. There's water. I look at myself every day. But I can't tell if I look senile. I don't know how other old people look. So tell me the truth.

"I left your world a long time ago. That world belongs to people like you. Thirty years ago now. Maybe forty. I haven't counted. There's no way to reckon time here. Yesterday's the same as today. Today's the same as tomorrow. I can't remember how many mornings or evenings. Over and over, the mountains turned green, then yellow. . . . I don't remember.

"I'm a deaf mute. The people here all take me for a deaf mute. When I arrived here I never spoke. Then nobody spoke to me. I was afraid I'd forgotten how to speak Chinese. Talking now to you, I see I haven't forgotten. I'm not really Chinese. My father's family were traders from India.

"Don't ask about that. I haven't had a name for years. What does it matter? I've lived all the same. They don't call me anything. They think I'm deaf.

"You're sharp. Nobody here can see I've been to school. My father's family was rich. I was the one who decided to quit studying.

"I never think about that. When I think about what I used to do, it seems it has nothing to do with me. Maybe it really has nothing to do with me at all. It doesn't matter whether it was me or somebody else.

"You brought something to eat? Wonderful! It's years since I've eaten hardtack. Delicious. All right, let's walk on toward the gullies.

"You'd never believe it, I have a gun. A twenty-shot Mauser. In a minute you'll see it. I don't know if it still fires after all these years. Where

I've put it, the rain can't get at it. Not a speck of rust. There are seven bullets. Nobody knows. Nobody comes here. Nobody climbs this mountain. They all think I'm stupid to climb it. If you're tired take a little rest.

"This way. If you're still tired, we can rest again in a while. I've been climbing this mountain since the day I got here. I'm the one who wore out this path. I went as high as I could. I worried about that gun. Come on. It's farther up above."

VII

He was old and feeble to look at, but his stride was more vigorous than mine. We went on talking as we climbed. I wasn't expecting wonders. At the same time I wasn't against seeing wonders. We walked and rested, walked and rested, and finally we reached the place he wanted to reach. He left me waiting a minute.

Suddenly, as if by magic, he was transformed from a pathetic old hunchback into a vicious, agile, armed bandit. From its shape, and the sound of his voice, I could tell the gun in his hand was real. He pointed its muzzle at my face. I thought of the seven bullets he said were left. My legs started shaking.

"Take all the food out of the backpack. Hear me? Hurry up!"

I was scared silly. . . . I just stood staring at the pitch-black hole in that muzzle. It was bigger than I could ever have imagined, like a cave, so big I could have walked inside it without bending over. I did what I guess anybody would have done: I grabbed the backpack, pulled out the first can of food I touched, and threw it on the ground. I tossed out more cans, a packet of chocolate, and the rest of the hardtack.

I was still hesitating whether to pull out the camera, when he laughed. "That's what I used to do, years ago. I wanted to try it out on a young person today. Just like before. Hee, hee! No change."

I clean ignored his laugh, with that cave before me.

Slowly he lowered the muzzle from my face. Like a worm in spring, my consciousness reawoke. I recollected what had happened. At last my mind processed his words.

But my brain was still half-numb. I didn't understand the real significance of what he did next. I watched him grip the gun in his left hand, click off the safety with his right hand, and raise his left in the air. The muzzle pointed to the sky. I stared at his left index finger hooked around the trigger. I saw it squeeze.

A roar pierced the air. Its echo filled the mountains close by, then the distant mountains. I felt the whole world was watching us. Far below, Machu village was bathed in noonday sunlight, so tiny it was unreal, like a village in a sandbox. I couldn't see people in the village, but I felt that they were all looking at us.

"Too bad there's only six bullets left. Not bad, after thirty years."

These two sentences I immediately understood. I realized the dream-world I'd been in had evaporated, but I still didn't comprehend the place these details would have in this masterpiece of mine.

Without my noticing it, he'd vanished among the rocks. When he reappeared, there was no gun in his hand.

He seemed to have forgotten me as he walked past me and started down the mountain with agile leaps, rising and falling, appearing and disappearing like a shepherd boy among the rocks. His tall, hunched figure grew tiny.

I squatted down and picked up the cans of food I'd thrown on the ground. By the time I stood up again, he'd disappeared. Now I got a notion to look for his gun.

I had a premonition. I verified my premonition. My premonition wasn't wrong. I couldn't find it. Maybe it didn't exist. Maybe it only existed in my imagination.

It was only on my way down the mountain that I remembered all my questions about the lepers. He'd lived for decades in this place full of lepers. Was he a leper? I didn't understand why I'd gone to look for him, why I hadn't gone into the village instead.

VIII

As I came down the mountain alone, I saw her house in the distance, right at the mouth of the ravine. I hastened my steps, surprised by a feeling of eager impatience.

I'd experienced such a singular night after leaving her place, and such a singular morning with the old hunchback on the mountain, that just to be able to go back to her room again seemed an incredible miracle. The sun hung overhead. Her little door and her staircase were enveloped in shadow. What a cool, what a joyful shade.

Approaching, I saw her sitting in the shadows alone on the threshold, motionless, like a cut-paper silhouette. When I approached, she stood up, walked inside, and shut the door.

I stood there on the step, at a loss. I was hungry. I didn't feel like strolling around the village on an empty stomach, so I sat down on the step, took out some hardtack, chewed it slowly, and tried to think over what to do next. If she didn't invite me in again, I'd have to find a way to break into their world on my own. I'd already lifted a corner of the curtain. But I realized that the final step inside would be harder without the help of the only two people in the village who spoke Chinese. Could I manage it without knowing the language?

Maybe it was because I was sitting in the shade. I started coughing until I gasped for breath. When I finally stopped, my lungs felt feverish and swollen. I was probably sick.

Behind me, I heard the door open. I sat there; I didn't turn around. I heard her steps coming down the stairs. One, two, three, four, five, six, seven, eight, nine, ten, eleven. She was standing behind me. I still didn't turn around. I wasn't going to be the one to speak first. I was pouting like a kid.

I started coughing violently, couldn't stop no matter how I tried, coughed until my face was red, my throat bursting.

She said, "Come upstairs."

My first thought was to shake my head, refuse. She wasn't anything to me. She wasn't from any world I knew. What right had I? Why should I?

I immediately rejected that despicable idea. Obediently I walked ahead of her, my brain counting the steps mechanically, all eleven. I went in the courtyard door. She followed me.

The scene in the courtyard was exactly the same as yesterday, except that her son now occupied her place at the far end. The other two women sat leaning against the wall, dozing, sunning themselves, naked from the waist down. She gestured for me to come into her room.

By the door was a cast-iron stove with a crackling fire burning inside. Steam shot up from a smoke-blackened teapot sending out the fragrance of milk-tea. I couldn't keep from swallowing.

I went in, sat down on the mattress, and what did I see? I couldn't believe my eyes—my backpack! I reached out and grabbed it . . . no mistake. And inside it was my ever-so-soft down sleeping bag, my cans of food, my dried rations too. I shoved it behind me and leaned back against it, comfortable as could be.

She said nothing, and I didn't speak either. She poured me a cup of tea and went out. Through the window I saw her rejoin the other two women, put her child on her lap, open her blouse, and give him her breast. The only difference between her and the other two was that she was wearing a pair of pants.

The tea was quite hot. I waited for it to cool, but before it cooled I fell asleep. I slept through the afternoon, dreamlessly.

During my sleep I went on coughing. My tongue and my whole mouth felt dry. I was so thirsty I could have died, but I was too tired to open my eyes.

The first thing I did when I woke up was look for a drink. I snatched a cup of tea off the table and finished it in a gulp—cool, fragrant tea. I realized it was getting dark. My head ached as if it had been given a hard knock. I reclined against my backpack. There was no one in the room, no one outside. I remembered the previous night and figured they must have gone off to the basketball court.

I hadn't realized what a frightful thing I'd done. I'd drunk a whole cup of tea from a leper's cup!

I couldn't get back to sleep. My dazed consciousness was like a wounded bird, unable to fly, unwilling to fall back to earth. I started coughing again until my throat felt as if it was going to split. For the first time in my life I lost all sense of time. Machu village became a thing of the past, as if it had all happened a long time ago. I couldn't remember the woman's features, but I longed for her to return, longed to have her at my side again.

I vaguely remember unrolling the sleeping bag on the floor and insisting I was going to sleep in it, but at last it was the little boy who slept in it. I also remember her stuffing some white pills in my mouth. There seemed to be a doctor there from whom she took the pills, a woman doctor.

That night I had a fever. I finally fell asleep at dawn. Afterward she said I'd been talking the whole night, that none of what I said made sense. She said she hadn't slept all night. And that's how I became her patient.

IX

For two whole days I couldn't go outside. She didn't let me, and anyway I was too weak. She permitted me to walk only as far as her door, so I sat on the old wooden chair and stared out at her little roof-terrace, bored out of my mind. From morning until night I watched her two neighbors. And I actually observed some interesting phenomena.

She usually went out during the day. Sometimes she took the child. When she left him home, he rarely went out to sun himself with the other two women, but sat motionless on the sleeping cushion, watching me. I felt he was studying me, and it was not an enjoyable experience. There were three shallow wrinkles across his forehead. His gaze was uncanny.

Having this little elf scrutinize me was just too disconcerting. I decided to stare back at him. As long as you believed your opponent couldn't guess your thoughts, it was a delightful little game. I resolved to see who blinked first . . . not just once . . . ninety-nine times. I had plenty of time on my hands, but the sad thing was, after nine times I lost all my confidence. Those nine times, I won just once, and only after he beat me six times in a row. It wasn't an even match. I'd lost heart. My eyes felt prickly. I had to stop. The only benefit of this game was that I'd momentarily forgotten that he was watching me.

Then I got a new idea. I was bored silly, so all my ideas were silly. I took him onto my lap—he was lighter than I could have imagined—got him to look me straight in the face, and stuck my index finger between my eyes, so I went cross-eyed. I knew I looked funny—my showstopper! And it made him laugh for the first time in the twenty hours I'd known him. He lost that attentive, scrutinizing expression, and didn't look so precocious.

I decided to teach him my trick. All I had to do was take my finger and point it between his eyes, and his two little eyes came right together— he looked inexpressibly cute that way. I burst out in a big laugh, and he laughed with me. But something went wrong. When I took away my finger, his two eyes stayed crossed. I called to him, yelled at him—no good. I grabbed his little head and gave it a couple of shakes. Still just the same. I was worried. Then I remembered a story about the old worn-out scholar who won first place in the imperial examinations and was so ecstatic he went out of his mind until his father-in-law finally gave him a slap and brought him back to his senses. I didn't give it another moment's thought, just let him have it with the flat of my hand.

He let out a wail. The two women turned to look at me.

When I saw the blood running from his mouth, I felt bad, but that slap ended this boring story of the little boy who went cross-eyed.

*   *   *

Isn't there a philosopher who said, "Of all states of mind one can fall into, the most terrifying is boredom"? After two days shut inside that room, I fell into it. But these others, shut up in this village all year round—the word "boredom" wasn't enough for their condition. Those two women, for example, my temporary neighbors—I watched them a long time, and took careful note. They said nothing to each other. The shorter, dull-witted one was always drooling. It was she who rose first in the morning and began going in and out of their room, wearing pants.

Each morning she left the courtyard just once. When the sun came up she helped the tall one, also in pants, to walk out to the wall, supporting her by the arm. She helped her sit, and after that they had little to do with each other. Each sat by herself in the same place every day. By the time the short one was looking up at the sky, she was already dozing off.

They sat like this for two hours, then began to get restless. The tall one stretched her neck; the short one reached inside her blouse and scratched vigorously, then the tall one pulled out a little steel box from somewhere under her blouse, carefully unscrewed the lid, delicately poured out a little bit of something onto her thumbnail, and lifted her thumbnail to her nostril. I saw her sniff vigorously, raise a grotesque face to the sky, and sneeze violently with a most satisfied expression. The short one watched the entire process, admiration filling her moronic eyes.

The tall one repeated the same preparation, this time for her companion. I watched, my eyes moist with tears, as she stretched out her thumb to the short one's nostril. The short one's mucus moistened the tall one's thumb, but the tall one didn't pay the least mind, as absorbed in watching the short one sneezing as if she had been the one sneezing herself. I didn't know whether this was snuff, but I realized it was their greatest spiritual pleasure. Too bad—the scene ended here, and in the following days I never witnessed it again.

Then they went back to their usual places, just as before, each by herself, motionless.

Toward noon it started getting warm. First the short one took off her pants and opened her blouse to let the sunlight caress her. A bit later the tall one did the same. She was even thinner than the short one. Both were deeply tanned. I couldn't understand why they were so crazy about the sun.

It was the short one who fetched lunch, an earthenware bowl filled with tsampa. Then she fetched a bowl of water and sat back down in her usual place. Each took water, kneaded some tsampa into a ball, put it in her mouth, rhythmically chewed a while, and finally raised her chin and swallowed with a great effort. They both had good appetites.

After lunch they sprawled out, went to sleep, and slept so soundly I believe a clap of thunder wouldn't have roused them. They woke up a couple of hours later, stretched their backs and legs, and didn't move again, sitting quietly until the sun was in the west. Neither went to the basketball court.

When it was getting dark they walked outside the gate—to piss, I guess. The short one supported the tall one. Then they returned, went into their room, and shut the door until morning. I suppose they ate their breakfast and supper inside. My landlady brought them all their water in a little wooden bucket. They didn't make tea.

Sometimes the boy went out and walked over to them. Whoever was closer to him would reach out and take him by the hand. I could see they were both fond of him, but I noticed they never hugged him. They were both happy to give him some of their time, and if he needed them to do something, neither refused.

At first I took no notice of the women living in the room below. They rarely spoke, and all their movements were quiet. It was only when I heard a door opening and closing that I realized there was another world down there. In all I saw five elderly women, each going around on her own, passing silently in and out like bit actresses in a pantomime, like ghosts. It was obvious that none had relatives living here in the village. They muddled along together with no interaction. I thought their very souls must be lonesome, if they really had souls. Each one's hair was completely white. My landlady said there were six people in all down below, "but one of them has been paralyzed a long time. She never goes out."

"Can't any of them speak?"

"They all can speak. They speak rarely. They have nothing to say."

"The two upstairs don't speak either."

"The short one cannot say anything. The tall one can speak, but she does not want to."

"Are all the people in the village Tibetan?"

"Some are Chinese, some are Chinese Muslim, some are Lopa."

"Didn't you say there was no one who spoke Chinese?"

"They are Chinese who were born near here. They speak Tibetan. No one here speaks Chinese."

"The old people down below all go out. What for?"

"I also go out. We go to spin prayer wheels. There are two holy trees west of the village. We go to the holy trees and spin prayer wheels."

"You believe in Buddha?" As soon as the words were out of my mouth, I regretted them.

"I must keep busy. I can't be like them," she pointed her finger outside, "always sunning myself like that."

I felt something tug at my heart.

X

"The villagers say that the old deaf mute has gone crazy. Usually he only goes out to climb the mountain. For two days he has not climbed the mountain. He gets up early and walks around the village, back and forth. He has never walked around the village. He walks back and forth, and everyone says he is crazy."

"Why would he walk back and forth around the village?"

"No one understands why he walks back and forth. Now he does not climb the mountain. He walks from morning until evening."

"Doesn't anyone know why he doesn't climb the mountain?"

"No one knows why anyone climbs a mountain, no one knows why anyone lies in the sun, no one knows why anyone spins a prayer wheel."

Maybe I was being self-centered, but I couldn't resist concluding that he was searching for me. He must have regretted letting me in on his secrets, and gotten all worked up. Was he searching for the person to whom he'd made those revelations, to eliminate me? I thought of the morning two days ago, I thought of that cave I could have walked into, I felt goosebumps, I felt a pricking like needles all over my skull. . . .

"I said I have gone to school, I know many Chinese characters."

My mind was in a turmoil. "What'd you say?"

"You are still sick. You are tired. Lie down. I will go out."

"You say you've been to school, you say you know many Chinese characters?"

"Sleep for a while. You must still sleep during the day."

She helped me to lie down, then walked out.

I didn't feel like going to sleep.

Why had she told me all that? She always spoke openly, never vaguely, never evasively. I'd noticed that she spoke simply, but at the same time in a unique way. I'm a fiction writer. I notice people's speech. I knew the way she spoke was extremely rare. Her way of thinking was not like the way most of us think. If you wrote her words down, there would be no question marks. Even if our thinking involves vast leaps of thought, there is always some uncertainty in it, some question. For us, thought without question would be a miracle. But for her, whatever was, was perfectly obvious, clear at a glance, no problem. Just now she said she'd been to school.

Headache.

I'd been shut up in this room too long. I was certain she'd left. I wanted to go out and walk around, but I didn't want to bump into her. It was still a while before dusk, and almost nobody was stirring in the village. She hadn't said anything, but since I'd arrived, her man, the little basketball player, hadn't come to see her. If he hadn't come, mightn't she have gone to his place? I would like to be able to say that this reflection was untainted by jealousy. . . . I can't make out whether it would be accurate to say so or not. Anyway, I decided that she'd gone looking for him.

I'd been sleeping a lot these last few days, from the moment I lay down straight through until dawn. The sky could have fallen, and I'd have slept off to death. I'd been on the mattress, and the little boy had been using my sleeping bag. When I'd gone to bed, she'd still been sitting on the floor, patting the child, and when I'd woken up she'd already been busy going in and out. She probably hadn't slept at all. Should I think about leaving?

Someone was following me.

I didn't look back. I knew who it was. I walked slowly to let him draw near. He didn't. He must have slowed up too. I didn't understand why he was acting like this. I decided to rush him. I gave myself the command for attack, I turned, I strode up to him, I stopped. He couldn't have anticipated this. We stood face to face. I was certain he'd panic. I said, "You haven't climbed the mountain for two days."

To my surprise, he ignored me and walked on past. I stood there stupefied. It was only after a moment I remembered: for decades he'd been playing the role of a deaf mute. He couldn't just simply drop his role out in front of everyone. I was the one who'd been rude. There wasn't a soul in sight, but someone might have caught us talking. I brushed past him once or twice more, cut him off, followed him down the little street. This time, he didn't turn back.

I didn't want to follow him, but I was destined to go where he lived. I'll get to that later.

It was almost dusk. I headed for her room. I remembered the question I'd just been pondering. Should I move out of her house or not? But this was hardly just a question for me. I decided to let her decide.

I never expected it—I went up the stairs, and there was the little basketball player! He was playing with his son in the courtyard. Now he turned and smiled at me. I discovered that I liked this person.

I went past them into the room. Wrong again . . . she wasn't there. So she hadn't gone to find him after all. I sat down on the sleeping cushion, looked out the window, and saw a picture of family happiness.

Daddy made all kinds of funny faces, and son kept giggling. Daddy put son on his back and hoisted him up. Son kept trying to peek round in front to look in Daddy's face. Obviously, it was their classic game.

They played hide-and-seek: Daddy hid his face by keeping it stuck to son's bottom. At this moment things took a dramatic turn. Suddenly

Daddy became distracted, terrified. Son's smile froze on his face. Daddy abandoned the game, and put his son on the ground.

She'd returned.

She paid him no attention.

He didn't look at her, but stubbornly kept his eyes on the ground. She walked past him, reached down, picked up the child, and took him with her into the room. He shot her a hurried glance, turned, and walked out the gate.

What was going on?

I took out a can of pork, opened it for dinner, and watched mother and son swallow it down in a few bites. I was happy. She said, rather embarrassed, "It's good."

XI

I was gradually getting my strength back. That evening I didn't feel like sleeping. I lay down as usual, with their one and only sheepskin over me. I turned toward the wall and lay there motionless, so as not to disturb her.

The room was pitch dark. I reckoned from the sounds that she'd lain down on the floor not far from me. I resisted turning over to see what she'd covered herself with. The night was cold, and I felt miserable.

I lay there without moving, my eyes open. Gradually I got used to the dark. To kill time, I counted—all the way to three thousand three hundred thirty-three. I still couldn't sleep. I could hear she was sleeping, so I quietly turned over.

I hadn't expected to see the faint moonlight shining in through the window. It must be a crescent moon, I thought. In its light I could see her rolled up in a Tibetan sheepskin robe, facing away from me, sound asleep. I could hear her breathing. One bare leg stretched out from under the robe, round and full, suffused with the dim moonlight.

The temperature had dropped. I curled up in a ball under the sheepskin. Sticking out, my face acted as a sensitive thermometer. The tip of my nose was ice-cold. I saw her unconsciously pull in her exposed leg. She must have been much colder than I was.

I'm a rough and ready man. I couldn't stand for this. I had my down jacket—I could do without the sheepskin. What was I waiting for? I groped around with my feet for my shoes, sat up, and covered her with the sheepskin, especially covered her bare little leg.

I sat back down on the sleeping cushion. An incomprehensible warmth welled up in my heart. Sitting there, looking out the little window filled with moonlight, I didn't feel a bit like going to sleep, didn't even feel like lying down. Might as well just close my eyes.

I thought of her sitting on the threshold waiting for me to come back. I recalled how my imagination ran wild after she'd shut her door. I felt I'd known her all my life. It all seemed so far-off, so warm and familiar. I couldn't work out how she'd found my backpack and brought it to her room, how she'd known it was going to rain that night. When I thought of that rain I couldn't help feeling a shiver in my heart, whereupon I became aware of the thick sheepskin pressing down heavily on my body. I felt the warm, mutton-scented sheepskin now. . . . I didn't open my eyes.

My down jacket slid off my knees to the floor. I had no thought of picking it up. Her shoulder was pressing tight against me. She was naked. We were sitting with the sheepskin draped over our shoulders, silent. I was the man—it was up to me. I put my hand on her thigh, she put her hand on my hand, and we began pressing at the same moment. There was no need to say anything. She had nothing on. Why were we sitting here? Let's get under the sheepskin.

It was fragrant and warm that night in Machu village.

I'll eternally remember her passion as we made love. I know that her passion may leave its mark on me for the rest of my life. Still, I can't regret it. I just wasn't sober at the moment. Her heat burned my rational intellect to ashes. But if I had the chance to choose all over again, I wouldn't want my damn rational intellect. I made a frenzied sacrifice of my reason on the altar of her passion. Afterward, we slept deeply, all sweaty under the sheepskin, holding each other in our dreams. I wished we could have slept until doomsday.

The sun rose again.

I'd been lying down a long, long time. I still had plenty of things to do.

XII

How many days had I been in Machu village? I thought this would be a simple matter to work out, but counting the days up on my fingers I didn't get very far. My notion of time relies on the clock, but I'd set off in such a hurry that I'd forgotten my watch that shows the date. I remembered I'd spent May Day in Lhasa. May the first . . . two days on the road . . . that would make it May the third. . . .

I'm inclined to rely on ready-made hypotheses. Instinctively, I decided that my time in Machu village was already half up—four days or so. So today must be day five. To tell the truth, I'm not too fond of five: it's a number with a gloomy aura. But what could I do?

The morning was overcast. The clouds were high, motionless. It didn't look as if it would clear soon. I rejected all thought of moving out of her place, and decided to go to the holy trees that afternoon. I'd already decided the night before what I was going to do that morning—the old deaf mute lived in the southwest corner of the village.

I wanted to determine something. I stood at the gate and raised my eyes northward. If my guess was right, at that moment he was making his way up the mountain. I thought since he'd found me yesterday he wouldn't be crazily rushing around the village anymore. He could return to his old routine now, so he must have gone to climb the mountain. I stood there a long time, searching carefully. Wrong again. No sign of him.

I worked out the direction, and set off the shortest way. It took just a few minutes to walk to his house—small and low, without the courtyard that all Tibetan houses have. His having such a tiny house must have had something to do with his hunchback.

I didn't want to give anybody inside the chance to prepare for my entrance, so I didn't knock. The door wasn't locked. I thought that by bursting in I might discover something marvelous. Silently, I opened the door and stepped inside. If he wasn't paying attention, he wouldn't notice me.

It was only when I got inside that I realized my mistake. There wasn't a window anywhere, and it was so dark that whoever was in the room could see me, but since I'd just come in from the bright light, I couldn't see them. I bumped my head on the ceiling, ducked, then heard the low, vicious snarl of a dog. I panicked, goosebumps all over, but I didn't jump back. I knew it wouldn't be long before my eyes adjusted, so I stood still.

In a moment I could make out the layout of the room. He wasn't there. On his sleeping cushion lay an old dog, a really old dog, its teeth all fallen out. But after all it was still a dog, its bygone fierceness ingrained in its memory. It employed the only thing it had left to intimidate me, its bark. Very effective.

Its baleful eyes brimmed with hatred. Why was it so hostile?

I've wrestled, I've boxed, what's a dog to me? I'm not even afraid of dogs with teeth. By the look of it, toothless, its bark was a bluff. It was funny. The position it was lying in was peculiar. It had only one front leg. It was a cripple, collecting a disability pension. The reason I'm going into such minute detail about a dog is that there was nothing else in the room worth mentioning. Besides, the dog was striking. Someone had cut off its ears.

I'd been in bed two days, bored to death, so I was eager for some action. I hoped this dog would pounce on me so I could pummel it. By its fierce look I reckoned it wouldn't let me take another step. So I took three steps. Strangely enough it stopped barking. As I approached, it curled up and looked just simply pitiful. It had a strange expression in its eyes. A miserable thing. I lost interest in it.

In the house of this old man with a gun who pretended to be a deaf mute and spoke Chinese, I thought I could find something extraordinary. I checked around carefully. There was an iron stove, an aluminum water bottle, and a stack of pine branches for firewood. There was a pair of old-fashioned leather shoes, completely worn out, a Tibetan table, a wooden bucket, a thangkug,[4] and two wooden bowls. The walls were bare, nothing stuck up on them. If this room concealed something, I guessed it must be under the bed.

I knelt, put my face down against the floor, and gazed under the bed. I couldn't see clearly what it was, but I could tell for sure it wasn't shoes. As I approached, the dog became even more agitated. To my surprise, it rolled over on its back, belly in the air, and started quivering.

I explored beneath the bed, and, with no great effort, pulled that thing out. It was an old military officer's hat, with the Guomindang insignia—the white sun on a blue sky! Now I got really scared. I hurriedly kicked the hat back under the bed. My heart was thumping. The door released a flood of sunlight into the room. He'd returned.

XIII

The same thing happened to him as to me: he didn't immediately detect that I was in the room. He turned round to shut the door. All of a sudden the dog gave a joyful bark. I started with fear. Every detail of that gun pointing at me came back clearly. I didn't want to alarm him. I decided to speak up and say something to let him know I was there.

"I've been waiting for you."

He wasn't surprised at all. He acted as if he hadn't heard what I said. "Why didn't you go climb the mountain?"

4. Thangkug: a bag for tsampa.

He walked over to the bed, reached down, and scratched the dog's belly. The dog appeared delighted, stretched up its belly and spread its hind legs as wide as it could. It was a bitch, and apparently it had never had puppies: its three pairs of little nipples were tiny and shriveled like a male's. A bitch that's never had puppies—that's rare. "Don't you remember me?" I said in a low voice.

He refused to hear me. I thought he was being careful: walls have ears. I lowered my voice and repeated, "Don't you remember me?"

Head down, he was absorbed in scratching the dog. I couldn't see his face, but I could see the dog was acting like it was in heat. My heart rose, I felt sick. . . . I didn't want to suppose anything like. . . .

I couldn't reconcile this shriveled, skinny old hunchback with the officer's hat and Mauser pistol. I got up the courage to bump him with my hand. He looked up—the portrait of idiocy. This he couldn't have feigned, I swear.

I doubted my own memory. I didn't know how to conceive what had happened on the mountain. He appeared now like that short retarded woman. Could his gun have been nothing more than my fantasy? Was I suffering from hallucinatory delusions? I stole a look under the bed. There was the officer's hat. What the devil did it all mean?

Maybe there was a different explanation: was he really like the villagers said, mad? In these two days, gone mad?

I pondered it. Tibet was liberated in 1950. So he'd entered Machu village thirty-six years ago. How could he not know leprosy was contagious? Why was he hiding here? If he knew it was contagious (I guessed he must know) and still came here, then avoiding capture must have been a matter of life or death. He'd committed some enormous crime. No enormous crime, no taking such an enormous risk—that was my conclusion. Maybe he'd been some important figure in the Guomindang who had escaped capture during the liberation of Tibet, and hid here for thirty-six years.

At this thought, my heart began trembling. I'd fallen into his clutches: I was in a grim predicament. But he appeared to mean me no harm. I stood there behind him, but he didn't act wary—still the image of idiocy. He was either mentally retarded, or else a terrific actor, and a devilish, vicious murderer.

I didn't want to sit there and wait for it. He wasn't watching me. This was my chance to run. Why not risk it? I glanced back at him and the old bitch. He was digging his index and middle fingers into the dog's vagina. Its eyes were closed with pleasure.

I fled that cave without the least problem.

But I couldn't understand why he was afraid inside his own house. Even if he was demented, he still could have said something. If he'd gone insane, his self-control would have been evaporated. He shouldn't have been afraid to reveal his identity. He hadn't paid me any attention. Why did he refuse to recognize me?

In the powerful sunlight I felt I was back in the familiar world I'd lived in for better than thirty years. I walked west from his little house, toward the trees. Unwilling to think about him anymore, I made a deliberate effort to forget every detail of him.

For half a day I succeeded. Thanks to the sacred trees.

XIV

I had to walk an hour west from the village.

I was going along a little path, quite narrow, only room enough for one person. I could see two people ahead of me, a long distance apart from each other. The ground was level, and there was absolutely no reason to follow the path, but in fact everyone followed this little path, which had been worn out over the years. I didn't feel like opening up a new path. Ordinarily I just take the ready-made path without a thought.

Gradually the terrain rose. I was walking uphill, getting out of breath. I stopped to rest and looked back at Machu. There was no sign of life: Machu village was like an abandoned ruin at the edge of a vast stretch of mud and rock that had slid down off the mountain. From a distance the little houses appeared like giant boulders. There was very little mud on this stretch of land, and little green. The boulder-strewn ground looked as if it had been created moments ago by some cataclysm. But behind me the two gigantic trees reminded me: this most recent transformation of the mountains was a tale of long ago.

There were two more people following behind me, far apart, a long way off, and I could make out they were women.

I continued on. The sacred trees weren't far.

Their two trunks were joined together. I didn't recognize the species, but these were the thickest trees I'd ever seen. Beneath the powerful sunlight, they gathered a broad expanse of cool shade. Their green leaves were fresh, dazzling, but only grew on the top branches, too far away. I heard a knocking sound, pleasant to the ear.

There were several people under the trees, walking around them counterclockwise. I grabbed my camera and photographed them from all different angles. I didn't seem to attract the people's attention at all. I remembered that the people who spin prayer wheels in Lhasa always walk clockwise, but I'd never understood why. Here they walked counterclockwise. And the people who spin prayer wheels in Lhasa aren't separated, men from women, but here they were all women. Another difference between the people here and those in Lhasa was that the people here held no prayer beads and didn't chant the mantra. My photographs recorded things here just as they were. I used genuine made-in-Japan Fujicolor film. All in all six women stepped into my viewfinder, walking in measured rhythm, eyes almost closed. I guess none was younger than forty-five.

Just as I ascertained she wasn't among them, she came up from behind me and joined the moving formation, legs advancing mechanically. She didn't look at me, but closed her eyes like the others. With everyone else so devout, I felt ashamed peering left and right, and I did my best to stop gazing around, but I just couldn't help regarding this solemn scene out of the corner of my eye.

When I'd taken my long-range shots, I walked in beneath the shade. To my surprise I discovered a man sitting in the crevice between the two trunks—it was *him* making this pleasant sound, hammering a piece of rock, an unfinished sculpture, the bas-relief of a human head! I'd never imagined he was a sculptor of buddhas. There were no prayer flags or khatags around the tree trunks, but there were several dozen small, round relief sculptures of human heads evenly spaced all around the two trunks. From my little knowledge of Buddhism, I could see these carvings weren't Buddha Sakyamuni, King Srongtsan Gampo, or the Lotus Master, nor any of the attitudes and expressions of the Happy Buddha. Anyway, he'd made some idols, and these idols coexisted with the holy trees, consecrated for the people to bow before and worship.

I'd walked all the way here in the sun, and felt prickly all over. What surprised me was that after I'd walked in the circle with them several times, without my realizing it, the prickly sensation had disappeared. Each one apparently went round a fixed number of times. I watched the ones who'd been there first leave, one after another. Then the ones who came afterward also left. She'd already left as well, without a glance at him or at me. By the position of the sun, it had to be lunchtime. I became the last one spinning a prayer wheel. My spirit felt limpid and cool, my mind as peaceful as a turquoise tidal pool. I might have continued on going round the trees if he hadn't waved at me.

I didn't understand what he said, but I understood his gestures: he wanted me to take his picture. Naturally, I was glad to oblige. I motioned for him to go on chiseling, and snapped his moods and attitudes at work from every angle. Then I took a full-length photo portrait of him, as a keepsake of the occasion.

I could sense his goodwill toward me. We walked back together without speaking. Now from the depths of my heart came a kind of shudder; for no reason I felt a profound anxiety. I didn't know why, I only knew something was going to happen, something big. As we entered the village and were about to part company I gave him a can of pork (the same kind I had given the woman and child to eat the night before). He accepted it happily, and told me by gestures that he wanted to give me one of his carvings. This I really hadn't expected. I got so excited I was trembling.

XV

I couldn't have said exactly why, but I felt the sorrow of one about to depart. For the second time, I arrived at dusk at the basketball court. Although I hadn't yet decided to leave Machu village next morning, my intuition told me that this was the last time in my life I would be among them. Although we're contemporaries and live on the same planet, our worlds are cut off from each other. They are abandoned children. That's putting it cruelly, but it's true.

I knew almost all the villagers were gathered here. Only a few retarded ones and old women weren't present. I wanted to walk among them, gaze into each one's eyes, watch the men play basketball, behold the rest become an enthusiastic audience of their own free will. I was no longer afraid of them noticing me. Slowly, I strolled among the crowd, noticing that many younger women and many women in their prime had lots of children, all about the same size.

That night, I asked her, "Seems like, I hear, the . . . I mean . . . your disease is . . . contagious?"

She said, "I am not sure. Other people fear us."

I said, "Especially . . . I hear it's hereditary. . . . I mean, if someone with the disease has a child, that child is born a leper. . . ." This was the first time the name of the disease had been mentioned in our conversation.

She said, "Everyone says this. What can we do?"

"I saw so many women with lots of children. When the children are born lepers . . . don't the mothers suffer? Couldn't they stop having them?"

"What else can they do? They must have children, so they have children."

"They don't understand . . . but don't *you* understand either? You've been to school, haven't you? Why do you want to have children? You're irresponsible."

"I have children whether I want to have children or not. Maybe I am pregnant again. Maybe I am going to have yours, and soon I will have it."

"Then don't get pregnant! Don't get pregnant!" I'd burst into hysteria. My voice was thick, agonized.

"This is not something women can decide. You must know this."

"Then why don't you . . . use contraceptives?"

"You said something I do not understand. Say it again."

I'd forgotten where I was. How could I clarify this new term, this new concept? I was getting more and more desperate. I said, "Then . . . men and women shouldn't sleep together."

"What else is there to do here? You have seen. Besides basketball, what is there for men to do? Besides sleeping with men, what is there for women to do? No other young women go to spin a prayer wheel. I am the only one. There is nothing else for people to do. Tell me, if they don't do this, what is there to do?"

I'd wanted to warn her to think of the children, but now all of a sudden I felt my words were hollow. I held my tongue.

Afterward I thought to tell her that the little basketball player was going to give me one of his sculptures. She gave a graceful laugh. "He likes you. You make people like you."

It annoyed me, her saying this. I wasn't a three-year-old child. I don't like people talking to me that way. Now I unexpectedly discovered a meaningful change: when she'd gotten angry with me she'd used a series of questions: "What is there to do?"—three times, one after another. Although anyone else might have thought it was nothing, I was pleased. I knew what this change meant. I didn't know whether or not I should tell her that I had noticed it.

She said, "You know he likes you."

Solemnly I nodded my assent.

She said, "You don't know he is a Lopa."

In fact, I hadn't known. I deliberately used my calmest, coolest tone to say, "I didn't know."

"They do not like Lopas. They do not let me have anything to do with Lopas. I have not had anything to do with him for a long time."

I didn't feel it was right for me to ask who she meant by "they." She had her reasons for not explaining. Maybe she didn't feel it was proper to explain. I remembered the first time at the basketball court: she had been so proud when she said the child was his. Then there was the time she had been so cold to him. Because other people ("they") didn't allow it, she'd gotten rid of him. This made me angry with her, made me hate her. This time I definitely was considering the matter without any trace of jealousy.

I said, "You're making me angry."

"You say things I do not understand."

"What you said makes me angry, makes me hate you, despise you. Now do you understand?"

She said, "Then despise me."

When she said that, I just didn't know what to say.

The most disheartening event of all came later. After I'd put my last ounce of strength into it, I was panting, exhausted. But she said, "Your strength is not real. You are not as good as he is. When he came here he did it all night and did not pant."

Could I tell her it was altitude sickness? I just couldn't get an excuse like that out of my mouth.

XVI

She was already asleep, her body relaxed, her swelling breasts and her thighs pressing against me. I loved them. I didn't care that her fingers and toes were half rotted away, that her nipples were rotted. She was a warm, fragrant woman. That was more important than anything. And I knew one more important thing. She loved me. And so there was even a moment when I thought of staying among them, of remaining by her side.

Just before I fell asleep, I felt that quiver again deep in my heart. I started reasoning with myself: how could it be an omen? It was just exhaustion. I had overindulged in passion. I hoped (so much! so much!) I could persuade myself and finally fall asleep. I was confident that once I fell asleep, when I opened my eyes again the sun would be shining bright through the window. I couldn't . . . couldn't . . . could . . . not. . . . Without realizing it I overcame the irrational fear that lay at the heart of my insomnia.

In the morning it was bright sunny skies once more. With a sky full of light, those anxious tremors had dissolved.

After I'd gone to the holy trees, I'd clean forgotten all about the old deaf mute. I thought of all that had happened the day before at his house, one detail after another. The Guomindang officer's hat. His retarded look. Sex with his dog. Then there was that day on the street, when he passed me by and completely ignored me. I believed I'd discovered the crux of the problem.

Half an hour later I was walking the path he had worn out up the mountain. I'd purposely donned my brick-red down jacket. I was climbing at an easy, steady pace, stopping every so often to turn back and look. The morning sun was up, and the air was warm. I felt hot. So, halfway up, I sat down to rest, deliberately positioning myself on a protruding rock.

From here I could see clear out across the brown, rocky ground that stretched off to the river, the two houses, small as matchboxes there on the bank, and the dark green current. The mountains opposite rose and fell, already suffused light yellow, lower than the mountains at my back, and more lovely.

I shifted my gaze, and now I saw a tiny figure moving through the village. He was coming. I'd succeeded after all.

He'd left the village and reached the foot of the mountain. I wanted him excited, so I rose and rushed up the mountain for all I was worth. When I turned back and looked, he was going all out. I couldn't help feeling pleased. I thought I might as well hide behind a pile of boulders.

At last he caught up. I'd forgotten he was an old, old man. I heard him panting. Like a flash I jumped out from behind the boulders and stood there before him, calm and good-humored. When he saw me, he collapsed to the ground, pouring sweat, fear all over his face. My heart filled with pity for him. I was profoundly aware he didn't deserve pity. He'd gotten what he deserved, rushing up this mountain as if his life depended on it. He had skeletons in his closet. He didn't have to live on pins and needles all the time. He could have chosen another way of life.

I stood there looking down at him as he lay there, still unconscious. He must have been eighty years old. There were liver spots all over his face, his neck, his hands. He was panting. His eyes were dazed, the light almost gone from his pupils. He was finished.

But he'd been so energetic just four days ago! He'd dominated me. These past thirty-odd years had been rough on him, sure, but after all he'd lived through them. I couldn't figure it out—how had these last four days brought him to the verge of death? Maybe he'd been suffering from madness all along. This locale was the perfect soil to nurture madness, no doubt about it. Maybe it was just because someone who spoke Chinese had come and roused the urge to talk that he'd been suppressed all those years.

How had he managed to endure living for three decades in a leper colony? How much more unthinkable that he'd sealed his lips to make himself a deaf mute! The deaf mute had spoken, and now it was all over. I had no way to tell whether he was a leper—the symptoms weren't apparent. But I could see he was a psychiatric case. He'd had a complete breakdown.

Maybe he was a fugitive, guilty of heinous crimes. Maybe he'd never done anything wrong. But there was some secret behind his voluntary self-seclusion in Machu village. I didn't care about discovering who he was, I didn't want to know what he'd done, I just couldn't bear to think that he'd chosen to live this way.

Contrary to anything I expected, he started talking.

"People here all take me for a deaf mute. I was afraid I'd forgotten how to speak Chinese. Talking to you now, I see I haven't forgotten. How old do you think I am?"

"How old are you?"

"Give me your first impression. Don't humor me. Don't just tell me something to make me feel good. Tell me the truth. Don't worry. It's all right, understand?"

"I think you're eighty. You hear? Eighty."

"My father's family was rich. I was the one who decided to quit studying. Nobody here can tell I've been to school. My father's family were traders from India."

"How about your mother?"

"I didn't talk. Afterward nobody talked to me. They took me for deaf. I haven't had a name all these years and I've lived all the same. They think I'm stupid for climbing the mountain."

"They don't understand why you climb the mountain."

His eyes looked straight ahead. "You'd never believe I have a gun."

"I know you have a gun. A twenty-shot Mauser."

He was staring blankly, straight ahead. Before he could start talking again, I cut in, "Do you want some more hardtack?"

He seemed to think a while, then said, "Hardtack? What do you mean 'hardtack'?"

I took a couple of pieces out of my backpack and put them in his hand. He stared at them, looked up at me and said, "You'd never believe I have a gun."

I said again, "A twenty-shot Mauser. I believe you."

With a dejected look, he took the first piece of hardtack and crushed it to bits against a rock. Then he smashed the second piece. This time he didn't look up, but said in a low voice, "You'd never believe I have a gun."

Impulsively I replied with irony, "Of course I don't believe it."

He finished proudly, "A twenty-shot Mauser."

I said, "I still don't believe it."

"In a while we'll see it. The rain can't get at it where I've put it. Not a speck of rust. Nobody knows. I've been climbing the mountain since the day I got here. I'm the one who wore this little path."

Only now I realized—everything he said I'd heard him say before. I didn't want any part of the role he was casting me in. I didn't want to go through a repeat performance of that melodrama of four days ago!

"Too bad there's only six bullets left," he said. "Not bad at all, after thirty years."

Last time it was six. This time it would be five.

But I'd worried for nothing. He never rose from the ground. He was too feeble. Climbing the mountain this time had sapped the last of his energy.

I reckoned he wouldn't be likely to get up soon, so I turned and hurried down the mountain alone.

XVII

Maybe it was from a guilty conscience. . . . I quickened my pace. I was afraid of a bullet in the back. I dodged behind a huge rock to rest. When I looked behind me, the old deaf mute was out of sight.

I was excited, tired. I had the illusion that the entire slope was sliding. I felt my heart tremble. My eyes went dim. I saw the whole side of the mountain slide down onto the boulder-strewn land below me. I was dizzy. I hadn't got my strength back. I couldn't bear it. I shouldn't have been rushing up and down this mountain. I continued down slowly, gradually. I kept looking back, but I saw no sign of him. I urged myself to be calm, to keep steady footing, but over and over I found myself quickening my pace. I was afraid.

I remembered now what I'd wanted to do. She'd said he was a Lopa. No wonder the way he spoke sounded strange, different.

There were only a few dozen houses in the village. I'd spent a little time here now. It would be no problem to find out where he lived.

The night before, she'd said, "You know he likes you." At the time I'd nodded. In fact I hadn't known. He'd been rather friendly to me, I could see that, but he could certainly see my relationship with her. Didn't he reckon I'd stolen his woman? I wasn't familiar with the local customs, but I guessed any man anywhere would get heated up about something like that. Could he be an exception? In any case, when she'd boasted how good he was, I knew how uncomfortable it had made me feel.

I saw it all clearly. She didn't belong to anybody, she was free, she belonged to herself. And he apparently had no objection to that. But I wasn't able to take things so philosophically. I couldn't bear the thought of her belonging to another man. My heart was getting all worked up into a jealous frenzy. She'd borne him a child. So in order for me to make a good showing, I ardently hoped that she'd conceived my child, and best of all, a boy. My son would surely be better than his son. I hardly felt like looking for him anymore.

No, out of the question! His stone carvings fascinated me. Besides, I'd already given him a present, so he should give me a present too. I didn't reckon the exchange would be a fair one, but I wasn't going to weigh the matter according to justice. I could certainly find out where he lived.

But it wasn't all that simple to find a person in Machu village. First, my language wasn't the same as theirs. Second, there was nobody stirring. Every single family shut their door and stayed inside, and I didn't feel like going up and knocking on somebody's door. For a while I walked around in vain, then finally decided to go back and ask her.

Now I discovered that I was afraid to encounter her. Our conversation the night before had put a distance between us. After all, we came from two different worlds. We couldn't understand each other, shouldn't even have gotten involved with each other. Two people embracing and making love generate all kinds of idle fantasies: for example, the contagion and prevention of leprosy; for example, who belongs to whom; for example, an unwarranted desire to sacrifice oneself for love, etc., etc.

I'm nothing but a Lhasa fiction writer who's cooked up a few extraordinary notions. I've read a few books, understood a few odds and ends of human nature, so I become a true romantic, galloping off like a celestial horse across the sky, into blind foolishness. There's nobody more useless than I am. I get worked up and indignant, red hot, sighing with feeling, blathering on, spouting a load of philosophy, then cool down and take care of my own business, tuck my tail between my legs and behave at last like a good human being.

I would roar a while, then get my ass out of here. What had I solved? Contraception? Hereditary disease, was it? Maybe I was leaving a little problem behind myself. The fact was, I had no power to change Machu village. But here I was tossing around civilized solutions, and who knew what the results would be? I realized what I'd said must have wounded her deeply.

Wait! She said he was a Lopa. Lopas don't live in stone houses. If he followed the Lopa custom, he must live in a wooden house. I knew there were only two wooden houses in the village, I just hadn't paid any particular attention. It must have been Lopas who lived in them.

The two houses were next to each other. I came upon them from the south. One of the doors stood open, and lying in the doorway was a big dog, the kind that drains your courage just to look at it. I sure didn't want to provoke that dog, so I went over and knocked on the door that was shut.

I heard the sound of a reply, and the door swung open. The woman who came out was extremely short, delicately formed, young, and dressed in Lopa attire. She appeared astonished at my visit. Once again, I didn't know what to do. She was definitely no leper: her skin was light—apparently she rarely went out of the house. All I could do was speak to her in Chinese. "Is your man at home?"

She shook her head. I sensed that she understood my question. I asked, "Where did he go?"

She pointed west, and as she pointed with one hand, she raised the other as if to say, "Tall." Apparently he was still carving statues at the sacred trees.

I asked, "Is he your man?"

She nodded proudly.

I spotted a little boy behind her, skinny as a monkey, his head level with her hip. The child was just the replica of him, except that it was only skin and bones. Its eyes, for such a tiny child, were too large. The child was doing its best to hide behind its mother, but couldn't help peeking out and stealing a glance at me every now and then.

From the room came a baby's wail. She immediately abandoned me and the little boy. The little boy ran and cowered behind her. I followed on my own into the room.

It would be too brutal to describe that room in all its painful detail. I found six children in it, one smaller than the other, apparently all his and the woman's.

I couldn't bear to observe whether any of the children bore marks of the disease. I saw the can of pork I'd given him yesterday, placed where the children couldn't reach it, like an object of veneration. My heart was crushed.

I was unable to endure that room any longer. Besides, I saw none of his carvings there. I decided to go once again to the holy trees.

It was almost noon now. The dog barked behind me.

XVIII

When I reached the western edge of the village, I saw the old women coming toward me. There was room for only one person on this path, so I stopped. I didn't want to violate the established custom. If I walked the opposite way, I'd have had to start wearing out another path. That would have been no good.

After they'd reached the village, I remained waiting alone on the edge of Machu. It wasn't until past noon that I saw him coming toward me off in the distance, carrying a heavy stone in his hands. He was walking, stopping, walking, stopping, while I watched with tears in my eyes.

He saw me too, and once again he gave me such a friendly smile. Now I understood: he really did like me. I liked him even more.

It was the piece of sculpture he'd been chiseling yesterday, with a pair of huge, exaggerated eyes—a perfect specimen of expressionism. The nose was nothing but a short, stubby strip. The face had a pointed chin, but no mouth. Strangest of all, in the middle of its broad, broad forehead he had carved a vivid mountain.

Solemnly he placed this carving in my hands, then, still facing me, he knelt at my feet. I hurriedly put the stone image on the ground and reached out to help him up. Then I understood: he was worshiping it. This was his god. I knelt down behind him.

After a while he stood up and walked off without looking back. I didn't move. I thought of a word in Tibetan: as he walked away I said in a loud voice, "Thugjeche!" ("Thank you!"). He looked back to show he'd heard. But now in my heart I was saying, "Good-bye, good-bye."

XIX

That same evening, something happened.

Packing, I rolled the carving up in my sleeping bag and stuffed it into my backpack. She was beside me, helping. The child didn't take me for a stranger anymore. He was sitting piggyback on my shoulders, my hair gripped tight in both hands, watching what we were doing. I had the flashlight on.

She said it was too heavy.

I said it was no problem, I could carry it.

She said I'd never come back again.

Then she said she liked me, as her way of speaking had said the night before.

I said I'd seen his woman, seen his and the woman's six children.

She said there were several other children of his in the village. "He is a man who can do it."

I didn't reply.

After a while she said there were always birds on the roof singing before it was light in the morning. She said tomorrow morning I could wake up very, very early and set off before dawn. Her voice was peaceful.

I turned away, didn't want to say anything. I forced myself not to make a sound.

She said that just before dark she saw the old deaf mute walking back down alone from the mountain. She thought he wasn't the same.

"How not the same?" I asked.

"He walked slowly. He usually walks very fast. You have seen him. This evening he walked slowly."

I said, "He just came down from the mountain?"

"He just came down from the mountain. I saw him on the mountain this afternoon. He always used to climb the mountain in the morning."

"I'll be leaving, then."

"You are leaving tomorrow morning?"

I said, "Yes, tomorrow morning."

"Anyway, you are leaving. Then leave tomorrow morning. In the morning everyone is asleep. I am asleep too. Leave in the morning."

"I'd like to take your picture for you, all right?"

"I do not understand taking pictures." She reached up and stroked her face, very slowly, weeping. Suddenly I understood why she didn't want to take a picture. She knew the disease made her ugly. She was a woman! Maybe she'd been a beautiful girl before she contracted the disease . . . definitely, she'd been beautiful.

"I do not understand taking pictures."

At that very moment, a gunshot rang out. Something had happened. I said I was going out. As I was walking toward the door, she said in the same tone of voice I'd heard a moment before, "Then leave tomorrow morning. I will be sleeping in the morning."

Solemnly I nodded in agreement.

XX

I perfectly understood that gunshot.

The white crescent moon had already risen to its zenith, and was waxing now. Machu village lay clear, immersed in moonlight. The path was smooth. I trotted through the entire village. The sound of my steps frightened the stray dogs that roved at night. One set off another, until the whole village was full of their barking.

The gunshot hadn't attracted the villagers' attention. That wasn't bad. I ran up to the old deaf mute's house. The door was wide open. He was dragging the bitch out by the hind leg. He'd killed it. He tossed it into the vacant field in front of his house like he was throwing out a load of garbage. From his movements I could see the disgust in his heart.

The gun wasn't in his hand. I had to beat him to the gun, to keep him from taking the next step. I made it to the door just ahead of him, and turned on my flashlight.

I saw the visored officer's cap with the Guomindang insignia, white sun on a blue sky, trampled to pieces. Then he was at my side, his eyes following the shifting beam of the flashlight. I could hear him panting. I didn't believe he'd try anything on me. Of course there was no reason for my self-assurance. I thought that he might have put the gun somewhere outside. Step by step I followed the flashlight beam out, alone. The moonlight poured down. The flat, rocky ground stretched away, desolate. The dead dog lay like a pile of rags, no visible sign it had ever been alive. So the end of a life was that simple.

I couldn't think where else he might have hidden the gun. My mind was preoccupied with the gun. I heard another shot, as if in a dream. Vaguely, I realized he'd had the gun on him all the time. I'd given him ample time calmly to shoot himself.

Whereupon I decided not to go into his house.

I decided to set out that very night.

I went back to her room. She was already asleep (or pretending to be asleep). Softly, gently, I picked up my backpack, then turned off the flashlight, and put it down beside the last three tins of food.

I wanted to kiss her, but in the end I only kissed the child. I put on my pack, walked out the door, and shut it. Next, I walked out the courtyard door, and shut it.

Last of all, I walked out of the village.

XXI

My pack was heavy. The road was long. I walked, panting, until at last, ahead in the distance, I saw a point of light. I clenched my teeth and kept going. I was tired to death, but tired as I was, I didn't put down my pack, didn't miss a step. I knew if I stopped walking, I'd never stay on my feet.

That point of light was blinking like the fireflies we used to catch when we were little. I walked and walked until, to my surprise, I started dreaming. I dreamed about my little kindergarten sweetheart. We were in bed, sleeping under a child's blanket. Then I peed. She burst out crying. It was only because I was so tired that I peed the bed and dreamed, and on account of that firefly, because I'd already reached the light.

I was so tired I couldn't keep my eyes open. I don't remember knocking on the door. I don't remember how the two Tibetan road maintenance workers wound up on one mattress sleeping on the floor so I could sleep on the other mattress. I slept on until morning without any notion of what was going on around me.

A rumbling sound awoke me. I went back to sleep and slept on until the sun was high. After I opened my eyes I kept dreaming. I couldn't figure out why I was lying in a strange room. I saw two men standing in the doorway, peering outside, talking.

I said, "Hey, what happened?"

The stocky one told me there'd been a landslide that night—half the mountain to the north had fallen. I leaped up and ran to the doorway, and all I could see, across the earth and stretching up to the heavens, was boulders. Machu village was no longer visible. The landslide must have uprooted those two big holy trees.

As I was still gazing north, the skinny one came back and turned on the radio. "Broadcasting live from Beijing Workers' Stadium, with today's May Fourth Invitational Football Tournament. Some of the top international teams are taking part this year—Italy, West Germany, Paraguay. . . ."

"Wait, wait!" I realized something didn't fit. And what was it? Right, the date. "Say, boss," I asked, "What day is it today?"

"Youth Day, May the fourth," the stocky one said.

"May the fourth," I repeated mechanically. Silently, I reckoned . . . left Lhasa on May first, spent the second and third on the road, all that time in Machu village. . . . May the fourth?

XXII

Dear reader, now that I've finished this tragic story, I have something important to tell you. It's all made up. I was afraid you might take it for real. My stay in the Peace and Quiet Hospital will only be temporary. Sooner or later I'll be coming back out among you. I'm tall, a male citizen with a full beard, I have a name. Many of you might be able to pick me out in a crowd. I wouldn't want literal-minded readers to think I was infected with leprosy and treat me like a pariah. I could get banned from public places, even get put in isolation somewhere like Machu village. So that's the reason for this epilogue.

I have a stone relief-carving, a valuable Lopa cultural treasure. I won't tell you where I got it, okay?

I've been to many places in Tibet. Tibet is a young mountain range (as the geologists say), and so you can see spectacular boulder-strewn plateaus all over. A plateau strewn with boulders is the material I like, with a life of its own.

My wife is a reporter. While covering a conference she met a woman doctor who'd worked a year in a leper hospital. My wife listened to her describe that hospital, came home, and told me. There's nothing my wife doesn't discuss with me.

I also happened to read a book by a Frenchman, *A Kiss for a Leper.*[5] Later I read a book about a leper colony by an Englishman entitled *A Burnt-out Case.*[6] This sensational theme fascinated me.

Recently, when the spring wind was at its height, I went to the south of Tibet. The Yarlung Tsangpo River flowed ever eastward, its water clear turquoise. Graceful white seagulls skimmed its surface. Behind me stood the mountains. Between me and the mountains there arose a silent understanding. Without a word we conversed across miles of open rocky ground. Beside me stood a Tibetan shepherd-girl: her shepherd song intoxicated me.

I came back to Lhasa by truck. The driver was a friend of mine, said he'd been all over Tibet. All of a sudden he stopped talking. I asked him what was wrong. He said a few miles north of the place we'd just passed there was a leper colony. He said he'd made it with one of the leper women, kind of plump, had a child too.

These are things I've chanced upon. I'm a writer. Finders keepers. I found something good.

I've added this epilogue to exonerate myself. My masterpiece might lose some of its luster from all these explanations. Of all the bloody luck! But what can I do? Just grin and bear it. Who made me seek out this damned material, this stinking profession? Nobody, of course. I'll just have to put up with the stink.

So now that I've presented you with this fabrication, just between you and me I'll tell you a secret. In its fiction is all my sorrow, all my satisfaction.

5. By François Mauriac.
6. By Graham Greene.

• 3 •

A Ballad of the Himalayas

Ma Yuan

Lingda is a little village, a dozen
families of Lopa people, amidst the lush
vegetation of the Himalaya foothills,
precise location 94 degrees north latitude,
29 degrees east longitude.

I

*T*o ride from Menling to Lingda took us most of the day. My black
horse was glistening with sweat. We followed the south bank of the
Yarlung Tsangpo River along an earthen floodbank that gradually
sloped down into an emerald-green field of grain. The mountains and
valleys blazed green in the June sun, and the morning air was fresh,
with a cool breeze.

I reined in my horse from a trot to a walk, and looked back. My Tibetan guide caught up from behind on his white horse. He'd told me he
knew this country like the back of his hand, though he hadn't been back
here in forty years.

"I still haven't asked your name," I said.

He said, "Norbu."

"Norbu," I repeated mechanically.

"I'm fifty-four," he said.

The path was just wide enough for our two horses. Up on the left
was a tortuous hillside, with an eagle lingering in the air above the
trees.

I asked, "Will we be there soon?"

Norbu said, "It's up ahead now, not far. First, there's a river." When we reached the riverbank I suggested we stop and rest. There was a primitive, sturdy-looking bridge made of logs lashed together. Where our path reached the river a track forked off up into a deep, silent green canyon, both slopes covered in fir trees.

The river flowed northward into the Yarlung Tsangpo River. Above it, the white mountain peaks glistening in the sun dazzled my eyes. We sat on the grass by the side of the path. I opened up a can of peaches. The horses grazed nearby, tin cans dragging on the ground from their hooves. "They're good horses," Norbu said. "They won't run away."

"When was the last time you went to Lingda?" I asked.

"Forty years ago. I was a boy. Dad and I used to go up that canyon hunting."

"What's to hunt up there?"

"There's everything—tigers, leopards. . . ."

"Snow leopards?"

"Snow leopards, gold-spotted leopards. Bears too."

"All gone now," I said.

"All still there," Norbu said. "Straight up that canyon, four days, cross the mountains—India."

I said, "It's farther than that to India." I found my map and showed him. "Look, India begins all the way down here. It's still a couple of hundred kilometers."

"Four days," Norbu said. "My dad was in India."

"Where did your family live then?" I asked.

Norbu stared at the horses, grazing indolently. Suddenly from nearby came the crack of a rifle. The black horse shied, his hide twitching. Norbu jumped up and grabbed the single-barrel firelock he'd laid beside him.

A little hunter suddenly emerged from the canyon, blowing into the barrel-mouth of his gun. A tiny puff of gunsmoke gushed out the loading chamber. He didn't glance at us. He was no more than thirty meters away from us now.

Norbu stood stock-still. The little hunter walked past us as if we weren't even there. Norbu sat back down. The hunter turned up the path the way we'd come. Another moment and he was out of sight. He wore a fur hat, a sheet of heavy Tibetan wool cloth with a hole cut out for his head thrown over his shoulders, a wide leather belt decorated with white shells pulled tight around his waist, and two knives, one long, one short, slung over his shoulder in wooden sheaths looped with brightly polished copper bands.

"That's them," Norbu said. "You saw his face. Lopa men all look like that."

I said, "All I saw was his knives."

"They're all that way. You meet them and they don't say anything. They don't even say hello to people they know."

I said, "I hear every Lopa man is a master hunter."

Norbu didn't reply. He rose, untied the horses, and we started off into the canyon. Soon we were going uphill. A rapid torrent flowed down past us on our right, shallow and clear. On the streambed beneath the current lay pebbles of all colors.

The way was steep. The horses walked slowly. Norbu rode in front, silently, head down, as if he had something on his mind. We entered a forest of red pine. To my surprise, the road widened out. I urged my horse up beside Norbu's. He started talking again.

"My dad was tough," he said suddenly. "All the hunters this side of Sela Mountain still remember him. He was seventeen years older than me."

I reckoned it up silently. The last time he'd come to the mountains, his father couldn't have been more than thirty.

"Dad often went up into the mountains alone," he went on in a low voice. "Just left me at home with some meat and curdled milk."

After a while he added, "From what Dad said, Mother was beautiful. Dad stole her from the pasturelands. She screamed and fought and bit his trigger finger off. After that Dad had to pull the trigger with his middle finger." Norbu pointed to the road ahead and said, "This is the way Dad always took, through this canyon. This is how we came the last time."

I said, "Could he speak their language?"

"Who? Dad?"

I nodded.

Norbu's voice seemed to hesitate. "Some of them speak Tibetan. Dad probably spoke a little of their language. I *think* he could." I noticed he never called them Lopa people, just "them."

It was noon when we got to Lingda, just a little village, a few scattered houses here and there, surrounded by lots of tree stumps, a dirt path twisting among them. I couldn't see anybody around. I couldn't figure out if we were going into one of the Lopa houses or not.

"The men are all up in the mountains," Norbu said, "hunting and farming."

"They farm too?"

"They grow barley and red peppers. Can't do without red peppers." He didn't mention them by name, but he seemed to know a lot about them.

We passed through the village. The cabins were small and primitive—four walls, just logs fastened together. They made me think of forts. The logs were thick, hardly even trimmed with an axe. The sunlight was glorious. At the end of the village we reached a wide clearing, as big as five or six soccer fields, and down below was the river. Next to the clearing was what used to be a stand of tall trees. Some of the remaining trunks were five meters high. Others had fallen almost to the ground, charred black. You could see there had been a big fire. A little path had been worn out through the spaces between the trunks. It was obvious this was the way the village people went up into the mountains. We found a place to sit down.

"Norbu, did this fire start by itself?"

"A fire that starts by itself burns more than this. It burns a whole hillside."

"Did *they* start it then?"

"They always burn the ground around their villages. That way bears can't sneak up and start trouble. Those big fellows won't go through a burn-off." Norbu froze. "Someone's coming," he whispered.

As we watched a man gradually approached. His clothes were just like the hunter's back on the trail. The only difference was he didn't have a gun. Hanging over his shoulder was a bow and a quiver of arrows tipped with eagle feathers. The quiver was half empty. He was old and tiny but his step was vigorous. We sat by the side of the road. He gazed our way but appeared not to have seen us. As he walked by I noticed three snow cocks slung over his back.

As he passed, Norbu never raised his eyes from the ground. Now he started talking. . . .

II

Little Norbu's heart was full of bitterness toward Dad. Months ago, Dad had promised to give him a gun. Of course this was a big event for Norbu. But if Dad really meant to give him a gun, why didn't he give it? Weren't they going together into the mountains to hunt? But Norbu didn't dare complain.

Tall Dad galloped ahead eagerly. Listless and cranky, Little Norbu followed him into Lingda. Dad dismounted, tossed Norbu the reins, told him to wait outside, and hurried into one of the low wooden doorways. There was a delighted scream inside the house. Little Norbu could tell it was a woman's scream. Norbu couldn't understand what she said, but he knew she was happy. At first she just went on talking, then she started to laugh like a duck quacking, and for some reason it gave Norbu a strange feeling. Then she began to groan in a funny way, went on and on, but it didn't sound like anything was hurting her. Norbu felt his heart jump. He didn't wait there to figure out why the woman was moaning. He led the horses away from the cabin. Now he heard the woman cry out "Ah! Ah!" in a voice of full of pleasure. He walked away quickly, his heart in turmoil.

Half an hour later Dad came out of the doorway. The woman followed him. She was beautiful. When Dad turned back, she threw her arms around his neck, stood on her tiptoes, and bit him on the chin. Dad wrapped both hands around her bottom and squeezed it to him. Norbu heard someone coming. It was a little man, in hunter's dress. Norbu saw the face of the woman hanging on Dad's neck change color. She hurriedly dropped her hand that held Dad's waist. Dad looked around, his two hands still on the woman's rear. Then he let her go and walked off, almost brushing against the hunter, without glancing at him, a proud look on his face, almost like he wanted to pick a fight, head up, looking off at the mountains. Norbu followed him with the horses, looking back over his shoulder. The hunter didn't look back any more than Dad did, just went straight into the cabin without a glance at the woman, who stood dazed at the door, staring at Dad as he walked farther and farther away. Norbu didn't peek back again. He caught up to Dad in a trot. They passed over the open ground behind the village and into the dense forest.

Two days later Dad's firelock shot a red deer. Dad had tracked the deer half a day. At last it was unable to leap out of Dad's sights. The dying deer's chest puffed out spurts of foamy blood as it madly crashed its enormous antlers against the surrounding trees until the antlers lay shattered on the ground. Then it lay down, blinking, perfectly content, and elegantly closed its beautiful eyes, noble and solemn. Watching, Norbu was filled with fear. He discovered he didn't like Dad at all. He couldn't forget the expression in the deer's eyes before it died, full of tenderness and contentment.

His right eyelid began to twitch, and it got him all worked up. He felt something dangerous was coming. There wasn't a sound. Why was he so nervous?

Dad skinned the deer with a practiced hand, spread the hide out on a frame of cut branches, and lashed it high up in a pine tree to dry. Norbu stood under the tree, picked up Dad's hunting knife, wiped off the traces of blood, and carved a woman's head in the tree bark. Dad climbed down from the tree, noticed the cut bark on the ground, saw the woman carved in the tree, and laughed oddly at little Norbu.

Dad and Norbu picked up some dried tree branches, preparing to light a fire and roast some deer meat. Little Norbu hesitated and hesitated, and finally told Dad something was going to happen.

"What do you mean? With me around what are you afraid of?"

Norbu didn't know what he was afraid of. A single phrase from Dad shut it all back up inside him.

Another day passed. Again, night fell. They were still camped in the same place. It started to snow, and soon the snow was piled deep.

With Dad there, he didn't need to be afraid of anything.

Next morning the sky was clear, extraordinarily blue. When he woke up Dad was still snoring. He didn't want to disturb him. He sat up quietly.

Now he knew his premonition hadn't been wrong. He saw it.

It was the spots like black pennies that caught Norbu's eye. Against the pure white background of the snow, its white fur looked a dirty, messy gray. It was like a big cat, calm, peaceful, with a cunning look too. It stood thirty paces away, looking without malice at Norbu and Dad.

Maybe its expression confused him . . . little Norbu wasn't afraid. He felt unusually calm. He poked Dad lightly with his toe. The snoring stopped. Dad mumbled something in a dream. Norbu went on bumping him until he finally woke up. Norbu didn't dare say anything, just signaled with a glance. Dad understood too. He rolled over and saw the snow leopard.

Its prints were all around them, some just a foot from where they'd slept. The deer meat hadn't been touched.

Dad didn't move either. He and the leopard stared at each other. Norbu saw the gun hanging from the tree, slung from the knife stuck in the trunk, three paces away. How could Dad get to the gun? Norbu couldn't think of a way out. Any sound, any movement, and the leopard might spring.

Only now could Norbu turn his eyes elsewhere. Since Dad saw the leopard, it wasn't Norbu's anymore.

His eyes drifted. He wasn't the least surprised to see the little hunter behind the tree, drawing his bow. The leopard was exactly halfway between them and the hunter. The difference was that the leopard only saw them. Dad was only looking at the leopard, and the little hunter was only looking at the leopard, and little Norbu was looking at the hunter. Dad hadn't seen him. The leopard hadn't seen the hunter, nor the arrow on his bow that was about to pierce its body.

A delicate moment. The hunter had obviously followed them here. Now Norbu finally realized for the first time what had really frightened him . . . damned premonition!

Norbu saw everything clearly: the hunter's right forefinger and middle finger clenched, released, the arrow quivering lightly, floating with a whistle from the arc of the bow, a tremendous roar, the leopard struck between the eyebrows, shooting like another arrow at the little hunter with his bow still in his hand.

Dad leaped up, dashed to the hunter, and drove his clenched fist straight into the leopard's eye just as its paws seized the hunter's shoulders. Blood splashed out, mixed with clear jelly. The leopard fell on its right side and died without a twitch.

III

Norbu said, "I've never told anyone before."

But he told this story of forty years ago so vividly that I knew he'd repeated it hundreds of times . . . to himself, at least.

I suggested we walk back to the village. We led the horses behind us. The houses were all log cabins, with the same low, narrow doorway that looked like a square hole gouged out of the logs. Each cabin had a yard in front, fenced with thin poles like a stockade.

Norbu stopped in front of one of the yards. Tied inside were three pian oxen, including a silky-haired calf. The oxen had trodden the yard into a quagmire. At one side of the cabin door lay a black dog that rose when it spotted us, big and powerful, built like a small donkey. It didn't bark, it didn't jump, but it had a dark, ferocious look. Glistening black fur made it look all the more quick. I was afraid if it hadn't been tied with a rope of twisted cow tendons, it would have pounced on us.

We'd been munching some dried fruit and bread, and our mouths were parched. I asked Norbu if we could go inside this house and ask for some yak-butter tea.

He fell silent, disconcerted. After a moment, still speechless, he tied our horses outside the yard. I saw the cow-tendon rope was short enough so the dog couldn't get to the door. That clever dog didn't try to intimidate us, didn't snap at us, didn't even bare his teeth. It just stood stock-still and watched us.

Norbu still hesitated. It wasn't the dog that was bothering him—he hardly noticed it. He had something else on his mind. After a minute, still mute, he led me inside.

Coming suddenly out of the piercing sunlight, I couldn't see anything. It was like walking into pitch dark. This lasted about half a minute. Then I could make out the shape of the room in the light from the door behind me. I saw there was another source of light, a vent at the peak of the ceiling. Directly under the vent was a fireplace, four rocks on the floor. The vent served as a chimney. In the middle of the rocks were a few chunks of charcoal burning with a dim red glow. A wisp of blue smoke rose continuously up through the vent. Cut by the rays of light coming in the door, the blue smoke gave the whole room a bizarre, disorienting atmosphere.

I walked over and squatted down next to the old man who'd brought back the snow cock. He was absorbed in what he was doing—smearing a beautiful snow cock all over with mud. It looked to me like he was concentrating more than he really needed to. All the time I was there, he never glanced up at me. He had a flat nose and hollow cheeks. The features of his face seemed all wrinkled together. His hair was just about all white. I saw that his right index finger was entirely missing, but the four remaining fingers were incredibly nimble.

I must have stayed there squatting at the old man's side for half an hour. Finally he finished coating the three birds with mud, stood up, carried them over and put them into a black corner, turned, and walked out the door. I looked around. Norbu had disappeared.

Only now I noticed there was someone else in the room, an old woman, emaciated, her wrinkled face all shiny black, her clothes worn and tattered. As she looked over at the snow cock, the whites of her eyes flashed. My heart jumped.

Rising to her feet, the old woman tottered. Still trembling, she walked over to the fireplace. She was tall and skinny, and looked almost ready to collapse. She took a few sticks of firewood and laid them on the embers, bent over, and started to blow. I stood across from her. After every puff, a red glow flared, lighting her shocking face—two great scars running from the corners of her mouth to her ears. She seemed to be sobbing and smiling at the same time. Her apathetic eyes showed no sign of life. I pulled a lighter out of my pocket, lit some of her dry pine twigs, and put them under her firewood. The fire caught with a crackle.

I shifted my eyes—I couldn't bear to see that face any more. She didn't pay me any attention, and I could look around all I wanted. I noticed a stone mortar in the corner where she'd been sitting, with a pestle in it as thick as your wrist. She'd been grinding peppers, and she'd already ground a lot—I reckoned twenty pounds or more—but she hadn't ground any since I'd come in, or I'd have noticed her.

And I saw all the hot peppers in the wooden bowl she ate from, more than half a bowlful, bright red, with a wooden spoon on top. They must eat them just like that. Of course there was the usual roast barley and dried meat too. In another corner I noticed a broken old wooden pot for making yak-butter tea. I recalled I'd wanted to ask for tea, and then realized I wasn't thirsty anymore.

She was roasting the snow cock on the fire. The mud was hissing out white steam that mixed with blue smoke floating up in the air. My mouth watered.

With an effort, I brought my eyes back to her face. She must have been about sixty. How had her face have gotten ripped apart like that? I could see that once it must have been beautiful. Then it all struck me and I rushed out.

The powerful sunlight made me shut my eyes.

If I figured it right, Norbu and the old man had gone off somewhere together. I followed the road back southward through the forest, the way we came, to a sloping field surrounded with thick reeds. Most of the trees had been cut down here. All that was left was a few tall trunks rising at least four or five meters above the ground, sawed off at the tops. The field was surrounded by a fence of sticks and reeds, and divided into separate plots with reed fences. As I entered the field, I saw that the plots had been ploughed and planted with barley and peppers. I spotted Norbu.

He was leaning on the fence, staring straight in front of him with a dazed expression. His right hand gripped the fencepost. If I'd guessed right, this field must belong to the old man who'd killed the snow cock. And there he was—not far from Norbu on the other side of the fence, cultivating the pepper sprouts in one of the plots. Had he and Norbu been talking?

The old man never looked up when I arrived, completely absorbed in his work, just like in the house.

Neither Norbu or I spoke. He turned and began to walk down the edge of the field. As I followed him along the fence to a gap, I could see he was trembling. He went through it and headed up the mountain. We climbed a long way. Far below us now, we could see the old man working in the field. Norbu sat down.

IV

The leopard was dead.

Dad and the little hunter didn't say a word, didn't even look at each other. It was a delicate matter from start to finish. First the hunter had risked his neck to save Dad by shooting the leopard, now as it turned out Dad had saved the hunter.

The hunter had followed Dad all the way here. It wasn't hard to guess what for.

Still Dad and the hunter paid each other no attention. Dad gathered up the deer meat and packed it on the horse, took the rifle off the tree and slung it over his shoulder, pulled out the knife and thrust it in the sheath on his belt. He didn't glance at the dead leopard, didn't even call Norbu. He just led his horse away from the site of the showdown.

Norbu knew this wasn't over. His heart was heavy. He knew he had to follow. As Dad finished packing, the Lopa hunter stood to one side, arms limp, head down. Now, unhurriedly, he took an arrow from the quiver and laid it on his bow. Norbu cried out—

"Dad!"

Dad didn't turn his head. It was if he hadn't heard the cry bursting from his son's throat. The bow was drawn, then it was empty. Norbu didn't look at Dad. He rushed like a mad dog, seizing the hunter's hand in his teeth. With one swing of his arm the hunter shook Norbu off, turned, and started down the mountain.

Little Norbu didn't need to go up to Dad to know he was done for. He had pitched forward in the snow, his face twisted to one side, his spirit proud even in death. The snow beneath his mouth was stained with frothy blood, dark red, like a flower.

At that moment, Norbu remembered, his mind was empty. He couldn't think. He was too little to bring Dad back home by himself. He just held on to Dad's leg and dragged him backward up the mountain.

Now he had reached the edge of the forest. Up above it was just brush. A little beyond that was the snow line. He was taking his dad above the snow line. Dad's other leg was splayed out, dragging along the ground. It kept getting caught in clumps of brush. The two arms were just as bad. It took all of twelve-year-old Norbu's strength. If he'd dragged his dad by the head, it would have been better, the legs and arms wouldn't have got caught, but Norbu didn't dare. He couldn't forget the red flower that Dad's mouth spat out.

Dad's bulk was so great that Norbu had to rest, going up the hill, more times than he could count. But all the times he had to stop to free Dad's leg from the brush, he didn't dare look into that face.

It took Norbu a whole day to drag his dad's corpse the few hundred meters uphill. He stopped at dusk. It was still a long way to the top, but already here the snow never melted. From down below they'd noticed that the frozen peak was a permanent glacier. Now he and his dad were on the glacier.

Norbu didn't have any idea where the rifle had slipped off. The knife was still there. That was enough. He only needed the knife. He knelt down on the ice, took the knife in both hands, blade facing downward as if he were scraping the earth, and sliced away the surface of the ice. He vaguely remembered the Lopa hunter standing there all the time, not far below. He had no time to pay attention to this man who'd killed his dad. He just scraped away with all his strength at the solid ice. All night his arms moved mechanically back and forth. The man stood there all night too.

With the first light of dawn, he finished. He couldn't stand. The heat from his knees had melted him a foot down into the glacier. He'd cut out a grave of ice, just big enough for his tall brawny dad to sleep in. Still kneeling, he scooped up handfuls of ice chips and scattered them on Dad's face, his shoulders, his body.

A white grave jutted out of the glacier.

V

Norbu stopped there. I said nothing to urge him to continue, waiting, though I didn't know myself what I was waiting for. He stared down at the field below.

"They make those fences to keep out bears and wild boars," he said. "There are lots of wild boars here, black bears too."

Finally I said, "*He's* the Lopa hunter."

Norbu said nothing. I reckoned that his silence acknowledged what I said was true. I'd guessed right!

I thought and thought. At last I made up my mind. "You didn't tell the truth."

Norbu turned his face to me, bewildered.

"Your father didn't die."

He looked at me, shocked. I thought he was playing dumb.

"*He's* your father."

His reaction was beyond anything I expected. He gave a bitter laugh.

"He's missing the index finger on his right hand," I said. "You said your mother bit it off. After that your father pulled the trigger with his middle finger."

He just lowered his head and stared at the ground.

"I don't know why, but you hate your dad. So you say he's dead. Your mother isn't dead either. That woman back in the house—is she your mother. Maybe it's on account of her you hate your father, because she betrayed your father with another man, and your father killed him, and then ripped her face with his bare hands . . . or with his knife? But you hate your father, so you say your mother's dead lover was your father— is that it? I don't know. I only know you didn't tell me the truth."

He opened his mouth, ready to say something, then shut it again.

The old man worked on: the tableau below us was frozen in time. I had to think of something. "Look," I said, "it doesn't matter. You don't have to stay here. I have friends in Lhasa—they'll find you something to do. We'll go back there and. . . ."

Norbu went on staring at the ground. Finally he smiled again, and gently shook his head.

VI

You say you're the one who bit off his finger. When he swung his arm to throw you off, his finger was left there in your mouth.

You got the elder of your clan and he got a gun and seven days later you came back here to Lingda. You went to his cabin. He wasn't there. The tall woman couldn't talk. Her mouth was ripped apart, top and bottom of her lips torn apart as far as her ears. With one hand over her mouth she pointed the way—up the mountain, right where you'd buried your dad. Her mouth . . . who'd torn it? Why had they torn it? You didn't understand.

Most important, you had to take your dad back and bury him in the river, so the Fish-god would bear his soul out to the sea. Your dad grew up with the Yarlung Tsangpo River. You wanted to give him back to Yarlung Tsangpo. Yarlung Tsangpo is Mother of All.

You tied the horses in the trees, and kept going on foot with your clan elder until you reached the place where you'd buried Dad. You stopped, horrified.

The grave of ice was empty, nothing left but a clean hole in the glacier. It was your clan elder who spotted the vultures over the mountaintop, but your eyes were keener—you saw the Lopa hunter kneeling on the peak doing something with his head bent to the ground. Like a madman you rushed to the summit. Your chest was heaving like a bellows. You could hardly keep going. The vultures swirled wildly over a single spot.

Your dad's clothes were already off. His sturdy body lay on the white ice, facing the sky. Unabashed, you saw that even dead, his strong male sex pointed powerfully to the sky. The Lopa hunter cut off a lock of your dad's jet-black hair with his knife and pressed it into the snow with a chunk of ice. Then with one slash of his knife he cut off your dad's penis, calling out to the vultures, raising it up to them in his left hand. Three of them shot down, then rushed back into the sky, snatching it from one another's beaks. Your eyes were full of tears, but you weren't really crying. The day your dad died, the whole night you buried him, you never cried once.

The knife slashed nimbly back and forth. The vultures snatched up your dad until soon there was nothing left but white bones. The Lopa hunter didn't smash the bones. Maybe he hadn't brought anything heavy enough to smash them with, or maybe this was how he planned it.

For many years afterward you'd wanted to come back to the mountain. You dreamed of coming back. The bare white bones one color with the ice, the bones and the never-melting glacier frozen together into the tip of the mountain.

At that moment you'd forgotten the elder of your clan. You went up to the Lopa hunter, face to face. You knelt.

He hung his head.

You remained on your knees, waiting for him to raise his head. The instant he raised his head, you were going to call him . . . "Dad."

But he didn't raise it. He just knelt there.

You never came back for forty years, because when he raised his head you didn't cry out . . . "Dad."

It wasn't that you changed your mind. It wasn't your clan elder standing at your side. In fact the elder was gone and you hadn't even seen him depart.

There was no other reason: he raised his head and you were terrified. Blood dripped from his eyes.

VII

Norbu asked me, "You mean you didn't notice he's blind?"

• 4 •

Encounter

Ge Fei

In the distant past a high lama of the Potala prophesied that in 1904—
the year of the wooden dragon on the Tibetan calendar—a great calamity
would befall Lhasa. On various occasions the lama described this future
catastrophe, but never indicated whence it would come.

In the early summer of 1903, an expeditionary force of English, Sikh,
and Gurkha soldiers stole down the Disita River valley into Gampadzong.
Now at last it became obvious.

I

Before reaching Gampadzong, Col. Francis Younghusband's expeditionary force encountered no obstacles but altitude sickness and torrential
downpours. Of the legendary Tibetan shepherd army, there was no trace.
The vast, lonely plateau appeared sound asleep.

Francis Younghusband was an adventurer in the true sense of the word.
After his graduation from Sandhurst Military Academy, he began his Indian military career in the Meerut region, then transferred to Kashmir. In
the autumn of 1886 he slipped into the Chinese hinterlands and trekked all
over northeast China, Mongolia, Xinjiang, and the Kunlun Mountains.
Younghusband thought he had been selected to command the Tibet expedition for his military talent and mountain expertise. This was not at all
Viceroy Lord Curzon's reason for selecting him. The first time he met
Younghusband, the viceroy was deeply impressed by the young officer's

1. To follow the course of Younghusband's expedition, see the lower left inset on the map.

headstrong character: an obtuse, impulsive man like Younghusband was unquestionably the best choice to wage war in so mysterious a place as Tibet.

In Gampadzong the expeditionary force camped beside a dark, glittering stream on a height of land that overlooked the Tarkang River valley. Snowcapped silver-gray peaks, one beyond another, glittered with a dazzling radiance. Lofty, distant Everest seemed near at hand.

It was June, the beginning of summer. Flowers bloomed everywhere. Colonel Younghusband sat dejected on a tree stump inside his tent, playing a game of Erlut chess[2] with Major Bretherton. It was a game they had just learned to play. Major Bretherton kept turning distractedly to peer out at the lonely valley. His intense, apprehensive stare roused Younghusband's repressed uneasiness.

Here in Gampadzong, Younghusband's troops had been plunged into an endless wait. In his most recent letter, Viceroy Curzon implied that Parliament was undecided whether or not the expeditionary force should continue on to take Chumbi, seize Gyantse, and advance on Lhasa. Younghusband feared that this dithering weakness posing as strength might give the Tibetans time to gather their forces. At the close of the letter Curzon warned Younghusband that there was no reason to do anything rash before the Tibetan and Chinese negotiators arrived in Gampadzong.

Bretherton was a close friend of Younghusband's youth. On the eve of his appointment to the command of the Tibetan expedition, Younghusband had arranged Bretherton's transfer from Katmandu to his own unit, and placed him in charge of the supply train. Bretherton was of an honest, frank disposition, loyal, dutiful, competent—a capable quartermaster. But as Younghusband later realized, not everyone was suited to a place like Tibet. From the day he entered Tibet, Bretherton was overwhelmed with anxiety. Constant dysentery had reduced him to skin and bones. The sound of lamas chanting sutras filled him with foreboding. Again and again he remarked to his companion and benefactor, "Maybe we'll never get to Lhasa."

The wind swept the mountain wilderness. The Tarkang River gurgled peacefully through the valley. Younghusband could see small groups of British soldiers gathering fossils, plants, butterflies, and insects amid the low brush and sparsely growing barley. The broad valley was covered with red azaleas, bright as burning coals. The highland wind blew down across the plain. An indolent silence surrounded the camp, broken only by the murmur of the stream.

---

2. Erlut chess: an Indian board game.

At noon, someone who looked like a missionary, mounted on a small Tibetan horse, came riding slowly up the narrow road along the river toward the English camp. Younghusband peevishly tossed a piece at the board and stood up. "Someone's coming."

"It looks like a minister," Bretherton said.

"It's that Scot we met a few days ago."

Bretherton remained silent. His eyes gazed uneasily at the figure of the clergyman there in the wilderness . . . as if the arrival of a minister was an omen of some unseen danger.

Just after ten in the morning, three men arrived at the command post to speak with Younghusband: a Scottish missionary, the Rev. John Newman; the abbot of Tashi Lhunpo Temple; and He Wenqin, a Chinese official posted in Tibet. He Wenqin had come three hundred miles by order of the imperial Qing court to speak with Younghusband, but since it was impossible for the British officer to meet all three men when lunch was so near, Younghusband followed his instinct and his personal interests and unhesitatingly chose just to see the Grand Abbot of Tashi Lhunpo Temple, leaving He Wenqin to linger in a wheat field outside the command tent in the company of the minister.

The British officers couldn't imagine what the missionary and the Chinese official could be saying to one another out in the broad field. From the informal spontaneity of their gestures, it appeared He Wenqin and Newman not only knew each other, but were quite well acquainted at that, and that the missionary was even celebrating this chance meeting. The missionary approached He Wenqin, all smiles, reaching out to embrace him. Master He drew back. The missionary seemed fascinated by the silk robe He Wenqin wore. He lifted the corner of it, twisting it in his finger. Neither in Chinese nor in British etiquette could such an intimate gesture have been considered anything but indiscreet.

The moment the abbot entered the command tent, he made an unforgettable impression on Younghusband. Years of cold, wind, and sun had left his wrinkled face as dry as a sheepskin. The abbot was so thin his scarlet robe swayed as if it were empty. His polite, benevolent demeanor befitted his clerical status. What shocked the colonel was that this lama from deep down in the labyrinths of a monastery had a fluent command both of English and of Chinese. The abbot was obviously no government representative, but had come, he said, to offer Younghusband his personal advice.

It was clear that the abbot was well versed in the art of diplomacy. He deftly avoided such sensitive terms as "invasion" and "occupation." From religion and medicine their conversation turned to witchcraft and miracles, before the two ultimately came to loggerheads on philosophy. As a student, Younghusband had casually gone through Spinoza and Leibnitz, so he knew enough on this subject to contend with the abbot. Their two-hour discussion was somewhat spoiled by the inordinate amount of time wasted debating the question whether or not the earth was round. But the conversation pleased Younghusband, and many of the abbot's strange, fantastic statements took root in the commander's memory without his realizing it.

II

It was past noon when the abbot emerged from Younghusband's tent. He did not return straight back to Tashi Lhunpo Temple in Shigatse, but set off on a different road.

Younghusband was a difficult man to cope with. The colonel harbored no resentment toward Tibetan Buddhism—he even betrayed a certain cautious curiosity about it—but his cold, disdainful pride rendered him unapproachable.

There was a huge gap between the Lhasa government's assessment of the dilemma and the real situation. The British had completed their preparation to press on into the heartland of Tibet, and their seizure of the holy ground of Lhasa appeared a mere matter of time. There were some things one could not simply say just because one wanted to, the abbot thought to himself with a heavy heart. Not only had he been unable to obtain any useful information out of Younghusband, he had found no opportunity to dissuade him from pressing on to Lhasa, which had been his chief object in coming.

As his horse trotted at a leisurely pace down the sunlit Tarkang valley, the abbot saw ahead the lone figure of the Scottish minister riding beside the riverbed. The Chinese official who had been waiting with him outside Younghusband's tent was nowhere to be seen.

Newman had not really come to Gampadzong to speak with Younghusband, but to meet He Wenqin. But Younghusband's rebuff had so bruised the feelings of the Qing official and left him so crestfallen that he had refused Newman's company and returned alone to his residence in the Chinese village of Cangnan.

The missionary's horse walked slowly. In a short time the abbot had almost caught up with him. A gap remained between the two men as they rode single file down the reddish-brown valley under the burning sun. The summer wind blew a breath of the snow's coolness down from the ridge. Magpie-ducks and snow cocks called among the trees. A waterfall up a nearby gorge roared monotonously.

Perhaps it was to dispel the loneliness of the scene . . . tentatively, the abbot began a conversation. Throughout the aimless dialogue that ensued, the abbot knit his brow, still worried about Younghusband's plans. As the sun set, the red and white Phari fortress arose from the highland landscape. The abbot pulled up his horse. Out of politeness, as a mere parting formality, he asked the Scottish missionary to join him in staying the night at the castle. A grateful, polite refusal formed itself in Newman's mind, but to his lips came an immediate acceptance—an instance of how difficult it sometimes was for the minister to restrain himself. A whole chain of unforeseen consequences was to result from this encounter. At the moment, the prospect of staying together under the same roof made both the Christian missionary and the Tibetan lama uneasy.

The castle stood on a hill in the middle of a plain. Tibetan horses were tethered outside the courtyard in front of the rambling six-story structure. Rows of ravens chattered and squawked on the courtyard eaves. In a gully to the left stood a nunnery. A group of nuns was lined up at the river to draw water.

Never before had Newman managed to obtain permission to enter a Tibetan castle. As they hurriedly ate some tsampa and drank some barley wine in the main dining hall, he asked the abbot for a tour. The abbot pondered a moment, then nodded.

A servant-boy brought them a yak-butter lamp. As Newman followed the abbot up a brick staircase, the gloomy labyrinth of the lower stories unfolded before his eyes. On the second floor he saw an enormous old armory, piled high with straw: barrels of gunpowder, and matchlock rifles, as well as rusted armor, shields, breastplates—discarded relics of ancient times, covered with a thick layer of dust. But in a shrine set in the wall above all these neglected weapons lay row after row of prayer wheels, polished bright from constant use in the grip of innumerable hands.

"Actually, we have never thought there was anything wrong with Christianity," the abbot said as he led the missionary up to the scripture room. "So we have never sent anyone to Scotland to teach Buddhism. All religions are similar in nature, but give rise to completely different customs. Westerners describe Tibetans' appearance as 'dirty.' And in fact, we

seldom wash with water, as you do by splashing in your bathtubs. Our custom is to bathe in a clean wind. To cure illness, the Chinese take the pulse
at the patient's wrist; you slide a thin piece of steel back and forth over
their chest; we decide if a person is sick or not from the froth their urine
makes in a wooden pail." Moonlight through the parapet cast a bluish
tinge over the abbot's face that sent a chill through Newman's whole body.

The minister considered religious debates with lamas part of his sacred duty. In this setting he felt that to dispute religion would not be to
his advantage, but since the abbot had already broached the subject, Newman could only do his best, out of politeness, to answer, amplify, clarify.
"One thing I have never understood," the missionary replied. "You believe
in Buddha, but how do you know Buddha really exists, or where he exists?
And how do you explain the sufferings of this world?"

"How do you Christians know God exists?" the abbot asked in reply.

"From miracles," Newman answered.

"What miracles?"

"For example, in the Bible Moses turns a wooden staff into a snake."

"That is nothing but sorcery," the abbot interrupted with a gentle
laugh. "In Tibet many itinerant magicians are skilled in such arts."

Newman's face turned red with embarrassment and rage. As he was
thinking up some stunning refutation, the abbot patted him on the
shoulder and said in a quiet, mysterious tone, "Come, I have something
to show you."

Guided by the light of the abbot's flickering lamp, Newman followed
him down a stairway. They passed through one corridor after another, all
blackened with smoke and soot, through a hidden chamber, and finally arrived in a small secluded courtyard at the back of the fortress.

"Do you see what that is?" the abbot pointed toward a tree in the enclosure.

"A tree."

"Walk closer. Look carefully." The abbot gave Newman the lamp. At
first glance this tree, from whatever angle, looked absolutely no different
from any other tree. Its crown was a chaotic tangle of disheveled branches
and twisted twigs. Its great limbs stretched out over the surrounding wall.
The missionary didn't know its genus and species, but the strange sound
the wind made through its leaves told him that it was different from any
ordinary tree.

Newman approached, light in hand, then halted in fright: on every
leaf was the distinct, lifelike image of some bodhisattva. The leaves were a
deep emerald green, some darker, some lighter.

"You can touch the leaves," the abbot called to him in the dark.

Newman carefully examined the leaves, soaked with dew, then reached out and stripped off a piece of bark. On the new bark beneath, the image of the Laughing Buddha reappeared.

John Newman had read that in 1884 a French missionary, Father Huc, had observed such a tree at Tar Temple in Qinghai Province. "Is this the kind of tree that Father Huc saw?"

The abbot nodded.

"How many of these trees are there in Tibet?" the missionary asked.

"Thousands," the abbot said. "Except for a few, most of them are unknown to man."

"Can I pick off a leaf and keep it?"

The abbot gave no answer, but merely laughed.

The missionary and the abbot passed the latter half of the evening on an open terrace on the roof of the fortress. The Union Jack flapped on the battlements. The fortress was already under British control. The conversation slipped, almost without their realizing it, to the British invasion of Tibet.

"There is only one way to keep the British army from marching on Lhasa," Newman warned the abbot.

"What?"

"Kidnap Younghusband."

A cool predawn breeze was blowing. Newman saw nuns kneeling in a grove by the riverbank, washing their sleeping rugs, loudly discussing something. Their uninhibited laughter rang clear from afar.

III

Guru canyon was the gateway to Gyantse, the first British objective on their advance to Lhasa. But the wretched winter weather aggravated the soldiers' altitude sickness and their reaction to the lack of oxygen: pneumonia and bronchitis ravaged the camp. And so Younghusband had to postpone his original plan for a Christmas Eve assault on Guru canyon until January. This delay gave the large Tibetan army time to anticipate the British attack and secure all the high points above the gorge.

Younghusband now faced his most difficult problem since he entered Tibet. If bad weather persisted for another two or three weeks, his already weakened transport crews would be unable to supply enough food for his troops. Parliament, on the other hand, was still urging him to make every effort to negotiate with the Tibetans. Younghusband feared that negotiations would give the Tibetans the impression that he and his troops had spent two years trekking over the Himalayas not for military conquest, but on a diplomatic initiative. This thought the colonel found unbearable.

On January 16, 1904, Younghusband advanced his Twenty-Third Engineers to the edge of Guru canyon. The next morning he proposed direct negotiations with the Tibetan military command: if the Tibetan army did not withdraw from Guru canyon within five hours, he was prepared, in spite of objections in Parliament, to give these reckless Tibetans, dreaming of their lama rituals, the lesson they deserved.

Younghusband's meeting with the Lhasa Depon, commander of the Tibetan army, took place on the sandy ground of the canyon floor. The two lay on a large Tibetan cushion, carrying on the dialogue through an utterly incompetent interpreter. The Depon insisted that unless the British withdrew to the mountains south of Yadong, "The earth will open and the world be destroyed." This ardent patriot then embarked upon a verbose account of the impending calamity. His self-assured obstinacy wounded Younghusband's self-esteem. The colonel pulled the interpreter to one side: "Just tell this Tibetan the world is Allah's, the earth is the Pasha's, the heavens are the lamas', but the British must rule them all."

In this way negotiations came to an end.

At twenty to three in the afternoon, January 17, 1904, Colonel Younghusband and Major Bretherton sat huddled in a tent in their temporary command post, gazing out at a detachment of one hundred British and three hundred Indian cavalry advancing into the silent canyon. Armed action was about to commence. Younghusband was solemn, his expression gloomy. Bretherton was apprehensive. The colonel reckoned that the Tibetan troops would be unable to restrain themselves when they saw the British cavalry enter the canyon, and would open fire with their matchlock rifles and their bows and arrows. The Maxim machine-gun brigade stationed on their flank would then have a pretext to cut them down.

Regrettably, the Tibetans showed enormous patience. In silence they watched the British troops enter the canyon without firing a shot. The cavalry detachment sent to create the provocation wandered aimlessly around the canyon floor for a while, then returned the way it had come.

Younghusband could hardly restrain himself. Instantly he issued a new order: the cavalry detachment was to advance, and "Drive the Tibetans out of the canyon the way the London police disperse demonstrators on Trafalgar Square."

The calamity occurred at dusk.

The British troops advanced in a broad line up the canyon, demanding that the Tibetan troops hand over their weapons. Pushed and shoved by the British troops, the Tibetan soldiers were in chaos. Under orders from Lhasa not to attack the British first, the Lhasa Depon realized that the course of events left him powerless. He couldn't restrain a cry of anger, drew his revolver and swung it at the jaw of a British soldier. The Tibetan troops heard no order to retreat, no order to resist. Unwillingly, they handed over their arms. The restraint and forbearance of the Tibetan officers in the face of the British provocation made a deep impression on English war correspondent Henry Naylor, a witness of the ensuing massacre of "these simple, innocent shepherds." Herded down the gorge like a flock of sheep, the Tibetan soldiers were raked with the fire of two Maxim machine guns and the rifles of three hundred British infantry. Bretherton warned Younghusband that firing on unarmed Tibetan troops was in clear violation of the expedition's objective—negotiation.

"War is war, not some kind of puppet show," Younghusband replied in a leisurely voice, as he lit a cigar. "Blood gives the soldiers a chance to let off steam."

In his tent on the bank of the Guru River, Younghusband had a dream. A tall, enchanting Tibetan woman stood on the shore of Lake Namtso, her scarlet headdress and heavy, intricate robes blown aside to reveal her graceful body.

At noon on January 20th, mounted on an enormous Indian horse, Younghusband set out, mighty at the head of his troops, through Guru canyon and on to Gyantse. In the riotous profusion of sunlight, the entire landscape—glacial valleys, forests, marshes—appeared as unreal as a painting.

The personal attacks against him on the home front did not dull Younghusband's appreciation of the scenery, resplendent and serene as the Swiss alps. Parliament's criticism of the battle of Guru had been predictable: denunciations of British soldiers' slaughter of innocent Tibetans. *Punch* had gibed, "We deeply regret to report a disastrous raid carried out against British troops in the Guru Valley by Tibetan forces whose dead bodies later grievously disfigured our British officers' photographs of the local landscape."

Only one thing preoccupied Francis Younghusband now. The city he dreamed of, the holy city Lhasa, lay only a few hundred miles away. Save Thomas Manning, over a hundred years ago, he would be the first Englishman to see it.

The trees along the British troops' line of advance filled the air with a chilly fragrance. Snow lotus, saffron blossoms, and scarlet crocus covered the valley. Pines and low brush stretched off like green brocade to the snowy peaks. Mani cairns and Buddhist altars stood everywhere.

At that moment, trouble was brewing, of which Younghusband had no inkling. A Tibetan force of one thousand six hundred Khampa men, traveling day and night, was approaching Tashi Lhunpo Temple in Shigatse. Prompted by the Scottish missionary, the abbot had prepared secret orders for the Khampas to slip into Gyantse and raid Younghusband's command post.

IV

An exhausting three-day journey from Phari fortress had brought the Rev. John Newman to the Gambala Mountains, twenty miles southeast of Gyantse. The sun rarely shone here in the village of Cangnan, but rainfall was plentiful, so that cherry trees and strawberry bushes grew luxuriantly. At the foot of the mountain lay a tumbledown village of crooked wooden shacks. From a distance they looked like collapsed bird nests. On the shore of a creek in the southwest corner of the village stood Newman's destination, a stone Ming Dynasty courtyard, the residence of He Wenqin.

Eleven years before, this Qing official, a former supervisor of grain transport on the Grand Canal, undertook a slow journey, half assignment, half banishment. After stopovers at Chagang in Gansu Province, then at Yushu in Qinghai, he finally reached Tibet in the autumn of 1893. Time passed. His conception of geography changed. His memory of hours spent in the bead-curtained chambers of Yangzhou's gaily painted pleasure boats grew ever more remote. Like a beetle eager to return to the stamen deep within the petals of a flower, he waited month after month for an edict from His Majesty the Emperor to recall him, longing for the twenty-four bridges of ancient Yangzhou, half hidden in the misty moonlight.

He Wenqin's house was near the hotspring. Every day he could see Tibetans bathing together with the foreign traders and pilgrims. If he hadn't seen the cheerful, uninhibited local women wash themselves in the hotspring of the oil and dried animal blood they smeared on their faces, he would never have discovered their natural grace and beauty.

The Tibetans of Cangnan knew how to have a good time, and they also knew the healthful effects of the iron and sulfur in the hotspring water. When the springs weren't warm enough, they lit horse dung to heat rocks and tossed these into the springs. And so a light scent of horse dung filled the air around He Wenqin's residence all day long.

One morning He Wenqin was startled out of a deep sleep by a commotion outside. From the window of his bedroom he saw a foreigner at the hotspring performing magic for the Tibetans. His maidservant told him that this foreigner had been in Cangnan for several days, and had as many magic tricks as a pomegranate has seeds. He Wenqin told his maidservant that she could invite him to his residence to perform his magic. That evening a foreigner in a black suit and straw hat followed the maidservant into He Wenqin's courtyard. Totally unfamiliar with Christianity, He Wenqin imagined the foreigner to be some sort of wandering Indian pilgrim who performed magic to make a living. This was the first meeting between He Wenqin and the Rev. John Newman.

The Jesuits had withdrawn from Tibet in 1785. The parishes they had set up were taken over by French priests of the Lazarist order. The Lazarist missionaries made no more headway in Tibet than had the Jesuits. A variety of misadventures brought them to despair of their objective. "In the eyes of the Tibetan people," one Lazarist missionary wrote back to his superiors, "their primitive religion is perfect."

After years of missionary work in the lower Yangzi valley, Newman returned to Scotland for a sabbatical. Previous missionaries' failure in Tibet inspired in him a deep sense of wonder for this mysterious land. His wide experience in the missions of China, he thought, would surely prove useful in Tibet. Though it would be impossible to convert every Tibetan overnight, he could at least open a door there for the Christian faith. In the summer of 1894, Newman trekked across the Kashmir basin in the company of a band of frontier traders, crossed the mountains of the northwest Indian frontier, and entered Tibet alone. With him he brought some of the latest fruits of Western civilization, hoping to rouse the interest of the Tibetans of the remote mountain wilderness with a camera, a telescope, several microscopes, a cigarette lighter, and two dozen books. His ten years' work would have succeeded but for an outbreak of smallpox that carried off three Tibetans who Newman believed would ultimately have become converts.

Patiently, modestly, with scrupulous attention to every detail, Newman demonstrated his black metal instruments, delighting He Wenqin's maidservant. Master He displayed no great interest. Finally, Newman produced a camera and a high-powered microscope. He explained that the camera could fix a person's image onto a piece of paper with no harm to the person himself, and that the microscope could render an invisible object visible to the naked eye. Master He shook his head in sign that he couldn't believe such bizarre talk. So Newman gave him a demonstration there on the spot. He snatched up an ant from the ground and placed it under the microscope lens. When He Wenqin saw the ant under the lens turn into a mouse, he was so astonished he was speechless. "For a moment," he later said to Newman, "I thought that time was playing tricks on me."

Master He, like many Chinese, had no aversion to Christianity. Wryly, the Chinese official told Newman, "If you can bring Western small-pox vaccine to Tibet, you'll have as many converts here in Tibet as there are sheep." This young official, tall, pale-complexioned, with his long, glistening black pigtail, refined bearing, and brocaded silk robe, looked to Newman more like a woman. The instant the missionary saw him, he was deeply attracted by his appearance. Newman was an old China hand from the Yangzi valley missions near the ancient cities of Jiangning and Yangzhou. His experiences there became an inexhaustible subject of conversation between himself and He Wenqin. The two became practically inseparable: drinking tea, discussing classical Chinese poetry, riding off to hunt in Moon Wood, journeying to the horse-racing festival in North Tibet. Gradually, in the obscure depths of John Newman's heart, his hope to convert He Wenqin began to surpass the bounds of missionary duty.

The close relationship that quickly developed between the two was not without aggravations for He Wenqin. Newman's immoderately warm embraces troubled and alarmed him. When the minister implored him to become a Christian, He Wenqin was still more displeased; but, out of politeness, he never expressed refusal.

The British Expeditionary Force's sudden invasion of Tibet in 1903 and the simultaneous Chinese national crisis marked a turning point in this friendship.

Unhurriedly, Newman rode his roan Tibetan horse up to the gate of He Wenqin's residence. The courtyard was peaceful. A grove of resplendent green orange trees, loaded with fruit, swayed in the wind. Creeping vines mounted the low courtyard wall. A Buddhist prayer flag slanted through the air.

The maidservant told Newman that Master He was taking his afternoon nap. He could wait in the library, she said. Her ice-cold tone made

Newman uncomfortable, putting him in mind of his uneasy parting with Master He at Gampadzong. A slight melancholy crept over him.

He Wenqin was in a room off the rear courtyard, not sleeping at all. Through his lattice window and a bead curtain in the library doorway he glimpsed Newman's fleeting shadow, but he didn't feel like getting up to meet him.

Whenever he watched the merchants' yak caravans pass through Cangnan westward for India and Sikkim, an irrepressible yearning for home welled up in He Wenqin. He dreamed of the ship masts on the Grand Canal in Yangzhou, of its deep, silent lanes, of the fragrant osmanthus on the rainy evening breeze.

Master He had set off to negotiate with the commander of the British Expeditionary Force, Colonel Younghusband, at the behest of the Qing emperor's Mandarin in Lhasa. If he had been able to prevent the British advance on Lhasa, or even merely to delay it, the Mandarin had guaranteed him his return within the year to a post in his home district of the Yangzi valley. But that arrogant, conceited colonel had refused to meet He Wenqin because "Your rank is too low."

Since the British army's appearance in the Chumbi River valley, Master He had repeatedly urged the Mandarin to petition His Majesty the Emperor to dispatch troops south from Qinghai for a decisive attack on the British on the Gyantse plain, before they could reach Lhasa. The Mandarin met these suggestions with a stern rebuff that sparked off a series of ominous conjectures in the thoughts of He Wenqin: the imperial court's control over this southwestern border region was a thing of the past; the emperor was transferring the Qinghai and Sichuan garrisons back to the coastal cities, to quell civil unrest; the ancient empire faced unprecedented calamity. He Wenqin realized that the deterioration of the national situation could not but lead to disaster in his own life.

That evening, when Newman came into the parlor with his usual radiant smile, he found He Wenqin standing in front of a map, gloomily marking it with a pencil. "Your men have already captured Gyantse," He Wenqin said.

"*Our* men?" the missionary said evasively. He felt the coldness in He Wenqin's tone, and his heart grew heavy.

"They killed a thousand Tibetan soldiers in the Guru valley," He Wenqin said with his back still to Newman.

"There's nothing to fear, Master He." Newman walked up to him. "The British will never reach Lhasa."

"Why not?"

John Newman was about to explain something to Master He, when a Chinese Muslim walked in, took a parcel wrapped in green cloth out of his shirt, handed it to He Wenqin, bowed, and left without a word.

"What's in the parcel?" the minister asked.

He Wenqin made no reply. He put it on the table and began carefully to unwrap it. Inside it was a brand-new German pistol. With a practiced hand Master He loaded a cartridge into one of the chambers, spun the cylinder, and pointed the gun at Newman.

The missionary stood petrified. His face went red, then white. "Master He . . ." he smiled unnaturally, "is this a joke?"

He Wenqin was calm, but a wild light flashed in his eyes. "If your Jesus is in heaven," he said, "he will protect you in the underworld." He pulled the trigger.

"Master He!" Newman cried, covering his face as if to ward off a flash of dazzling light.

He Wenqin unhurriedly pulled the trigger a second time. Again, the gun clicked. He gave the pistol a disappointed look, heaved a sigh, and casually set it on the table.

The skin of Newman's face was twitching. Tears sprang from his eyes. Agitated, confused, he stood in the middle of the room. After a few moments, he seemed to recover himself. "Master He! I don't appreciate these nasty theatrics of yours!" he yelled in a strange, unnatural voice. "Not one bit!"

He Wenqin gave a smile and reached for his teacup.

V

Word of the British attack reached Tashi Lhunpo Temple. A young lama spinning a prayer wheel brought the abbot the news: the British army had killed dozens of Tibetan soldiers in Guru canyon.

Two days later a pilgrim brought a more detailed report: among the boulders in the gorge, herdsmen from Gyantse had found the corpses of three hundred twenty-one Tibetan soldiers. (To dispose of all these bodies presented an unprecedented problem for the only two sky burial masters in Gyantse.) The whereabouts of an even greater number of Tibetans taken prisoner was unknown. The news stunned the abbot. He had had a premonition of all this, but now that it had actually happened, the practiced ascetic could not restrain himself from weeping.

Reports came one after another: the British had passed through Guru valley . . . had entered Gyantse. This information caused the abbot to hasten to enact his plan to kidnap Younghusband. Specially recruited for the mission from among the shepherds of the southeastern mountains, twelve hundred Khampa men appeared in Shigatse in a single morning, tall, red-turbaned, ruddy-brown in complexion. The abbot greeted them at the edge of the road outside Tashi Lhunpo Temple. In accord with an ancient local rite, he laid his hand on the head of each one.

On the abbot's orders, the Khampa tribesmen were to reach Gyantse by May 3rd, attack the British command post at midnight on May 4th, carry off Younghusband to a forest on the shore of Lake Yamdrok Yumtso, and there await further orders.

"But how will we recognize this man we must capture?" the tall young Khampa leader asked.

"Oh, I almost forgot," the abbot gave a laugh, patting himself on the forehead. From beneath his robe he pulled a stiff piece of paper. It was a photograph of Younghusband, sent to him several months before by the Scottish missionary, John Newman. The man in the photograph was lean, with a thick moustache. Epaulets and braiding decked his uniform. The Khampa leader's eyes went wide with terror. He threw the photograph to the ground as if he'd been scorched by a hot coal.

"Don't be afraid," the abbot said gently. "It's not a paper mirror, it's not a demon. It's a daguerreotype, something a Frenchman invented."

The Khampa force set out before dawn on April 25th. The abbot accompanied them to the far end of the pass. The sun was high now. A mountain road came into view, thin as a sheep gut. The abbot took the young Khampa leader off to the side of the road, by the bank of a mountain torrent.

"This road leads straight to Gyantse," the abbot said gravely. "When your attack has succeeded, tie your red turban to a big log. Drop the log into the water. The river will carry your good omen here."

The leader nodded, turned to depart, then anxiously thought of something. Hesitantly, he turned back and asked, "What if we fail?"

"Fail?"

"What signal should I send you if we can't capture this man?"

This question paralyzed the abbot. He thought a moment, patted the leader's shoulder, and replied, "We won't fail."

When the Khampa troops had departed, the abbot did not return to Tashi Lhunpo Temple, but quietly sat down in the pleasant, warm sunlight on the bridge, crossed his legs in the lotus position, and never moved again.

A Kampa man. (Photo by Fosco Maraini)

Over the few past months, the war had entangled the abbot in the most extraordinary incidents of his life. Plans for this raid on Gyantse had involved him ever more deeply in military and political affairs he ordinarily abhorred. He had devised the plan to kidnap Younghusband all by himself, since report of it to Lhasa might have given rise to unnecessary controversy there that could have thwarted his plan, frail as it already was. And even if Lhasa approved the plan, word of it might then have leaked out, alerting the English. How could he know whether the gods in darkness would protect his strike force? The scope of the undertaking was greater than the abbot's power even to imagine. After the murderous British attack at Guru canyon, the buddhas had remained silent—how could his plan not be contrary, then, to their hidden purposes? These tangled questions shattered the inner tranquility that had taken the abbot a lifetime of meditation to achieve. But if the raid to kidnap Younghusband could stop the British from invading the holy ground of Lhasa, it was worth the risk.

The river rippled peacefully, swirling in eddies behind the bridge pilings and swaying the water plants in the current along the shore. Milk-white henbane and withered canola blossoms filled the wilderness. Flocks of titmice called among the trees. On the opposite bank stood a small village. Billows of pure white cloud pressed low over the narrow roofs of blackened straw. Multicolored prayer flags streamed from one roof over the next, linking the houses. One flag blew through the trees, reaching the end of the bridge. A flock of fat ducks perched on the bridge wall.

At midday, the abbot saw a group of women trudge past him across the bridge, bent beneath their baskets of dried horse dung and of ice that they carried down from the peak on their backs. Hacked from the mountain, the great ice cakes glistened like diamonds. The women kept stealing glances back at the abbot as they walked off into the village, whispering.

That evening at dusk the women reappeared, with tsampa, sweets, and barley wine, and a thick Tibetan rug to keep off the cold. Not to disturb the abbot's meditation, they laid these things at the end of the bridge, and quietly went away. The abbot remained sitting at the end of the bridge, silent as a stone. The ice-cold wind swept his face. The evening frost congealed on him. Next morning the women brought new food and took away the old, untouched.

One after another, monks, incarnate lamas, and pilgrims arrived from local temples to accompany the abbot. Though they did not know why the eminent lama had chosen this place for his meditation, they quietly sat down around him and began to beat their drums and chant the sutras. As evening approached, they stole nearer the abbot to ward away the chilly May wind with their bodies.

VI

Four days after John Newman returned to Cangnan, an English soldier in Tibetan disguise brought him a secret message from Gyantse. The soldier found Newman alone outside He Wenqin's residence, waiting for Master He. He passed Newman a handwritten note from Colonel Younghus-band, ordering Newman to report immediately to Gyantse, but without specifying any particular reason. The maidservant had told Newman she had seen Master He walk off early that morning toward the forest with a double-barreled shotgun over his shoulder, as if he was going hunting. Newman waited until sundown by the tiny brook outside He Wenqin's residence to say goodbye to Master He, with no sign of his return. At the English soldier's constant urging, Newman finally set off for Gyantse in the falling twilight, with a lost feeling in his heart.

The missionary arrived in Gyantse the next morning. Major Brether-ton met him outside the command tent. The young officer appeared even thinner and more deeply tanned than when Newman had met him at Gampadzong. Insomnia caused by these bizarre, alien surroundings had traced deep lines in his face. Bretherton told Newman that as the British troops plunged deeper and deeper into the Tibetan heartland, the fighting would be grimmer and casualties were sure to mount. So Colonel Younghusband hoped that Newman would remain with the expeditionary force to serve as their military chaplain.

Newman told Bretherton this was out of the question. He was a mis-sionary and had neither reason nor interest in undertaking any other duty save what came to him from his church in Scotland. "And so much the less," Newman explained, "as I can't stand the smell of blood."

"Reverend Newman," Major Bretherton smiled patiently, "you are at Colonel Younghusband's combat headquarters, not in some Scottish parsonage. I'm sorry that you can't stand the smell of blood, but if Colonel Younghusband ordered you to drink a pint of it now, could you refuse?" Bretherton's words apparently left the missionary no room to bargain.

It was the rainy season in Gyantse. The days passed monotonously. Newman had been assigned quarters in a Turkish tent pitched in a barley field on a barren, rocky mountainside near Barje Temple. Every day a fine drizzle commenced at noon and continued until dusk.

The whole camp was losing patience in the gloomy, cold rain. The attack on Guru canyon had raised Parliament's opposition to the expedition to fever pitch. For the past few days Younghusband had been constantly downcast. Frowning, he told Newman that even if Parliament immediately approved his plan to march on Lhasa, the advance would have to be put off until the end of the rainy season. If his forces attacked in the rain, the Tibetans could easily cut their long, vulnerable supply line.

Bretherton was more approachable than Younghusband. He often came to Newman's tent for a chat after lunch. With a reverent expression, he told Newman of his impressions of Kashmir. "Wherever I looked, I saw before my eyes peaceful mountains and green pastures, the Promised Land of the Old Testament flowing with milk and honey." Bretherton had studied the history of religion in school, but his interest in the subject was limited to matters of scholarship and textual criticism, and never touched on faith. But like certain mystics, Bretherton felt an intuitive assurance of Jesus's existence. He told Newman that when he'd been stationed in the profoundly Buddhist regions of India and Kashmir, he'd sensed the spirit of Jesus so strongly that it "seemed to hover before me in the air."

In southern India Bretherton had been taken to a dark, secret chamber. According to the hints of local Buddhists, Jesus had managed through his profound yoga powers to survive his crucifixion, and passed his old age as a recluse here, meditating in this hidden chamber and surviving to the ripe age of eighty-one. Newman's reaction to what Bretherton told him was like a man's reaction to a woman—a perplexed mixture of contempt, disgust, and all-consuming desire.

Bretherton was a man possessed by a powerful imagination and, in certain respects, a good person. From the moment this young officer who'd grown up on the banks of the Thames entered Tibet, its strange, secret worship of the spiritual had terrified him. Absurd fantasies wrapped him in a continual sense of foreboding. More than once, he said to Newman, "Disaster is creeping near."

VII

Waiting in Gyantse under the heavy rain and driving sleet, the British soldiers fell into despair. Reports flowed in upon Younghusband one after another: soldiers had raided Barje Temple and the Gyantse antique market, stealing jewelry, raping women. The Gyantse Tibetans became less meek and gentle. Two English noncommissioned officers had disappeared without a trace.

But the worst news came from England. Viceroy Curzon had been suddenly discharged from his post, replaced by the senile Lord Ampthill. Younghusband had lost the last supporter of his advance on Lhasa. In the middle of April he received a telegram from London: a high-ranking government official tactfully urged him to resign his command.

Moreover, the Tibetan government officials had abandoned all hope of negotiating with the British. Khampa troops flowed in a steady stream into the mountainous region north of Gyantse, where they began to build fortifications and a defensive wall at the southern foot of Kharo Mountain. These new troops were equipped with relatively modern weapons, including Zanger rifles with a range of over two thousand yards. An advance party that Younghusband sent to probe the Tibetan forward positions met with stiff resistance.

At noon on May 2nd, the dark, overcast sky finally showed signs of clearing. Before the sodden grass had begun to dry, some English soldiers started a game of football on the muddy slope. Another group of soldiers came down to the bank of the Gyantse River to strike up a chat with some Tibetan women washing clothes. The women ignored the soldiers' jokes. The moment the remarks passed certain boundaries, the women hurried away.

That afternoon, the British interrogated several wandering Nepalese beggar-monks making their way past Gyantse Fort. The monks gave Newman startling news. Along the road they'd happened upon the greatest Buddhist assembly they had witnessed in Tibet, a thousand monks and incarnate lamas in a huge circle on both banks of the river. The sound of their chanting was audible a mile away.

That evening, Newman slipped out of Gyantse and hurried toward the site of the assembly, unaware that the abbot of Tashi Lhunpo Temple had been sitting there in meditation for seven days, near death now from hunger and cold.

If he didn't strike them a mortal blow before the Tibetans finished their fortifications, Younghusband feared that their defensive wall, stretching off for miles in both directions, would be an insurmountable obstacle to the British advance. Before dawn on May 3rd, after a sleepless night, Younghusband ordered the greater portion of his troops under the command of Colonel Brander to storm Kharo Mountain. This plan met with the tenacious opposition of Major Bretherton: if the main British detachment proceeded north to Kharo Mountain, the command post at Gyantse would be left exposed. Once the Tibetans knew of the British troops' advance, they would attack the post and wipe it out.

Bretherton's worry was by no means groundless, but it enraged Younghusband. In the presence of the other officers he sternly rebuked his quartermaster: "Our adversary isn't Napoleon's Grand Army. It's a band of mountain shepherds."

That evening at dusk, seven hours after the main British force had left Gyantse, several dozen Tibetan prisoners who had been receiving treatment in the British field clinic mysteriously vanished. At the same moment the Tibetan maidservants and porters whom the British had hired suddenly departed without a word. Scouts reported catching sight of a caravan of yak drivers slipping under cover of dusk into the dense woods on the opposite bank of the Gyantse River twenty miles from the command post. Where they had come from, no one knew.

Younghusband did not pay the least attention to this ominous news. After dinner he went to Bretherton's quarters for their usual game of Erlut chess. Perhaps he realized that his dressing-down of Bretherton before the other officers had imperiled their long friendship. Now, as they sat peacefully across from each other over their chessboard, all unpleasant feelings dissolved like smoke. These last few days Younghusband had actually grown rather tired, and now, with the game half-finished, he dozed off in his cane chair. At midnight the usual heavy rains began falling again, thunder began to rumble, and a wild wind began snapping the tent.

At two in the morning, undetected in the roaring wind, the twelve hundred Khampa raiders slipped up to the British camp. The British had taken no precautions. The camp lights had been extinguished. Everything was pitch dark. In the forest outside the camp a few ducks and cuckoos called nervously.

A new Indian recruit, sleepless from diarrhea, had just come out to the latrine when he noticed the human forms flitting outside the perimeter. Then, in a flash of lightning, he saw the rifle barrels protruding in through the loopholes in the barricade. Numb with terror, the green recruit stood in the dense curtain of rain several minutes before he came to his senses and fired his gun to sound the alarm.

The gunshot startled Bretherton. He roused the sleeping Younghusband with a shout, then rushed out of the command tent with several guards. At first Younghusband was unable to figure out what was happening. Flustered and confused, he emerged from the tent in his pajamas as the Tibetans' fire burst through the air. Gurkha soldiers were scurrying about inside the enclosure. The old regimental doctor stood trembling in their midst in his white undershorts. The officer in charge of camp security, Major Murray, rushed up to Younghusband with the guards. The whereabouts of the attackers were still unknown.

But the Tibetans were utterly ignorant of assault tactics. If, at the beginning of their raid, they had stormed over the barricade into the camp, the surprised British would have been completely overwhelmed. But now, firing blindly into the compound through the loopholes in the barricade, they gave the British time to organize an effective counterattack.

The Tibetans continued firing until five in the morning, when the first rays of dawn pierced the darkness, and the raiders, shooting from atop the barricade, lay entirely exposed to the firepower of the British Maxim machine guns. Over one hundred corpses soon lay to the left of the camp, where the British drove the Tibetans southward along the Gyantse River. To the right of the camp, thirty Khampas had taken refuge inside a stable. Major Murray said that his men could easily capture them all at once, but a badly shaken Younghusband ordered the machine guns turned on them. After one long, furious burst of fire, the plan the abbot of Tashi Lhunpo Temple had ruminated for months came at last to naught.

The British Expeditionary Force's casualties were extremely light: five killed, including one cavalry lieutenant. The moment the attack was over, Younghusband summoned war correspondent Henry Naylor to his command tent, to whom he dictated a battle report for urgent dispatch back to England. The communiqué raised the number of British killed in action to sixty-three.

"The Tibetans could never have dreamed that this silly raid of theirs would prove to be such a help to us," Younghusband told Bretherton on the way to the field hospital.

"You think this will persuade Parliament to approve our advance?"

"This raid is the key that will open the gate of the Potala," Younghusband said as he lit a cigar. "We're on the road to Lhasa."

Bretherton wanted to say something more, then changed his mind. Their lucky escape hadn't relieved his depression.

Tibetan wounded lay everywhere on the grass around the crowded shed that served as a field hospital. Tense-faced doctors and nurses bustled about. Bretherton noticed a wounded Tibetan soldier displaying no emotion as his leg was being amputated without anaesthetic.

"When do you plan to attack?" Bretherton asked Younghusband after a moment.

"Tomorrow." Younghusband quickened his pace. "We'll take Tapan Temple next week."

VIII

When He Wenqin returned at dusk from hunting in Moon Wood, the maidservant watering the irises in the courtyard told him that the Rev. John Newman had waited for him all day, then left Cangnan at dusk. "It looked as if he had something to tell you," she said.

Without a reply, He Wenqin threw down the game he'd killed, two snow cocks and a small antelope, and went straight into the back courtyard. Although he disliked Newman more than ever now, the missionary's departure left him with an empty, desolate feeling.

As the British Expeditionary Force closed in on Kharo fortress, Tibetan and foreign traders poured out of Cangnan. Even if this village, a few miles from Gyantse, would not be the site of the battle, it would still be on its fringe. Every day large contingents of Tibetan troops passed through Cangnan with their yak carts. They'd trekked a long distance on short rations, and appeared utterly exhausted, trudging off through the chestnut trees along the bank of the Masog River toward Kharo fortress.

On May 21, 1904, a Chinese courier arrived at the residence of He Wenqin, bearing a personal letter from the High Mandarin in Lhasa. The Mandarin reprimanded He Wenqin for "letting slip an opportune moment through your inept negotiation." The Mandarin rebuked He Wenqin for his association with the British missionary, hinting that such a secret friendship had encouraged the British to push on toward Lhasa. "And what's all this about your rank being too low?" the Mandarin continued. "You bore the dignity of an imperial envoy of His Majesty the Qing Emperor. Younghusband is nothing but a colonel." In view of this malfeasance, so grave as to render him unworthy of His Majesty's continued favor, the High Mandarin commanded He Wenqin to lock himself away and consider his mistakes while awaiting his punishment.

There was a downpour again that evening. Rain lashed the paper windows.[3] Damp night air carried the cool, heavy fragrance of the trees

3. At this period, Chinese windows were still made of translucent paper.

into the library. By the light of the yak-butter lamp, He Wenqin sat gazing out at the tassels of water that dripped from the eaves, and never slept all night.

In his hometown, the ancient city of Yangzhou, the rainy season came just as the plums were turning ripe. In the continuous downpour the drenched leaves of the jasmines and the blooming scholar trees gave off a seductive fragrance. By the faint candlelight He Wenqin used to sit alone in his little house listening to the wind and the rain.

Now he was cut off from all that. The thick branches, the ubiquitous curtain of rain of his youthful memories seemed dead, remote, silent. The High Mandarin's letter did not specify how the emperor, beset with enemies from within and without, would punish him, but He Wenqin could read his fate between the lines. The way back to the home that filled his every dream had silently shut. History had swept him aside.

Next morning at dawn, He Wenqin mounted his tiny yellow-maned Tibetan horse and rode alone out of his courtyard toward the forest of oaks and chestnuts by the riverbank. In his drunken daze, he saw the servant woman run out after him, and pulled on his reins. Tears streamed down her face. Her raucous voice rang in his ears, but he could not understand what she was trying to tell him. From across the Gambala Mountains came the faint sound of scattered gunfire.

He lashed his little horse, and it raced off across the stony ground under the trees. The maidservant's figure grew smaller and smaller. He Wenqin gave a heavyhearted laugh, and waved to her.

The warm, indolent sun flashed on the river's curving ripples. Pheasants and ravens flew up from the rocks on the bank. He Wenqin whipped his horse to a gallop. Rushing water, clumps of blooming iris swept past. The pleasant warmth of the sunlight and the cool wind against his face gave him a carefree feeling he'd never known before. He had no idea where he was going. The peaks around him rose one beyond another, higher and higher off into the distance. He let out a roar, and distant echoes reverberated through the valley.

Near Lalo, the Masog River turned to the northeast through a misty, black forest. He Wenqin saw the snowy peak of silver-gray Kharo Mountain.

The Tibetan army was camped on a broad mustard field north of Kharo Pass. Soldiers with gloomy, expressionless faces huddled around blazing campfires, their old matchlock rifles across their knees. The odor of burning horse dung mixed with the scent of the woods and fields. One group near the ancient, blue-walled fortress played Tibetan mandolins, singing. Their song reminded He Wenqin of boatmen's chants he remembered from the canal towns around Yangzhou: deep, crude, rhythmless, mournful.

Master He rode slowly among the troops. When he reached the barricade at the edge of the camp, an adjutant of the Lhasa Depon blocked his way.

"You can't go on," the adjutant told him in halting Chinese. "Three hundred yards ahead—the British forward line."

He Wenqin seemed not to have heard him. He lashed his horse down the slope of the pass, and the gathering darkness quickly swallowed him.

"The British machine guns will tear you to raw meat," the adjutant shouted after him.

He Wenqin did not know why he wanted to go toward the British camp. He had no notion where his lean little Tibetan horse was really taking him. And in the end, he never reached the British line. His horse carefully picked its way around a wide stretch of glimmering swamp, and turned into dense forest about a hundred yards from the British line, on the shore of Lake Yamdrok Yumtso. By this time, He Wenqin was slumped forward in his saddle in a drunken sleep.

When he awoke next morning in the cold dawn wind, he found himself lying on the bank of a creek, his body thickly covered with frost. He heard his horse snort as it drank from the current. A scarlet turban appeared and disappeared among the tangled vines and branches on the far bank. A tall Khampa was chopping down a birch tree, his ax resounding with a hollow echo through the forest. He Wenqin took his horse by the reins, splashed across the creek, and went up to him.

The young Khampa had a bullet wound in his leg, and walked with a limp. He Wenqin helped him fell the birch tree, then the two sat down on the sandy bank.

"Did you just come from the battle at Kharo fortress?" He Wenqin asked.

The Khampa shook his head. "From Gyantse."

"Gyantse?"

"We attacked the British command post. The British drove us into a stable, set up a machine gun, and shot us down. I hid, waited until dark, and escaped."

"Why did you cut down this tree?"

"It's like this," the Khampa said. "When we captured the British commander, I was supposed to send a signal to the abbot of Tashi

Lhunpo Temple—tie my turban to a log and throw it in this river. But our plan failed. . . ."

"Then send the signal for failure," He Wenqin said.

"That's the trouble. We never thought our plan could fail."

He Wenqin frowned, comprehending the Khampa man's predicament. "What will you do?" he asked.

"Kill me," the young man replied with a gloomy look, "and tie my body to this log. Then the abbot will understand everything."

"I understand what you mean," He Wenqin regarded him sympathetically, "but I can't kill you. Take your time and think of something else."

He Wenqin stood up as he finished saying this, preparing to depart. The sun was up. White butterflies fluttered in the sunlight that fell through the leaves. As He Wenqin led his horse away, considering which direction to take, the Khampa had already stolen up behind him, knife in hand. All of a sudden, Master He felt an ice-cold thrust into his back, flowing instantly all through his body. The Khampa dragged him, still alive, toward the river. The riot of light pierced his eyes so sharply he could not hold them open, but he smelled the pure, fresh fragrance of the vegetation and felt the sun's warmth. Then he felt himself floating downstream, as his face sank into the icy water.

IX

Ten days the abbot had kept watch on the bank of the Gyantse River, without seeing the auspicious signal, the red turban tied to a log. The ancient prophecy of the Potala high lama was confirmed.

The Rev. John Newman arrived to find the abbot on the verge of death. This great lama left a verbal testament about one of the great secret legends of Buddhism. The only one who heard, Newman, sensed the abbot's hesitation before recounting it.

Long ago, after a journey of many hardships and dangers, a young Jew named Jeshua arrived alone at a monastery in the foothills of the Himalayas, and embarked upon an intense study of the sutras and the practice of meditation. His powers of understanding were beyond the ordinary; in a few short years his meditation bore fruit in the blossoming of extraordinary powers. Tibetan, Indian, and Kashmiri sutra masters, foreseeing his remarkable future, did all they could to persuade the young man to remain and preach in the regions of the Himalayas, but one bright moonlit night he set out secretly on the long, long, road back to Jerusalem.

"This young Jew was Jesus," the abbot told John Newman. "The sutras that record his story are preserved in a secret chamber in the Jokhang Temple in Lhasa."

The abbot of Tashi Lhunpo Temple died quietly at midnight. In commemoration of him, the people built a pagoda where he passed away, sitting in meditation.

One morning, when this pagoda was nearly complete, the body of He Wenqin floated down the Gyantse River. The fish had eaten his rotting flesh clean away, but Newman recognized the tattered Chinese robe. He pulled the remains from the water, buried them in a field of poppies beside the pagoda, and planted an orange tree at the head of the grave.

Soon after he buried He Wenqin, Newman left Tibet. He hired a Tibetan horsecart to take him to Yadong, the first stage of his journey back to Scotland. With him he bore a prayer wheel and He Wenqin's glistening black pigtail. Often on his cold and desolate journey, Newman gazed at the pigtail, his eyes full of tears. Though it no longer drew sustenance from He Wenqin's body, the pigtail went on growing.

When Newman was changing horses at a post station near Yadong, a British officer told him that the expeditionary force under the command of Col. Francis Younghusband had captured Lhasa.

That evening, in the dim candlelight of the inn, the Scottish missionary lay awake long into the night, unable to sleep. As he casually turned the pages of his Bible, a dried leaf fell to the floor. Newman picked it up with tweezers, placed it under his microscope, and examined it carefully. The leaf from the sacred tree looked no different from any ordinary leaf: the image of the Buddha had vanished.

On July 30, 1904, the British Expeditionary Force under the command of Col. Francis Younghusband reached the bank of the Yarlung Tsangpo River, twenty miles from Lhasa. But Major Bretherton was never to see the flame-like golden roofs of the Potala. His foreboding of doom became reality. As the British troops forded the Yarlung Tsangpo, Bretherton and two Gurkha soldiers slipped and disappeared in the current.

Three days later Younghusband rode at the head of his troops into Lhasa. The lamas dispatched negotiators of every rank to dissuade him from entering the Potala, but an undeterred Younghusband commanded his troops to storm its gates, and burst into the resplendent, mysterious temple.

Bretherton's death was only the first of a series of misfortunes that dispirited Younghusband as he had never been before. On September 7th, with neither orders nor authorization from the British government, Younghusband concluded and signed a treaty with the Tibetans—a document over which one would not know whether to laugh or cry. Soon afterward, the General Minister for Indian Affairs dispatched a letter to former Viceroy Curzon, characterizing Younghusband as "crude, ill-bred, and uncultured. What he has done in Tibet proves his lack of an adequate understanding of the twentieth-century political situation between Europe and Asia. For the sake of Britain's honor, it would appear we have no choice but to remove Younghusband from command."

On the eve of his departure from Tibet, Younghusband rode alone to the shore of Lake Namtso. Since he had entered Tibet all his most fundamental, deep-seated notions had somehow incomprehensibly changed—even his notion of time itself. Now, under the snowy peaks of the Nyenchen Tangla, Colonel Younghusband momentarily lost consciousness of where he was. Ringing in his ears was the feeble voice of the abbot of Tashi Lhunpo Temple. It was in his command tent at Gampadzong as he and the abbot had been hotly arguing the basic facts of geography. With incredible obstinacy the abbot insisted, "The earth is not round. It is a triangle, like the shoulder bone of a sheep."

• 5 •

Tibet: A Soul Knotted on a Leather Thong

Tashi Dawa

$\mathscr{I}$t's rare nowadays, in the year 2000,[1] that you hear that simple, lingering Peruvian folksong "El Condor Passa." But I've preserved it on my tape recorder. Every time I play it, I see before my eyes peaks and valleys, flocks of sheep scurrying through clefts in the rocks, scattered plots of sparse crops at the foot of a mountain, a watermill by a stream, tiny, squat peasant houses built of loose stone, mountain people shouldering heavy loads, copper bells on leather cords, lonely whirlwinds, dazzling sunlight. This scene isn't the Peruvian Andes at all. It's the Pabunegang Mountains of southern Tibet. At first, I couldn't remember whether I'd really been there or if I'd just seen it in a dream. I'd been so many places that I just couldn't recall. It was only later, when one day I finally went to the Pabunegang Mountains, that I realized the scene in my memory was merely an exquisite nineteenth-century landscape from the brush of John Constable.

Although Pabunegang is still a peaceful mountain region at the start of the twenty-first century, these isolated people have begun to enjoy the advantages of modern life. There's a small airport with five helicopter flights to Lhasa every week. There's a solar generating station. Here in the little restaurant by the gas station where the road enters Telu there's a chatterbox with a big beard sitting at my table, the chairman of the board of the renowned Himalaya Transport Company, the first in all of Tibet

1. The story was published in 1985. In its elaborate time scheme, the fictional narrator portrays himself completing in the year 2000, sixteen years in the future, a story he had begun to write in 1984. The description of Tibet in the year 2000 in this opening passage is a fictional futuristic portrayal of a modernized Tibet set a decade and a half after the story appeared in print.

with a fleet of Mercedes Benz tractor-trailer trucks. When I went to visit a rug-knitting mill, I found the designers contriving new patterns on computer. A five-channel ground–satellite station offers viewers thirty-eight hours of TV programming every day.

But no matter how modern material civilization forces the natives to abandon their traditional culture, Pabunegang people still hold fast to some of their old ways: as I was speaking with the head of the village, a Ph.D. in agriculture, he sucked in a mouthful of cold air and murmured the traditional expression of humble submission, "Los, los."[2] Somebody who asks a favor still sticks out his thumb, shakes it back and forth and utters an entreating "Kuji, kuji. . . ."[3] When a stranger from the distant city walks past, old people still take off their hats, hold them in front of their chests, and stand to one side in respect. The government standardized the system of measurements long ago, but to express a length people here still stick out one arm and hack it with their other hand at the wrist, the forearm, the elbow, or the shoulder.

Incarnate Lama Sangye Dhapo is dying. He is the twenty-third reincarnation of the Incarnate Lama of Zatroe Temple, and has lived to the venerable age of ninety-eight. There will be no reincarnated heir to take his place, so I'd like to write a special report. I've met him before. Now that one of the most profound and mystical of all the world religions, Tibetan lamaism (with its various sects), has no more reincarnated heirs, and so no more leader great or small, it appears to be nearing its last day. "External form determines consciousness," I said.

Incarnate Lama Sangye Dhapo shook his head in disagreement with what I said. His pupils were slowly dilating. "Shangri-la. . . ." His lips trembled. "The war has begun."

According to scripture, there is a Pure Land, heaven on earth to the north, Shangri-la. Yoga, it is said, had its origin here, and here the first king Sodrak Donagpo accepted the teachings of Buddha Sakyamuni and began to spread the mystic doctrine of the Diamond Sutra, which records that a day will come when a great war will take place in this land wrapped in snow-covered mountains, Shangri-la. "In the midst of the twelve heavenly generals you shall command twelve heavenly armies, ever galloping onward without a backward glance. You shall cast your spear at the breast of Halutaman, leader of the demon hoard against Shangri-la, and they all shall be annihilated." So reads the eulogy of the last king, the Warrior King of the Wheel, in the *Oath*

2. Los: Tibetan for "yes."
3. Kuji: Tibetan for "could you please."

of Shangri-la. Sangye Dhapo of Zatroe once spoke to me about this battle. He said that after a fierce struggle lasting many hundreds of years the demons will at last be wiped out, the grave of Tsongkhapa in Ganden Temple will open of itself and the doctrine of Sakyamuni will once again be preached for a thousand years. Then will come a great wind to afflict the earth, and finally a flood will engulf the whole world. When earth's last day arrives, survivors will be delivered by the gods and taken up to heaven. Then the whole earth will be formed anew, and religion will arise once more.

Sangye Dhapo of Zatroe lay on his bed, entering a mystic vision, speaking to some invisible person before his eyes, "As you climb across snowcapped Kelong Mountain and stand in the lines of the palm print of the Lotus Master, do not pursue, do not seek. In prayer you shall understand, in understanding you shall see a vision. In all the lines of the wrinkles in Lotus Master's palm print there is only one path of life that leads to the Pure Land among humankind."

I seemed to see the Lotus Master rise from this world: a chariot descended from heaven, he mounted in it, and, accompanied by two maiden immortals, he soared aloft toward the distant south. "The two young Khampas are looking for the road to Shangri-la," murmured the Incarnate Lama.

I looked at him, exhausted. "You mean . . . in 1984 . . . the two Khampas who came here, a man and a woman?"

He nodded.

"And the man got injured?" I asked.

"You know this too," the Incarnate Lama said. Sangye Dhapo of Zatroe shut his eyes and recalled in broken words how in the year 1984 two young people had come to Pabunegang, and as he began to recount what the two told him of their experiences along the way, I realized that the Incarnate Lama of Zatroe was reciting a story I had made up. I had never shown this story to anyone, but kept it locked away in a box because I hadn't been able to finish it. Now he was reciting it word for word. The time was 1984. The setting was village X on the way to the Pabunegang Mountains. The characters were a man and a woman. I hadn't shown this unfinished story to anyone because I didn't know where the characters were going. Now the Incarnate Lama had resolved the dilemma, and at last I understood. The only difference was that where I had abandoned the story my main character was sitting in a tavern, and an old man was telling him which way to continue on his journey, but I hadn't been able to figure out what destination the old man was talking about. Now the Incarnate Lama was telling me—and here was a coincidence: both the old man and the Incarnate Lama spoke of the palm print of the Lotus Master.

Other people came into the room and formed a circle around the Incarnate Lama. With half-open eyes he gradually entered the state of thoughtless unconsciousness.

From my reading in ancient scriptures about the art of dying, I knew by the Incarnate Lama's skin color and the dilation of his pupils that he was entering into the third of the seven stages between death and reincarnation.

The people began to prepare for the Incarnate Lama's funeral. The Incarnate Lama of Zatroe was to be cremated. I know some people wanted to collect and preserve the Incarnate Lama's sheli as an eternal memorial.

After I parted with Sangye Dhapo of Zatroe, on my way back home I began to ponder the sources of literary creation.

When I got home, I opened the lid of my box inscribed, "My Beloved Abandoned Children." Neatly arranged inside were over a hundred manila envelopes—all my unpublished works, including works I didn't want to publish.[4] I took out binder number twenty-eight, untitled, about the two Khampas going to Pabunegang. Here are the words of that story.

Halfway down the mountain Chung paused with her twenty-odd sheep. A black speck was moving unhurriedly, like an ant, along the vast, meandering gravel path of the dried riverbed. She could make out it was a man, and he was walking right toward her house. With a wave of her whip, Chung drove her sheep down the mountain in a rush. She reckoned he wouldn't arrive until after dark.

The only homes in all the wilderness were these two low houses of cut stone on this little hill, and behind these houses was a sheepfold. There were just two families here in all, she and her dad, and the fifty-year-old deaf woman. Dad sang the epic *Song of King Gesar*. Distant villages often invited him to come and sing, sometimes for a few days, sometimes a few months. A messenger would ride up the little hill leading a spare horse, and ask Dad to mount. Dad would sling his long-necked six-string mandolin over his back. Then lonely copper bells in time to the beat of the horses' hooves, sounding for a long time, farther and farther off into the silent wilderness. Chung would stand on the hill, one hand stroking the

---

4. The "unpublished" story that follows begins in the Tibet of the mid-1980s, when "Tibet: A Soul Knotted on a Leather Thong" was indeed first published.

big, black sheepdog standing at her knee, and watch the horses disappear around the bend of the mountain.

Chung had grown up to the monotonous rhythm of the horses' hooves and the copper bells. As she sat on the rock tending her sheep, lost in reverie amid the solitude, that sound became a wordless song floating from the distant mountains, and out of that song, filling the life and loneliness of the wilderness, came a desperate yearning.

Every morning, the deaf woman stood on the little hill and cast a handful of peas and tsampa toward the sky, calling on Bodhisattva Chenresig. Then, spinning a grimy prayer wheel in her hand, she muttered her prayer to the east. All day long the deaf woman worked at her loom, weaving woolen cloth. Once in a while, Dad would climb out of bed at midnight and clamber up the hill to the woman's house, return in the dim light of dawn with his long sheepskin robe pulled up over his head, and climb back under his sleeping rug. At dawn Chung would get up, do the milking, then make tea, eat a bowl of tsampa gruel, stuff the sheepskin bag with barley for the day's meal, sling the black pot on her back, go behind the house, pull open the bar of the sheepfold, wave her whip, and drive the sheep up the mountain. Such was her life.

Now Chung prepared food and hot tea, climbed under her sleeping rug, and waited for the guest. When the dog barked outside, she rushed to the door.

The moon had just risen. She gripped the dog's chain, but saw no one around until a head came up over the slope.

"Come on, it's all right, I've got the dog," Chung said.

Arriving was a gigantic fellow with an indomitable look.

"You must be tired, brother," Chung said, and led the fellow inside. Beneath his hat brim a shock of scarlet tassels hung beside his forehead. Dad wasn't home. He'd gone to sing *King Gesar*. From the deaf woman's house next door came the clack-clack of her mallet as she pounded her cloth on the loom.

When the fellow had eaten and thanked Chung he dropped exhausted on her father's bed and fell asleep.

Chung stood outside the door for a while. The myriad stars burned in the sky, stillness everywhere, no sound from nature. The open gorge before her was bathed in the pale white of the moonlight. Fastened on its chain, the big black dog was going round and round in a circle. Chung went over, squatted down, and hugged its neck, thinking of the childhood and youth she'd passed on this bare, lonely hill, of the men, always silent and withdrawn, who came to fetch Dad, of Dad mounting the horse, of this traveler, sound asleep in the house, come from afar, going far off again tomorrow. She wept. Kneeling, her face in her hands, she silently prayed for Dad's forgiveness. Then, wiping her tears on the dog's fur, she got up, went back inside, trembling feverishly all over, and climbed without a word under the fellow's sleeping rug.

As soon as the morning star had risen in the east, Chung rolled up her own thin sleeping rug in the flickering light of the yak-butter lamp. Into a cloth sack she stuffed dried meat, a leather bag for kneading tsampa, some coarse salt, and a piece of yak butter. She slung over her shoulder the little black pot she used to boil her tea every day up on the mountain, tending her sheep. Everything a girl should carry she had on her back. She glanced around the little room to check. "Okay," she said. The fellow took a last pinch of snuff, clapped the last bits of it off his hands, stood up, stroked the top of her head, and put his arm around her shoulder as the two of them ducked their heads under the low doorway and walked out into the pitch-black west. Chung was fully loaded. Her burden clanged with every step along the road.

She never thought to ask the fellow where he might be taking her. She only knew she was leaving this lifeless stretch of ground forever. All the fellow had in his hand was a string of sandalwood prayer beads. He strode ahead, head high, like one full of faith about the boundless journey ahead.

"What's that leather thong you have hanging from your belt, like a little dog with nobody to lead you?" Tabei asked.

"It's to count the days. Don't you see it has five knots tied on it?" Chung told him. "It's five days since I left home."

"Five days? What's that? I've never had a home since I was born."

She followed Tabei. Sometimes she spent the night on a village threshing floor by the side of the road, sometimes in a sheepfold, sometimes she lay in the corner of a ruined temple wall, sometimes in a cave; if she was lucky she spent the night in a peasant's shed, or a shepherd's tent.

Every time they entered a temple, they prostrated themselves before the pedestal of every bodhisattva, one by one, striking their heads each time on the ground.

Outside temples, beside roads, next to rivers, in mountain passes, wherever they saw a mani cairn, they always picked up a few little white stones and laid them on top of it. There were Buddhist faithful along the way who prostrated themselves and struck their heads on the ground at every step, wearing aprons worn through at the chest and the knees, patched over with layers and layers of canvas, also worn through. Their cheeks and noses were covered in dirt. Their foreheads bore bumps the size of eggs, covered with blood and earth, from incessantly striking their heads against the ground. As they bowed and prostrated themselves, the protective coverings of iron-plated wood that they wore over their hands scraped deep tracks in the earth. Tabei and Chung did not bow to the earth, but walked, and so they passed them.

The dense mountains of Tibet stretched off into the distance, one beyond another. Plumes of smoke rose from the chimneys of houses, few and far between. They walked for several days without seeing signs of any person, let alone any village. A cool wind whistled through the canyon. Looking up a moment at the blue heaven, Chung felt her body rise and drift up, ready to leave the earth beneath her feet. The mountains of the high range lay sound asleep beneath the broiling sun, ageless, infinitely still.

The blazing sun beat down, the earth was burning. Vigorous and nimble, Tabei leaped from one treacherous rock to another, step by step up the mountain. He clambered up a boulder, looked back, saw Chung a good way behind, and sat down to wait.

They said nothing to each other as they hurried on their way. Sometimes, finding the silence unbearable, Chung would suddenly burst out in a song like a mountain she-beast howling at the sky. Tabei wouldn't even turn around to give her a glance, just kept his mind on the road.

After a while Chung stopped singing; all around it was still as death. Head bowed, she followed him, speaking only when at last they stopped for a break.

"Stop bleeding?"

"Doesn't hurt at all."

"Let me have a look."

"Catch me a few spiders. I'll crush them onto my leg, spit on them, and it'll be better."

"There are no spiders here."

"Go look in the cracks between the rocks and you'll find some."

Chung turned over half-buried rocks, conscientiously searching for spiders. In a while she'd caught five or six, walked back clutching them, pulled open Tabei's hand, and laid them in it. He crushed them one by one, and rubbed them onto the wound on his shin.

"That dog was vicious, I was so scared," Chung said. "I ran and ran. The pot on my back banged my head until it felt like it was spinning."

"I should have pulled out my knife and butchered it right there."

"That woman did this at us." She imitated an obscene gesture.

Tabei grabbed another handful of dirt and scattered it on the wound, then held it up for the sun to shine on it.

"Where did she keep her money?" Chung asked.

"In a cupboard inside the tavern, a wad thick as my hand. I just took ten."

"What will you buy?"

"Buy? Tsegu Temple is up ahead. I'll give some to the bodhisattvas. I'll keep a little too."

"There, fine! Are you better now? Stopped hurting?"

"It doesn't hurt. Say, my mouth is so dry it feels like there's smoke coming out of it."

"Can't you see I've got the pot on? I'll go collect some more dry brush."

Indolently Tabei lay down on a rock, pulled his broad-brimmed hat over his eyes to shade them from the sun, and chewed on a piece of dry grass. Chung lay on her stomach, face against the ground, in front of three white rocks she'd arranged into a fireplace. Her cheeks puffed, blowing at the fire. Shoots of flame appeared as the wood began to catch, crackling. She jumped up and rubbed her eyes, stinging from the smoke, pulled her bangs down and looked at them. The tongues of flame had singed them.

Two black figures appeared on a distant peak, shepherds probably, one tall, one short, like black vultures perched on the rocky summit, motionless.

Chung saw them and waved her right hand round and round in the air, calling. The tall one rose to his feet and waved a circle back to her in greeting, but the distance was too great. They could call to each other until they tore their throats, but neither would hear the other.

"And I thought we two were the only ones here," Chung said to Tabei.

"I'm waiting for the tea." Tabei closed his eyes.

Suddenly Chung remembered something. From inside her blouse she pulled out a book. Pleased, she showed Tabei her own loot from the village where they'd put up last night, snagged from the back pocket of a little guy who'd poured sweet talk into her ear but wasn't so prim and proper in what he did next. Tabei looked it over. He didn't understand the strange characters the book was written in or the drawings of machines. On the cover was printed a tractor. "This dumb thing's no use." He threw it back to Chung. A dejected Chung tore off page after page to fuel the fire for the next pot of tea.

They'd walked until dusk, now rounded the bend of a mountain and gazed at a distant village surrounded with green trees up ahead. Chung's spirit was roused once more. She started to sing again, swung her walking staff, began to dance wildly in the indigo weed at the side of the road. Very cautiously she raised her staff and poked Tabei's armpit, then his back, to tease and tickle him. Tabei grabbed the end of the stick and flung it away, so that she lost her balance, staggered, and fell.

When they entered the village Tabei went off by himself to drink. They agreed to meet at the construction site next to the town school where they would spend the night in one of the half-finished buildings, still without windows or doors. A movie screen hung from a wooden pole in the town square—there was a movie showing that evening.

A crowd of children climbed some nearby walls and surrounded Chung as she picked up firewood in a little grove. They lay on their bellies atop the walls and threw stones at her. One hit her on the shoulder, but still she didn't turn around. Finally a young man in a yellow cap came along and shooed them away.

"They threw eight stones, and one hit you," yellow-cap smiled, holding up his calculator, flashing "8." "Where are you from?"

Chung looked at him.

"How many days have you walked?"

"I don't remember." Chung held up the leather thong. "I'll add them up. Help me count."

"Each knot means a day?" He knelt in front of her. "Interesting. Ninety-two days."

"Really?"

"You never counted them?"

Chung shook her head.

"Ninety-two days, twenty kilometers a day. . . ." He jabbed the calculator. "One thousand eight hundred forty kilometers."

Chung had no conception of mathematics.

"I'm the accountant here," the little guy said. "No matter what's the problem, I use this to work it out."

"What is it?" Chung asked.

"An electronic calculator. It's fun. Look, it knows how old you are." He pressed a number and showed Chung.

"How old?"

"Nineteen."

"Am I nineteen?"

"How old are you, then?"

"I don't know."

"We Tibetans never used to reckon our age. But this knows. Look, it says nineteen."

"That doesn't look like nineteen."

"Really? Let me see. Oh! Not used to it yet, I just bought it."

"Does it know my name?"

"Sure."

"Okay, what is it then?"

He pressed eight digits one after another until they filled the screen.

"See, it knows."

"So what's my name?"

"You mean you can't even read your own name, dopey?" He held it up.

"That says 'Chung'?"

"1 2 3 4 5 6 Chung. How about that?"

"Wow!" she cried excitedly.

"Wow? Foreigners have been using these a long time. Now here's a problem. We used to work all day long. If labor expended is proportional to the value of production. . . ." He blabbered on about the value of labor, value of goods, add subtract multiply divide, and showed her a number, "Look, it comes out negative. That means we'll be holding out our hand for government grain. And that's against the laws of economics. . . . Hey, what are you staring at me like that for?"

"If you don't have anything to eat you can have dinner with us. I've got firewood to boil tea."

"Damn, did you just walk out of the Middle Ages? Are you one of those extraterrestrials?"

"I come from a place far away. I've walked. . . ." She held up the thong again. "How many days did you count?"

"Let me see . . . eighty-five days."

"I walked eighty-five days? That's not right. Just now you said ninety-two. You're tricking me," Chung started to giggle.

"Oh, tsk, tsk! Buddhas and bodhisattvas," he shut his eyes and murmured, "you're driving me crazy."

"Do you want to have supper here with me? I still have some dried meat."

"Girl, let me take you to a place where young people have fun. There's music, beer, disco music. Throw away that rotten tree branch in your hand."

Tabei squeezed out of the darkened mass of people watching the movie. It wasn't the liquor that made him drunk. It was the multicolored shadows on the screen flashing back and forth in images and human figures—now tiny, now huge—that sent the blood rushing to his head and exhausted him till all he could do was drag his feet back to the empty building. The little black pot stood balanced on the cold rocks. All Chung's things were in the corner. He picked up the pot and gulped a few mouthfuls of cold water, leaned back against the wall, faced the chilly sky, and racked his brain. The farther they went the more the village evenings lost their natural peace and quiet, the noisier and more raucous they became, full of the roars of engines, songs, shouts. The road he was following didn't lead to an even noisier city filled with pandemonium. Definitely not. The way he wanted to go was. . . .

Chung staggered back, stumbled, and leaned against the adobe wall by the doorless entry. Tabei caught the odor of a liquor on her that was sweeter than the smell of the cheap stuff on him.

"Was that fun! They were so happy," Chung said, half laughing, half crying, "happy as gods. Brother, let's stay on here and leave . . . the day after tommmorow. . . ."

"No." Tabei never spent two nights in the same village.

"I'm tired, I'm worn out," Chung's head swayed.

"Tired? You don't know what tired means. Look at those legs of yours, strong as a yak's. You were never tired since the day you were born."

"No, listen, I'm not just a body." She jabbed at her heart.

"You're drunk. Sleep," he pulled Chung by the shoulders, shoved her down on the floor covered with ashes and dirt, and finished by tying another knot on her leather thong.

Chung grew daily more and more exhausted. Whenever they took a short break on the road and she lay down, she didn't feel like getting up again.

"Stand up. Don't lie around there like a lazy mutt," Tabei said.

"Brother, I don't want to go on." She lay in the sunlight, squinting up at him.

"What did you say?"

"Go on alone. I don't want to go on following you every day, walking, walking, walking. You don't know where you're going, so you just roam around forever."

"Woman, you don't understand anything." On the contrary, he was one who did know which way to go.

"No, I don't understand," she shut her eyes and curled up in a ball.

"Get your ass up!" He kicked Chung in her backside, raising his hand. "Or else I'll hit you."

"Devil!" Chung pulled herself up groaning. Tabei set off ahead, and she followed, leaning on her staff.

When she thought the moment was right, Chung ran away. They were sleeping in a cave. She got up at midnight, and without forgetting to sling her little black pot over her shoulder, she fled by the light of the moon, back the way they'd come, feeling free as a bird that's escaped its cage. At noon the next day, as she rested by a cliff on the crest of a canyon, a black speck appeared on the opposite ridge, like the one she saw that day as she came back home from tending her sheep. Tabei had cut her off. After a while, he drew near, and walked up beside her. Trembling with rage, she swung her little black pot for all she was worth, aiming a blow at his head powerful enough to fell a wild bull-yak. Startled, Tabei raised his hand and dodged. The pot flew out of her grasp and rolled clanking down into the canyon. They looked at each other, listening to it clanging down the slope. At last, all Chung could do was climb whimpering down into the valley. It took her an hour to recover the pot, covered all over with dents big and small.

"You're paying for my pot," Chung said.

"Let's see." He took it. The two checked it over carefully. "Only one crack," Tabei said. "I can fix it."

Tabei set off. Chung followed crestfallen. "Ai—" she began to sing in a voice so loud and startling she set all the canyon ringing.

There probably came a day when Tabei tired of Chung too, and thought, "I've rejected evil and followed good, stored up karma, accumulated wisdom and blessings in my past reincarnations, so I wasn't thrown into hell, or born into a false faith, or changed into a half-witted hungry ghost, but reincarnated into this human body. And as I walk on middle earth in the final stages of the way to my soul's liberation from suffering, women and wealth are nothing to me but external objects, stumbling blocks."

By this time Chung's thong was clustered densely with knots.

They arrived in a village called X. To their surprise throngs of villagers met them at the town gate, beating drums and gongs to welcome them. The people's militia formed an honor guard on both sides of the street, semiautomatic rifles strapped on their backs, the muzzles stuffed with rolls of red cloth. Pairs of villagers disguised as yaks danced by the side of the road. The village chief stood at the head of the crowd accompanied by girls carrying a khatag and silver teapots, the spouts garnished with tiny figures sculpted out of yak butter. It turned out there had been a long drought here, and a soothsayer had foretold that today at dusk two people would enter the town from the east, bearing nectar-like rain to bring the crops to harvest. And here they were.

Wild with joy, the people helped Tabei and Chung to climb onto an Iron Horse tractor draped with more khatags of white silk. A crowd clustered round them as the tractor bore them into the village. Men and woman, young and old, had donned their new clothes. Every family had raised a brand new multicolored prayer flag on their roof peak. Somebody discerned in Chung's facial features, her bearing, and her manner of speech the likeness of an earthly incarnation of Mother Goddess Boka, whereupon Tabei was cast aside in neglect. But Tabei knew for certain that Chung was no incarnation of Mother Boka; asleep at night she was ugly, her face sagged, and saliva ran out of the corner of her mouth.

He went off alone, depressed, to the tavern. Tabei was itching for trouble. All he needed was someone to act disgusted at some thing he did. Then he could start something. If the guy pulled a knife, so much the better.

The tavern was full of flies. There was just one old man, drinking alone. Tabei sat down opposite him with a belligerent air. A peasant girl with her hair in braids put a glass on the table, and poured it full.

"This rice wine tastes like horse piss," Tabei said in a loud voice.

No reply.

"Is it like horse piss or isn't it?" he demanded of the old man.

"Horse piss? When I was young I drank it, put my mouth under the stallion's thing there. That's no lie."

Tabei gave a satisfied laugh.

"Chased my sheep and yaks from Getse all the way to the Taklamakan desert. Trying to get them back from Amilier's rustlers."

"Who's Amilier?"

"Hey! She was a bandit leader from up in Xinjiang, a Kazakh, came down this way, oh, thirty, forty years ago. She had a big name up in Ngari, and all around northern Tibet. All a chieftain's cattle, a herd bigger than you could count—she swept them off the grasslands in one night. He came out of his tent the next morning and looked . . . the whole grassland was empty. Nothing left but thousands and thousands of hoofprints. Even the government soldiers couldn't catch her."

"And then?"

"Horse piss? Right. I slung my musket over my back and chased my yaks and sheep over that big desert. That's when a few mouthfuls of horse piss saved my life."

"And then?"

"Then Amilier caught me, and wanted to keep me as her. . . ."

"Husband?"

"No, her herdsman! I was that chieftain's son! But her, damn, she was as beautiful as the sun. You didn't dare look straight at her. I ran away back here. So outside of hell and heaven, where haven't I been?"

"You haven't been where I'm going," Tabei said.

"Where do you mean to go?" the old man asked.

"I . . . I don't know." For the first time Tabei felt uncertain about his destination. He didn't know which way he should continue.

The old man understood what was on his mind. He pointed out the window to a mountain behind him and said, "Nobody's ever gone that way. Our village used to be a relay station. People came and went all different ways from here, but nobody ever went that way. In 1964," he recalled, "they started the people's communes. Everybody talked about the communist road, but nobody then could say just what communism was . . . some kind of heaven. But where? They asked people who came from Western Tibet—'Not there.' Asked people from Ngari—'Not there.' People from the Qinghai border hadn't seen it. The only place left nobody'd ever been was Kelong Mountain. A few people in the village sold off their belongings, said they were taking the road to communism, slung their tsampa bags over their backs, set off across Kelong Mountain, and never came back. After that not a single villager headed up that way, no matter how hard things got."

Tabei clenched the rim of the cup in his teeth. His eyes trembled, gazing at the old man.

"But I know a little secret about what's over Kelong Mountain," the old man winked.

"What?"

"You want to go there?"

"Maybe."

"You climb seven days, you reach the peak at dawn, you'll hear a strange wail, like the wail of an abandoned bastard. That's just wind blowing through a crack in the rocks. Don't hurry right down the other side until it's getting dark. In the sun the snow glare can blind you."

"That's no secret," Tabei said.

"Right, that's no secret. What I really mean is, when you've been going down the other side of Kelong Mountain for two days and reached the bottom, you'll see ravines, deep ones, shallow ones, more than you can count, crisscrossing and twisting off in all directions, like you've walked into a labyrinth. Right, that's still no secret, don't interrupt me. You know why there are so many gullies? That's the palm print of the Lotus Master. In the old days the Lotus Master had a wild battle there with a demon named Shebameiru. For a hundred and eight days neither one could over-power the other. Lotus Master used all his supernatural powers, but he couldn't get the best of Shebameiru until at last the demon turned himself into a tiny flea, thinking Master wouldn't be able to see him. Lotus Mas-ter raised his marvelous right hand, shouted a terrible curse, snapped his hand down over the earth and shoved Shebameiru down to hell, and since that day Lotus Master's palm print has always been there. All anyone needs to do is walk in there and they'll lose their bearings. They say there's only one way out of all those gullies. All the other roads lead to death. And the road to life has no markings."

Tabei looked gravely at the old man.

"That's a legend. I don't know what kind of world that road leads to," the old man murmured, shaking his head.

Tabei decided to go that way. The old man asked Tabei a favor. The old man said he managed an electric grain mill, and his wife managed a couple of dozen acres of farmland. Past generations had never been so wealthy, past generations had never been so busy. Not long ago, the old man said, he was sent as a representative to a big city meeting of "Pio-neers in Stamping Out Poverty and Promoting Prosperity." He got a certificate of merit and a prize, and the newspaper published his pic-ture, four inches high. These days everybody wants to buy farm ma-chines. Early in the morning, the rumble of machinery drowns out the birdsongs of ten thousand years, and the horse carts and donkey carts are forced off the road. When people drink from the clear brook that runs down from the mountain, they catch a whiff of diesel fuel in the water. He had a son who'd just bought a mini-tractor, and needed a daughter-in-law to look after the housework. So he asked Tabei for Chung.

As they were talking the old man's son walked in and pulled out a roll of colorful banknotes to show off in front of the outsider. The son wore an electric wristwatch, a smart new walkman on his belt and headphones on his ears, shuffling his feet to the rhythm of some inaudible music. He'd mastered rich city kids' style. Tabei paid him no attention: the chugging of the mini-tractor the young fellow had left running outside was pulling at Tabei's heartstrings. He got up, walked out to the tractor, and stroked its steering wheel.

"All right, I'll leave Chung with you," Tabei said.

Maybe the fellow had already got a little something from Chung—his eyes brightened in a vague smile.

"Can I try this thing?" Tabei asked.

"Sure. Half an hour and you'll know all about running it, I guarantee you." His new pal gave him an explanation of the controls: the throttle, the gears, the clutch, the brakes.

Tabei started the tractor and sailed off down the dirt road through the village and into the dusk. Chung watched him from the roadside. The young fellow came up and whispered something to her. She cried with joy. She was going to stay!

Now a huge, powerful Iron Bull tractor with trailer in tow came bearing down on Tabei from behind. There was a shallow ditch by the roadside, so Tabei couldn't pull over. He didn't know what to do. His pal yelled at him to pull off the road. Tabei jumped into the middle of the road, his tractor went slowly by itself into the ditch, the Iron Bull put on the brakes too late, and Tabei was struck down by the rear end of its trailer.

He'd been hit in the back, but he said it was nothing, nothing. He climbed back up, brushing himself off. Everybody heaved a sigh of relief.

The first time he'd fooled with a machine and it bit him. It was time for Tabei to leave. He embraced Chung, and they touched foreheads in farewell. Tabei left village X and set off toward Kelong Mountain.

That evening it began to rain. The villagers sang for joy. Tabei entered the mountains and began climbing alone. As he went, he vomited blood: he'd suffered internal injuries.

The story ended here.

I decided to go to Pabunegang and climb over Kelong Mountain to search for my character in the maze of the Lotus Master's palm print.

The road from village X across Kelong Mountain to the palm print of the Master was much longer than I expected. My rented mule collapsed from exhaustion, lay on the ground frothing at the mouth, and gave me a dying look. All I could do was unstrap the pack from its back and put it on my own back, break up a few pieces of hardtack and leave them by its mouth, and carry on alone.

At the summit of Kelong Mountain I heard a wailing sound like the roar of the sea. The snow on the slope below me churned like clouds, the snow under my feet swirled like a tidal wave. But I felt no wind. The air was as still and tranquil as on a windless winter night. I set off down the mountain without waiting for the snow glare to subside at dusk—I was wearing snow goggles. The entire snow-covered mountainside formed a smooth, glassy slope, with no visible obstacles, no protrusions, no hollows. So with my pack on my back I zigzagged slowly down. The heavy pack gradually slipped from my shoulders and slid down my back. I shrugged my shoulders to hike it back up, the sudden shift of weight made me lose my footing, and I fell forward head over heels. I knew I couldn't get back on my feet, I was already sliding downhill fast, so I tucked in my arms and legs, pulled myself into a ball and rolled toward the foot of the mountain, everything whirling around me. Luckily I didn't fall into a crevice. When I awoke I was lying on powdery, level snow, looking up from the foot of the mountain at the long deep track I'd left into the misty, snow-swept sky, vaguely visible above.

On the peak I'd taken a look at my watch: 9:46 a.m., August 11, 2000. Now I looked at it again. The hands showed 8:03 a.m. I passed below the snow line. Grass and lichens were growing around me. Farther down were meadows, alpine plants, then groves of small trees, and as I went lower, dense forest. The forest gradually thinned out to reveal barren rocks, steep and desolate. Along the way I frequently looked at my watch, comparing the time and date it should have been with the time and date on its dial. When I'd crossed Kelong Mountain time had started going backward. The hour and date on my fully automatic solar-powered Seiko wristwatch were going backward at fifty times normal speed.[5]

The farther I went, the stranger the landscape: the egg-shaped leaves and withered, pale yellow limbs of pipal trees slid calmly past my eyes. At the side of the road were the ruins of an old temple. Across a broad plain an elephant came walking, its legs as long as skyladders. The scene reminded me of Salvador Dali's *Temptation of St. Anthony*, so I very carefully avoided it, turned the other way, hastened my steps, didn't look back, and only stopped to rest when I'd reached a hot spring. Steam leaped into the air. I was terribly tired, but didn't dare go to sleep because I was afraid, since time was going backward, that once I shut my eyelids I'd fall into an eternal slumber and never wake up again.

Ahead through the steam I could make out a golden saddle that had been left here in some bygone age, bows and quivers of arrows, suits of armor, swords and shields, prayer wheels, temple horns, and a tattered yellow flag. It looked like an old battlefield. If I hadn't been so tired I'd have walked over and taken a look, maybe even done some archaeological research to determine whether this was one of the battlefields described in *The Song of King Gesar*. But now all I could do was sit and gaze from a distance. Years of heat from the hot spring had softened and

5. The narrator has set out from the year 2000 in which, according to the story's fictional time scheme, he writes. To search for his characters Chung and Tabei in the story, which he has set in 1984, he has to travel backward in time.

melted the metal of the weapons over the ground. They had lost their original shapes, dissolved, flowing in formal order, running off in all directions into inextricably interwoven symbols like Mayan hieroglyphs. At first I suspected the entire phenomenon before my eyes was an illusory change in the shape of external objects, an effect of my prolonged solitude. But immediately I rejected that notion. My thoughts were still logical, my memory and analytical faculties were still functioning. The sun was still traveling from east to west, the universe was still following the laws of physical motion, day and night still followed one another. But my watch was still racing backward, and the day of the week and the date were still reversing, and all this must have confused my biological clock and given me the sensation of disembodiment.

Finally, at some dawn, I awoke and found myself beneath an enormous red rock. I was at the intersection of countless gullies converging and radiating in all directions. It must have been the damp, cold wind gusting from the depths of the gullies all around that woke me and set my teeth chattering. Hurriedly I climbed the wall of bizarre, twisted rock, raised my head and took a look. All round me was the horizon. I had reached the palm print of the Lotus Master. Countless dark gullies stretched off like devils' claws, cryptic runes, unbridgeable crevices that the centuries had worn into the parched earth. Some appeared bottomless. There wasn't a tree, not a blade of grass. The desolate wasteland reminded me of the final scene from a nuclear war film I once saw: on the charred earth's last day the hero and heroine, a world apart, slowly raise their heads, and with an agonized effort begin to drag themselves toward each other. The world's two survivors crawl together and embrace. All they have suffered is in their eyes. Freeze. They are the new Adam and Eve.

Incarnate Lama Sangye Dhapo's remains have been cremated. People have probably found bits of his precious sheli in the blazing ashes. But I can't find my hero anywhere.

"Ta . . . bei!" I shouted, "Where . . . are . . . you?" He could never have found his way out of this place. My voice resounded far off over the wasteland. There was no reply.

Then, a miracle. A distant black dot, a couple of miles away. I rushed along the ravine, calling my hero's name. When I saw the figure clearly, I stopped, astonished. It was Chung!

"Tabei is dying," she approached me, sobbing.

"Where is he?"

She led me to the bottom of a gully. Tabei was lying on the ground, his face pale, sallow, his breathing heavy. Water trickled from the moss-covered stone of the ravine wall, gathering into a pool. Chung dipped her thong and held it up, dripping water into his half-open mouth.

Tabei opened his eyes and gazed at me, "I'm waiting, Prophet. I know God will enlighten me."

"The wound on his back is horrible," Chung whispered in my ear. "He has to keep drinking."

"Why didn't you stay in village X?" I turned to her.

"What for?" she replied. "He never agreed to let me stay. He plucked out my heart and tied it to that cord around his waist. I couldn't go on living without him."

"Not necessarily," I said.

"He keeps wanting to know what that is," Chung pointed behind me.

I turned and looked up. We were in a deep, straight ravine. In the distance at its end rose the gigantic bloodred rock under which I'd passed the night. It was only now that I could see the snow-white "Om" carved into its heart, invisible to anyone standing beneath—the first syllable of the mantra "Om mani padme um." Either this was a place frequented by gods and demons, or else some great hero lay buried here. On the bank of the Chumi Shinggo River that flows from Gyantse to Phari there stands a great rock carved with the syllable "Om" in memory of Depon Lhading the Second, leader of the Tibetan army, who fell there in battle against the English invaders in 1904. But all this I felt Tabei had no need to know.

Now, too late, I discovered the truth: these abandoned children of mine were endowed with a life and will of their own. Letting Chung and Tabei walk out of that manila envelope had been an irreparable mistake. Why to this day have I been unable to portray the image of the "new man," the "new woman"? Now that I've created these characters, their every action has become an unalterable fact. If someone were to call me to account why in this great age I've permitted them to exist, what could I answer?

Finally, trusting to luck, I lowered my lips to Tabei's ear and tried to persuade him, whispering explanations he could almost understand, that the place he wanted to find didn't exist, that it was only like Thomas More's Utopia, nothing more.

Too late. It was impossible now, at his life's last instant, to persuade him to cast aside a faith forged over so many years. He rolled over and laid his ear to the ground.

"Tabei," I faltered, "you'll recover, just give me a minute. My things are right over there. I have a first aid kit in my bag, and. . . ."

"Shhh," Tabei stopped me with a gasp, his ear pressed tight to the cold, damp earth. "Listen! Listen!"

For a good while all I heard was a feeble murmur in the intervals between my own heartbeats.

"Help me up!" Tabei called, waving his hand, "I want to go up there!" I had no choice but to help him. Chung climbed ahead. I supported him from beneath, surprised how heavy he was. I carefully protected his injured back with one hand, gripping sharp rocks with the other, helping him bit by bit to climb the ledge, searching for footholds on projecting stones. I clutched a rock and it cut my hand so it seared with pain. Warm blood ran down my sleeve. Chung lay on her stomach and reached down to grasp Tabei under the armpits. She pulled from above, I pushed from below. It took all our strength to lift him to the rim. The sun was just coming up over the horizon. The east shone, dazzling.

Tabei greedily drew in an agonized breath of dawn air and alertly gazed around, searching. "What is it saying, Prophet? I don't understand. You must know. Hurry, tell me, I beg you." He rolled over, prostrating himself at my feet.

His ears had caught the signal a few minutes before mine: now Chung and I both heard a very real sound coming down from the sky. We listened, deep in concentration.

"It's the bell ringing on a temple roof," Chung called out.

"It's a church bell," I corrected her.

"Frightening! A landslide, oh!" Chung said.

"No, this is the music of a spirited drum and bugle corps, a chorus, thousands of voices singing," I corrected her again.

Chung gave me a perplexed look.

"God is beginning to speak," Tabei said in a solemn voice. This time I didn't dare correct him. It was the voice of a man speaking in English over a loudspeaker. How could I have told him that this was the opening ceremonies of the twenty-third Olympic Games in Los Angeles, U.S.A., carried live on television and radio via satellite broadcast to every corner of the planet? The hour hand and date on my watch had stopped: 7:13 a.m. Beijing time, July 19, 1984.

"This isn't the voice of God, my child. It's a summons to struggle for all the world—bells, horns, a chorus." This was all I could say. I don't know if he heard me or not. Maybe he understood everything. He curled up as if he were cold and closed his eyes as if he was going to sleep. I laid Tabei down, knelt at his side, and smoothed out his tattered clothing. Beside his body I arranged stones in an "Om." My right hand had left a bloodstain on his shirt. I felt guilty. Was I the one who had killed him? More than once in the past I've sent other protagonists of mine off on the road to death. It's something I have to examine myself about.

"Now there's only me. I'm all alone," Chung lamented.

"You're not going to die, Chung," I said. I looked up at her. "You've endured the ordeal of this journey, and I can gradually shape you into a new human being." And in her sincere eyes I saw hope.

The thong around her waist dangled in front of my nose. I grasped it. I wanted to work out the number of days since she'd left home. Intently I began counting from the top: "five . . . eight . . . twenty-five . . . fifty-seven . . . ninety-six. . . ." It was a hundred and eight, just the number of prayer beads on the cord around Tabei's wrist.

The sun rose in imperial splendor, irradiating heaven and earth in luminous gold.

I took Tabei's place, Chung followed me, and together we set off on the way back. Time recommenced from the beginning.

• 6 •

The Glory of a Wind Horse[1]

Tashi Dawa

*U*gyen walked into the camp, forty or fifty tents squeezed together on a stretch of ground that looked like a garbage dump. It had just rained. The blazing sunlight brought forth steaming odors from the tents: human piss and shit; dog piss and dog shit; damp, moldy leather; horse dung; the musty stench of damp sheepskin; the sour smells of fermenting wine and human sweat; gasoline and plastic; a dog carcass; the decomposing breath of death from old people's bodies; cheap perfume; rotting leftovers. Ugyen felt sad.

Something flashed above him. He looked up: an airplane soared over the city, leaving behind it a gigantic roar. Then the entire earth was marvelously still: not a breath, as if the roar of the plane had sucked away every other sound. On the ground lay the body of a dog covered so thick with flies it was impossible to tell whether it was dead or asleep.

This empty, lifeless, dirty, ramshackle, abandoned camp was no ideal hiding place for him. His every move was open to surveillance. At this very moment someone could be watching him, peering out through a slit or hole in a tent. He paused beside a waterlogged hollow. In the

1. The Chinese title, "fengma zhi yao" (literally "windhorse's glory"), involves an untranslatable bilingual pun. The Chinese word "fengma" (a mare in heat) is a reference to the Chinese proverb "Feng ma niu bu xiang ji"—literally, "You can't mate a bull with a mare." The expression connotes a spurious attempt to establish a deceitful connection between two unrelated subjects, i.e., a red herring. In this sense, the title of the story reads "The Glory of a Red Herring." But "fengma" also translates literally from Chinese as "wind horse"; a wind horse, in Tibetan "lungta," is a piece of paper inscribed with a verse of the Buddhist scriptures; the piece of paper is released into the wind, and the scripture verse is carried off wherever the wind blows it.

back of his head something rang like a bell. It was a premonition. A boy scurried out from someplace and walked up to him. The boy's head was wrapped in a filthy towel. Over his shoulders was draped a grown man's coat like a cape reaching down below his knees. Under it, the boy's stomach was covered in mud. He had a cigarette in his mouth, and a red firecracker in his hand that he raised to the cigarette. He walked up to Ugyen. The hissing, smoking firecracker flew toward Ugyen's face. With a sweep of his hand, Ugyen snatched it as if he were catching an insect. The twisting, burning fuse prickled his palm like a fly beating its wings. Before he had time to open his fingers, it exploded, and he ran around waving his hand like crazy. He felt something wet in his palm. He thought it was blood. A clear yellow liquid smeared his fingers. He sniffed it. It was urine. He pressed his burning hand to his trouser leg and ran after the boy, searching here, searching there, but the kid must have ducked into one of the tents.

Supporting the tents were vast networks of crisscrossed cords fastened to wooden stakes and metal pegs driven into the ground. It had just rained, the ground was a quagmire, and some of the pegs and stakes had pulled out, cords had gone slack, sides of tents had collapsed. Ugyen began pushing stakes back into the ground with his foot, but it was futile. Still damp and slack, the cords couldn't support the tents.

He raised the doorflap of one tent after another, but found nobody inside. Finally, he discovered an old woman sitting cross-legged, her back arched, bent over some ancient coins. When she heard Ugyen at the door, she plunged her head between her knees and froze, as if she'd been caught doing something shameful. In another tent someone lay asleep, head covered. In a third a girl lay on a cowhide rug playing with a dirty, ragged pack of cards.

"Hey there, kind man!" he heard a voice say from inside a tent. Ugyen went over and raised the burlap bag that served as its doorflap.

An emaciated woman lay on a bed cushion, her hair in disarray. Her sunken eye sockets looked like a pair of glasses painted over her eyes. Her body was covered in all kinds of old clothes. A swaddled child lay beside her. A strange, powerful odor—like the stench of some weird, monstrous beast—suffocated Ugyen.

"Brother, I'm thirsty," said the woman, pointing. Outside the door a pot stood propped on three rocks, with some tea at the bottom of it.

"It's cold," he said.

"Doesn't matter. Here's a bowl."

He dipped out some tea and gave it to her. "A boy or a girl?"

The woman didn't reply.

"You haven't changed the baby. This smell's unbearable."

The woman didn't reply.

Ugyen held his nose as he spoke. "I, the hero, didn't come here to give you tea, ma'am. I'm looking for someone."

"My man left a long time ago!"

"I'm not looking for your man. I'm looking for somebody called Pockface Sonam Rigzin from Gonjo."

"What do you want with him?"

"Nothing to do with you, woman." Ugyen let go of his nose, took a breath, and held it again.

"The one you're after—he's my man. Left a month ago!"

Ugyen knew she was lying. Beside the woman he saw a square black tray with a black-tasseled awl. They were for black magic rituals. The woman was a witch. If he made a false move she could probably make thick, foul, black blood gush from his nose. He saw the child stir. A head appeared from the swaddling clothes. Between its eyes was a tiny green horn. Its face was covered with wrinkles, horribly ugly. The sickening odor must have been coming from this little monster. Ugyen covered his nose, terror-stricken, and backed out of the tent.

Three men stood by the waterlogged hollow where Ugyen had been standing just a few moments before, every one of them tall—well over six feet—and stalwart. One, slightly taller, had black tassels coiled round his head. A younger man had a fierce, savage face. The third played with a ring on his finger. They were looking at him.

"Hey, brother, can you tell me. . . ." Ugyen called to them.

They stood motionless as statues looking him up and down with narrowed eyes.

"If you're not going to open your mouths, just forget it," he said. Ugyen sensed the three were bored, just looking for a reason to start a fight. He didn't want to stir up any more trouble.

"The doors of our ears are not shut," said the one with the black tassels.

"Where's Pockface Sonam Rigzin from Gonjo live?"

"He died," the savage-looking one said after a moment.

Ugyen was confused. In the back of his head a dog barked. He gave his head a knock. The sound disappeared. "How long's he been dead?" he asked.

"Oh, four or five months . . . so I heard," said the one playing with his ring.

Ugyen didn't ask any more questions, just kept blinking his eyes as if a little bug had fallen into one of them. He turned to go.

"You're his relative?" the one playing with the ring asked.

"No. You saw him?"

"It's what I heard. Everybody wants to find out something about him—isn't that right?"

"There's nothing worth finding out about him," Ugyen retorted.

The youngest one growled malevolently, yawned languidly, and started walking off. Ugyen felt there was something wicked about him: he'd said Pockface Sonam Rigzin from Gonjo was dead.

"You're Ugyen?" the one with the tassels asked in a somber voice.

He didn't know what to reply, so he just nodded.

"Evening the day before last, the police were back again, searching the place. With your photograph."

"Three days ago, Ngawang Melong," corrected the one playing with the ring.

"Doesn't matter," said the one with the tassels. "Where were you that night?"

"Robbers' Forest," Ugyen replied.

"That's what I guessed," Ngawang Melong said, nodding. "My grandpa hid out there in the old days. Did nothing big. Ran off with some Nepalese peddler's radio. Never seen a radio before. Tore the thing apart. Never found the little guy inside who did the talking."

"The police won't come tonight," said the one playing with the ring.

"I don't care," Ugyen stared off.

"Find someplace for him to hide, Dhargye," Ngawang Melong told the one playing with the ring.

Dhargye gave Ugyen a look. Dhargye seemed to like this murderer, standing here out in the open while the police were running around hunting for him. "You're not going to be carrying your next victim's head back into my tent in the middle of the night, are you?"

"Listen, I don't like that kind of joke."

"Right!" Dhargye said with a grin.

"Hey there, time to go," the youngest one said, waving from a distance.

"Find tent fifty-three," Dhargye said. "Fix yourself something to eat. If you're tired, sleep on the bed by the telephone."

"You've got a telephone? Where's it hooked up?"

"Up my asshole. I found it and put it there for looks."

"Remember, don't let the gatekeeper get a look at you," Ngawang Melong warned. "He's the eyes of the police."

"Yeah, yeah," Ugyen waved impatiently. "I didn't come here for orders."

"Right, you came here for Pockface Sonam Rigzin from Gonjo, murderer, but he's dead. So I hear," Dhargye winked. He was an optimistic, uninhibited young guy.

When the girl in blue jeans and a low-cut blouse heard he was looking for Pockface Sonam Rigzin from Gonjo, she shook her head and said she'd never heard of him. There was a guy named Sonam Rigzin all right, but his face wasn't pockmarked, and he didn't look like somebody from Gonjo. She pointed to a young man in a suit sitting over by the wall. Ugyen rushed in the bar entrance, his mind a blank. Just inside, red neon lights swirled in dazzling, incomprehensible letters. They seemed to soak him in fresh blood. On a wall by the door hung a sign embossed with regulations in a foreign language. Somehow or other those few lines of foreign words and those neon letters burned themselves into Ugyen's brain so that he'd remember them the rest of his life. During the subsequent investigation, he recalled them exactly, reproducing every last detail, to the bewilderment of the police, and triggering the fatal denouement.

The people coming into the bar were dressed in flashy clothes. Their walk was rough, their laugh was crude. They all looked like foreigners. The bar had an unusual odor, a disgusting atmosphere. Red and green lights flashed to the beat of the music, and made the people look like they were swaying back and forth. Ugyen stood in the aisle, staring around. A couple of grim-faced, hefty guys in motorcycle jackets walked toward him, helmets in hand. Ugyen was a tough Khampa with a knife stuck in his belt, but they shouldered him aside. Everybody here acted like a fearless desperado. Nobody paid him any attention.

Sonam Rigzin was sitting alone at a table with a cup of strong black coffee in front of him, looking rather bored, as if his friends hadn't shown up. He certainly seemed like a regular. Ugyen quietly sat down opposite him and coldly stared him in the face. He wasn't sure this was really Pockface Sonam Rigzin from Gonjo. The fellow was dressed immaculately, like a real city gent, not like someone from Gonjo at all. Ugyen couldn't make out the color of his suit in the pulsating light. All he could see was that the material had a fine, almost invisible stripe. The tailoring was exquisite, a perfect fit. His tie was embroidered with golden thread, in a pattern like the eyes of mad beasts glaring in the dark. His jet-black hair was combed neatly and elegantly. He was probably the only other Tibetan here. Ugyen never thought it would be like this. He'd always thought he'd be facing a Khampa who looked like himself. He didn't like facing this clean, tidy, stylish guy.

"Mister," said Ugyen, leaning closer and striking up a conversation. Perhaps from his work, Sonam Rigzin was used to meeting all kinds of people. In a very friendly way, and even with interest, he replied to Ugyen's questions one by one. "Right, I'm the one you're looking for." He stroked his face, laughing with embarrassment. "So, after all these years there's somebody who still remembers my nickname. Only somebody from my hometown could remember it. How could people give me that nickname? In fact there isn't a single pockmark on my face. Maybe I had pockmarks when I was little—I don't remember. Right, I'm from Gonjo County. Like something to drink? Don't like coffee? How about a beer? Sure." Ugyen phrased his questions carefully. Sonam Rigzin cooperated fully. In detail, he conclusively verified his identity as Pockface Sonam Rigzin from Gonjo.

"Tell you something about my father and mother? Ha, ha, you're a funny one all right. You must be one of those relatives of mine who're always creeping out of the woodwork, eh? Every damn one I run into is just as poor as you. What's your name? Ugyen, is it? What do you want to know about my father and mother for? Dad's name was Abo Delang, right. Mama's was Drachang Chodon. Yes, they were minstrels. You seem to know all about us. You know, I'm thinking of writing something about them. The old days are vanishing." Sonam Rigzin propped his cheek in his hand, shut his eyes, and, carried off by a sudden impulse, recalled the trials and feats of his father. Abo Delang was a wandering acrobat, famous everywhere. Stirring up thick clouds of dust, the minstrel troupe's wagons would rush into town, and children would race out to meet them, shouting with joy. Dogs ran behind the wagons, barking. Young girls stood shyly on the roofs, watching the merry minstrel troupe singing and dancing. Then Abo Delang began his elegant performance: the one-legged whirlwind. Seventy-two coins in a circle on the ground. The whole clan beat drums and rang bells as his father balanced on one leg and sprang, face up at the sky like a giant eagle, a great writhing dragon. Seventy-two times he would soar, whirl, and crouch, snatching one coin after another until not a single one was left on the earth. Cries of praise and wonder would pour from the villagers.

But these endless, roving performances made for a dangerous life. In the loneliness of a desolate mountain valley a distant gunshot reverberated glorious and eternal, shattering the dream of little Sonam Rigzin there at his mother's bosom. Opening his eyes, he saw the white clouds in the blue sky, the yellow valley, the minstrel troupe's horsemen in single file along the little winding path on the valley floor. When the sound of the gunshot

"The caravan of the minstrels is passing by." (Photo by Fosco Maraini)

died away, it was deathly silent all around, just as before. He felt the urgent rocking of his mother's horse that set the tiny bells on its neck jingling—and another gunshot, glorious, interminable, resonating throughout the valley. His mother screamed and held him close. As her powerful hand thrust him back under her robe into the drowsy moisture of her bosom, he saw a man ahead fall softly off his horse. Only many years later did he learn that this was his uncle who played the zither. In the excitement, he got pushed so far down his mother's bosom that he couldn't breathe. A roar filled the silent valley, a horse neighed in fear, people whispered curses, bullets whistled by. Oblivious to danger, he forced his head out of his mother's robe and stared wide-eyed at the gun battle. He saw the tiny figures of men high up on the hill. From all around him in the valley burst a cry full of wild power: "*Ah-hei-hei. . . .*"

His father Abo Delang was not only a master acrobat, but also a crack shot. He saw his father calmly roll over behind a rock, calmly, coolly raise his rifle, aim at a black figure on the hill, and pull the trigger. The tiny figure swayed and toppled to the ground just as his mother's hand shoved him back down into her bosom so tight he couldn't squirm out to watch the rest of the gun battle. It was only much later, after years of watching his father bent over as if he was looking for cow dung, that he realized that a wound from the gun battle with the bandits had bent him like this. The injury to his father's back got worse and worse. The man who'd braved the itinerant life died with the one regret that he would never pass his art on to his son, who was only just learning to walk.

Ugyen knew that all Sonam Rigzin had said was true. What he, Ugyen, had seen during the battle was what Sonam Rigzin had seen. He too had witnessed the unforgettable scene from his mother's bosom, high above on the valley rim. Ugyen rose and walked round the table. Sonam Rigzin stood, watching him in helpless panic. Maybe if this son of the minstrel clan, now dressed in a suit, had learned his father's unique trick, he could have dodged the mortal blade that Ugyen calmly, coolly, effortlessly thrust into him now. The long knife in Ugyen's hand plunged through the layers of Sonam Rigzin's clothing and into his stomach with as little effort as if his suit had been a sheet of paper. Ugyen thrust upward with all his might, probing for the heart. He heard bone crack, saw the bloody tip of the blade come out through Sonam Rigzin's clothing behind his shoulder blade. Ugyen had thought it would be difficult to plunge a knife through flesh. Now he knew he had strength enough to drive his knife through two bodies at once. Half of Sonam Rigzin's face twitched to the left, half to the right. He groaned a cold laugh, his head dropped, his body collapsed.

The bar went quiet. The patrons were either used to this sort of business or frightened out of their wits. In silence they stared at Ugyen. No one moved. At last, one real man tossed down a card with a practiced hand, jabbed his neighbor with an elbow, and tapped the table, meaning, "Your play." His neighbor looked at his own hand, pulled out an ace of spades, and took the first man's lead. When Ugyen wiped his knife on the dead man's suit, it left no bloodstain. He thought the suit must have been bloodred. He'd never seen a suit that color. He walked out of the bar, knife in hand. Nobody stopped him.

Maybe the girl in the blue jeans and low-cut blouse leaning on the door frame hadn't seen what happened. She paid no attention to his knife, just stood with a cigarette in the corner of her mouth, arms crossed, glancing indifferently out of the corner of her eye. It made him think of a girl he'd seen in a movie. "Dirty whore," he muttered.

There were no streetlights. No one ran after him. No one tried to stop him. All around him it was black. He heard a roar. He thought a crowd of people must be applauding somewhere in a big square. As he walked aimlessly through the dark, his head rang with the awesome undulating melody of a gunshot in a lonely mountain valley. Nobody in the future would ever again hear such a stirring sound. Now he was finished with all that. He felt light and easy. He'd searched painfully all these years, worn out many pairs of boots, worn himself out, gone without sleep, exhausted himself. Now it was all finished. In the future, whenever they mentioned his name, people would give an admiring thumbs-up in tribute to him. He didn't care if he never saw them do it.

Suddenly, he sensed a vast crowd of shadows following him. He turned to look. An expanse of green stars glimmered behind him, flashing like the stitching on the dead man's tie. A pack of stray dogs lurked close behind, ready to pounce and tear him to pieces. Could his victim's soul have turned to a stray dog and come after him for vengeance so soon? He hefted his knife, ready for a fight to the death, then looked down in confusion. The knife he'd clutched since he'd killed his victim had turned into a shank of dried mutton. He raised it to his nose and sniffed: it stank of bloody human flesh. He threw it away in disgust. In a flash, the pack of dogs pounced on it. A warm, putrid stench swept past him on the breeze. From where he'd thrown the shank came the yapping of curs fighting over their food. Ugyen heaved a sigh of relief: the knife he'd carried all these years was no good to him anymore. He sure didn't want to kill a second man.

Hey! Those dazzling magic letters—what country could they be from? Coiling and twisting together until they made you feel like dancing, like getting it on with a woman. When Thome Sambhota created writing, he sure wasn't thinking of those letters. And that writing on the sign— what was it, anyway? If he had the chance, he'd go back there, just for a drink. The beer wasn't bad. And if the stinking whore at the door . . . he started reckoning how long it had been since he'd slept with a woman.

Early in the morning, the Khampa vagrants came out of their low, cramped tents and greedily sucked in the fresh, clean air. Men and women with swollen faces and disheveled hair stood at their doorflaps, pulling on their clothes, doing up their belts. Puffs of blue smoke rose, laden with the pungent odors of rubber, oil, and chemicals. The old people had gotten up early and already finished circumambulating the Potala. The elderly Khampa vagrants always tried to be friendly and chat with the old Lhasa people they met as they walked together around the city, spinning their prayer wheels. But for centuries there had been bad blood between the Lhasa residents and the eastern Khampa people. The old Lhasa people walked cute little Pekinese dogs on leashes and led fat, tame sheep they'd rescued from the butcher. They wanted nothing to do with the grizzled old Khampa vagrants, who had nothing in their traveling bags, who once might have been robbers, swindlers, bandits, or horse thieves. Feeble now and shaking like candles in the wind, the old vagrants didn't care what the Lhasa residents thought. They worshiped the same Buddha as the city folks, they walked the same road, they prayed the same prayers. And as for the bliss of the life to come, well, they thought, we'll just walk along, spin our prayer wheels, and see. At every turn they invoked blessings on the holy Potala. Then, still spinning their prayer wheels, and their parched tongues still murmuring prayers from dry throats, they turned back toward the campground.

Around breakfast time, a blue police car with a flashing red light on its roof entered the campground gate. Five policemen jumped out. The vagrants who lived in the campground were used to the gentlemen of the police force bursting in at any time of day. Whenever anything happened in the city, the manhunt would always start here. The police usually carried out their raids at night. Piercing sirens would wail. Policemen with urgent, hectoring voices would flush naked men and women out of their tents. The officers would gape in amazement at the stolen items they found: automobile engines; tires; all kinds of auto parts; brand new motorcycles; bicycles, new and old; a dark green safe, still unopened, full of cash; rolls and rolls of cloth; countless boxes of

Pilgrims spin prayer wheels, praying at the Nechung Temple, Lhasa, 1988.
(Photo © 2001 by Galen Rowell, Mountain Light)

canned food. They found a maternity ward birthing chair, and a high-tech flush toilet from some hotel's restroom. They even recovered a golden-haired, green-eyed European baby that people said was stolen off the back of some foreign tourist couple—who knows what for? The police nicknamed the vagrant camp the Launch Pad. In a cold, majestic voice, a policeman in dark glasses announced through a loudspeaker their reason for coming. He commanded each family to leave one person behind to watch its tent. Everyone else was to line up and go to Cultural Palace Square to witness a mass public trial.

Many people couldn't figure out what the trial had to do with them.

"It's to scare us so that we'll behave here in Lhasa," Ngawang Melong said. He was tying on his boots. "They're going to kill somebody," he growled with a swipe of the hand across his throat.

"It's a shame," Shega said. She poured Ngawang Melong and their savage-faced brother Dorje bowls of tea, put a little leather bag of tsampa between them on the table, and set a spoon on top of it.

Dhargye hadn't come yet. He lived in tent number fifty-three, the one with the telephone.

"How come you didn't put butter in this tea?" Dorje grumbled to his sister.

"I had to keep it for Buddha Tsuklakhang's lamp."

"Don't give me that."

"Where's Dhargye—doesn't he want his tea?" Shega asked.

"Kill somebody—hunh!" Dorje said.

"Shut your mouth," she spat.

A couple of policemen walked up to the tent, bent over, and looked in. One of them pointed to his watch. "Hurry up. You leave at eight-thirty."

"Dog!" Dorje said.

The policeman didn't hear.

"Who'll stay behind?" Ngawang Melong asked.

"Shega, you," said Dorje.

"No. I'm going with you," she snapped.

"Listen, you," Ngawang Melong snarled, "my fist's just aching to let you have it."

"And who's going to get your lunch for you then, huh?"

"All right, you stay here," Ngawang Melong conceded. "We'll come back. Just make some tsampa for lunch, and some tea."

Dhargye was at the door. He bent over, looked in, and said, "Hey, we might see Ugyen on the platform today."

The others didn't make a sound.

"He's going to die today," Dhargye said, entering.

"Don't talk like that," Shega said.

Dhargye gave Shega a nod in greeting. She returned his surreptitious smile, passing him a bowl of tea.

With no butter in it, the tea was clear. This probably put something in Dhargye's head. He took the first mouthful and discovered phantom images appearing and disappearing in the bowl. First he saw a pile of white rocks with a prayer flag thrust into them and a mani cairn wrapped in wool. Next he saw strange, twisted, luminous letters drifting up out of a still green lake, then the mark of a human body left on the sand of a pure white beach.

Trembling, with the bowl still in his hand, he rushed off to old Longna's tent. In her youth Longna had been a village soothsayer. Now her toothless mouth uttered curses against these new times. "This is an age, when hoards of demons arise and stir up trouble," she said, "when the bodhisattvas fall silent and even the awesome heavenly guardians can't hold back the demons' power. Oh yes, the glittering golden temples around Lhasa still celebrate solemn festivals, and the deep resonance of the lamas' long copper horns still pulsates back and forth over the city, and fierce scarlet-robed lamas in yellow cockscomb hats, their shoulders padded so they look like sparrow hawks, strike rhombus-shaped clubs of bronze-inlaid iron against the earth over and over, terrorizing pious pilgrims from the countryside until they don't dare look up from the ground"—old Longna closed her eyes—"but they don't vanquish the evil spirits! It's just for foreigners to take pictures now," she said. Then she would cover her nose with her sleeve and mutter about the sinister dust polluting the air of the holy Tibetan plateau. Then she'd throw dust that she'd combed out of her graying braids into the fire, where it crackled and sparked. "That's a few more demons dead," she'd say, laughing in delight. Folks said all she'd killed were a few of her lice.

Longna stretched out a long fingernail and stroked Dhargye's face in sign of welcome, then listened, eyes shut, as he told her why he'd come. The two crouched shoulder to shoulder: two pairs of eyes gazing into the tea like people staring at goldfish in a bowl. There were definitely some strange images in that tea, but Dhargye couldn't decipher them. Longna took a crystal lens out of her bosom, spat on it three times, wiped it on her sleeve, and began a vague incantation. The images in the bowl gradually became distinct. She gave Dhargye a little pat on the back and pushed him into the bowl. A hot breeze swept the desolate pastureland. Foul, mosslike grass knit the dusty yellow soil. An indistinct trail stretched away among slopes that rose and fell off to the horizon. The scent of moist horse dung drifted on the air. Dhargye could hear the faint tinkling of a bell like celestial music, swinging from the saddle of some distant, lonesome traveler. He set off into the wilderness, searching for its ephemeral ringing.

The wilderness vanished—or had he reached the end of it? A dizzying abyss yawned at his feet. Up from this canyon blew gusts of frigid air. Far below, a river churned and swirled. From the brink of the precipice, Dhargye saw Dorje and a woman far below, walking to the temple, followed by Pockface Sonam Rigzin from Gonjo. Dhargye looked carefully. The woman was Shega! Around her neck she wore a sacred jade unicorn. Dhargye recognized it as the one the Chinese emperor had presented to the Fifth Dalai Lama, who had preserved it in the Potala until somehow it had found its way onto Shega's neck. And Pockface Sonam Rigzin from Gonjo had spotted it! As Dhargye watched in impotent rage, Sonam Rigzin slid his lust-crazed eyes from the jade unicorn hanging from Shega's white neck down over her breasts, down to. . . . But her brother Dorje was right there watching, and when he saw Sonam Rigzin slip his hand around Shega's waist, he reached to the sheath at his belt. Dorje and Sonam Rigzin danced back and forth, waving their knives. One quick slash of Dorje's blade, and Pockface Sonam Rigzin from Gonjo lay dying in a pool of blood. Shega ran to the dying man, embraced him, raised him up! As Dhargye looked on from afar, Shega took off the precious jade unicorn and hung it round Pockface Sonam Rigzin's neck, then touched her forehead to his. Dhargye couldn't get near. He wanted to run to Shega, but he couldn't get near. It was as if a glass door stood in his way.

Brother and sister didn't even glance at Dhargye, but floated off, propelled by some invisible force. Now Dhargye was standing next to the body of Pockface Sonam Rigzin, lying on the sand. A shepherd and a peasant girl passed, spotted the body, then eyed Dhargye suspiciously. Dhargye got flustered. He didn't know how to explain that he had nothing to do with the murder.

And right then who should burst in but Ugyen! In the corner of his tent Dhargye was gazing at Shega's white neck, sliding his arms down lower, slipping his hand around her waist—Ugyen didn't pay attention to what the two of them were doing, just walked in and pulled up the pile of worn felt carpets and a sheet of plastic, then lifted some wooden planks to reveal an enormous hole, big enough to hide a yak. The hole was filled with stolen goods, mostly scrap metal. Ugyen was rummaging for something. Dhargye heaved a sigh and let go of Shega. She straightened up her hair, straightened her clothing, spat out, "That Ugyen's just a jinx, damn him!" and walked out of the tent.

"What the hell are you looking for?" Dhargye demanded.

Ugyen didn't reply.

Who did Ugyen think he was, Dhargye shouted, a pillar of the community? The police were looking for him all over, and here he was swaggering around in broad daylight where anybody could spot him. Dhargye muttered something about reporting him to the police if he kept bursting in and spoiling his fun with Shega like this.

"Where's that camera I left here?" Ugyen asked him.

"Sold."

Ugyen put the planks back down over the hole and sat on them. "How much did you get for it?"

"Three hundred."

"Is that all!" Ugyen scratched his head, dejected. "I almost got caught grabbing it off that foreigner!"

"You told me to sell it."

"Did you think it was junk, selling it for three hundred?"

"The guy said one of the parts was broken."

"He robbed you."

"What did you want with it?"

"I made a deal—I give this guy the camera, he'll tell me where to find Pockface Sonam Rigzin from Gonjo."

Dhargye pushed him away from the hole, pulled the carpets back into place, picked up the telephone from where Ugyen had knocked it to the ground, and solemnly replaced it on the empty soapbox by the bed. "He's dead," Dhargye said.

"He's not. I know."

"I saw him die myself," Dhargye said, "I think."

"Maybe . . ." Ugyen said, lost in thought, "there's nobody named Pockface Sonam Rigzin from Gonjo."

"Can you see him clear?"

"Seems like the third one on the right."

"No, it's not. You can't see that far."

"I don't like it. What a crowd! My head's bursting."

"The bodhisattvas aren't happy about this."

"The wind will rise in the afternoon."

Tall and robust, Ngawang Melong, Dorje, and Dhargye stood outside the meeting ground, their hands on each other's shoulders. They looked as if they were standing around Tromsikhang market, bartering jewels. A policeman came over and told them in a low voice to get inside with the rest of the crowd. They paid no attention to him. Police began to surround them. People near them became nervous and moved away. Ngawang Melong could tell from their green uniforms that these were military police. When the three of them hung around, they usually rested their hands on the handles of their knives, but the police had made them check their knives with the officers who stayed at the camp. Now that they didn't have anyplace to put their hands, they just swung them idly back and forth.

The police herded the two hundred Khampas into the square. Fond of a joke no matter what the occasion, the native Lhasa people saw this confused gang straggling in, staring around at everything, and immediately cheered and applauded as if the Khampas were the honored guests. The Khampa men appreciated the joke and started laughing too. One of them complained that his seat was so far from the platform that he couldn't see anything: "Hey, mister! What's the show?"

"*The Last Judgment.*"

"Never heard of it. Something about a goddess?"

This silly question started the Lhasa people laughing again.

A row of criminals stood on the platform. Three of them had already been sentenced to death. When the public sentencing was complete, they would be driven to the execution ground outside of town. One was a Lhasa teenager who had shot and killed a policeman; the second was a peasant who'd stolen three hundred thousand yuan from a bank; the third was the murderer and escaped convict Ugyen. In a valley outside of town, the police had found a body. From the testimony of eyewitnesses—a shepherd and a peasant girl who identified Ugyen, from evidence discovered at the scene—fingerprints taken from the handle of an English-style bayonet, from the accused's hair under the victim's fingernails (which indicated that there had been a struggle before the murder occurred), and footprints found near the scene; and from the relationship of the victim with the accused before the crime, it was conclusively established that Ugyen was guilty of premeditated murder. The victim was Sonam Rigzin, also known as Pockface Sonam Rigzin from Gonjo. The motive: a revenge feud that originated with the murder of Ugyen's father by the father of Sonam Rigzin.

Ugyen knew nothing of legal procedure. As soon as he was captured, he admitted committing a murder, but the time of the crime, the location of the crime, and the victim were different. Ugyen simply and straightforwardly confessed all the details. The time—one evening. The place—a certain bar in the city. The victim—a man wearing a suit, called Pockface Sonam Rigzin from Gonjo. In addition to describing the bar, Ugyen recounted in precise detail—and even drew—each stroke of the letters in neon lights inside the bar's entrance and on the sign. The police didn't recognize the place. They felt the case was getting complicated. They began to wonder if he'd committed a second murder. In a police car, they drove Ugyen up and down every street and lane of Lhasa without finding the bar. He said it was at night and he couldn't remember what part of town it was in. The police concluded that the crime Ugyen was describing was nothing but a fiction that he'd invented to confuse the investigation. First, they reasoned, no other murder had been reported. A murder before so many witnesses, such as Ugyen had described, would surely have been reported. Second, the letters Ugyen was talking about . . . the devil knew what they meant. Maybe just some nonsense he dreamed up. As for neon signs . . . let alone shady, crowded low-life bars—even the luxurious, modern Lhasa Hotel didn't have neon lights. There wasn't a single neon light glittering in all of Lhasa. It's impossible to use them because Lhasa's high altitude produces too large a temperature differential between the inside of the light and the surrounding air. Ugyen was all confused. He'd admitted committing one murder, but the police said it was all a hoax and that he had committed a different one, which he didn't know anything about. He didn't know law, he didn't understand science. All he knew was what he had seen and what he remembered. So he broke out of jail and lived underground, trying to find the bar and prove it existed. But before he found it, they recaptured him and put him back in jail. Maybe he originally could have avoided the death sentence, but everything he'd done had only added to the weight of his crime. His name was put on the execution list.

"They've got it all wrong." Dhargye shook his head.

They'd been herded to their seats among the sea of spectators. The sun shone down. People held newspapers, books, and handkerchiefs over their heads to block its rays.

"It wasn't *Ugyen* who killed him. I know," Dhargye said, and gave Dorje a significant look.

"I suppose that crazy old Longna put all these ideas in your head," said Dorje.

"She pushed me into the tea bowl, and I saw it all clearly," Dhargye replied. "What I still can't figure out is why they've never mentioned the jade unicorn. But I know who killed Pockface Sonam Rigzin from Gonjo." He spun round to face Dorje. "It was *you!*"

Dorje gave him a look up and down. "You've got a problem in your head!"

"You knifed him, then Shega threw her arms around him, and hung that jade unicorn round his neck," he said in an low, tense voice.

"Damn! I'll knock the shit out of you!"

"Go ahead, knock the shit out of me," Dhargye said. All of a sudden he pointed stealthily at Ngawang Melong. "What's he up to?"

Ngawang Melong had squeezed himself up against old, white-haired Longna. The two of them had their heads together. It looked like they were hatching some plot.

"He knows there's somebody Ugyen killed," Dorje said, "but he knows he's innocent of the crime they're accusing him of, and he wants to save him."

"How?"

"There's always a way," Dorje said mysteriously.

Ngawang Melong walked up to the magistrates' platform. In about fifteen minutes, he returned. He had told the police he was Ugyen's friend, and asked them to give him a ride to the execution ground so that he could take care of Ugyen's body. A couple of friends, he added, would come along later to help him. The police knew Ugyen didn't have any relatives in Lhasa, so a policeman agreed to save him a seat in one of the vans.

Soon the sentencing was over. The assembly ground grew noisy. People walked around on the sun-baked mud, stretching their aching backs. A crowd mobbed the platform, trying to get a good look at the three criminals bound for execution. Ngawang Melong said he was going with the motorcade straight to the execution ground, and told Dhargye and Dorje to follow on foot.

Police and soldiers were everywhere. Guards escorted the condemned men onto an open truck. The motorcycle police started their engines and pulled into formation, ready to clear the road. Pious men and women thronged the truck, pleading with the soldiers not to sin by taking the condemned men's lives. Guards lined the edge of the truck bed, their rifles at the ready. People in the crowd spat at the soldiers and police up on the truck, clapped their hands in derision, cursed them. A few rocks came flying, thrown by stealthy hands. The soldiers remained motionless, stiff as ramrods. The military police kept order along the road, pushing back the mob. Up ahead, the formation of motorcycles cut through the crowd like the prow of a ship slicing the sea. The long motorcade started off. In its wake followed a dozen motorcycles—fellow gang members of the policeman's murderer, his funeral procession.

Photographs from an exhibition in a Tibetan village in 1992, showing two Tibetans executed for taking part in the Nyemo rebellion (1969). The X marks over the names indicate that the executions have been carried out. (From Resistance and Reform in Tibet, *ed. Robert Barnett, Indiana University Press, 1994; photo courtesy of Tibet Information Network)*

The peasant bankrobber's family already had a tractor waiting for his body outside the police cordon at the execution ground. Dhargye and Dorje had no transportation, so they had to walk as fast as they could.

Dark, rolling clouds blocked the sun and covered the mountains. Soon the wind would rise. They talked on the way to ease their sorrow.

"I'm moving back home in a few days," Dorje said. "How about you?"

"I want to stay. If I settle down here, my children will be Lhasa people."

"I'm taking Shega, but she doesn't really want to go. She likes you. Everybody sees it. Someday, if you really want, come to our town—we'll have a wedding."

Dhargye stared fixedly at the road ahead, pondering. "Maybe some incarnate lama used that bowl Shega gave me my tea in, and it was his power that made me see all that stuff."

"Holy treasures of heaven!" Dorje said, "I don't know. Maybe I really did kill somebody in a past life."

"Maybe everything I saw is going to happen in the future. Who knows?"

"We don't know anything. We're stupid as donkeys."

"Ugyen! That guy owed me three hundred yuan."

"It's not fair!" Dorje shouted angrily. "He's unarmed. His hands and feet are tied. He's a man, not a sheep!"

"We're all just sheep. I heard an incarnate lama say that Compassionate Bodhisattva Chenresig is shepherd of the Tibetan people. He came to earth to gather us into the safety of his sheepfold, and as long as there's a single sheep left outside the fold, he won't abandon us and go back up to heaven."[2]

"Hail Three Jewels, present everywhere," Dorje turned to the Potala, rising far off in the distance. He joined his hands and closed his eyes, murmuring, "Holy ground, supreme wisdom, protect us travelers far from home."

They walked a couple of hours before they reached the execution ground, a bare, sandy slope at the foot of the mountain—empty, silent, lonely. It was all over: only hawks remained, circling in the sky. In the distance they saw Ngawang Melong sitting by Ugyen's body that lay in a pool of blood. He waved his broad-brimmed hat over Ugyen's face to drive away the flies. Dhargye and Dorje came up and stood silently behind him. The setting sun cast their three shadows far across the desolate hillside. In their shadow, the pool of Ugyen's congealed blood looked like a patch of oil on the ground.

Ngawang Melong's face was expressionless—no grief, no suffering. His outstretched hand continued to fan Ugyen's face, like a shashlik vendor fanning the flames beneath his skewers of meat. He murmured, "It's okay . . . one bullet and it was all over . . . didn't say a thing . . . looked up as if he'd never expected me to come . . . sure I came . . . these filthy flies. . . ."

The wind rose. Swirls of sand blew past their feet, rushing at Ugyen's body as if to hurry it off the face of the earth.

Far off, amid the swirling sand, a vague, terrifying figure came riding toward them on horseback. He looked like some wandering hero, the brim

2. Chenresig is the Tibetan name for the Bodhisattva of Compassion, in China called Guanyin, in India Avalokiteshvara. Tibetan Buddhists believe that in order to lead all to the bliss of Nirvana, Chenresig remains on earth in the successive reincarnations of the Dalai Lama.

of his hat pulled down over his eyes, with an indomitable, haughty expression on his pockmarked face. His jaw worked as if he was chewing a
piece of dried meat. He glanced at the three men, then at the body of
Ugyen, hands tied behind his back, lying in the pool of blood, and he
smiled faintly. "Don't even think of trying to kill *me*," he drawled.

"Hey! Are you Pockface Sonam Rigzin from Gonjo?" Dhargye called
out boldly. This wasn't the man Dorje had killed!

Pockface Sonam Rigzin from Gonjo gave a contemptuous laugh,
jerked the reins, and kicked his horse. His chestnut stallion neighed
shrilly, and the man raced off into the depths of the hazy, windswept
desert.

The medical examiner who checked the corpses found a piece of
paper inside Ugyen's shirt. On it the executed man had printed some foreign letters, and, below them, a couple of lines of foreign writing. At the
bottom, the note said, LOOK EVERYWHERE. THIS PLACE EX-
ISTS. The medical examiner immediately passed the piece of paper to the
detective who'd been in charge of Ugyen's case. The detective's wife
worked as a translator in a travel bureau. She took one look and knew the
writing wasn't English or French. An interpreter from Beijing who happened into her travel bureau immediately recognized it as Spanish and
translated it for her. The flashy letters read BLUE STAR, and the script
underneath, 57 AVENIDA DE LA PLAYA, CALLE. It looked like an
address. With the help of his son who was in high school, the detective
pored over countless maps of the Spanish-speaking world until he discovered that Calle was the name of a port on the Peruvian coast. Blue Star
was probably the name of a bar. The words underneath must have been
the bar's address. What mysterious connection could there be between this
Peruvian address and a Tibetan revenge murder? Could Ugyen have gone
to a seaport bar in Peru and killed somebody there? But that was absurd,
preposterous, impossible. The riddle continued to trouble the detective.
He knew he would never solve it. "But even if Ugyen went to his death
denying that he committed the murder in the valley, this bizarre address
doesn't prove his innocence," the detective reassured himself.

That gunshot in the valley when he was an infant determined the
vagrant road Ugyen was to travel as a man, the holy mission out of ancient myth he would take upon himself, solemn, tragic, a road stretching
on and on over the endless Tibetan plateau, following the spirit of his
ancient ancestors, pointed and hardened into the tip of a steel knife

blade . . . lone, self-reliant, resolute, throwing down the gauntlet to this modern society catering to foreign tourists. At the pulsating sound of that melodious gunshot, he saw the rifle fall from his father's hands. His father turned. A strange light glittered on his twisted face. With an enormous effort he seemed to twist himself into an iron rod. A froth of yellow snuff smeared his sparse beard. A rope of saliva hung like a muscle from the corner of his pale lips, stretching, contracting, dropping to his chest. He staggered, collapsed to the ground, rolled over, then miraculously stood, raised his slackening feet and, with his dying strength, walked, then fell again. He fixed his eyes on his wife, standing before him with their child at her bosom, motionless as a stone. He'd been beaten, struck down by the shot from that wandering acrobat down in the valley. He should never have set out to rob those minstrels. He never imagined the famous Abo Delang was such a crack shot. He had fought his last battle with his robber clan. He would never train his son to be a famous bandit. His young wife shook her head in pity for her dying husband. He crawled to her side, and marked a bloody hooked cross on their son's pure-white forehead. With a laugh, he spoke his last words: "Damn. Killing everywhere. Knives. Guns. That's life."

Ugyen watched his mother pull his father's knife from his belt and solemnly lay it on him there inside her robe, passing the legacy to him. The icy blade on his face made him shudder as from an electric shock. The cold steel of the knife pressed against his chest so heavily that he couldn't breathe. His father stroked his face, laughed contentedly, and died.

Twenty years later, on a hazy afternoon, in the final seconds of his life, as the executioner took aim at his heart, Ugyen felt that of all the sorrows of living in this world the greatest was not defeat, not death, but his entanglement in an enormous, unfathomable riddle: why had he set out to kill Pockface Sonam Rigzin from Gonjo whom he'd never even met? Whether he really killed him or not . . . whether he killed anybody . . . whether or not the bar with the neon lights existed . . . what he really desired. . . . All at once he understood—a man's greatest desire in this world is to have a son. The overpowering desire to survive and reproduce exploded through his body, tied hand and foot. With a tremendous howl he leaped like a lion. His every nerve, artery, bone, every muscle struggled to free himself.

The gun roared.

With his last ounce of strength, Ugyen sprang forward violently, his wide-open mouth panting. Everything went dim before his eyes.

Sssst. Someone struck a match and raised it to a half-burned candle. Between him and Dhargye, the telephone without a cord was ringing loudly, shuddering on the soapbox. The two of them gazed at it suspiciously. Dhargye picked up the receiver, trembling. "Hello?" He passed it to Ugyen. "It's for you."

Apprehensively, Ugyen took the receiver. "Who's there?"

He could hear the sound of someone's peaceful breathing. Instinctively, Ugyen knew who it was.

After a moment, a voice said, "Still searching for me?"

"No. Not anymore." Ugyen shook his head.

"What do you want now?"

He thought a moment. "A son." When he'd spoken, Ugyen hung up.

"Pockface Sonam Rigzin from Gonjo?" Dhargye asked.

Ugyen didn't reply.

"We met him. At noon, on the execution ground."

"I'm not dead?" Ugyen asked, perplexed.

"Go ask Ngawang Melong and old granny Longna. They'll explain." Dhargye cradled the telephone in his arms, checked all round it. He gave it a pat and said, "Funny telephone. No cord, still rings."

Ugyen folded his hands behind his head and looked up through the narrow slit in the tent roof at the crystal-blue stars. The execution ground appeared vividly before his eyes. He didn't know if he was alive or dead, but he knew he could still think. And he had one idea. He wanted a son. He was sure this was a good thought.

• 7 •

For Whom the Bell Tolls

Tashi Dawa

The magistrate's son shoved his hands into his pockets. His bored, melancholy face was fresh and soft as butter. He walked around the spacious, quiet courtyard, unwilling to go back into the house.

Maddened by the bright color of the indigo flowers, a flock of butterflies fluttered up and down.

High walls surrounded the boy. Rarely did he get the opportunity to go outside. He was always shut up here in the family's courtyard. Every morning his father set off to work, surrounded by his secretaries and the rest of his entourage, while his mother sat the whole day in the parlor reading a little book that she never finished, occasionally glancing out the window to keep an eye on the gatekeeper sunning himself by the main gate.

The high stone walls of the magistrate's white two-story mansion had witnessed the passing of many years. White birches and clumps of weeds filled the rear of the courtyard. Cold and damp permeated the air here. Weeds burst through the cracks between the stones. It was desolate, lonesome. Here, the magistrate's son was allowed to play by himself. In the rounded corner of the wall, stone steps led up to a small platform that the first owner had built as a lookout post. The boy wasn't quite tall enough to see over the wall, so a servant had piled up enough stones so that he could just peep over the edge. His perspective expanded—he could see the world beyond the wall: a road, an abandoned field, a river, a bridge, and beyond the bridge, across the river, the common people's district. Off in the distance were mountains. But it was all monotonous, dull, lifeless.

The magistrate's son made friends with the gatekeeper, a solitary old man who liked to sun himself sitting at the base of the wall. The old man's body had a metallic smell, like a broken-down, abandoned war chariot. He'd spent his whole life opening and closing the gate for so many magistrates, one after another, that he couldn't count them all. He wasn't too fond of the present master of the mansion, a man whom he never saw smile. Nor was the gatekeeper fond of the magistrate's wife, constantly reading that little book that she never finished. Her broad parlor window faced the main gate, and she kept gazing out at him, as if trying to fathom some dangerous tendency in the gatekeeper's mind.

The magistrate's son stuck a piece of candy into the gatekeeper's mouth and sat down beside him in the sun. Sucking the candy, the gatekeeper mused to himself about the latest rumors he'd heard from the other side of the river, "Well, isn't that life? It never changes, eternally the same, but every few years somebody starts thinking they're tired of phony life, and yearns for meaning. So they start a revolution, change everything, then gaze out, pleased as can be, on a new heaven, a new earth. After a while, somebody else thinks that life looks phony, and turns the whole world upside down all over again."

One day the magistrate's son wasn't careful and fell into the courtyard well. After running around in circles, frantic servants finally managed to pull him out and brought him into the parlor, dripping wet. His father remained lost in a newspaper full of extraordinary news. The son watched his father's severe eyes suck in every word. His father crumpled up the paper, fixed his gaze on his son, and announced, "We live in turbulent times. Why does this happen to *us?*" His wife sighed, reluctantly laid down her unfinished book, still open, on the table, and told the servants to take her son to his room upstairs. They carried him off rolled up in a rug, still in his wet clothes.

Whether it was from the fright he'd gotten, or from the damp and cold, he lay trembling on his bed. On his forehead was a big cut where he'd bumped his head against a stone protruding inside the well. His mother stuffed a pill in his mouth to calm him down, and told him it would keep him from having nightmares. When he'd swallowed the bitter pill, he looked up from his bed, saw his mother's back as she was leaving the room, and cried out, "Mama, I love you!"

The woman gave him a puzzled, frightened look, shouted, "Damned kid, go to hell!" and slammed the door.

A dreamless night.

The magistrate's son stood on the platform looking over the wall. A young monk was sitting in the abandoned field by the side of the dirt road, resting his feet. He raised his eyebrows in surprise to see the head of the little boy sticking up over the wall behind him.

"Hey, little boy, are you sneaking into that house to steal?"

"I live here!"

Hearing this, the monk was filled with deep veneration. "So your dad is a big official!"

The boy nodded. "I hear people say that."

"Once I saw him when he came to make a donation to our monastery—young, self-confident, energetic. Even our Incarnate Lama bowed and stuck out his tongue to him.[1] I should call you 'Young Master.'"

"Nobody calls me that."

"Well, anyway, I'll call you that. You live here, so you're Young Master." An anxious expression crossed the monk's face, and he stood up and said, "I can't talk any longer." He gazed around, then said secretively, "A mob is coming to loot your house, Young Master."

And in fact a commotion was brewing across the river in the common people's district. On all sides shouts arose, "Revolution! Revolution!" Up on the platform, the magistrate's son could see a dark crowd. People on the square waved flags and banners. Shouts of angry slogans rolled like muffled thunder toward the magistrate's mansion.

The servants had already fled, all but the gatekeeper, who lingered on as if the whole thing had nothing to do with him. The magistrate, pacing back and forth in the parlor, told the gatekeeper to lock the gate—their lives depended on it. In this age of upheaval, law and order had vanished. A catastrophe was imminent. Any minute the barbarians would burst in and sack this blessed domicile. "We have to hide our valuables and secret documents," he cried out. Nobody dared venture outside, so the valuables had to be buried in some remote corner of the courtyard. The magistrate gave the gatekeeper a small bar of gold to keep his mouth shut, and told him to drink two bottles of liquor and sleep for three days, so he wouldn't see where his master had hidden his treasure. The gatekeeper requested five bottles of liquor, and told his master to lock him up in the cellar.

The magistrate had just chosen a spot to dig when he looked up. There stood his son, watching him. He gave the boy a suspicious look. At a moment like this, he trusted no one but his wife. Still, he needed his son to keep watch up on the platform.

He hung a bronze bell in his parlor, attached a long cord to it, then ran the end of this cord out onto the platform, where he told his son to

---

1. In Tibet, sticking out one's tongue at someone is a gesture of greeting.

keep his eyes open and watch everything that happened on the opposite bank of the river. "The moment the mob rushes over the bridge," he told his son, "pull the cord and sound the alarm."

Alone, the magistrate began digging his hole. Meanwhile, his wife began selecting precious objects to hide.

Their son mounted the platform, excited as never before. His whole body shook. Far off amid the uproar in the common people's district, he heard a shuddering roar: "The Great Age Has Arrived!"

Swirls of people formed into ordered ranks advancing toward the bridge. They came to a halt at the opposite bank, apparently in no hurry to cross it, but spread out in lines along the shore, screaming, throwing rocks toward the near bank. The rocks landed with splashes in the water.

The young monk came running by along the base of the wall. On his back he carried a scripture-scroll rolled up in yellow damask silk. When he saw the magistrate's son still up on the wall, he stopped and yelled out, "Young Master! Still standing there admiring the view! Hurry! Any minute those people will storm the bridge. Then, look out!"

"If they cross, I'll pull this cord."

"And blow up the bridge? Lord Buddha! You're a hero!" Breathless, shocked, the monk was flustered for a moment, then took a deep breath, sat down on the ground, and wiped the beads of sweat off his forehead. But as he chatted with the magistrate's son, he gradually realized that the cord in the boy's hand was no marvelous weapon, but only attached to an alarm bell inside the house. He gazed around anxiously and asked in a low voice, "Young Master, do you want to escape with me?"

"Where?"

"To a place far away, a place that's peaceful, a place that's . . . fun!"

"But how could I get down from up here?"

"That's up to you to figure out. The wall's too high—I can't help you."

The magistrate's son raised his head and thought. He decided to leave home. Telling the monk to wait for him, he ran back inside the house. All was in chaos. Open boxes lay scattered about, clothing and papers were strewn all over the floor. His mother was carefully cramming the last few valuables into a crate. The sight of her son standing at the door gave her a start.

"What's happening across the river?"

"They're standing on the opposite bank. Nobody is crossing the bridge."

"What are you doing back here then? Didn't I tell you—keep watch, and when they cross the bridge, pull the cord!"

"I thought. . . ."

"Get back where you belong!"

Glancing down, he saw his mother's book lying forgotten on the floor. While she wasn't looking, he reached down, picked it up, and stuffed it in his shirt. Near the doorway, he snatched up a small knife.

When she saw him still standing there, his mother shouted, "What are you waiting for? Get going!"

Hurrying out the door, he stooped and resolutely cut the bell cord. As he returned to the platform, he rolled up the cord, then tied one end of it snugly around the trunk of a large birch tree and threw the other end over the wall.

The monk, waiting at the foot of the wall, burst into a happy cry, and raised his hands to catch the magistrate's son sliding down the cord.

"I stole something from the house." Excitedly, the boy pulled out the book and showed it to the monk.

"What sort of treasure can this be?" The monk took the book and read the title. "'*Anarchism*, by the Canadian George Woodcock.' What kind of book is this?"

"It's a good one. My mama reads it every day." He took it back from the monk and stuffed it into his shirt.

Ahead lay the road to freedom.

"Long live General Lobsang Gendun!" yelled the government army, charging Sanglung[2] Temple.

"To hell with these devils! The gods will triumph!" screamed the thousands of monks from their commanding position high on the opposite hillside.[3] On the temple wall and on every roof of the temple complex, ranks of bald heads bobbed, flashing in the sun. The monks' shouts and the shots of their guns reverberated throughout the valley.

After a brief, tentative advance, the government troops withdrew. This had only been an exploratory attack. The government army had not yet committed its main force, only two companies. The troops retreated to Dasong Manor to await further orders. With their wives and children, the soldiers set up their tents among the groves of the manor,

---

2. Name of a mountain in southeast Tibet.

3. Armed clashes between government troops and forces of armed Buddhist monks are not uncommon in Tibetan history, and have continued since the Chinese occupation in 1950.

lit campfires, and began to cook supper, drink, and gamble. Blue smoke drifted through the trees. Horses and mules dashed around the manor grounds, nibbling plants, trampling flowers. People and animals were shitting everywhere.

The officers had requisitioned the manor as a headquarters, and were meeting at this very moment inside its main hall to devise their battle plan. A crowd of jobless, derelict tramps gathered outside the gate of the manor, singing in sharp, delirious voices,

> The army are eagles, marching ahead,
> We, their ravens, follow behind.
> The noble army eat the feast,
> We the ravens gnaw the bones.

At this moment, the army's spy was slipping through a little gate in the east wall of the temple, left open for him by a collaborator inside.

The army's intelligence unit had received information that the monks were equipped with a radio transmitter. They assumed that the monks would use it to summon monks of other temples to their aid. The spy's mission was to find the transmitter and codebook, and send a message to the nearby monasteries to cancel Sanglung Temple's call for reinforcements. This way, the army could quickly subdue the Temple. Above all the government wanted to avoid a civil war with monks all across the country.

Inside Sanglung Temple, throngs of noisy monks rushed hither and thither like chickens with their heads cut off. In this chaos, the spy, in his monk's disguise, moved about freely, shocked to see the quality and numbers of the monks' weapons. When he observed the heavy artillery set up on the roofs, he realized the government army had seriously underestimated its enemy's strength. This battle would cost his side dearly.

At this very moment, the spy knew, the temple's supreme council was holding an urgent meeting. He slipped into the heart of the monks' command center, the second story of the main hall. Heavily armed monks stood guard along the corridor. The spy stole down a passageway, around a corner, and looked out a window. Off in the distance he spotted an antenna on the roof of some monastery official's residence—that must be the transmitting station!

He took from his pocket his universal passkey and unlocked the door of the room next to the meeting hall. It was a small scripture room, simply but elegantly furnished. From a table of offerings before the statue of Buddha, he picked up a white bowl. He tossed the rice offering on the floor, held the bowl to the wall, and put his ear to it. He could just make out what was being said in the next room: the monks of Sanglung Temple were planning a large-scale set battle, a fight to the death. Their purpose—to defend a certain stupa in the temple. What puzzled the spy was that they made no mention of communications with other temples by means of the radio transmitter.

He set down the bowl, slipped from the main hall, and hurried across a square to the stupa of Incarnate Lama Gewang. To defend this stupa was the object of all the monks' battle plans. It stood in the corner of the main temple square, immediately behind the Dekyi Debate Hall, where it was sheltered by rows of scholar trees and elms. Its protected position shielded it from the government army's artillery.

Outside the stupa, all was pandemonium. Inexperienced in the ways of war, the monks were invoking Incarnate Lama Gewang in wild abandon, burning juniper boughs in braziers, and throwing on cypress branches, sweetgrass, tsampa, and liquor. The billows of smoke attracted fervent women who hadn't yet fled the temple. Armed monks shot their guns in the air.

This stupa held the remains of Incarnate Lama Gewang, who had developed supernatural powers through prolonged fasting and meditation, but committed suicide after his conspiracy against General Lobsang Gendun failed. After his death the Incarnate Lama's spirit remained on earth to haunt General Lobsang Gendun until the leader began to lose his head at critical moments and members of parliament whispered that the general was going insane. Their call for his resignation grew louder every day.

The general asked the national oracle to divine the cause of his affliction. The oracle performed the appropriate rite and told the general that the spirit of Incarnate Lama Gewang, dwelling in Sanglung Temple, was taking secret revenge on him. The general resolved to destroy the stupa, and dispatched representatives to negotiate with the temple's supreme council. In twenty days of discussions, neither side would budge—the monks worshiped the Incarnate Lama at this stupa, calling on him in times of danger. Negotiations broke down, and the general ordered his troops to attack.

The monks keeping watch along the wall let out a shout. More monks down below climbed onto the walls and roofs, screaming wildly. The spy clambered onto a fortified roof and gazed out. It was a European-style attack! In the vanguard came a military band marching in hollow square formation playing "God Save the Queen" on their drums and bugles, Tibetan flutes, and sunna horns, under the direction of a bandleader who waved his metal baton back and forth like a magic wand. Next came the flag bearer holding aloft a huge military banner that fluttered in the wind. At his sides marched two color guards. Close behind, the infantry advanced in square formations at a vigorous parade step, their rifles mounted with fixed bayonets flashing in the sun. Then came the officers of the battle command, with murderous faces. Last came soldier-monks, chanting incantations from the Diamond Sutra. Behind this grand, mighty formation came a jubilant crowd of soldiers' wives with babies in their arms and leading their children by the hand, urging on their horses, donkeys, and mules with loud cries, ready for the booty. On their animals' backs were empty sacks, wicker baskets, shovels, and drills. The soldiers' families had first priority, but at their heels came a mob of hoodlums and beggars, the scavenger ravens, cheering on the government army with raucous cries.

The monks on the temple fortifications stared wide-eyed at this outlandish formation. They hardly knew whether they were facing an attack or watching a military parade. The rhythmic tramp of thousands of feet marching to the booming beat of the drum shook the monks' hearts. Some quaked and fled the ranks in despair, moaning fearfully as if they'd seen a devil. The frightened monks didn't fire a single shot at these orderly, advancing ranks of demon-warriors.

The spy couldn't restrain his rage at the disgusting arrogance of this government army—marching with puffed-out chests, not even bothering to fire, as if their opponents were nothing but a squeaking pack of rats. The army's ranks had reached the foot of the mountain. In perfect formation, they surged up the uneven slope.

One monk, gripping his submachine gun as he staggered like a drunken man, suddenly raised it and fired—the first shots of the battle! The resounding burst shook the monks out of their stupor. They opened fire down the mountain. The rain of their bullets threw the enemy's formations into confusion. The vanguard of band musicians turned and fled, clutching their instruments. Dead bodies littered the slope.

The army commanders regrouped their forces and changed tactics— they reformed their troops into skirmishing parties. The bugle sounded another charge. The soldiers' voices rang out in their war cry, "Long live General Lobsang Gendun!" and up the slope they came from every side.

Awakened anew from their nightmarish trance, the monks fired point-blank into the oncoming ranks with machine guns and mortars. The enemy troops dove for cover. Now, from many groves all over the open ground, the general's artillery opened fire. The great English howitzers gave an earthshaking roar. The shells screamed over the temple, and on over the peak behind it. After what seemed a long pause, a sickening blast burst from the other side of the summit. (Only afterward was it learned that the artillery fire had flattened a village.)

The gunners adjusted their aim. The next salvo landed on the peak. The next landed halfway up the slope behind the temple.

But at the moment when it seemed that shells were about to fall on the temple itself, the artillery crews ran out of ammunition. To the mournful call of a bugle, the infantry withdrew. Empty-handed, the soldiers' exhausted wives beat a bitter retreat, resentfully fleeing among the ranks of the troops, driving before them their pack animals, now laden with the wounded. "Great! You're our first aid team!" the soldiers called sarcastically. The wives repaid this compliment of their husbands with strident curses.

The commanding officers were shocked at their heavy losses.

Jubilant monks mounted the temple walls. They raised the backs of their robes, stuck out their bare backsides, and slapped them in derision at the retreating soldiers.

"We've beaten off the enemy, now we're hungry, let's go back for lunch." In small groups the monks vacated the battleground, chatting and laughing as if they were leaving an outdoor carnival. In the sutra hall a huge cauldron of rice fried in yak butter awaited their triumphant return.

In the midst of this enormous crowd, the spy spotted the monk he had been looking for. With the passage of years, the young monk who had led him on the road to freedom had become an abbot at Sanglung Temple, portly and imposing, walking now with the typical pigeon-toed monk's gait, boasting to the two younger monks at his side how many enemy soldiers he'd taken care of with the Mauser pistol stuck in his belt.

The spy bucked up his courage and approached. "Do you remember me, Master?"

The old monk squinted, then shook his head, unable to recognize in the bold, craggy features of the intrepid spy the magistrate's young son.

From inside his robe the spy pulled out the little book, *Anarchism.* "Remember me now?"

These many years, the old monk's memory had been occupied only with sutras. So the spy had to recall to the abbot the little boy peering over the wall. Finally the old man remembered. Excitedly, he seized his hand. "We're monks in the same temple! How is it I've never bumped into you? What tratsang are you in?"

"Can we find someplace to talk alone?"

The abbot dismissed the two young monks at his side and led the intelligence agent through a quiet hall to his own luxurious quarters. Here the magistrate's son revealed himself. The abbot sprang up to face him. "You're . . . a spy?"

"A government intelligence officer," he replied with a nod and continued to explain his purpose in entering the temple, to look for the broadcasting station and the codebook, and send a message to trick the surrounding temples into calling off their reinforcements, and thus bring a quick end to the battle. He did all he could to persuade the old abbot that if the monks of other monasteries were to concentrate their forces here at Sanglung Temple, they might defeat the government troops and even advance on the holy capital itself, but then the government would only amass still greater forces from all over the country. Although the monks might deal the government a temporary blow, a massing of the monks could only lead to a full-blown civil war, the result of which the old monk could easily imagine.

"The suppression of Buddhism!" the abbot cried.

Solemnly, the spy nodded. He explained that the only way to avert such a disaster was to locate the temple's broadcasting station and send a false message to call off the reinforcements from other temples, then to direct the government army to bombard and destroy Incarnate Lama Gewang's stupa. "Master," he said, "we two must decide the course of history."

The abbot heaved a heavy sigh. "You are right, my son. I've long realized that the stupa of Gewang would bring an evil fate upon us. But what must we do?"

"Find the broadcasting station."

"What broadcasting station?"

"You don't understand? It's a machine. You put on a pair of earphones, you push a button."

"And then?"

"It sends news somewhere else, hundreds of kilometers away, where they have the same kind of machine in touch with the one here by means of invisible waves that travel through the air."

"I understand. It's a sky mother. I've read about it in many sutras."

"No, no, it's a machine invented by a foreigner. We paid a lot of gold for one."

"What a waste! Better to gild the Buddha's face with that gold and seek his infinite munificence . . ." the abbot rambled.

"Let's talk about what to do right now," the spy said. "You're a member of the temple's supreme council. You must know where the secret broadcast station is, who operates it, and where they keep the codebook."

The abbot swore there was no such thing anywhere in the temple. "How," he asked, "could anybody believe someone had really built such a thing?"

The spy asked him to come and see for himself. He led the abbot up to the roof. The antenna was in plain view. At last the abbot realized what the spy was talking about. He pulled a long face. "That's just an aerial for the temple magistrate's shortwave radio. He likes to listen to classical music on Radio Moscow, and 'Current World Affairs' on the Voice of America."

The abbot led the spy to the magistrate's apartment. After a careful search, the spy had to admit the abbot was right. The antenna on the roof was hooked up to the back of an ordinary Phillips radio in the lama's bedroom.

"You mean you monks really plan to resist alone until the government army destroys the entire temple?" the spy asked the abbot, shocked. "Why don't you surrender?"

"You're right, you're right!" the abbot kept repeating. "But who can stop the battle now?"

"Where's the temple's gunpowder?"

"You're . . . going to blow up the stupa!"

"There's no broadcast station. I have to do something."

"Meet me in two hours under the willow tree outside the Dekyi Debate Hall," said the abbot.

That afternoon, the government army launched an all-out attack, even throwing their rear guard into the fray. This time they employed encirclement tactics. A dense mass of troops ringed the slope. Two attack squads, experienced in siege warfare, moved quickly round the front corners of the temple wall. They surrounded the monks on three sides, then quickly breached the temple walls with concentrated, high-power mortar fire.

Monks rushed in and out of the two breaches in the temple wall like swarms of wasps, hither and thither, first on one side, then the other, unsure where first to oppose the assault. Army snipers shot down fleeing monks like scurrying grouse as they tried to escape up the slope.

The greater portion of the monks confidently retreated deep within the recesses of the maze-like temple complex, intending to carry on the defense of the temple alley by alley, passage by passage. Suddenly an earth-shaking roar stunned them. The stupa of Incarnate Lama Gewang flew into the air. Just as the battle had reached its critical moment, the stupa exploded of itself! An act of the gods! The monks crawled out from beneath heaps of shattered roof tiles, wiped the dust off their heads and faces, looked up, and saw the government army's flag fluttering atop the main temple hall where the spy had hoisted it. As one man, they submissively laid down their arms and raised a white flag of surrender.

It was over.

In his passion for revenge against Sanglung Temple, General Lobsang Gendun had intended to destroy the entire monastery. When the stupa exploded, the monks surrendered so fast that when he arrived on the scene, the furious general realized that if he were to destroy the temple now, after the monks had laid down their arms, the news would incite other monasteries to rise, an even larger force of armed monks would advance against him for revenge, the conflict would ignite a civil war, and he would be held responsible. He had no choice but to spare Sanglung Temple, much against his will.

The army command were furious with the spy for exceeding orders and blowing up the stupa. They had suffered heavy casualties, and the booty-sacks of the soldiers' wives remained empty.

The spy was stripped of his commission and driven out onto the street, where he was forced to work as a coolie. One day he noticed an old beggar. It was the monk who had been abbot! The old man told the former spy he'd been expelled from the monastery after an investigation revealed that he had supplied the gunpowder to blow up the stupa. The old man's eyes shone like the eyes of a sage. The two men looked at each other, laughed knowingly, and pressed each other by the hand. The former spy was about to walk on, when the old man caught him by the sleeve and asked, "Do you still have that book you left home with?"

The former spy pulled out the little volume he had treasured for years. "I've never read it. If you like, I'll give it to you."

The old man took it and stroked its cover: *Anarchism*. "These days," he said, "I'd better start reading some heretical literature."

One day, having tasted experiences of the world to the full, the magistrate's son returned to his hometown, covered with the dust of strange lands.

The cord was still where he left it, hanging down over the wall. He climbed up the cord to the platform, gathered it up, and returned inside the house. His mother had finished packing three large crates full of valuables. She was an old, doddering woman now with silver hair, too feeble to move the heavy crates, so her son came up to help her, but she pushed

A Tibetan man. (From Tibet, *ed. Nebojsa Tomasevic, © 1981 Jugoslovenska Revija)*

him away. "How come you're always running in like this? Didn't I tell you to keep watch outside."

"I've been outside a long time, Mama."

"Your daddy will have the hole dug soon. He'll come and move these crates. Go keep watch!"

He tied the end of the cord back to the bronze bell, unwound it as he climbed back up on the platform, and gazed off in the distance.

There on the opposite bank of the river, the common people were still waving banners and signs, listlessly shouting slogans, raising slack hands like withered flowers.

To welcome a great age is no simple affair, he thought to himself. The crucial thing for you is to pull this.

Whereupon he pulled the cord over and over. The courtyard rang with a sound like the peal of a funeral bell.

For whom does the bell toll?

• 8 •

An Old Nun Tells Her Story

Geyang

$\mathscr{T}$he month I was born, my mother dreamed that there was a gold Buddha as long as her arm inside our stove. As she was carefully lifting it out, the Buddha's head fell off. Several days later I was born. My father had wanted a boy.[1] My mother told me that if I'd been a boy, I wouldn't have lived because her dream showed that it wasn't her fate to have a boy. Except for my father, everyone in the family was happy about my arrival, especially my sister. Before I was born, she was lonesome. My five brothers, by my father's other wife, spurned her company. The afternoon Mother gave birth to me, my sister was in the sutra room, praying for a girl. When, years later, she told me this, I was quite moved.

My father was an able merchant. By the time I was born, he owned a silk-goods shop, a tea and porcelain shop, and an estate in Toelung[2] that he had bought from an impoverished aristocrat. But the estate was not completely ours—we still had to pay annual rent to the Kashag government.[3] It had thick groves of willows on the banks of a little brook gurgling past the back of the house, and a garden that overflowed with the scent of roses. But we only stayed on the estate for short periods, every now and then. It was only after I was grown that I realized the soil on the estate was poor, and its irrigation system so inadequate that the harvest sometimes wasn't enough to pay our rent.

1. "Little Buddha" is a common term for a precious baby boy.
2. A locale west of Lhasa.
3. The previous government of Tibet. This name is still used to refer to the Tibetan government in exile.

Father was of pure Khampa ancestry. When he was fourteen, he left the tiny temple where he'd been a lama and came to Lhasa to seek his fortune. He had realized that the powerful ambition surging within him would be a kind of desecration for a monk living in a monastery. The wealth and influence he acquired proved the wisdom of his decision.

Father had two wives, so I had two mothers. They lived peaceably, like sisters, and together bore my father five sons and two daughters.

Old Mother[4] was a devout Buddhist. She passed the greatest part of her day in our sutra room. As far back as I can remember, she ate vegetarian food, rarely eating with the rest of us. Sometimes she fasted. Despite this, she was fat; so I think whether one is fat or thin is probably fated by heaven. She wasn't my natural mother, but it was from her that I received most of my childhood education, just as my brothers and sister did theirs.

Without any doubt my natural mother was a beauty. She was fond of dressing up, and gave herself a fresh, new look every day. It was she who managed all the affairs in our home, and under her direction, everything was kept orderly and neat as a pin. She liked to sing and play the dramnyen[5] and knew all the street-singers' popular songs. The trouble was that she was so busy she never had time for us children, who needed her care and attention.

My lone companion was my older sister. I always gave in to her whims, and she always discovered something fascinating for us to do.

The year I was five, Father and my eldest brother set out on a long business journey. They were gone almost two years. When they finally returned home, I thought, why are these strangers hugging us and kissing us? I didn't dare approach them.

Barely three years older than I, my sister had the opposite reaction, and threw her arms around Father the moment he entered the room. I found this strange because she'd told me that she hated Father so much she hoped he'd never come back. Pretense isn't always a bad thing; sometimes it makes us lovable.

When I was eight, my natural mother told me I would be taken to a convent near Gyantse to become a nun. She dressed me in a reddish-brown skirt and robe and told me I looked lovely. I stood a long time looking at myself in the mirror, worrying that I wouldn't be beautiful after my hair was cut off. As I look back now, I realize how ridiculously vain I acted. Fortunately, reddish-brown becomes me.

4. The author coins this term to designate the protagonist's senior "mother"—the senior of her father's two wives.
5. A Tibetan-style guitar.

Who decided to send me to be a nun—my father or my mother? I hadn't the experience to consider the question then. I only hoped the place I was going to would be as beautiful as our country manor. So, bewildered and confused, I left my family and home.

It was a fine temple: the solemn, magnificent sutra hall, the glistening snow-white stupa, the great, heavy gate painted with elaborate designs, the narrow, steep stone stairway up the hillside, the green trees, the bright many-colored flowers, the little birds whose names I didn't know. I couldn't help immediately falling in love with it. It was so much more beautiful than I had imagined.

There were seventy or eighty nuns. When I looked into their placid faces, I hadn't the least doubt that I would become one of them. We were so tiny, so insignificant. We could only kneel before our master, the incomparable Lord Buddha, and pray—not only for our liberation from our own misdeeds, but also for the liberation of all sentient beings.

Convent life was austere, but once I had grown accustomed to it, it didn't seem so. It was monotonous, but once I accepted it, it no longer seemed monotonous.

The convent had a dozen yaks and a few dozen sheep. Winters, the nuns took turns tending these animals in the fields. Summers, the temple turned the animals over to herdsmen who took them to distant mountain pastures. All this followed an ancient practice: when summer comes, the herdsmen pack up their tents and take the animals up to the mountains to graze, leaving the lowland grass to grow for the herds in winter.

The winter pasture was quite a distance from our temple. More often than not, we were completely exhausted by the time we reached it. Still, I liked being sent there, liked the boundless grasslands, lying on the grass looking up at the sky, and the feeling I got watching the smoke rise into the heavens as the tea brewed over the fire. Sometimes the nomad herdsmen teased us with brazen jokes so that we blushed until our ears turned red.

We went to the pasture in pairs. I was usually paired with Nechung, who was four years older than I. From the time she was little, she had neither father nor mother and was brought up by her brother and his wife, and so she knew how to do many things I was ignorant of, but she was sympathetic and understanding, and didn't mind my mistakes. She was not beautiful, but in my eyes she was lovable. The year she turned fourteen, a young herdsman fell in love with her and was always thinking up ways to get near her.

One sunny afternoon, Nechung and I built a fire, made our tea, ate the tsampa we'd brought with us, and lay down on the grass. A light breeze was blowing. The sun was so dazzling that we couldn't keep our eyes open. Gradually, we fell asleep.

I'm not sure how much time passed before a cry awoke me. The young herdsman was clutching Nechung in his arms and kissing her. Presently, he stood up and walked off a few steps. Previously, he'd put his arms around her to tease her. I felt it was all silly, lay back down again, closed my eyes, and fell asleep. When I woke up, Nechung was sitting at my side with a blank stare on her face. She glanced at me. Something in her expression made me uneasy.

"He made me sleep with him," she said calmly. "He was so strong I couldn't stop him."

I knew she was upset, but I didn't know what I could do for her. We went back to our temple, returned the livestock to their pens, filled the water jars, ate our supper, chanted the sutras, and went to bed. I woke up in the middle of the night and heard Nechung crying. Terrified, we sat with our arms around each other until dawn.

Looking after the livestock was no longer something beautiful. The moment we set foot on the pasture, fear came to our side. Fortunately, the weather warmed up early that year, the herdsmen soon took the herds off to the mountains, and we no longer had to look after the livestock.

I was only ten at the time, too young to understand what had happened to Nechung. I couldn't comprehend her anguish, and she was afraid to give voice to it. I realize now that she didn't expect a ten-year-old girl to help her solve her problem. She just needed me at her side.

Before this, though no one ever came to visit her, she had been a happy girl. Her faith told her that everything that happened to her was determined by her actions in her previous life, so she wasn't worried about her present life. She believed that if she just tried hard, her next life would be filled with good fortune. And so she chanted more sutras than other nuns, worked harder, and bore the misunderstandings and burdens that others created for her. But with this calamity, her purpose in life was snatched away: she believed she had defiled herself in the eyes of Lord Buddha.

Worst of all, she was pregnant. We only understood this months later, when her stomach was so swollen it was impossible to hide. If we hadn't been so naive, perhaps we might have realized it earlier and thought of something to do about it, perhaps. . . . But until our teacher explained it to her, we were paralyzed by anxiety and didn't know that inside her slender body a tiny life was stirring.

She told her teacher everything. But it wasn't a story that everybody could believe. Probably all the nuns except me doubted her story to some degree. I was disgusted with everyone around me, but I realize now that I ought not to have blamed them. Anyone with common sense would have had some misgivings.

One morning our teacher came to tell Nechung that the abbess would permit her to have the baby in the convent, but then Nechung would have to leave. Nechung was devastated. She told me that she didn't want to go on living. To leave the temple, she thought, was to forsake all hope for a good life in her next reincarnation.

In the convent barn, among piles of hay, Nechung gave birth to a sturdy, healthy boy. The sight of the baby dissolved the nuns' misgivings and moved the abbess's heart: if Nechung and her child were to leave the temple now, how would they survive? The abbess said Nechung might remain a year. And so she was to enjoy a year of peace and security, during which her wounded soul might have healed. But this was not to be.

A second nun got pregnant, and the rage of the abbess fell like lightning on Nechung. The abbess said that the second nun got pregnant because she had punished Nechung too lightly. These two pregnancies had blackened our convent's reputation for purity and upright conduct. Nechung and the other nun were to leave in ten days—never to return.

For two whole days Nechung spoke to no one. There was no resentment in her eyes. She accepted expulsion as her fate. She gave no thought to where her path in the world might lead. She was looking for death.

When punishment for another's misdeed falls on us and crushes us, may we put an end to our life? May we ignore the teaching that, by choosing to die, we terminate the cycle of our reincarnations and suffer in hell for eternity?

It was my turn to take out the herds. Out of breath and panting, I reached the pasture with my new companion, a girl of infectious merry spirits. Our laughter attracted a crowd of other children who were watching their livestock. Someone began singing, and we danced around in a circle until we were worn out. I lay down on the grass.

Suddenly, my thoughts returned to Nechung. When I got back that evening, would I find her dead by her own hand? The boy who'd violated her was nearby, cheerfully drinking his tea. An irresistible impulse impelled me to my feet. I rushed up to him.

His eyes shifted nervously as I stood before him. I discovered that I was frightened too. How should I begin? He had made love a pretext for doing what he pleased, and had no thought for the suffering he'd caused. I wanted to chastise him, curse him, beat him, stab him, kill him. I didn't dare. I couldn't even scold him.

In a stammer, I blurted out everything—what I should have told him and what I should have kept back—as if I was telling a touching little story. When the story was finished, I had nothing more to say.

There was an awkward silence. He sat quiet.

I walked away. Had I run all this way just to tell him he had a son?

When I got back to the temple, I was relieved to find Nechung still alive. She rushed up to me and said, "He's here."

"Who?"

"The boy who. . . ."

"What for?"

"I don't know."

"Where?"

"With our teacher."

Like criminals awaiting sentence, we sat silently side by side, gripping each other by the hand as if we would never see each other again. The sound of approaching steps jolted us out of our daze. Nechung clutched her baby; he was standing there before us. "I confessed everything to your teacher," he said. "If the abbess won't let you stay, there's a place for you in my tent." He looked at the baby, reached out, stroked it, and said, "A child without a father. . . ."

The abbess changed her mind and permitted Nechung to stay in the convent, but now Nechung insisted on leaving—with a man she'd hated. "It isn't my fate to serve Lord Buddha in this life," she declared. "Heaven sent that man for me to take care of. But I'll keep everything I've learned here in the temple in my heart."

I was so young I didn't understand what it meant to part. I assumed she'd remain in the pasturelands nearby, but though I later searched and searched, I never found her. She and her man had disappeared forever.

My only friend was gone. I grew lonely again. Luckily, people from home came to visit me, bringing alms for the temple, as well as things that I needed.

Sometimes I left the convent in the company of other nuns to go begging in distant cities. Often we would stop several days in towns along the way, and so I saw something of the varied, colorful life of the world. But it did not make me want to change my life.

When Old Mother died, the family sent a servant to bring me back home. As I stood again at the gate of the courtyard where I was born, my heart grew anxious. How much had changed in four years? How much had I forgotten?

The face of my own mother seemed strange to me. My sister watched me from my mother's side, dressed in violet satin pume[6] and matching yellow puyod.[7] Could this beauty be the girl I'd slept with in the same bed with when I was little? Her skin was so fair! Suddenly I thought of my own face. How long had it been since I'd looked in a mirror? Did I look like her? I must look like her—we had the same mother! But maybe I didn't— maybe I didn't look like her at all. . . . As my imagination ran wild, my father walked into the room as solemn and majestic as ever. He acted genial, even smiled at me, but I was still afraid of him.

Several of my brothers were there, but I couldn't tell them apart. I must have been a stranger in their eyes as well.

Though Old Mother had died when I arrived, she is the only person who stands out distinctly in my memory of that time. Once a year she had visited me at the convent. The donations she brought made me proud. Her words, her tone of voice, the expression on her face gave me courage.

The whole house was grief-stricken. Father had lost a good wife. My mother had lost a friend and sister. My brothers and sister had lost a compassionate mother. The servants had lost a benevolent mistress. She had treated everybody kindly, did whatever she could to help people, never caused trouble for anyone. A person like her was sure to be reborn into a beautiful new life and enter the way of future reincarnations in peace. If we were grief-stricken merely because we would not see her again and benefit from her kindness, wasn't there some selfishness in our sorrow?

I stayed on at home for four months, gradually becoming reacquainted with my family. They were especially attentive to me. But still, I spent most of my time in the sutra room.

I don't know what kind of shock I would have gotten in a truly rich house, but the luxury in our own family startled me. I recalled our little temple, where we considered radishes a treat, where we had our tea with just a tiny lump of yak butter or nothing at all, where we never thought of cake and candy. We worked so hard, got up with the stars still hanging in the sky and recited so many sutras. Yet it all made sense. Watching the life of my family helped me to understand how impossible it is to set out on the road that leads to self-liberation and peace without deep faith and prayer in our hearts.

My sister turned sixteen that year. Beauty is always good—her loveliness delighted me. My brothers were frequently away from home, ab-

6. A type of fashionable, high-quality woolen cloth.
7. A second type of high-quality cloth.

sorbed in their own affairs. I never bothered to discover what they did. My mother was still the same: elegant and graceful. The daily round of life in the house went on beneath her watchful eye, as before. She had two more helpers now: my two new sisters-in-law. And my sister took no trouble to conceal her strife with them.

A merchant who was a friend of my father gave him a piece of beautiful White Russian[8] cloth. To this day, I can't tell what kind of material it was, but its texture, its sheen, its pattern—everything about it mesmerized my sister and my sisters-in-law. It was only big enough to make two skirts. I knew that dividing this piece of cloth would create a conflict. Without the least hesitation, my father gave it to my two sisters-in-law, and my sister was heartbroken for an entire week.

Finally I returned to the remote little temple, where there were always tribulations, but nothing to make me think there was anything wrong with life there.

I next returned home three years later. What a difference between one person's death and another's! My sister's death hurled me into depression.

If only she had lived, several months later she would have been a bride, mistress of an aristocratic home, borne beautiful children, devoted her life to her husband, become a radiant star in society. Her illness had snatched away a vibrant, lovely girl with such magnificent hopes. . . . Death was truly omnipotent.

My one companion was gone, and our home seemed alien to me.

My sister's death had aged my mother. The first wrinkles appeared on her face. She was my own mother, but we had never been close, never confided in each other. Still I loved her, and her anguish troubled me.

I'd been home half a year, and still there was no sign of any preparations to send me back to the convent. Early one morning, when I was chanting my sutras, my mother came to me carrying a matching light-blue robe and skirt with a pair of black leather shoes. She told me to put them on.

"Why?" I asked, surprised.

"Your father wants you to wear these. Guests are coming."

She looked over my hair and seemed quite satisfied. Though it was only an inch long, it had a natural curl and probably didn't look too unattractive.

She left. Bewildered, silent, I changed my clothes. In the past when guests had come for dinner, nobody had asked me to join them. I always

---

8. After the Russian Revolution, many White Russians (i.e., Russians of the anticommunist side) fled to China.

ate alone in the sutra room. After I changed into the new clothes, I felt ashamed. I didn't return to the sutra room. To sit on the cushion dressed like this, reciting my sutras, would somehow be improper.

When Mother came to call me, she had reassumed the radiance she'd lost after my sister's death. There was only one guest, a man thirty or forty years old, not very tall or robust, a very ordinary-looking person. As I sat at the table and started to eat, I found myself doing such ridiculous things that I regretted having come. I dropped food in my lap. My spoon clanged against my bowl. The noise I made taking my first mouthful of soup was so loud that I couldn't bear to go on eating it. My hands were shaking. I must have blushed to the roots of my hair. For the first time in my life, I felt like an ugly little buffoon.

I was weak with the realization that I was embarrassing my father and mother. Thank heaven, dinner finally ended. Alone again in the sutra room, I realized that the life I'd led in the convent had been so remote from everything my family had experienced that I could never be like them again.

Another month went by, and still there was no sign of preparation to send me back to the convent. My mother now insisted that I begin wearing bright, colorful clothes, and taught me how to match the colors. She made me put on showy rings and bracelets. Was this how she thought a nun should dress? She gave me jars of fragrant facial creams, a box of face powder, and a makeup kit and taught me how to use them. In the convent, we just rubbed our faces with a bit of yak butter and never gave it a second thought. Now I sat like a variety shopkeeper's daughter, perplexed by this dazzling display of glittering objects before me.

When she went out to play mahjongg with her friends, she insisted I accompany her, and along the way she would explain how to walk, smile, eat, and talk in public. She taught me how to use a phonograph. She even wanted me to learn to sing. Everything she said made me feel uneasy. I began to have a premonition.

I had always been a good daughter and believed it would be wrong to defy my parents. At the same time, I gradually began to understand my position in the family and in society. I sat and reckoned to myself—it had been a whole year since I'd left the convent.

"Mama, I think I should go back."

"You don't like it here at home?"

"No, no. But my teacher won't like it if I stay here longer."

"If your teacher says it's all right, will you stay?"

"I'm a nun. I should live in the convent."

"No, you're not. You've left the convent. We arranged it all for you six months ago. You don't belong to the convent anymore. You're our only daughter now, you belong here at home, and your father and I have decided to arrange a better life for you." Mother gave me a little hug. "We know you probably haven't gotten used to it yet, but you will in a while. Remember, from now on you're not a nun, you're the young lady of our family. We're not aristocrats, but we don't lack for money, and one day you'll become a true noblewoman."

Her words startled me. To become a true noblewoman was probably my mother's greatest dream, but such a notion had never entered my head.

Half a year later, I was married. My husband was the man who had come to our house for dinner—the only man outside my family with whom I'd eaten at the same table. Though his family was far from prosperous, he had pure aristocratic blood. By marrying him, I'd become a noblewoman, and my mother rejoiced.

My father had originally picked him out for my sister. If she had lived, she would have made him a fine wife. Her beauty, warmth, and charm would have assured his happiness. Stupid and clumsy as I was, I made up my mind to please him. I had to do this for my sister.

And so another phase of my life began. I was nineteen, he thirty-nine. Our life was uneventful, even dull. We had four children, and I discovered the joys of being a mother. I had learned many things at the convent. I realized that I was a knowledgeable mother. Of this I was proud.

My husband never shouted at me or hit me—unlike in my own family, where I'd seen my father strike my mother brutally. And my husband was a good father. I still recall the tears in his eyes when our son fell down the stairs.

His father had died when he was young, and his mother had gone blind, so his only sister, who was older than he, had left her convent and returned home to manage the household. She had never married. I was terribly frightened of her. Through the disgust and contempt in her eyes, I came to know the arrogance and prejudice of aristocrats. To her I was just a little beggar-devil, and she took every opportunity to humiliate me.

The family took its meals in a dark-red room. I could see in the elaborately carved walnut table and chairs the luxury of bygone days. Although the family's financial circumstances were nothing like in the past, their lifestyle had barely changed. My husband's sister obviously believed I was not worthy to share this splendor and ostentation. Her hostile, overbearing glare so spoiled my appetite that I always left the table half-hungry. My husband simply thought I just couldn't eat any more. As a nun

I had learned to make an effort to look on the good side of trouble: I had my sister-in-law to thank now for my slender figure.

In my new home, I undertook many things that I'd never attempted before, and discovered that I learned quickly. The convent taught me that life involves hard work. Gradually, I became accustomed to my sister-in-law's slights and provocations. I did my best to ignore them, and when I had to cry, I went off to cry alone. After a time I found that her trouble-making left me unmoved, and I wasted fewer tears, until eventually I became indifferent to it all.

I assumed she could never like me, would never cease trying to provoke me, then one day she started being nicer to me. I didn't know what to make of it, but in fact it made me happy. As we began to get to know each other, I discovered that she was really a most sincere person, a woman who held nothing back. If she hated you, she hated you to the marrow of your bones; if she liked you, you never needed to keep up your guard. My arrival had caused turbulence in their family; the turmoil subsided, and everything became quiet again.

My husband had two younger brothers. One had left the family and become a monk. The other lived at home. He and his wife were mild, gentle people who never bothered anyone. Ten years after I joined the family, this brother fell ill of some disease that baffled the physicians, and he died. For the sake of stability in the family, their uncle asked my husband to take his brother's widow as his second wife.

I didn't mind. Hadn't my own father had two wives? My sister-in-law was a good woman, my husband was a good man. Why shouldn't two good people come together?

But my husband refused.

He said to me, "I don't see any need for it. She's still part of the family. I can fulfill my responsibility to my brother by taking care of his widow and children. Besides, you and I have a good life together. Why should someone else come between us?"

In the ten years of our marriage, my husband had treated me well, he'd looked after my health, but he'd never revealed anything of a husband's feeling for his wife. I had always thought his concern was nothing more than a father's for a daughter. But the emotion I saw in his eyes now could only be love!

To accept the love of a man nearing fifty and try to love him in return. . . . Although it might have been called late love, there was nothing incomplete about it. For the first time, I knew the incomparable joy of being a woman. Ten years I had remained aloof. I thought that as long as

I looked after him and bore his children, I was fulfilling my duty. Deep in my heart I had always thought of him as my sister's husband. It took me ten years to begin to understand him, to let him into my soul.

Our children were growing up now. Several years later his sister-in-law remarried and left the household. Then his sister died, and I had to manage the household expenses myself. As soon as I realized our situation, I persuaded my husband to sell our unprofitable manor in far-off Kham,[9] dismissed some of our servants, and cut our expenses. Things were easier for a time, but after a few years we were again short of money.

My husband had little understanding of finances, and his health had begun to fail. If I'd explained our situation to him, he would have never stopped blaming himself, so I kept my lips sealed. My one consolation was that our eldest son was now a grown man, and my chief support.

Now I faced the greatest calamity of my life: my husband was ill, the family's finances were collapsing. I had nothing but prayer to keep me from despair. One evening my husband died . . . at dusk, in my arms. Fortunately by then I had become indifferent to death.

He was gone, I remained. I called my children together and told them that from then on we had to be tough, learn to bear hardships, live by our skills. They hardly understood the full significance of what I told them. We had no choice but to sell our home, and now, except for our noble name, we had nothing. When, half a year later, my children found themselves trudging along the streets of Lhasa, penniless, my one hope was that they would keep their courage.

They were the tender spot of my heart. I'd brought them into this world. When they came in the door dejected over some opportunity lost through their own mistake or stolen because someone cheated them, I tried to bolster their confidence, reminding them of past successes. I saw their vulnerability, their frustration, their sufferings, and their toil. Most often hard work leads to defeat, of course, but now I saw that they had begun to understand how to face defeat. Reversals and disappointments, bumps and bruises are unavoidable out in the world. From what I endured in those days, I learned that the most beautiful thing in life is not splendor and luxury, not wealth and rank, not occupying a position of power, but the self-assurance that comes from having overcome obstacles, step by step, through your own perseverance.

It is a beautiful thing to raise children. So many things you do not experience directly, you experience through them. Children represent hope

9. A region in southeast Tibet.

for the future. But what do the elderly represent? My braids are silver-white now, but still I have hope.

My children were busy with their own affairs, and at last my spirit was free to find itself a home. I'm a common, ordinary person, and like most elderly people, I've chosen an ordinary way to spend my remaining years. I left my family to become a nun. At sixty, I've returned to the little convent where I lived as a girl, shaved my head, and put on a reddish-brown robe again.

Many of my sisters of bygone years are still alive. As we tell each other the stories of our lives, everything we've suffered becomes something beautiful. And we discuss our hopes for the future, after this life. The pasture where I tended livestock as a child is as vast as when I was young, the sky as blue. The white stupa, the red walls, the green leaves . . . nothing has changed, and I realize now that the tumultuous life of a human being is nothing more than a passing flash in the timeless world of nature.

A God without Gender

Yangdon

$\mathcal{S}$he gazed around. Everywhere were lustrous purple willows and houses. She didn't understand what the steward shouted to her, turned, looked up, saw the dome of a gigantic white stupa towering between lofty twin mountains. At its base vague human figures were stirring. A sparkling scarlet ring crowned its pinnacle. She shut her eyes against its burning light. "Second Little Miss, wake up. Look!" She opened them again, perplexed, staring up where the steward pointed to a shining precipice cut by brown fissures. Its crest blazed.

"The Potala, Second Little Miss! You remember?" No, it was no dream—it was her nanny's hoarse voice that called to her. "The Dwelling of Bodhisattva Chenresig, Ah mo mo!"

A fresh, cool breeze swept her face. She awoke from her stupor. From the foot of the mountain a steep stairway wound up through dense, tall trees. On their branches hung wisps of greenish smoke from burning juniper boughs. The ringing of bells and the drone of prayers poured from the windows of the red-walled palace, and scattered trembling smoke down through the forest.

She joined her hands and recited the mantra "Om mani padme um," merging body and soul into this holy sublimation of the powers of apprehension.

Gaslights blazed in the courtyard. The steward helped me down off my horse.

"Second Little Miss has arrived."

The glaring, hissing lights hurt my eyes. I couldn't see the people around me, but only heard the voice of the steward, the sharp, broken cries of servants, the pleasant sound of the Lhasa accent. I walked into a broad corridor.

Three women in splendid satin gowns stood before me like painted ladies on a vase, but thinner, and covered with jewels. They smiled at me. The one a little older took my hand: "Little girl, who's your mama?"

I looked behind me. My nanny bowed, beaming. I pointed to her.

The older lady turned to the two behind her. "Ha, ha! Doesn't even know her own mother!" The three ladies laughed, so gracefully.

A second lady walked up to me and stroked my face with a long hand that wore a diamond ring. "Just like a peasant girl."

"Hair all matted with dirt!" exclaimed the third.

"When you've had some tea, Governess, "[1] said the tall, older lady, "please take her for a bath."

"Yes, Mistress."[2] A tall, thin woman with sunken eyes stared at me, and approached me.

My nanny[3] touched foreheads with me, and blew out the candle. "In the Holy Land of the Lord Buddha, you can sleep soundly. Good night, Miss."

There was a fragrance in the quilt that made my head ache. I felt sick to my stomach. I'd ridden on horseback eight days, now I couldn't sleep. It was terribly muggy. I sat up. Moonlight streamed in the window. The sickening fragrance congealed in the moonlight gray-white, gray-white. I heard the hiss of the gaslights, the clack of mahjongg tiles, voices, laughter, but I didn't know where they were coming from. I'd lost my sense of direction. A dark light flashed in the corner.

That person in the mirror . . . maroon silk robe, smooth-shaven head . . . was it me? How had I changed . . . to a nun!

"You don't like it?" Governess asked me. I noticed that she knit her eyebrows.

1. The governess is the head female servant, manageress of the household.
2. The author uses the term "Mistress" to designate the senior of the three wives of the master of the Lhasa house in which the young protagonist comes to live. Having grown up apart from her mother, a junior-ranking wife, the protagonist is unable to recognize her.
3. The protagonist's nanny has accompanied her from the countryside to wait on her as a personal servant in the new home of the protagonist's mother.

Her teacher told her a story. . . .

A continuous spiral of smoke rose all the year long. A crisscross of gullies, an ominous mountain, weeds scattered everywhere. The smoke from the brazier of burning juniper branches drifted out over the valley, scattering marvelously into an auspicious hooked cross. Villagers from beyond the mountains realized that an incarnate lama of deep compassion and clairvoyance with awesome magic powers dwelt in this valley. In search of spiritual growth and mystic teaching, they climbed up along the little brook, through the tiny pass.

Tashi, the lama's disciple, watched all this in consternation. At first he thought the stream of people would ebb when autumn had passed, but every day more and more pious believers flooded into the valley, prostrated themselves, touched their foreheads to the incarnate lama's feet in deeper and deeper veneration. Their ever-growing numbers dismayed Tashi.

Besides diligently serving the incarnate lama, Tashi assiduously studied the sutras. Observing this, the lama took Tashi up to the top of the mountain, pointed to a little cave barely visible among the lofty cliffs, and told him to meditate there for a month. . . .

Head down, Tashi emerged from the mountain cave. His pale, sunken face was distraught. He had meditated a month, endured hunger and cold, but no sign had appeared. He had seen no vision, heard no miraculous voice. Reeling down the slope, he suddenly smelled an unbearable odor. He covered his nose with his hands, and searched for its source. A swarm of flies buzzed round a sick, ugly bitch lying flat on the ground, countless maggots wriggling in her dark red anus. "Ai!" Compassion welled up in his heart. He stripped himself of his robe, tore off its bottom half and spread it on the ground. Squatting down, he gently picked off the maggots, one by one, between a pair of twigs, and placed them on the torn half of his robe. He drove away the flies, carried off the maggots wrapped in the piece of robe and buried them, then covered the dog in the other half of his robe, and continued on his way down the mountain, shivering in his sleeveless shirt.

He knelt in shame before the incarnate lama. Teacher, I failed. I meditated a month in vain.

You did not fail. Stand up.

What? He raised his head and gazed in bewilderment at the lama.

On your way back you saw a sick dog. And what did you think? A live dog covered in maggots—how pitiful! The lama nodded. Your month's meditation was barren because your heart was impure. You thought of the prestige and status that success in meditation would bring you. But your meditation has borne fruit. The root of the dharma is compassion. Tashi reached out and received his whole robe from the lama, with no mark of repair.

"How did the lama get Tashi's robe, Teacher?"

"It is only a story. A story can say anything."

She stood on the slope amidst green grass and trees with her teacher. A tiny path wound from their feet down to the bottom of the mountain. Quietly, wild goats meandered by a murmuring brook at the side of the valley. Beside the path grew wild pomegranates, dazzling bright. "What the incarnate lama taught Tashi was not secret magic arts or profound Mahayana doctrine,[4] but a pure heart and love." Teacher tossed away a stone, and walked down the slope.

The light, delicate scent of wild pomegranates filled the air. Today, the convent was sending her back to the city for the first time to gather alms. The drifting fragrance seemed to merge with the brook and the bright, clear calls of the birds. She wanted the little path to continue forever, but also she wanted to go home to see her mother and nanny.

"Don't hurry." Teacher bent over again with difficulty, picked up another stone from the road and tossed it away. "Throw away the one under your foot too."

She threw away the stone, gazing down on the pass at the foot of the mountain. "When I get to the city, won't it be dark?"

"To clear the obstacle of sin from the spirit, making travel easy for all those on the way is also compassion."

Their red robes wafted in the leisurely wind like prayer flags.

"Is that a way to accumulate virtue?"

"Of course." Teacher caught up from behind, panting slightly: "Why are you wearing these funny gloves? To clear away obstacles and plant good karma, you cannot avoid filth. Please take them off." Obediently, she pulled off the gloves. They were exquisitely knitted of fine white wool with a tiny hooked cross embroidered on the back in yellow thread. They didn't cover her fingers, but left them naturally bare.

Funny gloves.

As soon as I awoke, I couldn't resist the impulse to leave the bedroom.

"I've brought breakfast to your room, Second Little Miss." A maid-servant caught up with me in the corridor, and blocked my way. "You can wash your face."

4. Mahayana: one of the two major Buddhist traditions (the other being Hinayana) and the one adhered to in Tibet. Mahayanists attribute to the Buddha a supranatural quality and interpret the historical Buddha as an earthly manifestation of a transcendent celestial Buddha. The Mahayanist strives to become a bodhisattva, one who has attained a state of enlightenment but postpones his/her Buddhahood and consents to undergo further reincarnation on earth in order to aid others in their search for salvation. Thus, in Mahayana Buddhism, compassion, the chief virtue of the bodhisattva, is accorded an equal place with wisdom.

"I want to go out," I waved her away.

Governess appeared. "What's this noise? The Mistress has just fallen asleep."

"I have to get out of that room. I don't want to smell that odor. I want to use my own woolen quilt tonight."

"Second Little Miss, it is only servants who do not use satin. I sprinkled it for you with French perfume. Of course, if you have better, please tell me." When she said this, she raised her eyebrows, then left, her face void of expression.

The lawn gave off a clean, plain smell of grass and earth. It gave me a cozy feeling, like being on the meadow back at the manor. But here the grass was fussily trimmed, and didn't grow unevenly as at the manor. A furry little dog came running up to me with its tongue hanging out, plopped down at my side, and licked its belly. Bees came buzzing round my head. I sat down on the grass, indolent as a bee, dreadfully bored. Through the light blue smoke drifting through the grove came a slow, leisurely sound that made me strangely uneasy.

I went to look for this song. At the back of the grove was a dark row of servant's cottages, tiny and dreary beneath the high walls. The melody was coming from the open door of a cottage with its windows covered in cheap white cloth.

Someone was sitting on a straw cushion, head down, knitting. Black cotton shoes, a Tibetan robe of black cloth, close-cropped hair, a white, white face on a slender neck. Suddenly the furry little dog appeared in front of him, and the man's voice abruptly ceased. He looked up and stared at me in alarm. After a pause, he set down his bamboo knitting needles, gestured, and said something I couldn't understand. I asked a passing maidservant who this was.

"Chinese Lobsang."[5] She said the lord of the house had brought him back from Chamdo.

He raised his head and smiled at me, his two eyes squinting into one long crease. The wrinkles covering his forehead looked out of place on so smooth a face.

Whenever she heard it she felt strangely uncomfortable. Though Governess forbade it, she often ran off to the servants' quarters to gaze at him as he knit with his bamboo needles, and listen to him sing his peculiar, desolate song. In broken Tibetan he told her it was an ancient song from his hometown, but what it was really about, he didn't know.

---

5. Of Chinese origin, the servant has been given the Tibetan name "Lobsang."

"Are you afraid of demons?" she asked him.

"In Tibet, Miss?" His needles froze. "Demons?"

"Yes! They come out as soon as it's dark!" She thrust her head in the window, opened her eyes wide, grinned, stuck her fingers out from her head like horns, and swayed back and forth, howling.

"Me . . . scared?" His two eyes squinted into a single seam and he burst out laughing, "You not be afraid. I come catch."

That night a sheet of low black clouds covered the moon and stars, and stirred a wild wind. The prayer flags on the courtyard wall blew with a peculiar cracking sound. The bewildered dogs barked madly. People went to bed early to escape the frenzied gusts. The last courtyard lamp went out. The wind fell silent. The dogs' barking ceased. Their eyes shone dimly here and there in the black.

A piercing scream rang out, "Mistress!" A dark shadow rushed from the servants' entrance into the courtyard and scurried up to the main door.

Lamps and candles instantly were lit in every room. People dashed out, terrified. All they could see was Chinese Lobsang standing barefoot on the steps in a pair of floppy underpants, waving his arms. "Demon! Mistress! Demon! In quilt!"

Mistress came out supported by her maidservants, trembling, her robe pulled over her shoulders, her hair in disarray. She shouted to Governess to light the gaslights, and ordered the steward to take every manservant to Chinese Lobsang's cottage.

The maidservants cowered together, their robes donned in haste, their hands over their bosoms, screaming.

Now two menservants dragged a great black shape into the courtyard and threw it on the steps. Whack!

"Ah mo mo!" the crowd cried, shrinking back.

A great bulging cowhide sack, its top knotted with a leather cord, its smooth, round bottom painted with a terrifying red face with a huge bloody mouth full of long sharp teeth. "The soul-sucking sack!"[6] the people cried in panic.

"From the Hall of Heavenly Guardian Tsimare in Tengyeling Temple!" the steward shrieked, approaching the sack with a look no one had ever seen on his face before. "Stolen from the temple! Who could have put it in Chinese Lobsang's bed? Heavenly Guardian Tsimare will be enraged! Light boughs, purify it with juniper smoke, or it will bring disaster on the house!"

6. Certain Tibetan monasteries (such as Samye Temple) possess a "sack of the last breath," on which is painted an image of the demon who carries off the souls of the dying. Such a sack is believed to hold the last breaths of people who have died.

The Mistress gasped. Her hair stood on end. Her long robe dragged on the ground.

"Give it here, give it here!" The steward snatched the smoking brazier from a maidservant who held it up, approaching the sack. "No woman must touch that sack!" Governess hissed at the maidservant. "It would suck the soul out of you!" A torrent of thick smoke merged with the cries of Chinese Lobsang and the susurration of the maidservants' prayers.

She sat beside her teacher, looking out over the valley. . . .

A flock of yellow ducks flapped their wings, quacking carefree and content in the grass. The wandering monk sat by the stream, scrubbing his clothes with deft, practiced hands. He spread them on the grass to dry, took out some baby yams from his bag and scattered them to the ducks. When he had finished feeding them, he rang his ritual bell and began a hymn. A fierce male eagle swooped down, calmly and unhurriedly snatched up the bell in its beak, and flew back up into the sky. The monk watched where the eagle flew, and saw it circle gracefully and set the bell down on a cliff high up on a distant peak, then fly away.

The wandering monk built a hut on the top of that mountain and lived there as a hermit, meditating. The mountain people brought him offerings of food. One day a rainbow appeared over the peak. The air overflowed with the delicate fragrance of wild pomegranates. The monk paused in his meditation. He felt a sudden burning, like flame pouring into his stomach. A perplexing feeling gradually filled his body.

The people bringing him offerings saw that the monk had changed. His voice became delicate and high-pitched, his face turned beautiful, his bosom swelled. Long, long ago, some old people had seen a sky mother appear on this precipice. The people now realized that the sky mother had taken possession of the monk's body. So the mountain dwellers all around, and, later, people from the holy city beyond the mountains, came streaming to help build the sky mother's temple, and many women offered themselves at this door as nuns.

The mandala turns, age succeeds age. Over and over people rebuild the wooden steps of this temple, over and over the chant leader appoints a successor, and still the fragrant smoke of the holy fire rises, vigorous, clear, and pure.

"I pray for the blessing of the Buddha, I pray for the blessing of the dharma, I pray for the blessing of the lamas. . . ." At her teacher's side, she knelt on a thin cushion in front of the tiny, gentle lamp burning before the simple Buddha-image in the ancient shrine, softly chanting the *Sutra of the Refuge of the Dharma.*

She and her teacher finished evening prayer, left the little hall, and were walking down the narrow stair when she heard in her mind that marvelous, desolate song. In an instant it shattered the peace of her mind into agitated distraction.

Chinese Lobsang entered the room behind the steward, wearing a pointed black Tibetan-style hat that he'd knitted himself. Around his long slender neck he had knotted a red silk cord into protective Buddhist talismans. How long had he been accompanying the steward to spin prayer wheels at nightfall on the Barkhor? As soon as he saw me, he joined his hands and bowed deeply: "Honored Jetsun!" The prayer beads between his fingers swayed slowly in the light of the setting sun. His black clothing made his face seem paler, whiter, more emaciated.

Since I entered the convent, everyone in the household except my mother had been calling me "Jetsun," and were respectful and reserved when they met me. Their courtesy reminded me of the old manor back in the countryside, with its big kitchen, its grain pile, and the clean scent of earth and rain.

Sitting out in the sunlight, I was peeling the scabs off little maidservant Tsomu's back. When oldest cousin had gotten angry, he'd poured burning coals down her neck. Tittering, she blew the white sheets of skin into the sky.

In the warm, dimly lit kitchen, full of the scent of burning yak dung, little Tsomu and I ate roast potatoes as we listened to the caravan drivers' loud, crude talk about sly shopwomen and the color of Nepalese women's skin.

The beating wings of the wild pigeons swept over the roof, bearing away their mellow cooing. The five-colored prayer flags fell slack against the background of the evening clouds. All around there was a solemn stillness. In the rose-colored evening the slow, bleak song came drifting from beyond the grove like a dream. My body seemed to dissolve and float into the evening fog. An inexplicable, overwhelming desire rose up in me.

His hands knitted with practiced ease as he leaned against the doorframe, gazing in reverie at the setting sun, singing. His usual expression had vanished as if the hand of some demon had wiped it from his pure, white face, leaving an expressionless mask in its place.

I walked up to him. "Tomorrow is the Day of Universal Peace,"[7] I said. "Won't you come worship Lord Buddha with us?"

---

7. The Buddha's birthday (12 June on the Western calendar). On this same day the Buddha's enlightenment is also commemorated. Tibetan Buddhists celebrate the day by climbing to the top of mountains where they burn juniper boughs in honor of the Buddha.

He turned to me. "Honored Jetsun!" Apprehensively he folded his hands and bowed.

I repeated my invitation.

"How I dare? How I dare? Mistress not allow me go. I am servant." He rocked his head oddly.

"Tomorrow is the Day of Universal Peace. Mistress will let you go."

He continued rapidly bowing to me, hands clasped. "Day of Peace, Day of Peace. My breath stinks. Blasphemy."

"But didn't the Mistress give you a box of tooth powder?"

"But . . . it does not wash out garlic stink."[8] He clutched his head, his whole face red.

"As long as you sincerely want to worship, and practice good deeds, Lord Buddha doesn't care about that." The setting sun was a disk of red. A burst of gratitude welled up in my heart. Thank you, Compassionate One.

"Thank you for the paradise fruit you gave me, Jetsun."

"Thank you for the beautiful gloves you made me."

May all follow the way of bliss.
May all sources of bliss increase.
May all beings extricate themselves from suffering,
And from the sources of suffering.
May all sentient beings cast off enmity and vain desire,
And be of one heart, one mind.[9]

She set down the book, still open, on her knee. The sky was clear azure. The mountain ridge blocked the sun. The valley was dark, translucent. The white stupa was suffused with a cold, clear, lonely light. A little calf kept close to the mother pian cow that roved back and forth by the bank of the stream among a herd of wild goats.

"You're doing well, doing well, my disciple."

Her heart shrank suddenly at this voice, her thoughts were thrown into turmoil. Angrily she shut her book. "Who is it?"

"It's me, your honored teacher!" The strange mannish voice sounded again behind her.

"It's you, Chungchung! You frightened me!"

She turned, took the pail from Chungchung's hand, and plunged it onto the stone step under the water in the stream. The two of them sat down on the bank.

8. The Chinese commonly use garlic; Tibetans find its smell offensive.
9. This is one of the most common Buddhist prayers, considered a summary of the essentials of Buddhist teaching.

"Look!" Chungchung shouted, pointing to the distant slope, where a figure quickly disappeared behind the rocks.

"It's Norlha, isn't it? Where is she going?"

"Down the mountain, maybe," answered Chungchung. "Her teacher gave her a scolding this morning."

"She didn't remember her sutra again?"

"No, said her shape had changed."

"Her shape had changed?" All Norlha had done wrong was to eat a lot of wild pomegranates. Her nose had turned black, she was often sick to her stomach, had gotten fat, and often vomited. Why had Norlha's teacher been so harsh to her? The scent of wild pomegranates burst over her with the ring of the trembling bells on the necks of goats in the weeds. Fear swept her . . . hadn't she secretly filled her own pockets with wild pomegranates whenever she went to collect firewood?

"What a shame . . . such a pleasing beauty," Chungchung leaned and stared at the distant slope.

"Don't call her that. Her teacher got angry when she heard someone call her that, and said that was the reason she hadn't memorized her sutra."

"The old biddy."

"There you go again! My teacher is going to have tea. I have to leave." Agitated, she wrapped her book in its yellow silk cloth and hastened away from the brook. . . .

Slowly she walked up the stairs with the sandware teapot. The yak-butter lamp shone on the little low table. A book with a threadbare brown woolen cover lay open on her teacher's knees. Teacher sat under a cloak, legs crossed, head swaying continuously from side to side as she whispered the praise of Lord and Protector Jampeyang Bodhisattva.

She shook the teapot and poured tea into her teacher's little wooden bowl. "Why don't you eat some tsampa?" she asked.

"Tea will be enough, I can eat at noon and in the evening."

"There's plenty of tsampa."

"No need to waste food. Many are hungry," Teacher said, and blew lightly on the butter that floated on the tea. "Why don't you eat something yourself?" She picked up her prayer beads, eyes already shut.

A silver teapot, a snow-white lace tablecloth, a silver tray covered with pastries dripping butter. Cups and cups of yogurt, Xinjiang grapes, Indian candied fruit, Arabian dates, Kashmiri apricots, apples from the estate. No one ate much. Now and then big sister took a cake, languidly broke off a piece, and gave it to the little dog. Her fingers were covered in butter. When a servant brought in more pastries, the dog feigned disinterest and snuggled up to me, drooping its ears. Little Brother and Little Sister[10] threw pieces of candied fruit at each other, laughing, then began to throw pieces at a passing servant.

"Don't do that," I called to them in a low voice.

Governess appeared at their side. "Sit still. Second Young Miss does not permit you to play in your own house," she said to them enigmatically. "You must listen to her." Her deep sunken eyes gave me a sidelong glance.

My nanny gestured to me, covering her mouth with her hand.

I ran to her. "Why should I keep silent?" I asked angrily.

"Speak softer, my Miss." She looked around and lowered her voice. "Old Master cast off the family and abandoned us all the day you came out of your mother's belly. Now your mother is one of the wives in this high-ranking official's residence." She picked a leaf out of my hair. "You must be obedient, so that new Master and Governess will like you."

An apple rolled to my feet. Little Brother and Little Sister were shouting and leaping in the bushes. From the corridor a pair of horrible sunken eyes were watching me, above lips that wore a cold smile. I wanted to raise my foot and crush that apple. Despite myself I picked it up.

She walked out of the temple at her teacher's side, filling her lungs with pleasant, cool air. Her heart was bursting with an inexpressible sense of accomplishment. The sky was so blue it seemed to be drawing her up to heaven, the realm of the Buddhas. Walking down the steps, supporting Teacher by the arm, she noticed the ache in her own legs. She had been sitting all day on the thin cushion, legs crossed, answering one question after another, until at length she had smoothly passed the oral examination. Now she would be a Chuzan, permitted to study *The Sutra of the Heavenly Guardian* with a new teacher from one of the three great temples in Lhasa.

"Most of us live in ignorance," Teacher said in a low voice. "As we practice compassion, our ignorance dissolves. But one must also study hard to clarify the spirit."

The clear chant of the sutras, the ring of the bell, the mysterious, dark wisps of the smoke of burning juniper boughs, the simple grace of the robes . . . marrow and pith of the temple. More and more she would know,

10. In a Tibetan household including several wives of one husband, a child of any of the wives was "brother" or "sister" to the child of any other wife.

would comprehend all these. As she stepped from the last stair onto the soft earth, the familiar yet strange song came drifting down from heaven.

I, Su Wu,[11] hostage of a western tribe,
Cherish my Han god.
I find no shame in loyalty.
Gulping sleet, chewing hides,
Nineteen years I have endured
Earth of snow, heaven of ice,
A shepherd in bondage
On the shore of a frozen sea.
The insignia has rotted
From my envoy's banner,
And I am captive still,
Finding in old trouble troubles ever new.
My heart is firm as iron.
At midnight I hear the alien flute
High up on the fortress wall
Bitter in my ear.

11. The words of Chinese Lobsang's song, which he himself says he does not understand, recount the story of an ancient Han Dynasty envoy, Su Wu, who was taken hostage
by a western non-Han tribe and forced to labor as a shepherd, but remained staunchly loyal
to his Chinese emperor during his long captivity, refusing to accept an appointment from
his captors to high office in their government.

· 10 ·

Wind over the Grasslands[1]

Alai

A dry, cold wind blew fiercely in their faces. It bent the grass, yellow from autumn frost, to the ground. When the gust slackened and the grass sprang up, immediately another gust drove it back down. Back and forth it swayed. As it rustled, its remaining moisture and green evaporated and faded. The wind whistled more and more shrilly. The dried grass snapped and blew off into the sky.

A steep mountain road climbed the ridge that filled the horizon. The two men traveling into the wind could hardly move. To try to take a step was futile now. Their worn-out horses couldn't budge. The drovers carried no whips to lash their horses—they simply led them by the reins.

"Let's stop," the long-haired one said.

"Right," the shaven-headed one replied.

They unloaded the packs off their horses and arranged them in a circle, knee-high.

The wind kept blowing off the shaven-headed man's fox fur hat. He put it on, and the wind blew it off again. At last he stuffed it under his sheepskin robe.

The two men shoved wooden stakes into the ground, pounded them in with rocks, passed the reins through metal rings at the end of each stake, and tied the horses, one to a stake. Their horses now formed a second, larger circle around the packs.

1. The story is set in the Tibetan region of Sichuan Province.

Only now did the shaven-headed man realize the wind stung his scalp. He wrinkled his scalp violently with his hand several times, murmuring a Buddhist mantra. His beard trembled in the wind.

The long-haired man wore a blue cotton hat with a drooping brim, its earflaps pulled down and tied tightly beneath his chin. The shaven-headed man silently observed the other's habitual satisfaction with his cotton hat and his long hair.

"Hey!" the long-haired man called to his shaven-headed companion. "Monk! Let's get a fire going."

"Fire?" the monk grunted. "In this wind you'll start the whole mountain burning till you've cooked everybody to roast meat . . ."—suddenly he clapped his hand over his mouth, but the inauspicious words were already out. The wind's sudden shriek gave him goose bumps, and his heart shrank.

As usual, the long-haired man didn't fuss over the monk's fear. "Then I'll roast you first, and eat you," he snapped at the monk.[2]

"Oh Amida Buddha,[3] I sinned."

"Ah! You sinned!" the long-haired man mimicked him.

The horses panicked a moment, then quieted down again. Inside the ring of packs and the ring of horses, the wind was not nearly so strong. Dried grass and leaves whirling through the air fell into this circle of calm. The two men crossed their legs in the lotus position, leaned back against the packs, and pulled their heads inside their sheepskin robes. Inside their robes it was quieter still. Silence—the most powerful defense against the violence of nature.

The sky was dark. The wind tore swaths of gray cloud down to the earth. The whole world seemed to have fallen back into primeval chaos. There on the slope, the horses raised their heads to the sky, motionless as great rocks, like mountain spirits, neighing zestfully. If an eagle had soared up into this wind, it would have seen these black, white, and red horses standing like a blooming wreath of flowers amid the desolation. There were no men to be seen. The drovers looked like two rocks that neither wind nor rain could erode.

*   *   *

The wind had swept all the carefree sentiments clean out of the young postman who led his horse alone amid the mountains: the verses

2. Besides the obvious taunt, the long-haired man obliquely alludes to the fact that Buddhist monks abstain from meat.
3. Devotees of the bodhisattva Amida repeat the phrase "Amida Buddha" in prayer.

he thought so marvelous had slipped out of his mind without him re-alizing it. He struggled forward against the wind, tugging the reins of his horse.

On this, his very first time out on the route, he hadn't expected to meet this sort of weather. This wasn't like roaring cockily up and down the high-way on a motorcycle, as he usually did. This route was two and a half days on horseback out to a tiny stockaded village of a few dozen families, and back again. Was it because he was sick of the smell of gasoline? Was it the repulsive sight of the stiff, arthritic old postman that made him fight for this route? Maybe it was his superficial reading of some Whitman poems.

At this thought, his steps regained some of their lost vigor. It must have been the inspiration of the thought of Whitman that revitalized his endurance and courage. He saw a little cave but didn't even stop and struggled on. A man keeps going! He bent his body against the wind, jerked the reins, and climbed up the mountain.

Gradually the ridge opened out before him: nothing but wild, surg-ing waves of grass. The ferocious wind swept the earth with no obstacle to block it, howling like a hungry wolf. (But this was just a metaphor—he'd never actually heard a wolf howl.)

It became harder and harder to walk. He panicked. His thoughts fo-cused on one thing. The more difficult it became to take a step, the more he repeated to himself, he must not stop. Whatever happens, do not stop, the old postman said. Otherwise, otherwise . . . the sun will rise tomorrow on your shrunken lips bared over clenched teeth. Those who find you will think you're smiling. But no, you'll be frozen to death. A smile more tragic than tears. The young man felt like weeping, but quickly controlled him-self. Crying would look bad. Girls would cover their mouths with their hands, laugh, say, "Ha ha, some man!" There were no girls here, of course. He'd wandered on among peaks shrouded in primal chaos. The mountains were hidden in cloud; still a man had to keep going. The horse bent its head and sniffed a confused labyrinth of fresh footprints. It flared its nos-trils and hunched its shoulders as if it had found something encouraging.

He seized the horse's mane, leaned his head against its neck, and struggled on. Gradually the ridge rose, growing steeper and broader as the wind rushed down on him more madly than ever. The horse had to exert more and more strength just to take a step. The wind poured into the man's nostrils so that he could hardly draw a breath. The blood that trick-led from his chapped, cracked lips congealed on his chin, dark red. At last he simply got behind the horse, grabbed its tail, and simply let the animal drag him along.

Gradually he neared the summit.

From depression, the young postman's mood swung to exultation. He thought of the wind, of the horse, of himself. Gripping the horse's tail, he felt its strength, its resilience, some ineffable spirit pulsing from the animal's body through the fingers and palms of his hands and into him. Here he was, hurling himself without stint into windswept mountains. "Damned fine horse!" he grunted. His verse should be rough now, he thought, to fit the scene. Over the summit, the road should be a lot easier.

He gazed off. The summit before his eyes was completely beyond anything he'd imagined. Half a kilometer wide, it stretched off endless, covered with wildly flailing waves of grass.

In despair, he sat down on the grass. Desperate as its master, the horse lay down, frothing at the mouth. The village was still a long way off. He realized that it had been a mistake to let the horse pull him up the hill as he held its tail—a mistake no self-criticism could ever atone for. Carrying the mailbag into the wind up such a long slope and pulling a man at the same time had exhausted the animal. Before the warmth of tomorrow's sun, his lips would spread in the stiff grin that the old postman had described to him. God! For a grown man like him to hang his life on a horse's tail!

The mailbag had begun to slip off the horse's back! The wind had blown it open, tearing corners off newspapers and half-sheets of letters out of the bag and swirling them up into the sky. His trip would be in vain! He rushed to the saddlebag. Clumsily—his fingers were frozen stiff—he retied its cord. Now he took the wind goggles from his belt, put them on and adjusted them. He pulled the horse's reins. It struggled unsteadily to its feet. He forged on, his arms wrapped tight around the horse's neck. The horse neighed, and the young man felt he was going to cry. He looked up. Above his head, the vault of heaven was about to collapse.

*   *   *

The monk shifted his head inside his sheepskin robe and stuck out an ear. The sharp whistling wind had risen to a low, powerful roar. He nudged the long-haired man. "It's worse."

"Like it's. . . ."

"Going to snow," said the monk.

The long-haired man stuck out his head, and squinted. "Seems like." He gave a long yawn.

"Who'd have thought it would snow like this today," said the monk.

"Didn't expect it," the long-haired man replied, and stretched.

The monk knit his brows. "We won't get down off the mountain tonight."

"You don't think so?"

"Open your eyes!"

"Then we'll just spend the night up here," the long-haired replied coolly. "We've got charcoal, right?" he asked, his voice suddenly serious.

"Right," the monk replied.

"Firewood?"

"Yes."

"All right." The long-haired man untied a pouch at his belt and took out flint and steel, and tinder. He stood up, gathered the grass that the wind had accumulated inside the circle of saddlebags, and shoved it inside his shirt.

The monk muttered a single phrase over and over.

The long-haired man gave the monk a sidelong glance. "Buddha—hunh! Fire's Buddha." He pulled his head back into the dense muttony odor inside his sheepskin robe. He was almost asleep again when the monk nudged him again.

"Behind us! A man with a horse!"

"You see them?"

"No. I've got a feeling. . . ."

"You've got a feeling . . . a feeling! You've prayed yourself into one of the immortals, huh?"

"No, no. The postman's coming to the village. Should arrive today. No wonder I've got a feeling that. . . ."

"Hah! That old guy's stronger than you are."

"That old man's not like the others. He's always delivering things for the villagers. A kind deed finds a kind reward," said the monk.

"Kind reward? If he weren't different from the others he wouldn't come up here into these mountains in the first place."

"That's true too," the monk said gloomily, and took a pinch of snuff. *A kind deed finds a kind reward.* This was the monk's lone article of faith. Whether his was a firm faith it would be difficult to say, but this was as far as his faith went. The monk thought of his own life, of the long-haired man's life—both complete contradictions of his lone article of faith. But he thought it was better to treat the stumbling blocks of experience as so many nightmare demons, fantasies, fleeting clouds that cover your eyes. Only death was real. Only death led to stillness, to peace.

"It's all fate," the monk said in a low voice.

"Fate?"

"Like the sky. Even such a great wind can't do anything to it."
"In this empty world you're nothing, and when you die you're an even littler nothing," the other replied. With these words, the long-haired man betrayed, in spite of himself, all his dejection.
"But dying's not easy either," said the monk.
"Ai!" the long-haired man sighed.
"Ai!" the monk sighed.
The monk's last words had touched the wound in both their hearts.

*   *   *

Deep down in the horse's mane, his hands felt the tendons of its neck tighten. It gave two low neighs, raised its head, and tottering, fought its way to its feet. The horse looked at its master, intimately flared its nostrils, then began walking. Without knowing why, he called out "Ai! Ai!", seized the horse's reins, and set out walking behind it as the wind blew up the flap of his cotton overcoat. Leaning forward, he trudged on, a fierce look on his face. The raised flaps of his overcoat were powerful wings and he was a bald eagle, a spirit . . . a nameless bird of prey parting the snow-filled air, beating his wings, spreading them over his faithful horse, over the warmth for girls in his own heart, over his own young self, thirsting for life. . . . Press on. Walk.

Still he recited verses that rose in him—he didn't know why. . . . *From fish-shaped Pomonock⁴ . . . this mountain so like the backbone of a great fish. . . . From. . . . —Ah!* Those lines had a real man's strength in them! They coalesced into one incessant theme—Walk!

His temples throbbed as though pistons beat inside them. He realized his own confusion. How could he be thinking his heart was the nest of a dove, and the letters were fluttering off, cooing?

The horse stumbled again, its legs gave out, it collapsed and lay down.

He untied the mailbag. How could a week's national, provincial, and local newspapers and a few letters weigh forty pounds? Then he remembered. At the bottom of the saddlebag he found articles that the old postman had bought for various villagers from the store. The old postman hadn't wanted to bother him with them, and now he regretted offering to bring them.

He uncinched the saddle, tossed it away, and swung the mailbag onto his back. The horse stood up again.

---

4. Pomonock: a native American Indian name for Long Island, which Whitman uses in his poetry.

The shrill ringing in his ears made his temples throb. The sky flashed black, over and over. Crowds of stars flickered all over it. Still he tottered on, his mind a blank, mechanically moving his feet.

As the wind dropped, he collapsed.

Sparse snowflakes fell. The horse lay down heavily.

Hunger and thirst burned him. He opened his mouth wide to catch the chilly snowflakes on his lips, on the tip of his tongue. His breathing grew steadier. He pulled out his last two steamed buns, took a big bite of one, and gulped the mouthful down whole. As he swallowed a second bite, he stopped and pondered. Awkwardly, he crawled to the horse, nibbling the grass by its muzzle. He broke the buns into pieces and shoved them into its mouth. When the horse had eaten them, it seemed to regain some strength. Its eyes grew brighter and it began to lick the snow. The young man couldn't help a smile flickering over his lips. He put his cold, stiff hands over the horse's nostrils to warm them and looked into the animal's eyes. They blinked. The young man saw tears run from them. The warm smile froze on his face.

He wanted to stand. The mad windy world of a moment ago had been swallowed up in this new world of softly swishing snow. He knew he couldn't stand. So this mysterious world could bring you down as easily as this. In this infinitely gentle, vast wilderness of snow he wasn't afraid to think of the word *death*. Still, he thought the horse had the strength to get up again. Yes, look! It rose to its feet!

But the mail!

Deliberately, he took off his overcoat and laid it over the mailbag, then wound the reins around his wrists and tied them tight. He would let the horse drag him on. *An old horse knows the way home.* Let the horse drag him to a pulp, drag the skin off him, so long as his hands were still fast to the reins.

The snow fell a long, long time.

*   *   *

The long-haired man stuck his head out of his robe. The snow fell faster, in clumps, in chunks. Much of the dried grass inside his shirt was soaked. He pushed what was still dry deeper inside his clothes, pulled out a little bottle of liquor, and took a savage drink.

Inside his robe, the monk cursed.

"What?" the long-haired man said.

The monk stuck out his head. Without looking at the long-haired man, he said "I can smell that."[5]

"Old mushroom," the long-haired man tried to laugh it off. This was a derogatory epithet he'd picked up from a cadre during the Four-Clean Movement.[6] The word the cadre had really used to criticize the monks of the monastery was "stubborn reactionary" (*wangu*). But the long-haired man couldn't understand Chinese—what he heard was *yuangu* (round mushroom). The long-haired man secretly admired this cadre's cleverness in coming up with such a sharp metaphor—the monks' twisting bald heads sticking up from their greasy robes looked exactly like round mushrooms!

The monk paid no attention. Crouching, he propped his hands against the ground and with a groan pushed himself up. He stamped the snow flat, then raised his robe to shelter this space. The long-haired man piled dry grass beneath the monk's robe, added tinder, covered this with more dried grass, then pulled out his flint and steel. He had just lit the fire when suddenly the monk spun round. Snow fell on the fire and snuffed it out.

"Stand still, you slut of a monk!"

"A horse neighed!"

"A ghost!"

"The postman?"

"Could be," the long-haired man said. "Let's get the fire going first." He lay down and struck his flint and steel again. Now the long, wretched neigh of a horse pierced the thick curtain of falling snow.

"Quick! In a moment he'll pass by!" Without tarrying to cover their firewood, the two men rushed to mount two horses and galloped off into the thick curtain of snow.

*   *   *

Snow continued to fall.

The young postman felt himself falling into a deep slumber.

The snow fell so gently, so ruthlessly. Just like a beautiful but cold-hearted girl. He felt sorrowful, and closed his eyes. His whole body was

---

5. A Buddhist monk's vows forbid alcohol.

6. A nationwide movement in China during the early Cultural Revolution, from 1963 to 1966, to attack antisocialist elements in politics, economy, bureaucracy, and ideology. Among the ideological targets were monks and monasteries. The long-haired man is a local Tibetan. He has trouble understanding the Han cadre, who speaks Chinese.

going numb. Endless numbness . . . was this eternity? It was nothing special then, a trance, far from life, from every ideal. . . .

The horse struggled, struggled, and finally stood. It gave two low neighs. The horse saw its master didn't stir, and nudged the man's cold face with its nose . . . a whiff of warm breath . . . its master gave a faint smile. Warmth. The horse. *The rumbling motorcycle was warm too . . . sunlight flashing in the rearview mirror, flashing. . . .*

Maybe . . . the warmth of a girl's kiss . . . he didn't know. His overcoat covered the mail. But the roan horse, red as fire, can't warm me. My body is no more. I don't know where I'm going. "Observe, observe these limbs, red, black, or white, flesh, nerves. . . ." That was Whitman too. Whitman can't save me. . . . The horse flew into the air neighing. It split the sky like a flash of lightening as the warm rain dripped down, glistening. . . . the horse raised its head and sadly began a shrill neigh. . . . oh, this merry green-coated angel raises its arms and rises into the sky. . . .

The horse seemed to know its master couldn't get up, and moved to shield him with its body. Vaguely he felt that the snow had ceased to fall on his face. *A snowflake . . . no . . . they were plain now . . . letters swirled like doves, crying, fluttering their whirring wings and scattering. . . .*

*   *   *

The world turned unreal. Even people were becoming unreal. Living and dying had become empty words! The monk leaned forward as far as he could, kicking his horse's belly over and over as if he were beating a drum. But with so much snow on the ground, the horse could go no faster. Evaporating sweat rose in a cloud from the monk's head, giving him a comical look.

The monk wiped the sweat from his brow. "Lash your horse!" he cried. "Lash it!"

"Stop howling like a hungry wolf," the long-haired man said coolly. He knew deep in his heart that even more than dying, what scared the monk was the word *death*. He had feared it too, and so he had despised himself, and despised the monk even more. Oh, this wind, this snow. . . . No sound—no human voice, no neigh of a horse. The silence itself seemed real. Even if something had appeared, the wind and snow would have swiftly wiped it away.

"Don't be afraid," the long-haired man comforted the monk.

The monk wiped the sweat off his head again, and nodded. He went on thinking of many things, all of them revolving around that single word he dared not pronounce, whether from superstition or from genuine fear. The snow fell so thick and fast that their field of vision was no wider than the breadth of a tent. The sky was like a tiny awning, accompanying them step by step. They could see only as far as an oil lamp would illuminate. Years ago the two had seen a movie, *The White-Haired Woman*. Whenever the tragic woman appeared, a halo of light surrounded her, just the size of the tent of light that surrounded them now. The monk had felt this movie was so mysterious! Enthralled, he watched it through to the end, walked halfway home without making a sound, then sighed aloud, "fate!"

The long-haired man, who'd drunk all through the movie, replied, "That was nothing but a light."

"Fate!" the monk had severely replied.

What appeared before their eyes now seemed just as illusory—a roan horse motionless, head down amid the swirling snow, sheltering its master with its great body. Snowflakes danced in the stillness. On the horse's body and the man's legs, which jutted out from beneath the horse, lay a blanket of snow.

The two men stared, and then, with an "Ah!" both slid off their mounts.

The trace of a stiff smile lingered on the young man's face. Who could tell what his last thought had been? The monk couldn't help trembling. "Dead?"

"Dead, my ass!" the long-haired man burst out. "Go die yourself!" He pulled out the bottle of liquor, took a big mouthful, pulled open the young man's shirt, and spurted the liquor over his chest, rubbing it faster and faster. The monk hurriedly brushed the snow off his legs, pulled off the young man's shoes, and rolled up his trousers. He opened his own shirt and pulled the young man's bare legs against his stomach.

At last the young man's chest flushed red. The long-haired man put his ear against his chest and listened. In his gratified smile, the monk too heard the sound of the young man's beating heart, and forgot to go on repeating his mantra. The monk's eyes flashed beneath his eyelashes, he closed his eyes, and a tear rolled down.

"Damn! Where's the old postman?" the long-haired cried out, looking up, and searching around. He saw something behind him, walked over to the snow-covered heap, pulled off the young man's coat, and picked up the mailbag. He looked back at the thinly clad young man and made a wry face. "Throwing away his life for this!" The long-haired man began cursing. "A few damn sheets of paper! What good is it anyway? Newspapers!

We can't understand it!"[7] Rage filled him. He cursed. "Not a soul in the village knows how to read this garbage!"

The monk wrapped the young man in his coat.

The roan horse neighed so long and loud that the curtain of falling snow trembled.

*   *   *

The long-haired man unloaded the comatose postman from his own back. "My throat is burning," he said. He grabbed a chunk of snow and stuffed it into his mouth.

The monk's legs buckled. He collapsed into a sitting position. The long-haired man rubbed the young man's hands, rolled them into fists, and shook them back and forth. "Light a fire!" he cried. "Fire!"

The monk rolled over onto his stomach. But their pile of grass and firewood was wet now from the snow. He could do nothing but stare at them.

The long-haired man pulled out his bottle of liquor and poured some on the grass. He struck his flint and steel, but the sparks wouldn't catch. His hands were stiff from the cold that had already seeped into his guts. He could feel the sweat freezing on his body. Desperately he gripped the flint and steel and again struck a shower of sparks. The liquor caught with a roar. He couldn't hold back a cry of joy that sounded like a suppressed groan. "Ah! Good liquor! Just a little's enough." He smiled, but soon the liquor was burned up. The tiny fire burned out with a small puff of smoke. The scorched grass hadn't caught fire.

He shook his bottle. Empty.

The sound of the monk's voice reciting the mantra rose. Trembling, the monk pulled a sheet of newspaper from the mailbag. "Try this!"

The long-haired man shot the monk a sneering glance, apathetically walked over, and sat down next to the young fellow's body. The monk knew what this meant: "You're not worth this little guy." The monk crumpled up the paper and put it on the pile of grass, picked up the flint and steel, and struck. It was futile. The paper was too wet to ignite from the sparks. The monk slumped to the ground in despair.

Slowly the roan horse approached, gave a low neigh, and lay down beside its master. The long-haired man took off his sheepskin robe and

7. Printed in Chinese, the newspapers are incomprehensible to people in Tibetan districts, who cannot read Chinese characters. The purpose of the media in China is to unite the public behind government policy. Cheap newspapers are made available everywhere.

wrapped it around the young man. Then he raised the young man so that he lay with his back against the horse's warm belly. The long-haired man put on the young man's thin cotton overcoat and leaned back against the mailbag. Silently the monk came over, sat down, and pulled the young man's feet inside his own robe, up against his stomach. He knew they could do nothing now but submit themselves to fate. The terror-stricken expression gradually dissolved from his face, and in its place came a look of calm.

"Hey!" the monk hesitantly brought out.

"Huh?"

To the monk's ears, the long-haired man's "Huh?" concealed so much disdain! But just to speak would unburden his heart so much. "Hey!" He wanted to speak about that thing drawing near them. "We've met this before. . . ." But he lacked the courage to say it.

"This? This what?"

The monk closed his eyes. Deep, deep inside his chest, with all his strength, he drew a long breath. "Death." As soon as he spoke this word, he felt a profound relaxation.

The long-haired man laughed coldly, then fell silent. After a long while he said, "This will be the third time."

Swirling snow still fell, but the sky had grown dark and the snow was invisible now. Its only sign was a broken rustling sound, as if a flock of ominous crows were wheeling above their heads, proclaiming the irresistible destruction of those who try to resist fate.

The long-haired man cradled the young man's head against his chest. "If it wasn't that I'm here with you today," he said, "I'd have forgotten we were both monks together once. How you disgusted me when you broke our discipline with that woman! Damn you!"

"You're right—damn me! But that woman was . . . good!" The warmth of the monk's feelings from a dead past revived. "Like a dream. Ai!" The monk's lips gave a faint echo of his thoughts, off in a bygone year. "Like a dream!"

The long-haired man couldn't help a tiny laugh.

*   *   *

The unreal feeling of the approach of death surfaced in both their thoughts. Now they were characters in a story. . . .

Shortly after the Communists defeated the Guomindang in 1949, the people told a story of the death of two young monks. The temple was closed, and reciting the scriptures was forbidden. The old lamas shut themselves up inside the temple, set it on fire, and burned themselves to death. Two young monks escaped the blaze. Many other monks fled too. These two became drovers, continued to recite the sutras and kept the monastic discipline. They transported tea, salt, and cloth to the townspeople. But the townspeople told a tale that these two young monks had refused to capitulate and had died like the old monks.

"In '68, I made a clean break with that woman," the monk hurriedly put in, as if he were confessing. And he shamefacedly smiled.

In that year, the villagers told a second story of the two monks' death.[8] For years the two had kept their monastic discipline. But now it was the Cultural Revolution. The work team[9] took action to eradicate superstition, and sent the two out to hunt.[10] They acquiesced. They lassoed a musk deer.[11] Its eyes gazed about wildly, so pitifully. For fear of the work team, the two men didn't dare let it go. So, to sin against it less, they decided to kill it as quickly as they could, not to make it suffer. They hit it with a big stick. They missed. They swung again. God, this was worse than dying yourself. If only they could stop!

"But I'm scared," the monk confessed.

"From now on," the long-haired man said, "killing is permitted, liquor's permitted. We can even grow our hair long."[12]

And so the people told the story that the two monks jumped off a cliff and died pointlessly, tragically.

* * *

The monk lost his fear. Half kneeling, he flattened out the crumpled newspaper and carefully replaced it in the mailbag. Then the two were silent.

Lying on its side, the horse occasionally blinked to keep snowflakes from falling into its eyes. The eyelids of the long-haired man dropped in sleep. The monk stared at the horse, and saw in its eyes the dusky sky and the dancing, ruthless snowflakes.

8. In that year, 1968, the Cultural Revolution was in full swing. All forms of religion were under fierce attack.

9. Work team: a small unit of workers on a people's commune.

10. To kill an animal is a violation of Buddhist morality, which enjoins compassion for all living beings.

11. Musk deer: a tiny deer, smaller than a sheep.

12. Monastic discipline requires Buddhist monks to shave their heads.

The young man lay against the warm belly of the horse. With his head against the long-haired man's chest and his feet against the monk's stomach, he began to warm up. Dense needles pierced his feet. The flock of white doves carried him back. The vision faded. The young man stirred. "Huh? I'm alive?" He gave a tiny groan.

"Better to die," the monk said mournfully.

"What're you talking about? Who says he has to die?" the long-haired man shot back.

The young man inhaled a breath of ice-cold air. The white doves swiftly scattered. All that was left of them were floating feathers— snowflakes, lovely snowflakes. Gradually he came to. A swarm of wasps stung his legs.

The long-haired man shook him. "Hey!"

"Cold . . ." the young man mumbled.

"Ai! No fire. Better go back to sleep," the monk said mournfully.

"Fire . . . fire?" The young man understood. His speech became a bit clearer. "I've got that," he said. He took a long breath, and with an effort he raised his arm and pointed to the pocket of his cotton over-coat, which the long-haired man wore. The latter reached in and pulled out a lighter.

Over and over he flicked it beneath the pile of grass. But the grass was too soaked. The monk began to intone his mantra. The young man propped himself up, took the lighter from the long-haired man, and opened its bottom. He pulled out the cotton wick, soaked in lighter fluid. This he lay on the damp grass. Urgently, he mumbled, "The cigarettes in my coat pocket!"

He pulled out the cigarettes and tore up the pack on top of the grass. Slowly, carefully, the long-haired man lay more grass on top. Again the long-haired man flicked the lighter. A blue flame licked up from the cot-ton wick! It climbed to the cigarette pack. The paper turned red, then white. The grass crackled, then caught! A reddish glow suffused their three happy faces. Hurriedly, the monk put on tiny sticks of firewood. Then he put on bigger pieces, and finally chunks of peat. The long-haired man took out a leather bellows and began pumping it to fan the fire. He leaned the young fellow back against his own legs. For a long time the three men warmed themselves in silence. Now that they had a fire, the long-haired man pulled dried meat from one of the saddlebags. They ate until they were full, then ate some more. Then, silently, they listened to the hiss of the snowflakes as they fell into the flames.

"How come the old man didn't come with the mail?"

"I wanted to take his place."

"Why?"

"I wanted to write some verse."

"What's verse?" the long-haired man said.

"You feel worse?" the monk pretended to understand.

The young man didn't know what to reply.

"So wet, and you didn't worry about dying?" A smile flashed across the long-haired man's face as he asked this.

"Not at first. Then I realized," the young man said quietly. He believed it was all a deep, heroic poem. Like one of Whitman's.

"You weren't afraid?" the long-haired man asked again.

"Afraid, and you used your coat to cover the mailbag?" the monk anxiously put in.

"What's the use of being afraid?" the young man said quietly.

"Why weren't you?"

"To die like that would have been worth it."

"Worth it?" As they had never heard of verse, they'd never heard of a value in death.

It was hard to explain, the young man felt. A poem never explains anything. And yet he couldn't help trying to explain. He swallowed his saliva and said, "To die with glory, like a man."

"Oh."

"We died like men too, those first two times," the monk said, lost in thought.

"Those two times don't count," the long-haired man said. "They don't matter."

"And doesn't breaking the monastic rules matter either, then?" the monk asked. Reluctantly he mused . . . had all those years transformed into three bare words—*They don't matter.*

"Not worth remembering," the long-haired man replied decisively.

"What?" The young man didn't understand.

"Nothing," the monk gave a soft laugh.

"Nothing at all," the long-haired man said.

Nothing at all. Nothing but the bonfire on the snowy ground, roaring with impervious might. Its flames rose and fell, now bright, now dim, in time with the beating of their hearts. Now their three brooding faces appeared profound and impenetrable, now strong and powerful. Besides this, there was only snow, and endless night.

· 11 ·

The Circular Day

Sebo

$\mathcal{C}$olorless, lusterless, textureless sunlight fell on the flagstones of the round square. In front of the square, old, twisted willows trembled in the wind. Their leaves, once light green, were darkened now and shriveled as if the veins had been ripped out of them. A row of peasant women from the outskirts of town with patterned towels wrapped round their heads sat to the left of the temple, selling pine boughs. Almost every passerby bought one and stuffed it into the enormous brazier of burning juniper that sent thick smoke and ash gushing into the air over the square. In comparison to the swirling smoke, the rough, jagged shadow of the watchtower seemed precise, eternal, more comfortable to look at than the sunlit places. The shadow looked as if it had been established on the square since Sheba created the world, no more related to the sun in the sky above than a birthmark on your ass, than scabies, than psoriasis.

The girl raised her hand to shield her eyes from the sun, lifting developing breasts that pushed up the school badge on the bosom of her blouse. The badge reflected sunlight onto a yellow prayer flag, fallen limp to the ground.

Beside the girl an old peasant woman sat by the crossroad at the foot of a wall. She wore a greasy sheepskin robe that exposed her right arm, revealing the filthy sleeve of her red blouse. In front of her, upside down, lay a hat. A humpbacked old man spinning a prayer wheel came out of the alley and threw a bill into it. The old woman sat absolutely still, staring at the golden roof of the temple with a dead expression. After a while she reached into the front of her robe, pulled out a bottle of cheap liquor, and took a couple of contented swigs. After every swallow she brazenly stuck out her tongue and scratched it with a swollen-knuckled finger.

From down the alley came a roar. Out raced a glistening red motorcycle. Its young rider couldn't take the sunlight, stopped, and covered his eyes with the pair of sunglasses hanging round his neck.

"Having a good time, brother Wangchen?"

"Sunday. Nothing's happening," the young man replied in a dull voice. "You?"

"I have something very important to do today," the girl said, "but first I have to go to Nida Temple with my mother. She's taking an offering there."

"Your mama's doing real well . . . taking care of that incarnate lama until his ears are good and fat."

"I don't know. I've never seen him."

"Go look. Who knows? Maybe he's your father."

"Ai!" the girl said sadly, and sighed.

The young man pumped his accelerator. The air shook.

"Brother Wangchen . . . going already?"

"Yeah."

"Sometime, why not . . . take me along."

"Too little."

"Where am I too little?" She spread her arms.

The young man looked her up and down, screwed up his eyes, twisted the accelerator, and sped off. On the back of his shirt, embroidered in metal thread, was a savage eagle.

The girl pouted.

Heavy smoke blocked the view down the narrow alley behind her. You couldn't tell whether the alley turned left, right, or went straight.

She cocked her head to listen. Not a sound of her mother. She walked out into the street.

The sun had nestled down between the rows of peaks that enveloped the river. Slanting sunlight poured from the mountains and cast all sorts of strange shadows over the broad street—blurry, incomprehensible, in sharp contrast to the sunlit places. The girl walked, walked, then looked back for her mother.

A window above a jewelry shop opened. From it came the sound, low but clear, of a hymn sung to the soft music of an electric keyboard. A plank was fixed with horseshoe nails to the bottom of the window frame. On it stood several pots of flowers. A plump, clean white arm reached out a

green plastic watering can and swayed it back and forth, showering one
flowerpot after another. The hand withdrew, the window closed, the song
ceased. In a moment, the other window opened, and the same thing happened again, but this time there were two rings and a bracelet on the hand.
The water from the nozzle was clear, transparent. It flowed without a trace
of mud along the edge of the board, then dripped down onto the patterned bricks of the sidewalk. As she walked into the shop the girl opened
her hand to catch a drop—immediately she pulled it back as if she'd received an electric shock.

The interior of the jewelry store was dark, bathed in the fragrance of
Nepalese incense. Visible through a raised door-curtain, a shaft of sunlight poured down aslant a steep staircase, white with swirling incense-
smoke and motes of dust. The song descended, sweet and ethereal,
through the tortuous, dark room. The girl was about to leave when a soft
hand took her arm. "I was only passing by," she said. "I have something
very important to do."

Steps resounded on the stair. "Come up," a woman's voice called.

On tiptoe, the shopkeeper reached over the counter for a peach-
shaped pendant. He hung it round the girl's neck. It fell right between
her breasts.

"You don't even know me," she said.

The steps fell silent. A robust, naked thigh was pressing against the
handrail, cutting off the light, swinging back and forth to the rhythm
of the religious melody, a sandal with a six-inch heel hanging from its
toes. The shopkeeper turned, looked, walked over, and pulled the door-
curtain shut.

"Come on come on come on," the woman called.

The shopkeeper wagged his head ambivalently.

"You know me?" the girl said.

"Right," the shopkeeper answered.

"'Right' . . . what d'you mean?"

"I hear people talking about you."

"Where?"

"Teashops . . . wineshops."

"Oh, I know," the girl said dejectedly. "They gossip about me."

The hurried steps resounded. The woman drew some indecipherable
sign on the other side of the door-curtain with her fingertip as she
hummed the song in her throat.

"It's true. They gossip about me, don't they?"

"No."

"They do. Otherwise . . . I'm grown up now . . . why doesn't anybody ask me out?"

"Look," the woman called merrily. Something covered her mouth, muffled her voice. "Ha, ha! Look!"

The girl stared wide-eyed.

"Don't pay attention to her," the shopkeeper said.

The woman gave a pleased laugh, wrapping herself in the curtain.

"Get the hell out of here, you she-devil," the shopkeeper roared.

"Get the hell out? Sure," she said, and, wrapped in the curtain, kicked a sandal at him. "Get the hell out?" she said, and kicked the other one at him.

The sandals—first one, then the other—struck the shopkeeper in the crotch. His face quivered. He snatched up a sandal and threw it. It hit her in the ass. She let it drop. "Okay," she said. Still wrapped in the curtain, she picked it up and slipped it on. The second one hit her in the breast. "Okay," she said, and slipped it on. Then she writhed wildly, screaming as she twisted herself tighter and tighter in the curtain until her every lust-provoking curve stood out. She cooled down for a second, then wriggled until her breasts bounced like two energetic, frightened colts. "How's that!"

The girl's eyes stared wider and wider. Savagely, her whistling nostrils sucked air. At last she turned and walked out of the jewelry store on trembling legs, hid in the corner of a wall, and wept as if her heart was broken.

Nida Temple stands on a triangular floodbank among bare, brown peaks. An earthen yellow path like an umbilical cord connects the temple to the main street. On the left side of the floodbank stands a stunted poplar, and on the right, a dead willow. A bald vulture had perched on one of its dried, blackened branches.

"Better wait under the poplar tree," her mother said.

"Why do I always have to wait under the poplar tree?" said the girl. "You want me to fall asleep in the sun like that ugly old man there?"

"It's shady under the poplar."

"It's not shady under the poplar."

"Nangsel!" her mother scolded.

The girl hung her head and kicked at the grass. "I'm going to take a look at the temple," she said.

"No."

"I just want to look, I won't call anybody Dad. I'm this old, and who have I ever called Dad!"

"Nangsel!" Her mother seemed about to say something, stopped, and just said, "You wait here."

Angrily, the girl walked over to the poplar tree.

Her mother heaved a long sigh, raised her head and stared, motionless, at the temple. Tied to her back she carried a bundle. Her dark face, running with sweat, looked like an asphalt road after the rain. She undid the bundle, tied it over one shoulder, flexed her arm a couple of times, and began prostrating herself.

From the road came the ringing of cowbells. A pair of men from the grasslands shouted at a herd of yaks they were driving to slaughter in Lhasa. Behind the herd, a woman on a horse stretched out her neck and sang:

> I open my mouth, she says I'm crazy,
> I hold my tongue, she calls me dumb,
> I stay at home, she says I'm lazy,
> I step outside, she calls me whore,
> Oh Mamaaaaa. . . .

A Tibetan girl doing prostrations in front of the Jokhang Temple, 1982. This practice was allowed again in 1981 after being banned since 1959.
(From Tibetan Nation, *Warren Smith, Westview, 1997)*

The woman's voice collapsed like a punctured sheepskin. Before she could pull herself together and take up the song again, she'd disappeared around the bend.

The river was broad, calm, blue as a lake. On the brown sand of the riverbank a flock of sheep patiently nibbled the grassroots. On the opposite shore was another brown sand beach, and further off, the mountains . . . a seamless expanse of peaks, rising and falling.

The girl sat in the shade of the tree, bored. She pulled a crumpled paper out of her pocket, smoothed it across her knees, and began to write. A whirlwind blew up from the opposite bank. It began low, tiny, then suddenly rose and swerved across the river. At the valley mouth it stopped and vanished as if it had been sucked away by a vacuum cleaner. On the black road where it had disappeared stood a scruffy American. He was quite young, blond, decked out in Tibetan women's clothing. He wagged his head, looked all around as if he hadn't collected his wits, then started climbing up the little path. A camera with a long-range lens bounced on his chest. He halted between the girl and the vulture, raised his camera, aimed at the vulture, snapped, turned, aimed at the girl, snapped, raised his head, and looked off with an exaggerated air, first in one direction, then the other.

"Nice weather!" he said.

The girl and the vulture looked up, squinting at the sky in more or less the same attitude.

The black sun was fixed in the center of the red sky like the center point of a circle.

The American walked under the tree and propped himself with one hand against the trunk, panting. His skinny shoulders rose and fell under his loose smock.

"Who are you?" the girl asked.

"Frank."

"Is that your family name?"

"Strunk."

The girl thought a moment, blew on the tip of her pen, and wrote,

Dear Frank Strunk,
What are you?

"Are you a devil?" she asked.
"What?" The American blinked.

"I saw you come across the river," the girl said. "Only devils go riding around on whirlwinds."

"No, no." The American got it. "I'm human. Don't believe it? I have a shadow. I'll stand out in the sun and show you."

He walked out of the shade. He cast no shadow. He looked all round, still couldn't find one. He got flustered, he chattered, yelled, he turned round in circles. Finally he had an idea, and raised his foot. . . . his shadow was under his foot.

"Here!" he cried out. A string of saliva dangled from his mouth. "Sssst," he sucked it back in. "My shadow!"

The girl wiped her own mouth.

"See?" the American said, embarrassed, hobbling back into the shade, "I was in the way of my shadow."

The girl wrote on her piece of paper,

I'm registering in a gymnastics class.

"And my temperature," the American said, kneeling against the girl's thighs, pressing his forehead against her forehead. "Feel it?"

The girl didn't reply. The American probably wanted to stick his lips on hers, but his nose was too big. His moustache brushed the girl's nostrils. She gave a loud sneeze. He moved away and sat down by her side.

There's a furry, blond guy from America,
a photographer. All day long, he takes
so many pictures of me there's no space
in my room to hang them all. I know
he wants to attract me. There are so,
so many guys all trying to attract me,
Americans, Germans, Italians. They all
take my picture.

"What are you writing?" the American asked.
"A letter."
"Who to? Your lover?"
"Yes."
"Where's he live?"
"Anywhere you like."
"OK!" the American shouted.[1]

1. The word "OK" appears in English in the original.

The sun stood still for a moment, then began its westward decline down the sky. A tractor cut across the green hill beyond the river, throwing up a long stream of dust, its engine droning languidly.

Today Mama's going to buy me a tracksuit
with a low, low v-neck. Oh! I'm embarrassed.
I shouldn't have told you that. But I can
tell you what gymnastics is. It's this:

A classy Land Rover back from Lhasa roared up and stopped. Two young lamas in monastic robes and sun hats scrambled out, waved to the driver, and started climbing up the path. One wearing earphones babbled a song in tune with his pocket radio.

Mother stood on the temple steps, composed, body erect, her eyes glittering with a vacant light. She held her cloth bag rolled up in her hand, empty. Its corner fluttered up in the evening wind off the river, fell limp, fluttered up again. Mountain mist, eggshell white, enclosed the temple. Hurrying along its red wall, the lamas looked like specters roving in the netherworld.

The girl crumpled the paper into the American's hand and flew up the little path.

"Nangsel!" her mother called.

"Mama!" shouted the girl.

"How much is the wool sweater?" a Han girl asked.

"What color?"

"Red."

"Forty-four yuan forty-four cents."

All sorts of clothing hung over the counter. So did an official certificate of merit featuring a single eye-catching word: "glamorous."

A beggar sat half blocking the entrance, clapping his hands. Mother threw him some money, bent over, and entered the shop. Her daughter followed.

"And the black one?"

"Forty-four yuan forty-four cents."

The mother stepped up to the counter, with her daughter behind her. "I want to buy the tracksuit," the mother said.

"Sold out."

"Sold out! Didn't you say I could pick one up today?"

The saleswoman looked her up and down.

"And the yellow one?" the Han girl asked.

"Forty-four yuan forty-four cents."

"You said you'd keep one until Sunday," the mother said.

"Why didn't you come on Sunday?" the saleswoman said.

"This is Sunday!" the mother said.

"I kept it until noon, then put it out on sale. An old peasant woman bought it . . . walked in, took off her hat, slapped it down on the counter—full of coins."

"That one?" the Han girl asked. "How much is that one?"

"Which one?"

"The one in red, black, and yellow . . . with 'OK' on it."

"Forty-four yuan forty-four cents," the saleswoman said fastidiously.

"Who said you'd only hold it until noon?" the mother said, turning away.

The girl was already gone. Customers were streaming in. The air was filled with the choking odor of ash.

"Hey! I get it!" the Han girl gave herself a smack in the head. Her face was moist and red. "They all cost the same!" she said in a loud voice, pleased. Outside the market, the girl was bent over the iron railing of a flower garden, weeping. Her mother waited patiently beside her.

On the sidewalk opposite, a liberated sheep snapped up a tuft of plastic grass from a Chinese Muslim peddler's mat and ran off with it. The sheep's back had been smeared red by pious Buddhists who had rescued it by purchasing it from a butcher. The Muslim peddler, in his brimless white fez, ran close behind the sheep stamping his feet, clapping his hands, shouting, "Spit it out! Spit it out!" He mingled coaxing with his threats, afraid just to snatch it back with so many Buddhists around. The liberated sheep paid him no attention, but casually ambled off through the crowd, stopping now and then to chew the plastic grass with evident relish.

"Let's go," Mother said, walking on. The sun was like a murky glass ball, about to be swallowed by the peaks along the river. She looked back for her daughter. The slanting sunlight cast dismal, blurry shadows across the road. On the iron fence that ringed the cultural palace hung a huge sign advertising a dance—the men's shoulders were enlarged, the women's buttocks were exaggerated. Beneath the sign sat a Khampa couple, the man's hand rubbing an arousing circle on the woman's breasts. But the woman was staring at the scene around her, popping a piece of chewing gum in her mouth like a Lhasa city-woman.

Near the couple sat a ruddy-faced woman from North Tibet. She pulled the head of her baby out of her bulging robe, played with the baby a minute, then pushed it back inside her robe again, where it kept wriggling.

Mother stopped and leaned on the gate of the iron fence to catch her breath, thumping her back with her hand.

Behind the fence, Wangchen rode his motorcycle up to the cultural palace ticket window, bought a ticket for the dance, and roared off in a cloud of smoke.

A group of old people walked around and around the cultural palace, spinning the music out of the dance hall by whirling their prayer wheels. An old humpbacked man left the circular concrete path like a drop of water spun out of a whirlpool. He searched around a moment, then walked, panting, behind one of the concrete pillars of the iron fence, took a piss, came back, turned to Mother, and looked her up and down over his wire-rimmed spectacles. She nodded to him with a little smile. He stuck his hand through the iron fence, pulled her ear up to his mouth, and said in a low voice, "Sometimes I don't really want to go to heaven."

When he'd said this, he let go her ear and walked off. But before he got to the concrete path, he turned and looked at her, raised his prayer wheel, and spun it. "Know why?" he called.

The mother shook her head.

He walked back, took her ear, and pulled it back to his mouth. "There's nowhere to piss there," he pushed her ear away and ran.

Mother rubbed her ear and went off into the circular square.

Ash lay heaped around the braziers. Clouds of it swirled through the air. The milk-white bulbs of the candelabra streetlamps were not yet lit, but already a large crowd had gathered beneath them around a young man in a Western-style suit and leather shoes, chanting the ancient epic *Song of King Gesar* as he strummed a guitar. In the coffeehouse on top of the watchtower, young men and women sipped coffee under enormous sun-umbrellas, gazing down on the empty drink-cartons kicked back and forth across the square, the scraps of paper blown back and forth in the wind, the bones carried back and forth in the mouths of dogs.

A tiny, deformed man shoved himself with fingerless hands over the square on a little wooden pushcart, tiny legs sticking out stiff in front of him. Presently he bounced down a curb, rolled off the cart and lay like a beetle flipped on its back facing up at the sky unable to fly, his little legs flailing feebly in the air. Mother walked over, stuck her hands under his armpits, and with practically no effort lifted him back up onto the cart.

"In my last life I sinned, Sister," he said in a twisted voice, "I pushed a high enlightened lama out of a horse cart, and so he put me in this body and made me spend this life on a little cart. I didn't know who he was. I didn't know I hurt his leg. . . ." He pushed himself along, repeating over and over, "I didn't know, I didn't know. . . ."

The old beggar woman was still sitting below the wall at the mouth of the alley. She'd taken off her red blouse and hung it on a stick she'd thrust in a crack in the wall, spreading the blouse over her head to shade herself from the sun. She'd pulled down her sheepskin robe. Beneath it she wore a tracksuit. Its overlarge v-neck exposed two triangular mounds of shrunken, shriveled skin that were her breasts. Dried, cracked, glittering scales shone among the wrinkles like metal in a desert, golden in the rays of the setting sun. Her hat lay upside down on the ground in front of her. Mother took out the money in her pocket and just threw it all in, then looked out across the square.

"Nangsel!" she called.

· 12 ·

In Search of Musk

Feng Liang

*W*hen he'd climbed halfway up the mountain he could still make out his and Erwan's motorcycles, like two red-shelled insects. And there was somebody in black and white loitering around them.

If he rushed back down, whoever it was in black and white would still have time to strip whatever parts he wanted off their motorcycles and walk away. So he didn't look back again.

When he reached the summit, he could see nothing. Rolling mountains blocked his view back to the man in black and white by the motorcycles. He still wanted to see what was happening back down there. He wasn't the carefree type who goes on working with one eye on his job and one eye on something else. He was still wondering what to do about the man by the motorcycles.

From the next mountain over he heard the crack of Erwan's rifle, then its prolonged echo. That gun he'd given Erwan had a fierce kick. Erwan's shoulder and the side of his face must be throbbing. By the time he got back down the mountain, Erwan's shoulder would be black and blue.

He gazed off over the receding peaks. The higher he climbed, the darker the green of the mountain. Down below, before he'd climbed, he'd figured there would be musk deer up here.[1] The slope was steep, but the footing was good. Nimble mountain sheep kept darting past. These ruts

1. Solitary and timid, the diminutive musk deer lives in mountainous regions from Siberia to the Himalayas. The male has a musk-producing organ, the musk sac, on its abdomen. Fresh musk is semiliquid but dries to a powder. Musk is highly sought after for use in perfumes.

were their hoofprints. When he reached the top, the ground was almost level. The bright sun gleamed down, and the dark green forest merged into the wide, unfathomable blue sky.

Now he regretted not taking the double-barreled gun he'd given to Erwan. There were musk deer up here for sure—bucks. He'd prudently sent Erwan over to the next mountain, but why had he let him take the double-barrel?

From this ridge he couldn't see anything. The brambles were too thick. He was alone up here. He was panting. It was over five thousand meters above sea level. If he could only see Erwan's face . . . it must be green . . . his must look the same.

He pulled out his binoculars and checked for movement, far off, then nearby. His father told him these old-fashioned binoculars were made in Germany. The gap between the eyepieces was so wide he could only look through one eyepiece at a time. Could a German's eyes really be so wide apart? The Germans who made them must have forgotten about the difference between white people and yellow people. His father said narrow-eyed men were too fussy. But then hadn't his father, a graduate of Huangpu Military Academy,[2] also peered over the battlefield at the enemy through these binoculars one eye at a time? Just as he was peering through a single lens now—for musk deer. His one eye could see nothing but luxuriant brush and sturdy trees. Another shot rang out from the next mountain, and at the same moment, his footfall flushed a couple of fat, brown grouse. They flurried off, invisible again in an instant.

Carefully he put the binoculars back in the front pocket of his dark-red photographer's jacket, gripped his rifle in both hands, and slowly stalked along the ridge. The soles of his feet luxuriated in the spring of the grassy earth. There was nothing to be anxious about. He knew a musk deer would appear.

He'd always been waiting for musk deer. Since he'd started hunting, he'd planned, calculated. How many musk deer had his father shot? It seemed his father had spent his whole life single-mindedly stalking and shooting musk deer, so many he couldn't count them, bucks, does. . . . His mother had stewed pot after pot of their meat to a mushy pulp, then poured it down his throat, into the fire of his belly where it churned around until he crapped it out. Another of his mother's chores was to preserve his father's innumerable dried musk sacs. All her life she gloried in

2. Huangpu (Whampoa) Military Academy near Guangzhou was the training center for the elite of the Guomindang command. Early in his career, Jiang Jieshi (Chiang Kaishek) served as its commandant.

dried musk sacs. Sometimes he felt that he, this marvelous son of theirs, was nothing but another musk sac that his mother cherished to forget her glory days in silks and satins. His father never sold a musk sac, never cut one open to smell the musk. His will pointedly stated that these musk sacs were the product of both his and his wife's labor, and that, except the few to be distributed to their children and grandchildren as legacies, the dried musk sacs were to be entombed with him and his wife. This will hung prominently in his parents' parlor. And for the sake of these musk sacs his mother forgot her youthful glory in silks and satins.

But his father hadn't spent his military career for nothing. He'd snorted through life with gusto in that banal semimilitarized agricultural district in the grasslands of Gansu.[3] The pressure of his father's enormous shadow smothered the breath he'd wanted to draw in his father's company. He'd resisted his short, fat father's pressure, but at the same time he lacked his father's dynamic spirit.

He was more inclined toward his mother. It was his mother who'd formed him. His father said he had womanish ideas. Those ideas were playing tricks on him now. He regretted asking that shepherd.

Halfway up the mountain he'd come upon a twenty-year-old shepherd listlessly calling his sheep. He'd sat down by his side, gazed at the mighty knife stuck in the shepherd's belt, at the spindle he was twirling in his hands, and asked him if there were musk deer on this mountain. The shepherd gave him a look, said no, and engrossed himself in his spinning.

He was confused now, anxious. He knew there must be musk deer . . . bucks. He regretted asking that shepherd. . . . He shouldn't have asked.

His self-assured father always invited four or five hunting companions along, then went leaping ahead of them, face shining, wings on his heels, to kill the first musk deer with his first shot. His blustering, yelling father was perfectly happy crawling in the mud, climbing trees, jumping into rivers. As soon as his father reached the place where he wanted to hunt, he would seek out the locals for all the tips he could get. As a result of this bravado, his father often had his gun confiscated along with his precious musk, and a fine to pay, yet his father didn't really care. But he cared.

In the mountains, he avoided people. Asking that shepherd had been out of character for him. He regretted it.

Erwan's gun sounded again. Little Erwan was good for nothing but rabbits. In these mountains there were so many thickets where rabbits burrowed and bred that killing twenty of them in an hour was no trouble.

3. A poor, remote province in northwest China.

One bullet and it was over. A couple of spasms, the rabbit was dead. What fun was that? Rabbit meat was so dry and smelled so bad, it wasn't worth eating. He'd let a dozen go by. He was waiting for musk deer.

But in July? Deer hunting season was October. And yet he knew he'd get a buck with a musk sac today. With one shot he could bring down anything that ran or anything that flew. But he couldn't read tracks. He'd tried for months to learn from a hunting companion, all for nothing. He couldn't get the knack of it. So he didn't watch the ground. He pulled out his binoculars again. After his father had given him the binoculars, people offered him five hundred yuan for them, but he wouldn't sell. Even though when his father gave him the binoculars he'd said, "You didn't turn out like me."

The fierce wind on the ridge swayed his tall, slim body. His stomach had never grown into a burdensome load like his father's. He was so bony . . . but there was nothing great about that either. His father had been right about one thing: the country's most snobbish university, where he'd gone to study, had been the right place for a skeleton like him. His father hadn't acted as if he were passing him a family heirloom when he'd given him the binoculars.

He'd never dared to ask his father for his grandfather's saber, half the height of a man. Later, his father had given the clanking saber to his grandson, passing on the family's grand military tradition over his head to the following generation.

He'd thought at one time that he could still get the saber, so he told his father he was moving to Tibet. His mother burst out in a piercing wail. To make amends, his mother had wanted to give him a musk sac. But all he wanted was the saber . . . or at least to see his father burst out for once in a wail like that. But his father, graduate of Huangpu Military Academy, maintained his natural poise, and just raised one corner of his mouth in a half-smile. So that was how he had come to Tibet, where he'd married, had a son, and started to hunt. And the only game he hunted was musk deer.

The sun had evaporated last night's rain. The green grass was already showing the first signs of its inevitable withering here on the hot, dry Tibetan plateau. The sunlight made his chest feel as if it were on fire. He kept seeing his father's face. . . . When he'd told his father that he was going to hunt musk deer, the old man had twisted his mouth and said, "Well, go nick one, if you want." July? This wasn't the hunting season.

On a mountain twenty kilometers from here, before dawn as Venus faded from the sky, one cold October morning he'd shot a musk deer. His marksmanship hadn't been as good then. The bullet struck the deer's skull. Purple night mist blackened the blood bursting from its head. The sky was growing rapidly light. It was a doe, her belly already swelling. The doe had probably just awakened and was looking for some of the night's fresh growth to eat when he'd shot her. Before the sun had risen, he'd dragged the doe and her unborn fawn down a steep dew-covered slope to where the footing was solid. This was the only musk deer he'd ever run across. At first, he hadn't really been sure it was a musk deer. He'd almost taken it for an overgrown rabbit. He'd depended on his father's German-made binoculars, but they hadn't helped him.

This time he didn't use the binoculars. He relied on his naked eye.

His throat was parched. His army canteen was still half full. He was doing his best to conserve his water. It was still five hours to sundown . . . but maybe he wouldn't need to be so careful. . . . He saw a flash of yellow! He held his breath. . . . It was his strong-thighed prey!

The mountain was silent. He spotted his musk deer again, clear now. The crickets were chirping, the birds were calling. He threw down the binoculars and heard the sturdy German lens crack against a rock. He knelt, thinking . . . could he have broken the binoculars? He'd never done anything like that before! Those were his father's binoculars. He raised his rifle.

A dazzling sun hung in the west. The wind had dropped. The yellow deer was running straight south on the gently undulating ridge, its legs so amazingly long he would have thought it was a mule deer. He pulled the trigger. The recoil of his small-bore rifle knocked him over. He lay on his back. The gun had kicked into his chest, but he felt no pain. He'd waited all day for a musk deer, then hadn't even nicked it. Wildly, he righted himself. The musk deer was standing where it had been when he'd shot, looking over its right shoulder into the sun with enormous, bright eyes, straight at him. The sunlit half of its body glistened. He curled up his long, long legs beneath him (and a musk deer's legs are long too, so, so long!) and stared back at the deer. His heart was pounding. It was a buck. It was still watching him. He shoved a cartridge into the chamber. Nearby, a shot rang out. Had Erwan come over to this side of the mountain? His stomach was churning. He wanted to vomit. He wasn't sweating. He was still down low, legs under him, holding his gun. He'd never go hunting again. He caught a glimpse of his father's German binoculars at his feet, slanted upward. He thought they were in pain. He aimed his rifle steadily at the head of the deer as it stared at him over its right shoulder. With his naked eye he could see its enormous, shining eyes. He shifted his aim behind its shoulder. The deer didn't move, still gazed at him. Open ground lay before it. He let out a yell, and knew he was pulling the trigger. He saw the deer in convulsions on its back (it had fallen on its back, too) exposing its pure white, translucent belly to the sun. He scrambled to his feet. His foot struck the binoculars. They rolled down the slope. He raced madly to the deer. Those binoculars were worth five hundred yuan, but so was the musk of the deer lying there on its back . . . worth a thousand in Guangzhou, Shenzhen, big cities blazing with flashing lights. But his mother could preserve this musk sac as a treasure like his father's.

The shuddering deer tried to stand. It sprang to its feet, fell, sprang up, stood steady, then without any warning collapsed on its belly, rolled over slowly, with difficulty, onto its back, then raised its head toward its stomach. He couldn't figure out what the deer was doing. He thought it was still struggling to get up. The deer's stomach was bright red with blood, white, frothy, pouring onto the level, gently undulating ridge.

His heart leapt. He saw the deer bite into the center of its stomach where its musk sac was, not yet emerged this early in this season. The deer's musk was bulging out. At last he understood. He flew forward. He wanted the musk for himself! His hunting career was over. He'd never wanted to kill. He loathed the red blood he'd spilled, flowing through his mind. He was his father's only son. It was all on account of his father. Without even looking, five feet from the deer, he knew. It had sunk its teeth in its musk sac! He bent down madly, pocketknife in hand. Why hadn't he shot it in the head? The deer gazed intently at him with its enormous, bright eyes, still full of energy and life, as it blissfully sank its teeth again and again into the musk sac in its navel. With a gasp, he seized the deer's front legs and shook them savagely. Its legs jutted from its neck, but its muzzle was still sunk in its navel. He let go of its legs and seized its head. The deer opened its eyes and flashed him a vibrant look, then shut them morosely. From its swollen musk sac oozed a stream of dark reddish-brown fluid. He reached out his hand to catch it. The deer's teeth, snow white, were still sunk in its abdomen.[4] In his right hand he held the knife.

Nothing like this had ever happened to his father. He could never have done what his father did: his father never needed a knife, just picked up a sharp rock and cut out the whole musk sac intact. He could simply have cut the deer's musk sac right out with his knife, but the deer hadn't let him. It had spilled its own musk.

4. According to Chinese folklore, the dying musk deer bites open its own musk sac.

Anyway, he hadn't done like some, taken the deer's testicles for its musk sac. A deer's musk sac was in its navel.

The reddish-brown liquid went on flowing, spreading gradually over his fingers. A sharp, pulsating itch prickled his hand. The musk was burning hot.

An exhilarating fragrance filled the mountain.

· 13 ·

A Blind Woman Selling Red Apples

Yan Geling

$\mathcal{A}$s we started up over the mountains, the sky began to clear. But after three or four switchbacks, the fog got as thick as curdled milk, and by the time we reached the peak it covered the whole sky. Even our driver, who had been shuttling back and forth over the Tibet–Sichuan border for years, stretched his head, looked up, and exclaimed, "How come it's so white!"

There hadn't been a latrine for hours. Everybody said they were going to burst, and all jumped out. We girl[1] soldiers stumbled off a good long way trying to keep our knees squeezed together, then four or five of us took off our overcoats and held them up standing round in a circle with their backs to the middle, and everybody took turns going to the toilet in the center. Tibetan women in their leather robes—they just squat down, stand up, and it's all taken care of gracefully.

By the time we got back to the truck, the boy soldiers were sick and tired of waiting, and yelled, "What were you doing there? Looking for a flush commode?"

As the truck started off again, a woman appeared around the bend. "Catch a lift?" she called. Most Tibetans can't speak Chinese, but this is one phrase they all know. She didn't look straight at us, but coquettishly twisted left and right like a teasing, spoiled little child. Everybody on the truck yelled at the driver to stop. Finally somebody got up the nerve to say what everyone was thinking, "That's a beautiful Tibetan woman!"

---

1. During the Cultural Revolution, when this story is set, young people joined the army in their early teens, or even younger. The members of this army entertainment troupe, male and female, are generally teenagers. (The author herself began performing with such a troupe at the age of twelve.)

By the side of the road we often saw Tibetan women threshing barley or churning butter. When they got hot from work they'd pull their
robes down to their waists, and those two shapeless things would bounce
around busily on their chests as if they were keen to help out with the job.
After you watched for a while, you forgot they were women.

This woman was completely different. The simple, inky-green robe
she wore must have been emerald before it got so dirty. Her shoulders and
neck were lean and slender, her chin was thin and pointed. Approaching
the truck, she raised her chin, stretched out her hands, and groped in front
of her. Somebody solved the enigma: "She's blind."

We helped her up into the back of the truck and put her in the corner with her shoulder pole and two buckets of apples. She looked around
outside the truck, she looked around inside the truck—we were all just
part of the landscape. She appeared to be about twenty-six, so we knew
she must be around sixteen. Tibetan women always look ten years older
than they are.

When we reached the Yajiang army post, she walked off by herself.

The Yajiang post is just a relay station for military transports, not
much more than a motel for long-distance army truck drivers. But it has
two big hotsprings. The minute we heard we could take a bath, our whole
performing troupe starting yelling "Wow!" Veteran soldiers say that after
you've been stationed in Tibet a few years, you can't take the grime any
more, you feel heavy with all the dirt on you—if a grain of barley slipped
into your belly button, it would sprout.

When the post took this place over, they walled up the hotsprings,
dug two deep pools, and lined the bottoms with cement. If some regional
commander came to Tibet, the post would reserve the pools for him alone
as long as he visited. Performers like us were permitted to use the bathhouses too—just once during our stay.

We girls went to the women's side, and there in the pool rose the bare
back of a man standing in the water, big and crude-looking with a gaping
lantern-jaw. When he saw a bunch of girl soldiers come in, he got all flustered, rolled down the legs of his trousers, and let them hang there in the
water. He'd been sent in to scrape the sulfur deposits off the bottom of the
pool. The layers of sulfur residue, one on top of the other, made a confused, mingled pattern like cloisonné enamel or the three-colored glaze of
Tang pottery.

We asked the man why crowds of Tibetans were gathering on the
knoll outside. He gave a start, looked all around to be sure that he was
the one we were talking to, and stammered "Ba . . . Bathing Festival

st . . . starting," in a Gansu[2] accent. His teeth were tea-colored. The sun that turns Tibetans' faces purple turned his dark green. He covered himself with the ragged, shapeless army jacket he'd tossed on the edge of the pool and left the baths to us.

By the time we'd finished bathing it was high noon. The temperature had soared twenty degrees. "I can't take this heat!" one of us girls said in a weak voice. Gummy water flowed out of the bathhouse, down into a makeshift ditch. A cloud of steam rose from this ditch, and in it was a crowd of purple bodies. The scum we'd washed off ourselves floated on their water like the fatty skin on a bowl of sour milk. Naked bodies stuck up everywhere out of the trench, men and women all mixed together. Before the army post converted the hotsprings into a men's and a women's bathhouse, the springs had been theirs, and they'd soaked at ease to their heart's content, and didn't have to wash in somebody else's bath water.

"Hey, what are we hanging around here looking at?" somebody blurted out.

As we fled the scene fearfully, joyfully, we saw the beautiful blind woman standing there, off in the distance. She had one sleeve of her robe pulled down. She kept her chest covered, without baring anything, but she still gave you an idea of everything she had there. The shoulder protruding from her robe was delicate and slender. She leaned forward in an attentive pose, "looking" toward the ditch. She'd spread her apron to display her little red apples. Now she took one, licked it all round, then polished it on the front of her robe. This was why the apples shone so.

The post had a strict regulation—no soldiers permitted near the hotsprings or the ditch during the Tibetans' Bathing Festival. There was always friction between the post and the Tibetans. Most of the time, each side kept to itself and minded its own business—during the festival, the Tibetans had a wild time among themselves, but if a soldier stood around watching, they got angry. Setting up the stage that night, we soldiers, boys and girls, were still giggling, stealing glances at the Tibetans bathing there in the ditch.

It was time to wash our faces and put on our makeup. The Gansu man carried in buckets of hot water on his shoulder pole until we had a half-dozen. Then he squatted down and started rolling a cigarette. A soldier came along and kicked him in the ass. No reaction. More soldiers walked up—one knocked the drooping brim of his old, worn army cap down over his face. He just kept smoking.

---

2. A poor, underdeveloped province in northwest China. As is made explicit later in the story, the army entertainers are from the more developed Sichuan Province.

Bathing in the Lhasa River. (From Tibet, *ed. Nebojsa Tomasevic,* © *1981 Jugoslevenska Revija)*

Finally the duty lieutenant in his red armband came up, crooked his finger at the Gansu man and called him like he was calling some little animal.

The Gansu man stood up, tall and gangling, slightly stooped, long arms hanging down, big hands dangling at his sides.

"At it again? Still staring, eh?" the lieutenant said, with a glance at the girl soldiers putting on their makeup. "Didn't get enough last time, huh?"

None of us knew what the lieutenant was talking about.

"What are you loafing around here for?" the lieutenant shouted. "More water!"

The Gansu man gave a grunt, his face a blank.

We all said we had too much water already.

The lieutenant put on a smile and said, "Give *him* a break? Get him out of here!"

The Gansu man put his pole on his shoulder and staggered off as if the earth was shaking underneath him.

"Son of a bitch!" the lieutenant muttered with a grunt.

"How can somebody that old be a soldier?" someone asked.

"Him—a soldier?" The lieutenant glanced at his receding silhouette, humped with muscle behind the shoulders. And so out of the lieutenant's mouth we heard his story. The Gansu man had been in one of the regiments that came into Tibet to put down the 1959 uprising. The hotsprings were wide open then. When the time came for the festival the Tibetans arrived, men and women, to play in the water. The Gansu man couldn't stop watching them, as if he were addicted. The Tibetans grabbed him and said they were going to beat him to death. The post sent some soldiers out to bring him in, then punished him—discharged him and sent him home to Gansu in the middle of winter. Next year he was back again, a walking skeleton. There'd been a famine in his town, and he was the only one in his family left alive.[3] The post let him stay. He wore clothes people threw away, picked up scraps from everybody's pot, did work nobody else would do.

Next day we drove to Yajiang city to take in the sights, and along the road we met the blind woman walking with the man from Gansu. On his pole he was carrying her buckets, full of little red apples. The blind woman had her hands free now, and gripped the flap of his worn-out army jacket. She took little steps, he took big steps. Somehow they just couldn't get in stride, so that her hands holding onto his jacket jerked from side to side.

---

3. The time referred to, 1959–60, is the period of devastating famines during the Great Leap Forward.

They didn't speak to each other. Their whole conversation was nothing but laughter back and forth—crazy, foolish laughter. He'd covered the blind woman's whole head with flowers stuck into her hair, like Mu Guiying's crown.[4] He'd hung a ball of flowers around her neck, that swayed back and forth on her chest, and another around his own neck. Flowers on the Tibetan plateau have such short stems that he couldn't tie them into a bouquet, only roll them into a ball for her.

When we finished our show that night, we conspired to sneak back into the hotsprings for a second bath. There was no telling when we could take another one after we left here. We were quiet as thieves for fear our captain might find out, since the bathhouses were off limits during the Bathing Festival. Our captain taught us not to discriminate against Tibetans. He also warned us that Tibetan men grab a girl soldier, put her in a big leather sack and carry her back up into the mountains to breed little Tibetans.

It was almost midnight. Tatters of gold and red still covered the western sky.[5] The hotsprings lay at the bottom of a small gully. You couldn't see them until you climbed to the top of the gully rim, then there they were right in front of you. The army of crows that had been hovering around in the sky all day had flown off who knows where. The fiendishly happy Tibetans who'd been running riot in the water had scampered off who knows where.

One of us whispered softly, "The sky looks like People's Road!"[6]

Everybody laughed at her. "Anything pretty you call People's Road— all you know is People's Road!"

She said, "I'm from a little Sichuan village, at least I know People's Road. That big Gansu devil—what does he know?"

Everybody chimed in. "He's so big he makes me want to puke," one girl said.

"Somebody up at the post said once when they got a load of oranges, he tried to eat his skin and all. Nobody told him you've got to peel an orange—everybody peeled theirs behind his back. They were so bitter he couldn't take it. Next time they handed out oranges, he gave his away."

The sky shone warmly. Halfway down the gully slope, we froze. Usually at a moment like this some dope would holler out, but this time nobody yelled.

4. An ancient Chinese woman general; in Chinese opera the character Mu Guiying wears a huge military commander's headdress.
5. Since the entire country of China is on Beijing time, in the western region, where this story is set, sunset occurs toward midnight.
6. The lively, colorful main street of Chengdu, capital of Sichuan Province.

The blind woman was standing in the ditch, cupping her hands and slowly pouring water over her body. She didn't realize how filthy it was. Most of the flowers had fallen from her hair. Only a few were left, scattered helter-skelter over her head. The water came up to her thighs. Her hips were lean and slender. Staring silently in front of her, she bent her legs, cupped the water in her hands and poured it over her body, again and again. The exact, monotonous repetition of this movement made her appear almost statuesque.

If the scene had consisted of her alone, nobody would have paid attention. What shocked everyone was him. Tall, huge, he crouched in the dark nearby, lantern-jaw gaping, looking at her, poised, every muscle taut. You could feel the energy of his tensed figure like an animal ready to spring.

Nobody reported this to the officers. We went to bed edgy and suspicious.

In the early hours, there was a big commotion in the post. They were going out searching for someone. Searching for *him*. The Tibetans had been keeping a close eye on the Gansu man and the blind woman, and that night they'd moved into action. Naturally he tried to run to the post to hide, but the post wouldn't let him in. The garrison was afraid the Tibetans would smash the place. So he ran off. The officers let the Tibetan mob in to search for him so they could see he didn't belong to the post. After they couldn't find him, the garrison went out to search with them, so we went along.

The search party followed him into a little forest, scaring up every crow in the world. Instantly the first rays of dawn lit the dark sky.

The Tibetans who caught him had wounded both his legs with their spears. His ragged old army pants were soaked with blood, his thickset legs were so wobbly he couldn't stand.

They brought him in, arms twisted behind his back, a soldier holding him on one side and a Tibetan on the other. He didn't seem too scared at all. By the look of him he still didn't know what was going on.

It got really hot. Flocks of screeching crows shot up into the sky. We were shocked to see how many Tibetans there were, as if they'd suddenly all just sprung out of the ground. You could search forever, and you'd still never find all their dens.

They dragged the Gansu man into the post courtyard and dumped him on the ground. There in the crowd the beautiful Tibetan woman turned her eyes to his bleeding body. She still carried her apples, full to overflowing with red.

The soldiers and Tibetans finally came to an agreement—tie him up, and send him under guard to district headquarters. He was so big and awkward they couldn't get him in the right position to tie up. He raised his head and looked around, worried and ashamed at how clumsy he was. A truck waited, its engine running. Everybody was getting jittery. As they were shoving him at last into the back of the truck, he groaned a couple of times, "Thirst." Everybody pretended not to hear.

It was time for our performing troupe to move on. All the people were listless. Even the truck, starting up, was sluggish. The garrison was somber too, resentful and discouraged about something.

As our truck was crossing the mountains, snow began to fall. Snow in these mountains in June is nothing to be surprised at. We rounded a bend, and there she was again. The truck slowed down—the driver waited for us to make up our minds. We kept as silent as a load of freight. She took a few steps in our direction. As she reached the truck, it pulled away abruptly, and left her groping in mid-air. She fell, and her red apples spilled over the ground like a filthy red wound festering in the snow.

• 14 •

Stick Out the Fur on Your Tongue or It's All a Void[1]

Ma Jian

III. The Weevil

I was in the Changthang pastureland of western Tibet, a place with many lakes, ideal for photographing grasslands scenery. The terrain was crisscrossed with rivers that cut off my line of travel, so I kept walking into dead ends.

Wispy clouds gathered off in the west, harbingers of the rosy clouds of evening. As the sun began to turn red, I sized up the scene: high, ragged peaks rose and fell to the east, snowless—by the look of it I had to cross them. While I was still climbing, the sun rolled down under the horizon. In the dying light I hurriedly looked around: the way back was pitch-black. Dusk covered the pastureland ahead, not a single light anywhere. I'd have to sleep out again. I stopped looking for anybody's fire, just found an open place on the mountaintop where the wind would drive off the mosquitoes, and sat down. I'd already finished the biscuits I'd bought in Panga,

---

1. In Tibet, sticking out one's tongue at someone is a gesture of greeting. *Stick Out the Fur on Your Tongue* . . . is a collection of five stories. Printed here are the third and fifth stories.

The author explains the title *Stick Out the Fur on Your Tongue* . . . as an allusion to Lu Xun's notion of the writer as a physician of society: the patient of the traditional Chinese doctor sticks out his or her tongue so that the doctor can diagnose the malady. The author explains the second half of the title, . . . *or It's All a Void*, as implying the futility of the act of diagnosis. Though the writer may analyze society's ills, there is nothing he or anyone can do to remedy them: the prospect for a cure is an empty void. The image of the void is associated with the Buddhist doctrine that all existence is nothingness.

In our interview, Ma Jian professed ignorance of the rude implications of sticking out one's tongue at someone in Western society.

so I pulled out a few dried-up cheese scraps from my jacket pocket. I'd swiped them in the marketplace. When I tasted the first one I almost threw the rest away, they were so sour. After I held them in my mouth for a while they softened. Too sour to chew, they still bore some flavor of milk—a taste we savor from birth. Before the evening wind came up I spread out my sleeping bag, jumped inside without taking my shoes off, and, lying there facing the sky, I reflected on the eternal theme of life. What you see in Tibet is different from the rest of China. First of all, Tibetans don't treat death as something sad: they just think of it as a change from one world to another. But all those men and women prostrating themselves, in temples, outside temples—incomprehensible. Why are they so frightened of punishment?

I was hungry. I had no food. My stomach was utterly empty. Air churned around inside me, shoved down through my intestines, and slipped out my anus.

I rolled over, and my stomach didn't bother me as much. It began to get cold. I thought about my previous experiences in this kind of night-lodging, raised my head, and checked the wind direction . . . not so bad—my scent was blowing northward toward a river, with open pasture beyond it. Even if wolves caught my scent they couldn't cross the river to get me. I pulled my dagger out of my pack, and tied it to my wrist. I was falling asleep when I started imagining a mad bull-yak rushing down and trampling me, a wild dog running off with my backpack, a ferocious wolf creeping up silently and snatching my poor neck, skinny as a stick of kindling, some little devils that hadn't had enough to eat in the hell surrounding me, chewing off my ears, nose, hands, and feet like radishes. Then I thought of women . . . the warm scent inside their bras. At that moment I'd have happily died just to stroke a breast.

I looked back: left of the way I'd come, I saw a blurry, motionless light. I pulled out my camera and took a look through the zoom lens. The light was shaped like the ventilation gap at the top of a tent. I climbed out of my sleeping bag and groped my way down the mountain.

It took me two hours to find that tent. I made a little noise. No dogs jumped out, so I lifted the doorflap. An old man sat motionless by the fire. I called to him in Tibetan. He turned around. He couldn't see me right away, likely because he'd been facing the fire, and he didn't discover I was Chinese until I sat down. He laughed and asked me in Chinese where I'd come from. I told him I'd come down from the mountains where I'd been photographing the sunset, that I'd been in Drokpa village the day before. He said he'd seen cameras, he'd been a construction worker rebuilding the

Danse macabre. (Photos by Fosco Maraini)

bronze Buddha at Sera Temple where Chinese and foreign tourists came every day. In a few years there he'd learned some basic Chinese. I put down my backpack and sized up his tent. There was nothing inside it at all. Countless fires had calcified the rocks of the fireplace. People must set up their tents here all the time. He'd probably arrived here during the last couple of days. I looked around to see if there was anything to eat, but there were only a few old sheepskins lying on the ground, the saddlebag off his horse, and an aluminum basin. I asked if there was any food. He said no. I stretched my hands toward the fire. He reached behind him and dragged out some cakes of dung, some wild grass, and some damp dwarf-willow roots that he'd gathered, and started chatting. I was awfully hungry, just replied now and then for the sake of politeness. He stood, did up his belt, and walked out of the tent. I laid out my sleeping bag, pulled one of his old sheepskins over me, and went to sleep.

Vaguely, I heard something funny: the desperate stamping of hooves just outside. I drew my knife and rushed out. He'd come back, gripping the horn of a yak in one hand, its nostrils in the other. It was pulling against him with all its might. I was going over to help him when he called in a hushed voice not to come near, clutched the yak's head under his arm, reached down, pulled his knife, plunged it into the yak's neck, and snatched off his hat to catch the blood. The yak was struggling wildly. Then he let it go, gave it a shove, and it staggered off. He came back with the hat brimming with blood in both hands, and gave it to me. Drink, he said. He went back to his old sheepskin, pulled out a cigarette, lit it, and sucked the dripping blood off his fingers. I put the hat full of blood down beside me and watched the froth and steam gradually dissipate. I didn't feel like sleeping now, so I started chatting with him while I waited for the blood to congeal.

He was a shepherd from the grasslands around Jiwa. Half a year ago he'd left there and gone to Shigatse to pray to Buddha. There he'd sold off all his yaks and sheep and given the money to Tashi Lhunpo Temple. I asked him how he was going to live. He said he was going on a pilgrimage to Mapam Yumtso in the Gangtise Mountains to wash away his sins. Then he said he had a daughter. I asked him why his daughter wasn't with him. He went quiet, with a searching glance all around him. I knew he wanted a drink, so I pulled out my roll of tobacco and tossed it to him. . . .

When he'd finished his story, the image came to me violently of a girl I'd seen, but I hesitated to speak about her. All the time I was there I never told him. First of all, I was afraid he'd pester me about it, and besides, finding out about her might have driven him crazy.

Here's the gist of what he said.

"I sold off all my animals, and went to Tashi Lhunpo Temple to pray, may Buddha bless my daughter with peace and safety, may Buddha grant me to meet her in heaven when I die, may Buddha bless my . . . all the way to the Hall of the Joyful Mandala, and forty-nine times around it, and then to heaven. It was all my sin.

"When I was a boy I sucked my mother until I was fourteen. Mama's milk never stopped. Daddy got killed the year of the rebellion. There are no other families in our grassland. When you get there, you'll see. I started sleeping with Mama when I was sixteen. I went every year to Jiwa village for the Spring Yogurt Festival and for the sheepshearing, and I met other women, but I was all confused. I couldn't get along without Mama. Sometimes she used to cry too, but what could we do? I was her one man, she'd never taken care of anyone but me, raised me up from a baby. Since Daddy died, she'd never even said hello to a passing herdsman. One year in Jiwa I heard that the lamas of Sera Temple were going to repair their bronze Buddha. I seized the chance to leave Mama and went to Lhasa. My daughter was already nine years old then. You understand? How could she have gone on living, if she knew it was my Mama who gave birth to her?

"Many things became clear on the outside, but nobody knew I was a man with a sin. Every day after work I went to the door of the main temple and prostrated myself for hours, over and over, to wash my soul. But I'd been in the habit of sucking nipples a long time. Those years, I chewed my fingers to a pulp."

I thought of him as he'd stuck his fingers in his mouth to suck the blood off them just now, greedy as a nursing baby. His face turned so dark it was frightening: a mass of wild hair tied with a red cord, the blood vessels bulging at his temples shining crimson in the light of the fire. He stretched out his hand as he talked, and a loose lock of his hair fell down, swaying back and forth as he swung his head. The look of him disgusted me.

"Five years went by. I thought my sin was washed away. I went back home. My daughter Machrung was thirteen. I brought her back some clothes and some boots.

"Machrung could already sew her own aprons. Sometimes she'd tumble down into my lap and have me do her hair like a town girl's. In two years she grew into a big girl, breasts and neck just like her mama's. Here in the grasslands women go bare-chested at midday just like men. Maybe you don't know?"

I said I knew. I asked him, "What about your Mama?"

"She died the year after I came back. When Machrung rode out herding the yaks with me, her bouncing breasts got me all worked up. One day I couldn't stop myself, grabbed a ewe and sucked its teats for all I was worth, to let Machrung see. From that day on she kept her robe up and wouldn't come near me when she went to sleep. I started drinking a lot. I knew my old problem was on me again.

"Last summer a guy came round selling leopard skins and old pottery. His name was Tubu, very cultured, said he'd been a labor cadre in Lhasa, but he was an evil guy, and when he dies he'll go to hell. He brought along things people need in the pasturelands—aluminum pans, plastic winepots, colored thread."

"Did he fall in love with your daughter?" I broke in.

"He laid his bedroll down next to hers, and that night he slept with her. I heard Machrung crying out in a low voice. I couldn't stand it. But I wanted Tubu to marry her, or I'd go back to my old sin. That night I started chewing my fingers again.

"Tubu stayed a few days. Every day Machrung brought him his wine, and roasted meat for him. He gave Machrung plastic hairpins and a pair of plastic bracelets. I went out to watch the herds, to leave them the tent. But Tubu was getting worse and worse—not thirty yet, and cursing women like an old man. If Machrung hadn't liked him, I'd have let him have it."

"The night before they left I got drunk. I really shouldn't have drunk so much that night," he started getting excited, staring at me as he talked on. I saw the blood was cool, so I took it in my hand, passed him back his hat, sliced off half the blood and handed it to him. He took it without looking at me, scooped out some with a trembling hand, and ate it. As I watched, I pitied him.

"Tubu poured me the wine," he looked up at me.

I realized he was lying. I lowered my head and noticed the blood in my hand: the fire reflected off the side I was slicing. The light off my knife flashed across his face.

"Tubu was probably drunk too. I started off telling him to take good care of my daughter, it hadn't been easy to bring her up. He promised to treat her well, and called me Daddy. I laughed, and told him Machrung was my mother's daughter. Machrung screamed, I remember. She told Tubu not to listen, that I was talking nonsense, but Tubu acted delighted, and poured me more wine. Then I started talking foolish, asked Tubu to give me Machrung to sleep with that night. He agreed. Machrung pounced on me, started hitting me, but Tubu said if you won't sleep with your Daddy I won't take you along with me. Machrung stared dumbstruck.

"When it was light I found myself on top of Machrung. I'd chewed her left nipple to a bloody pulp. I'd let out everything I'd held inside me for years on Machrung's body. At first I thought I was dreaming, and went out to piss. When my head cleared from the wine and I went back inside the tent, I saw Machrung holding up her clothes to cover herself from me. I went back out, got on my horse, and fled.

"When the frost came in the pasturelands, I drove the herds to Chala. I knew she would never call me Father again; still I wanted to find her. When I started asking around Chala, people said she wasn't there. I heard in the cart-shop that a skin-trader had come through a couple of months before, who had a woman with him. The shop-owner asked me if the woman I meant wore big hairclips like flowers, made of turquoise, a round face, and eyes a little swollen. He said this trader was always cursing her. From his accent, the owner said, this trader sounded like he was from Shigatse. So I sold my herd and went to Shigatse.

"When I got there I didn't dare tell people I was looking for my daughter. I asked around and found a lot of guys named Tubu until finally I met a skin-trader on the street who told me he knew Tubu, but he'd gone off buying skins. About ten miles out of town, I found Tubu's house. Machrung wasn't there. I asked Tubu's mother, said I was from the grasslands where Machrung came from, and had a message for her. 'You're looking for that bastard?' the old woman said. 'I wouldn't let that stinking woman in my house. I threw her out a long time ago. Nyangmala lhunchu sabho!' She called on Bodhisattva Chenresig to send her quick to hell.

"Then I went to Tashi Lhunpo Temple, and walked round it prostrating myself, praying many days. People spinning their prayer wheels said there'd been a woman, not twenty yet, who let all the idlers in the district do whatever they liked with her. They said she depended for food on the pilgrims who came to spin their prayer wheels and pray to Buddha. They'd heard she was from the Jiwa grasslands. After a while her body had begun to stink, so no man would touch her. The old people cursed her father pitilessly. I felt awful. I prostrated myself all day long to expiate my sin, praying Buddha in his compassion to grant me a chance to find Machrung again."

He went on with a lot more, but that was basically how it stood. He truly longed to die. He'd heard that people who go on pilgrimage praying all the way to the Gangtise Mountains and walk round and round Mafu Mucuo, praying until they die there on the mountain, go to a high place in heaven. To return alive meant nothing to him. I looked up at the wind-flap in the top of the tent: it was already getting light. The blood in my stomach wasn't digested. It let out a burst of stinking air. I found a couple of cloves of garlic in my pack and ate them, then got sleepy. He slumped over on his old sheepskin, with the aluminum basin for a pillow, his lips mumbling, "Om mani padme um." The tent was full of his foul breath. As I lay down I recalled the girl I'd seen on the Barkhor in Lhasa: round face, cheeks blown purplish-red by the highland wind. There were no flowers of turquoise in her hair; it was like a pile of yak tails. She kept pushing it back as it fell down in front of her face. When she noticed someone watching her she'd abruptly look up and give the passerby a smile. If you just stood there without throwing her anything, she'd stick out her tongue at you.[2] Her lower eyelids were puffy, but as soon as she smiled, her eyes shone gently. Her lips were red and firm—the smile of a simple, miserable, selfless woman of the highlands, a smile broad and open as the plateau. Begging, she constantly had to keep looking up to those passing by. Her forehead was covered with wrinkles. The crowds, the dust, and the ceaseless noise of the market engulfed her. To avoid being trampled she crouched against a butcher's stand. When she noticed someone stop and give her a compassionate look, she bent her head, raised her left breast to her lips, sucked it, then gazed up and smiled. From being so much in her mouth, her nipple was round, transparent. Dogs scurried around her, waiting for scraps from the butcher's counter.

V. The Final Aspersion

Calm, cool, the barren mountains rolled off hundreds of miles in the afternoon sunlight. Dusk fell. I saw the great stretch of wild peaks tremble like flesh, bloodied by the setting sun. Finally, in the twinkling of an eye, the red sky of evening sank beyond the summit, and as one final curve of red hung dying between heaven and earth, I began to climb, groping for the wild pulse of life in this wall of rock. That pulse plucked me out, washed me clean away, and the filthy, empty body that was left stood up and walked back to the main road, cursing, scratching itself, then smiling.

That was the day after I left Kaga. I hadn't taken the main road. I thought that climbing these desolate mountains would reveal what this damned silly thing life is. What other choice did I have? The whole day I went around in circles, frantic, no way out, beaten, humiliated, sobbing like a child. That's the problem with artists—one fit after another.

2. A gesture of greeting.

Every inch of ground on the Tibetan plateau is steeped in religion—a mass of legend and myth. Some sufferings are unintelligible to
modern, civilized man. By writing down this story today, I begin to forget it.

They discovered her nine days after the death of Incarnate Lama
Tenzin Wangdu. She was nine days old, surveying the people and things
around her with wide-open eyes. The house was made of bricks of mud
mixed with straw. A yak-butter lamp shone on her mama's nipple and on
the red and green patchwork squares of mama's apron. It was a poor family. Mama heard a noise outside and stuffed her into the sheepskin robe.
Suddenly people outside filled the doorway like a mass of pitch-black cattle. Mama stood to invite the guests inside. They were of high rank, lamas
from Tenpa Temple.

Their leader, Ritual Master Sonam Jigme, said, "I've heard your child
was born nine days ago."

Mama replied, "Yes."

Whereupon the ring of lamas folded their hands and began to chant.
Sonam Jigme sent one back to report that the incarnate lama's reincarnation had been discovered. And he asked, "A boy or a girl? What is her
name? Sangsang Dolma? From now on she will be called Sangsang Tashi."

Then they performed the solemn ritual for the discovery of an incarnate lama, and Sangsang Tashi's entire family moved into Tenpa Temple.

By the time Sangsang had reached the age of fifteen she had already finished reading the entire Fivefold Treatise, and begun the study
of Nenriba traditional medicine. The first time in her life that she had
stepped outside Tenpa Temple was to take the hour's walk to the Nenriba study-house. These last few months she had not allowed anyone to
accompany her. A feeling had been troubling her that she couldn't put
into words. She felt that here, as she walked along the path, she was
able to think. For the past fifteen years she had never left the temple,
and all she had done there was learn to read, memorize sutras, and
study yoga. This road terrified her, even in her sleep. Actually, she had
been walking the first half of it for years. When she opened the door of
her meditation cell there it was, that little road, paved in stone, winding down the slope, with the dormitories of monks of the various
houses of study on both sides. Now she reached the turning, beneath a
high red wall. Within that wall was the heart of the temple, venerable
Sakyamuni and the sixteen great bodhisattvas. Below the red wall was

"The body is like a garment that you put on and take off"—a boy incarnate lama.
(Photo by Fosco Maraini)

the path pilgrims walked as they spun their prayer wheels. Here Sangsang Tashi often met an old woman who'd been continuously walking around the monastery for twenty years. Whenever the old woman saw Sangsang Tashi she prostrated herself and struck her forehead ceaselessly on the ground. Opposite the wall was the Grand Magistrate Lama's gate, where the usual dogs were chasing each other and copulating. Further on, turning to the right, she saw the street that led through the main temple gate, filled with masses and masses of pilgrims who had come for the Feast of the Exposition.[3] Sangsang Tashi often came to buy bracelets and earrings from the Indian merchants who pitched their tents here. Squeezed among the tents were the stonecutters' and beggars' huts, primitive structures of unmortared stone. The way to the Nenriba study-house led along a little path that turned left down through fields of buckwheat and peas. Pepperwort grew luxuriant among the clumps of dwarf willows along the road. In the morning the scent of white campion filled the air. Sangsang Tashi often stopped here. Looking back, she could see Tenpa Temple: above it all, halfway up the mountainside, lofty and pure, unsullied by dust, rose the platform for tomorrow's ceremony of her manifestation as Incarnate Lama. When the wind blew, she could hear the sound of the prayer flags on all the buildings, snapping as if they were being torn to shreds. Hundreds of tiny stupas rose in rows along the contours of the mountain. Farther on was a little stream, gathered by the mountains into the sparkling Nyangchu River, below. Just across the river was the house of Nenriba.

Whenever she reached this path, she forgot that she was an incarnate lama, the reincarnation of Tenzin Wangdu. Here she knew she was not a man. The smell of the open country intoxicated her. She even wanted to stand on that wooden plank bridge and watch the water plants sway in the current. Beyond the Nyangchu River lay bare, desolate mountains.

Tomorrow they would perform her aspersion from the diamond scepter of Buddha's heavenly guardian. In this solemn ceremony, the final aspersion of her body, Amida, Buddha of the Western Paradise was to subjugate her greedy, concupiscent nature, and she was to manifest the Tathagata. It was autumn now. The believers were flowing in an endless stream down from the mountains for the ceremony of her manifestation

3. Chinese "shaifojie": a feast during which a statue of the Buddha is placed in the sunlight.

as Incarnate Lama that was to follow her aspersion, as well as for the alms-giving. Tashi had no interest in any of these ceremonies. She only wanted to be alone to think.

She arrived as usual at the school of Nenriba medicine. In the middle of the vast, desolate hall, a corpse had been laid out. Today the master was to discuss the locations of the breath, the vital centers, and the arteries. It was precisely this that Sangsang was impatient and eager to learn. Master waited until a servant-monk had set the altar, then plunged in his knife. He cut open the chest, dug out the organs, and laid them out in offering, separating the heart and pointing out the position of its eye. A foul smell nauseated Tashi. The dozen other students all stared with fixed attention at the master. Although she was the only woman here, with her head shaved she looked no different from the other monks. Close by her side was Geleg Paljor. He was a monk of Peling Temple, an adept who had already finished studying the Diamond Sutra, sent here for advanced study. Whenever Tashi attended class, she always stood next to him.

The master told the students to shut their eyes, enter into trance, and visualize his thought. After a moment, four lamas told what they had seen. The master called on Sangsang Tashi. She was the youngest here, but she was an incarnate lama. Immediately she concentrated, but since she had only studied yoga for six years, the eye of her heart was not yet clear. She recited her mantra to readjust the artery of her heart and grasp her guardian-bodhisattva. Her heart's eye grew brighter but it was still blurry. Now she felt a ripple of heat in her toes that gathered into a mass, entered her leg, and flowed up into the eye of her heart. She silently recited the mantra of the purification of karma to steady her consciousness, and gradually saw a frozen river take form in the master's mind. Then, just as she passed out of the state of concentration and was returning to the sensory world, she saw herself naked in this ice-covered river. She gathered her thoughts, and told the master.

"What you have seen and told me is not something you saw with the eye of the heart, it is what *I myself* saw in you," the master said, "with my eye that beholds the future." The master began to dig through the corpse's temple into the skull. Sangsang's heart was in tumult. The master hadn't told her why she was in the river. Was that her future? She was shocked at seeing herself naked, like the sky mother in the paintings with the Buddha.

Master picked out a soft nodule from beneath the pituitary. "This is the eye of the future. Through this eye, with long practice, you can see the hidden diseases of a person's body, and the devils that surround it. When I saw Sangsang Tashi in the frozen river, I was seeing her destined place several days from now in the ordeal of the six virtues and three roots of suffering. It is ordained for her by the augury of the stars.[4] Listen well, Sangsang Tashi—your yoga can keep you in that frozen river three days without harm."

Sangsang Tashi's thoughts were in turmoil. She had only seen that river from afar. In freezing weather she could pass several days outside in the snow without feeling the least trace of cold, but what would it be like in the river? She thought of the wave of heat she had felt just now in her toes. That wasn't from her own skill. She looked beside her: all she could see was a floating halo of light revolving around Geleg Paljor's head. She smiled at him. She understood that Geleg Paljor's yoga had surpassed the master's, that he had never revealed this to anyone before now.

The master raised the soft nodule from the corpse's skull with the tip of his knife, saying "This one lived a life without understanding, enmeshed in this world, so the nodule is yellow. When your meditation reaches the state of trance, the nodule becomes transparent. Meditation, mastery of the emotions, and mystic doctrine all come down at last to this soft bone. Only this can enable you to see the world of the buddhas, to reach illumination, and to distinguish the spirit in everything in the universe." Then Master dug out an eye, pricked it, regarded the dark liquid running from it. "Those of the world see through this eye," he said. "Because its nature is dark and turbid, the vulgar worldly ones are entangled in the five poisons and cannot purify their consciousness."

Sangsang Tashi fixed her gaze on that mutilated body—a middleaged man, with big, white teeth. Flies swarmed over the organs.

That afternoon Sangsang sat alone in her room. Mama was terribly ill. She had just been to see Mama, using the medical understanding she had acquired in several months of study with the Nenriba master to treat her, but nothing really worked. Last month she had cast some of the disease's evil spirits into a dog, and immediately the dog died. But her master Labrang Chantso said all things have souls, so it is forbidden to expel evil spirits into other creatures. She could see her mother gradually

---

4. The augury of the stars: an oracular ritual that interprets an individual's physiognomy in conjunction with signs in the heavenly constellations.

withering away. She tried once again, but she could not settle her mind to meditate. Her aspersion would be performed tomorrow, and then, after that, the ritual of her manifestation—the most solemn ceremony ever celebrated for her since the death of Incarnate Lama Tenzin Wangdu, whose reincarnation she was. But her heart was not in it. The old prayer flags on all the temple buildings had been changed for new. Craftsmen had repaired the long ceremonial trumpets, unused for years, and every day now lamas practiced blowing them. The lamps in all the temple halls had been filled with yak butter, burning day and night. Nervous and frightened, she stared blankly at the lamp, thinking.

The monks had hung red tapestries and lit yak-butter lamps beneath the murals all around the walls of the meditation hall. In the middle of the hall stood a great mandala, adorned with images of the buddhas, and on it, servant-monks had laid out all sorts of sacrificial offerings. At the north point of the mandala were the organs of the dissected corpse, the intestines washed clean and coiled in a golden bowl. Four braziers full of incense burned at the mandala's four points. At the south point they had laid out several large cushions where she was to perform the ritual of the unification of her two bodies.

This time, as usual, it was her master Labrang Chantso, Tenzin Wangyal, who would perform her aspersion as the heavenly guardian who bears the diamond scepter.[5] At the thought of actualizing her two bodies with him, Sangsang gasped as if she were about to suffocate. She sensed that Master Labrang Chantso was disgusted that his elder brother had been reincarnated in her, and loathed her. But Master Labrang Chantso was proficient in mystic doctrines. It was he who taught her all the Five-fold Treatise and sprinkled her with sacred water at her rite of initiation. She thought of Master Labrang Chantso's forehead, full of wrinkles that twisted when he looked at you . . . his tiny eyes that looked as if they were squeezed into his face . . . his gigantic body. . . .

She thought of the mural on the wall: the Buddha's joyful heavenly guardian sitting in meditation, unifying his two bodies, masculine and

---

5. In this fictional ritual, Incarnate Lama Sangsang Tashi, who incarnates the heavenly guardian bodhisattva's female body, unites with Master Labrang Chantso, who becomes the male body of her heavenly guardian bodhisattva. In the course of the ritual she is to practice meditation and yoga, in order to receive the spiritual powers of the heavenly guardian bodhisattva's male body. (See Glossary, "Incarnate Lama.")

An old lama holding a bundle of incense sticks. (Photo by Ma Jian)

Male and female deities in sexual union (in Tibetan: yab yum, literally "father mother"). (Photo by Fosco Maraini)

feminine. Tomorrow she would mount the guardian. A naked feeling, damp and hot, stirred her. Master Labrang Chantso's face flashed before her, with no trace of a smile. Immediately she drove away these agitated thoughts and entered the state of meditation. The mantra of Sakyamuni gradually filled the breath of her heart. Three sky mothers appeared and told her that tomorrow the Buddha's joyful heavenly guardian would grant her his own body. One in red turned back and smiled at her. Then her guardian-bodhisattva himself, Jampeyang, appeared, sitting opposite her on the mandala. She felt the inside of her body go hot, her seven pulses flashing like bright lights in her heart. Her buttocks, her thighs, the hollows of her knees, the upper surfaces and soles of her feet felt light as feathers. Now Geleg Paljor appeared. She felt stark naked, overcome with shame, and her concentration was broken. Her heart was in a flurry. She drew the Buddhas of the Four Directions into her meditation, but now her meditation held nothing of herself. Her brain buzzed. All the sounds outside her entered her heart. Again, she had to break off her meditation, thinking of what the three sky mothers had said.

From outside came the fragrant smell of frying cakes. She felt hungry, struck the wooden fish to call a serving woman, and asked her to bring a bowl of yak-butter tea. Then she shut the door. It was already dark outside. She stared at the calcified black knot at the tip of the lamp's wick, wondering how she would appear tomorrow. At the thought of herself lying there naked, her heart leapt up. She felt a pang of fear. She tried to expel these thoughts, disrespectful toward the buddhas, and to meditate with undivided mind, but for some reason she couldn't focus her consciousness. She couldn't remain still in the lotus position. It was the first time in years she was unable to concentrate. She realized that she had violated monastic discipline. Her whole body tensed. She relit the two lamps that had gone out, and recited the bodhisattva mantra of the five mysteries, "Bentsa sandu samaya, nano panaya, bentsa sadu tenu padeta, dritu minpeya, sudu mone monpaya, o nuratu minpaya," and gradually her mind entered the trance.

When she awoke in the early hours of the morning, she felt herself completely woman. The sky was still covered in hazy moonlight. She felt it begin at dawn. First the blood. The peacefully flowing blood was coursing all through her body. Her inner clothing pressed against her breasts until they throbbed. Her thighs, her pelvis, and the soft place in her loins were lithe and graceful, wet and slippery. As she sat up, her breasts trembled. They rubbed against her underclothing and she felt a flash of dizziness that spread now to her vagina. She couldn't help pressing her hand there. A feeling like fire burned her. Her groin throbbed. Feminine sexuality had woken on the sly within her. She thought that soon she would be brought forth naked before the people and anxiously hugged her shoulders as her teeth began to chatter.

She watched it gradually turn from purple to red outside, then gradually the sky grew light.

A crowd of several hundred lamas filled the meditation hall. Fires were lit. Horns and drums sounded. In a yellow robe, with scarlet beads strung around her neck, Sangsang Tashi walked to the center of the carpet and sat facing Master Labrang Chantso, her legs crossed, hands on her knees, palms upward in invocation, chanting the fivefold incantation of Dorje Semba. Her mind was agitated, her hands trembled. Embarrassed, she pressed her feet tight into her thighs. The horns sounded again. She knew that she had not realized the state of concentration. Bewildered, alarmed, she seized on the talamma mantra, to invoke instantaneously the presence of her guardian-bodhisattva, but the words came to her out of order, there wasn't time enough. . . . She opened her eyes and saw Master Labrang Chantso walking toward her, undoing his robe. An imploring light flashed in her eyes. Her heart palpitated. Master Labrang Chantso dropped her to the carpet. She was dazed by the piercing, swelling ache between her thighs and the weight of the body pressing down on her until she nearly fainted. She felt the woman who'd entered her flesh that morning torn apart all at once by Master Labrang Chantso.

The sweat ran down her back and neck. The ache in her loins passed. She was conscious of herself instinctively twisting in unison with the body on top of her, as she floated into a black hole. From her thighs a twitching rose up through her whole body. She was alone in the black hole, and this brought her a moment's calm. Desperately she called to mind that in the completion of the masculine and feminine aspects of her body, she was to rely on her breathing, her seven pulses, and her vital nodes to reach the wisdom in the body of Master Labrang Chantso. Only thus could the wisdom of the heavenly guardian in Master pass into her. She must immediately activate the breath of wisdom; but Master Labrang Chantso pulled her up standing, took one of her legs in his hand and wrapped it around his waist, and his shuddering movements made her forget the ring of her pulses. Now she felt her own body wither gradually: Master Labrang Chantso was absorbing her, magnetically sucking out her marrow and vital spirit. She collapsed, unable to keep herself from letting him manipulate her at will. When Master sat into the lotus position again and pressed her against his body, she squatted like the sky mother on the mural, her legs skillfully hooking around his back. Her breasts that she had seen burgeoning that morning were dry and shriveled now as an old woman's. Suddenly she felt the bitter ache in her abdomen begin to spread down to her groin, through her pelvis, into her tailbone, and up her spine, making her gasp for breath. She opened her eyes. Sunshine filled the ritual hall. Trembling incense floated all around her. Above the incense Buddha Sakyamuni appeared with his golden smile. She shifted her face away from Master Labrang Chantso's stinking chin, looked down, and caught sight of Geleg Paljor among the mass of shiny heads. Instantly she shut her eyes, clenched her teeth, and hid her face against Master's chest.

The final aspersion ended at noon. When she awoke, Sangsang Tashi discovered herself lying on the cushions on all fours, like a dog. Her whole body twitched spasmodically. Her shrunken breasts were soaked in sweat. Two nuns approached and helped her to stand. With water from a golden bowl they wiped the sticky, bloody sweat from her loins. She couldn't move. Her legs were numb. The thought of her dying mother came violently over her. When she stood, horns blew in unison all around her. The chants and the blare of the horns merged with the clear smoke of the incense. Now the golden bowl full of organs was laid in offering at the center of the mandala. Master Labrang Chantso had donned his robe and seated himself on his reed cushion, his face flushed. Her legs still quaking, Sangsang awaited the close of the ceremony. This morning, she realized, the yoga she had studied these many years had left her. But she knew now that she was a woman, and it no longer astonished her that every organ in her body was female.

Sangsang Tashi died in the evening, the day after they put her into the frozen river. The incantation to generate fire, in which she had always been extremely proficient, never returned into her body. According to the ritual she had to remain three days in the river-nirvana in order to manifest the Tathagata. Three lamas kept guard over her, taking turns to hack away the ice that froze around her neck.

Day was about to break when Ritual Master Sonam Jigme left the campfire, stepped cautiously out across the ice, and observed Sangsang

Tashi's body, sunk just below the surface. They pulled her out and found that her body was transparent as the ice. Where her breasts and knees had been bitten through by the fish, there was not the least trace of blood. Her eyes were slightly open in the face's usual expression in meditation, as one nourishes oneself from the light.

At dawn, a contingent gathered to receive the Incarnate Lama. The people wore magnificent festive apparel, their horses adorned in multicolored silk. As far as the monks were concerned, the outcome was the same whether the Incarnate Lama lived or died, yet for a while they stood around Sangsang in astonishment. She lay on the ice, frozen. The sun shone down, neither hot nor cold. Her body was as transparent as ice, and inside it all the organs were visible. A fish that had gotten in somewhere was cruising through her intestines.

I've got Sangsang Tashi's skull here. The man who sold it to me said it was passed on to him by his grandfather, who'd studied witchcraft as a young man at the Nenriba medical school. Sangsang Tashi's skull was a sacred object preserved in the temple, only used in the final aspersion ceremony. It's turned yellowish-brown. On its left side is a crack, full of dirt and grime, a result of its falling to the ground in who knows what bygone age. The fissures on the dome of the skull ripple like the waves of an electrocardiogram. A doctor friend of mine told me this trait distinguishes the skull of a girl who hasn't reached puberty. The skull-bowl is set inside a brass ring with an inlaid design. Inside the skull-bowl is a layer of metal, fit to the shape of the skull. The man I bought it from quoted me a price of five hundred yuan, but I got it for a bargain at one hundred. Anybody with some U.S. dollars you don't know what to do with, just get in touch with me. The price has to cover my travel expenses all the way back up to the northeast.

Glossary

Amida: Bodhisattva associated with the western paradise, place of eternal light and life, especially worshiped by devotees of the Pure Land sect, widespread in China.

Aspersion: Buddhist rite of consecration or initiation. In the first aspersion ritual, water is sprinkled or poured upon the head of the one consecrated. In some sects (as in Ma Jian's "The Final Aspersion"), the rite, repeatedly carried out in a series of varied forms, marks the progressive steps of initiation into esoteric knowledge.

Barkhor: Main street of Lhasa, running in a circle around the Jokhang Temple.

Bodhisattva: In Buddhism, one who has attained enlightenment, but delays entry into the bliss of Nirvana and consents to incur further reincarnation back into the world in order to help humans on earth to discover the way of salvation.

Buddha: Literally "Enlightened One"; applied to anyone who has attained ultimate enlightenment, but preeminently to Sakyamuni.

Chenresig: The Tibetan name for the Bodhisattva of Compassion, in China called Guanyin, in India, Avalokiteshvara. In Tibet, the Dalai Lama is believed to be his incarnation. Tibetan Buddhists believe that in order to lead all to the bliss of Nirvana, Chenresig remains on earth in the successive reincarnations of the Dalai Lama.

Chuzan: A term of rank for a Tibetan nun who has passed certain basic examinations.

Circumambulation: The practice of pious Tibetan Buddhists who walk in a circle around a holy site as they spin their prayer wheels.

Dorje Semba: A bodhisattva; in Sanskrit, Vajrasattva.

Gang Rinpoche: Tibetan name for Mount Kailash, elevation 6,714 meters.

Heavenly Guardians: Four warlike bodhisattvas who guard the Buddha; their associated symbols include the diamond rod (or scepter) and the thunderbolt.

Incarnate Lama: Reincarnation of a bodhisattva; a person identified, or "discovered," to be the reincarnation of a recently deceased incarnate lama and thus inheriting the incarnate lama's clerical position.

Jampeyang: Sanskrit *Manjusri*; the defender of wisdom, an important bodhisattva in Mahayana Buddhism.

Jetsun: An honorific term of address for a Tibetan religious devotee of either sex. The literal meaning of the term is "spiritual guide."

255

Jokhang Temple: One of the three major temples of Lhasa.

Khampa: One of the group of Tibetans who speak their own distinctive Khampa dialect of the Tibetan language, and dwell in Kham, the eastern region of Greater Tibet, lying partly outside the boundaries of the present Tibetan Autonomous Region, within Sichuan Province.

Khatag: A ceremonial sash of white cloth, usually silk or muslin, used (often in religious contexts) as a token of worship or esteem.

Lopa: A hill tribe who live near the border between Tibet and Bhutan. "Lopa" is the Tibetan word for "aboriginal."

Mahayana: One of the two major Buddhist traditions (the other being Hinayana) and the one adhered to in Tibet. Mahayanists attribute to the Buddha a supranatural quality and interpret the historical Buddha as an earthly manifestation of a transcendent celestial Buddha. The Mahayanist strives to become a bodhisattva, one who has attained a state of enlightenment but postpones his/her Buddhahood and consents to undergo further reincarnation on earth in order to aid others in their search for salvation. Thus, in Mahayana Buddhism, compassion, the chief virtue of the bodhisattva, is accorded an equal place with wisdom.

Mandala: Circular representation of the cosmos, symbolic of spiritual unity, employed as a focus for concentration in meditation.

Mani cairn: A cairn of rocks, each of which is engraved with the words of the mantra "Om mani padme um." In Tibet such cairns are commonly found at the side of a road, especially at the highest point of a mountain pass.

Nenriba: Tibetan traditional medicine.

Pian ox: A cross between a bull cow and a female yak.

Potala: The chief monastery of Tibetan Buddhism, located in Lhasa; pious Buddhists circumambulate the Potala as they spin their prayer wheels, walking around it in a circle.

Prayer wheel: A rotating cylinder containing a written prayer, fixed on a handle. Tibetan Buddhists, praying, spin the handle as they pray, and the prayer is deemed to have been recited each time its written text revolves.

Sakyamuni: Siddhartha Gautama (c. 563 B.C.–c. 487 B.C.), the historical Buddha, founder of the Buddhist religion.

Sheli: A relic of tooth or bone that remains after the cremation of an incarnate lama, employed in rituals.

Shigatse: The second largest city of Tibet, site of Tashi Lhunpo Temple.

Sky burial: Traditional Tibetan funeral rite, in which the body of the dead person is cut into small pieces, and the bones smashed to bits; these remains are then consumed by vultures and other carrion birds.

Sky Mother: Goddess in Tibetan Buddhist mythology possessing certain special knowledge.

Stupa: Sacred building, which often houses the relics of a saint.

Tashi Lhunpo Temple: A major monastery, located in Shigatse; its chief abbot holds the office of Panchen Lama, second-ranking cleric of the dominant Geluk sect of Tibetan Buddhism, the sect headed by the Dalai Lama.

Tathagata: A title of the Buddha, in his role as source of all creatures; literally, "He who has thus gone."

Three jewels: The three essentials of Buddhism—the Buddha, the dharma (the teachings of the Buddha), the sangha (the monastic community).

Tratsang: A semiautonomous unit of a large Tibetan monastery.

Tsampa: Ground roast barley, the staple Tibetan food.

Tsongkhapa: A monk (1357–1419) posthumously regarded as founder of the Geluk (System of Virtue) sect, the dominant sect of Tibetan Buddhism, both in terms of number of monks and of political power. The Dalai Lama serves as its leader.

About the Authors

Alai

Alai (pinyin equivalent, Ahlai[1]) was born in Maerkang County, Sichuan Province, in 1959, to Tibetan peasant parents. He attended local primary and secondary schools. In 1980 he graduated from Maerkang Normal College and began teaching in a primary school in the rural village of Dawei. Soon he began to teach in secondary schools, first in Jiaomuzu, then in the town of Maerkang. It was at this time that he began to write.

In 1982 his first published work, the poem "Soar, You Wings of the Spirit," won the first award in a five-province competition for Tibetan writers. In 1984 he commenced working in the literary association of Ahba prefecture as a professional writer. In 1989, his first collection of stories appeared, *jiunian de xueji* (Bloodstains of the Past). In 1990 he published *suomohe* (Suomo River), a volume of poetry.

From this point on, Alai abandoned poetry to concentrate solely on fiction, publishing short stories and novellas in such periodicals as *shanghai wenxue* (Shanghai Literature) and *renmin wenxue* (People's Literature). His major works from this period include the short stories "huaihua" (The Flowers of the Scholar Tree), "qunfeng feiwu" (A Swarm of Bees), and "yueliangli de yinjiang" (The Silversmith in the Moon), as well as the novellas *nieyuan* (The Brink of Sin) and *xingxingren eryi* (Eryi the Executioner). The year 1998 saw the appearance of his novel *chenai luoding* (The Dust Settles). A number of his works have been translated into English, French, and German.

Alai's works portray life in the Tibetan areas of Sichuan Province, beyond the borders of the Tibetan Autonomous Region. He writes from a perspective outside that of the traditional Tibetan Buddhist heritage, describing the Tibetans who had been under Chinese government long before the Chinese occupation of Tibet in 1951.

Lately, Alai has turned to the theme of Tibetan culture. Published in 1993, his *caoyuanshang de taiyang* (The Grasslands Sun) is an account of the work of the Tibetanist

---

1. Tibetan authors' names are given in romanized Tibetan, with the pinyin equivalent in parentheses.

and educator Lobsang Nima. He also contributed to *ahbazhou zangchuan fojiao shilue* (A Short History of Tibetan Buddhism in Ahba Prefecture, 1990) and has written television scripts on Tibetan cultural subjects.

Alai is married. His wife, a Han, works as an English teacher. They have a twelve-year-old son. Alai currently lives in Chengdu, the capital of Sichuan Province, where he works on the staff of the magazine *kehuan shijie* (Science Fiction World).

Feng Liang

Feng Liang was born 1963 in Xide County, Liangshan Prefecture, Sichuan Province, into a family of the Yi minority nationality, a group scattered through Sichuan, Yunnan, and Guizhou Provinces of southwest China. She completed primary and secondary school in Liangshan, then, in 1980, enrolled in the Chinese language and literature department of the Central Institute for Minority Nationalities, Beijing, from which she graduated in 1985. The same year she volunteered to move to Tibet, where she served until 1998 as an editor for Tibet People's Press.

In her editorial work, Feng Liang has played a role in the publication of Chinese-language fiction on Tibet by a number of writers, both Han and Tibetan. In 1989 she edited the fiction anthology *xizang xiaoshuoji* (An Anthology of Tibetan Fiction), in which eight of the stories included in this present collection appear, among them her own "xunzhao shexiang" (In Search of Musk). She has edited a number of Tibetan writers' work, including Sebo's anthology *yuanxing rizi* (1991).

Her first fiction appeared in print in 1986. The author's original Yi name is Jihu Shini. For a time she continued to publish under that name, but her works now appear solely under the Han name "Feng Liang." Her collection of short stories *qingxu* (Dejection) appeared in 1995. In 1998 her novella *dishao* (A Low Fever) was published in the anthology *lingting xizang* (Listening to Tibet). The same year saw the appearance of her novel *xizang wuyu* (A Tale of Tibet). Her fiction generally portrays Tibet, whether urban or rural, as indistinguishable from urban or wilderness settings in the People's Republic of China.

In 1986 Feng Liang married the painter Zhai Yaohui. She gave birth to a daughter in 1992. In 1998 they moved to Beijing, where Feng Liang now works for the Chinese language editorial department of Nationalities Publishing Company (Minzu Chubanshe), a Chinese government publishing house for works by writers of minority nationalities.

Ge Fei

Ge Fei is the pen name of Liu Yong, born in 1964 in Dantu County, Jiangsu Province. In 1981 he enrolled in East China Normal Institute in Shanghai, where he remains today as a teacher of creative writing. He is married and has one child.

The region of the author's childhood, the lower Yangzi River valley, is the setting of many of his works. In some, which include his earliest published story, "ren kanbujian cao shengzhang" (People Can't See Grass Grow, 1987), the imagination overpowers the real world to portray reality in a dreamlike atmosphere. In other stories like "qinghuang" (Blue-Yellow, 1988), "hese niaoqun" (A Flock of Brown Birds, 1988), and "yelang zhi xing" (A Trip to Yelang, 1989) his narratives tend toward surrealism.

In a second group of stories from the same period, Ge Fei uses the historical setting of the tumultuous period prior to the founding of the People's Republic of China to create a kind of antihistorical fiction. In "mizhou" (The Mystified Boat), "danian" (New Year's Eve), and "fengqin" (Harmonium), a web of misunderstandings, conspiracies, and counterconspiracies enmesh the characters in a net of shifting points of view until history becomes the mere product of the interplay of contradictory perspectives, the result of caprice, with no possibility of genuine meaning. Ge Fei's major early works are collected in *mizhou* (The Mystified Boat, Beijing, Renmin Chubanshe, 1989).

In a third, smaller number of works, Ge Fei employs a traditional narrative line. One of these is "Encounter," his only venture, thus far, into the subject of Tibet. The story is the result of a two-month trip Ge Fei made there.

Ge Fei's works include two novels, *diren* (The Enemy) and *bianyuan* (The Border). His stories are collected in *ge fei wenji* (Ge Fei's Collected Works, Jiangsu Wenyi Chubanshe, three volumes, 1995).

Geyang

Geyang was born in 1972 in Dagyab, a small town in the Kham region of eastern Tibet, of Tibetan parents. In 1989 she entered Nanjing Meteorological Institute. She began publishing her fiction in 1996 and studied writing from 1996 to 1997 at the Lu Xun Institute in Beijing. While sharing the strong interest in Buddhism of Tibetan writers of the eighties, her work also shows the stylistic influence of the New Realism school of Chinese fiction of the nineties. Her first story, "xiaozhen gushi" (A Story of a Small Town), won the first annual Tibetan New World Literature Award. In 1998 she won the National Minorities Literature Award. Her stories and novellas include "tianzangshi" (The Sky Burial Master), "meng kaishi de difang" (Where Dreams Begin), "rang ai manman yongheng" (Let Love Slowly Persevere to Eternity), "linghun chuandong" (A Soul Passing through a Cave), and "wo shi chung de lasa pengyou" (I'm Chung's Friend from Lhasa). Geyang currently works for the Tibetan Meteorological Bureau and reads the nightly weather report on Lhasa television.

Ma Jian

Ma Jian was born in the port city of Qingdao, Shandong Province, in August 1953, the youngest of four brothers. He grew up in poverty in the years of the Great Leap Forward and the Cultural Revolution. In the Great Leap Forward famine, he and his family survived on a diet that included mice, toothpaste, leaves, and fish bones. "When I was little, I wanted to free all humanity when I grew up. It was only when I reached the age of thirty that I realized what I had to liberate was myself."

After completing school, Ma Jian became a photographer and reporter for a Beijing daily. He married and had a daughter. During this period, he was a devout Buddhist, chanted the sutras every day, and underwent the ceremony of aspersion. He has since given up Buddhism.

In 1984 he divorced his wife and married a Hong Kong resident. The next year, he gave up his job and began a journey through twenty different provinces of China, earning money along the way as a hairdresser and decorative painter. His purpose on this journey was "to search for popular culture and for myself." Photographs he took in various minority areas were exhibited in Guangzhou and Beijing with the "Anonymous Artists" group, and later published as *ma jian zhi lu* (Ma Jian's Journey, 1987). His travels took him, in 1986, to Tibet, where he spent three months, a stay that provided the material for *Stick Out the Fur on Your Tongue or It's All a Void.*

As the husband of a resident of Hong Kong, Ma Jian was able to move there in 1986, before the Chinese publication of *Stick Out the Fur on Your Tongue.* . . . This collection of five stories appeared in the prominent review *renmin wenxue* (People's Literature) in 1987, just as the Communist Party launched a movement against "bourgeois liberalism." On February 2, 1987, three *People's Daily* articles on *Stick Out the Fur on Your Tongue* . . . denounced Ma Jian for "sensationalistic language" and for describing characters who were solely "motivated by sexual desire and greed." The articles criticized the work for "grave harm to the brotherly solidarity of the nationalities,"—that is, in this case, between Han and Tibetans—and condemned it as an example of "the rise of bourgeois liberalism. . . ." Ma Jian was already in Hong Kong, safe from the storm but unable henceforth to publish in the People's Republic of China. Since the censoring of *Stick Out the Fur on Your Tongue* . . . Ma has published only in Hong Kong and Taiwan.

After moving to Hong Kong, he published his collection of stories *ni la goushi* (You Hunk of Dogshit, 1987) and the novel *si huo* (Confused Thoughts, 1989). The raw physical detail of *Stick Out the Fur on Your Tongue* . . . appears again in *lamianzhe* (The Noodlemaker, 1994). The folkloric element of *Stick Out Your Tongue* . . . is again evident in *jiu tiao chalu* (Nine Sideroads, 1995), a novel that describes the experiences of a group of urban youth sent down to the countryside to live among a tiny minority nationality in southwest China during the Cultural Revolution.

Ma Jian has also published a collection of essays, *rensheng banlu* (Life Companion, 1996). A second collection of his stories and novellas, *yuanpai* (Sign of Enmity), appeared in 1995. None of these works is available in the People's Republic of China, where his work subsequent to *Stick Out the Fur on Your Tongue* . . . remains almost entirely unknown.

Shortly after Hong Kong reverted to the control of Beijing in 1997, Ma Jian accepted an offer to teach Chinese at Ruhr University, Bochum, Germany. He now resides in London, England, where he continues to write.

Ma Yuan

Ma Yuan was born in Jinzhou, Liaoning Province, northeast China, in 1953. As a high school student he, like millions of other "educated youth," was sent to live among the peasants during the Cultural Revolution. His four years' experience working in the countryside provided him the material for "maozi" (The Cap,—later reprinted under the title "cuowu"—A Mistake). His metafictional style is already evident in this early story.

Ma Yuan returned from the countryside to continue his studies, first at Shenyang Railway Technology Institute, where he studied engineering, then at Liaoning University, where he majored in Chinese literature. On graduating from Liaoning University in 1983, he moved to Tibet. "I went to Tibet," he told the translator, "because I wanted to go someplace different from the rest of the world. I'm Chinese, I couldn't leave China. The most exotic place in China is Tibet. So I moved there."

Ma Yuan worked in Tibet as a reporter and editor. There he married the writer Feng Li (pen name Pi Pi). Their son was born in 1987. During the seven years he lived in Lhasa, Ma Yuan wrote the innovative stories that established his reputation. The novella *gangdisi de youhuo* (The Spell of the Gangtise Mountains) interweaves the lives of two young Han writers in Lhasa with tales they hear and with their fictional creations. The author strikes a different tone in the novella *xugou* (A Fiction), which explores the male attitude to the other—to woman and to alien races—in the tale of the narrator's love affair with a Tibetan leper. The calculated aura of mystery with which he surrounds Tibet in such stories as "youshen" (Vagrant Spirit) derives both from his extensive reading (in translation) of contemporary Western postmodernist fiction and his abiding interest in the Daoist master Zhuangzi. Many of his significant early novellas and stories on Tibet appear in *xihaitian fanchuan* (Sailboat in the Sky over the Western Sea), published in Lhasa in 1987. Ma Yuan also has written several metafictional novellas set in Han China, the most prominent of which is *jiusi* (Old Death), the narration of a rape entangled in a web of fictions.

In 1989 Ma Yuan developed heart problems from the effect of the Tibetan altitude. He returned to Liaoning, divorced his wife, and began working in television as host of the series *Wenxue Changcheng* (The Great Wall of Literature).

In 1992, after he received an invitation to attend a conference in the United States, officials of the Chinese government denied him a passport. It was during this period that Ma Yuan adopted the lifestyle that he follows to this day. He began to travel constantly back and forth over the length and breadth of China, spending time in Hainan Island, Guangzhou, Tibet, Beijing, and Liaoning. He attempted to start an advertising agency, which failed, but he continues to write freelance advertising today. After finally obtaining a passport to travel abroad, in the mid-1990s he briefly worked with a Chinese television crew in Holland.

Ma Yuan has also turned his hand to drama. His plays include *junmao* (The Army Cap), based on his early story "maozi," *guole yibainian* (A Hundred Years After), and *ai de jijie* (The Season of Love). In 1997 he published *lasa de xiao nanren* (The Little Men of Lhasa), a collection of his works from the 1980s, interrelated stories and novellas about a group of young Han and Tibetan artists in Lhasa. Ma Yuan's collected works, *ma yuan wenji*, appeared in four volumes in the same year, published by Zuojia Chubanshe (Writers' Publishers, Beijing).

Sebo

Sebo (pinyin equivalent, "Se Bo") is the pen name of Xu Mingliang, a Tibetan born in Chengdu, Sichuan Province, in 1956. His family subsequently moved to Fenghuang County, Hunan Province, an area of mixed nationality population: Tibetan, Miao, and Tujia minorities, as well as Han.

In 1973 he enrolled in medical studies at Liaoning Medical Institute, in Shenyang, Liaoning Province, northeast China. After graduation in 1975, when he was not yet twenty, he began practicing medicine in Motuo County, Tibet, later transferring to People's Hospital, Lhasa.

In 1982, he began to write fiction as well as critical essays. The next year, Sebo took a position as a literary editor with *lasahe* (Lhasa River) magazine. Throughout the mid-1980s, in stories published in various journals, he developed his own distinctive style. In addition to his fiction, he is also the author of essays and criticism. In 1988 he became fiction editor for *Xizang Wenxue* (Tibetan Literature). The next year he was appointed general secretary of the Tibetan Writers Committee. In 1990 he left this post to join the Tibetan Literary Association (Xizang Wenlian), to devote himself to the writing of fiction.

Sebo's most prominent works are structured according to a Buddhist conception of existence as an eternally recurring cycle. His representative stories include "yuanxing rizi" (The Circular Day), "huanming" (An Imaginary Cry), "zai zheli shangchuan" (Get the Boat Here), "zhudi, chuoqi he meng" (A Bamboo Flute, a Sob, and a Dream), "zuotian wanshang xiayu" (Last Night It Rained), and "chuanxiang yuanfang" (Heard from Afar), which won the Tibet Literature and Fine Arts First Prize. His novella *yongbuzhixi de he* (Eternal, Ceaseless River) also won a Tibetan literary award. His stories are collected in *yuanxing rizi* (The Circular Day, 1991).

The author's first marriage, in 1982, ended in divorce two years later. In 1991 he married Yang Xuemu, a manager with a medicine firm in Chengdu. The couple's son was born in 1993. In 1998 they moved back to Chengdu, where Sebo currently works with the Sichuan Provincial Literary Association.

Tashi Dawa

Tashi Dawa (pinyin equivalent, "Zaxi Dawa") was born in Batang County, in the Garze Tibetan Autonomous Prefecture of Sichuan Province, in 1959. His father is Tibetan, his mother Han Chinese, both Communist Party cadres. He describes himself as a Tibetan author who writes in Chinese.

At the age of ten Tashi Dawa began to move back and forth with his parents between Sichuan and Tibet. After graduation from Lhasa Middle School, he worked as a set designer and scriptwriter for the Tibetan National Drama Company. His first fiction appeared in 1979. Its depiction of Tibet's advance into the modern age attracted attention in official party circles. His novella *xizang yinmi suiyue* (Tibet: The Mysterious Age) and his story "xizang: xizai pishengjieshang de hun" (Tibet: A Soul Knotted on a Leather Thong) deal with Tibet's transition from Buddhism to modern technological culture. In 1986, the latter story won China's National Short Story First Prize.

Tashi Dawa cites as a major influence on his work the Chinese translation of *One Hundred Years of Solitude* and likens his writing to that of Gabriel García Márquez in its combination of realistic and nonrealistic details. In this way, he says, his stories are comparable to ancient Tibetan chronicles, which contain both factual history and mythical narrative. The magic of his fiction appears most strongly in such stories as "fengma zhi yao" (The Glory of a Wind Horse) and "sangzhong wei shui er ming" (For Whom the Bell Tolls).

In the eighties and early nineties, Tashi Dawa was by far the most prominent Tibetan writer in the People's Republic of China. "Tibet is a sensitive subject," he told the translator, "and I can't write everything I want." Well known in China for his portrayal of a Tibet on the verge of modernity, Tashi Dawa has been almost entirely ignored, in China at least, as an author who deals with Tibet's struggle for cultural survival and for justice. Neglect of these themes in his work may well be a result of deliberate camouflage on the part of the author, who obfuscates political implications beneath the complexities of his magic realism. The perplexing conundrums of time and space in "The Glory of a Wind Horse" cloak the implications of Ugyen's futile search for truth until the soldiers of the regime finally carry him away for execution. The magical time changes of "For Whom the Bell Tolls" cloak the allusion, in the battles between monks and the "government army," to the many battles over the past decade and a half between Buddhist monks and Chinese army troops.

Tashi Dawa's first novel, *saodong de xiangbala* (Turmoil in Shangri-la), was published in 1993. His major works are collected in *xizang yinmi suiyue* (Tibet: The Mysterious Age, 1996). In recent years he has been writing scripts for television. His recent Tibetan-language documentary film, *Barkhor, No. 16*, a film record of the events of a single day in a Communist Party neighborhood office in downtown Lhasa, has achieved acclaim in the Tibetan community around the world. Tashi Dawa now divides his time between Lhasa, Beijing, and Chengdu, where his parents still live. The author serves as chairman of the Tibetan Writers Association.

Yan Geling

Yan Geling was born in Shanghai and attended primary school there until the Chinese school system closed during the Cultural Revolution. In 1970, at the age of twelve, she entered the People's Liberation Army and served in ballet and folk dance troupes, officially stationed in Chengdu, Sichuan Province, but spending most of her time on the road with her troupe, performing at various military installations, including a total of eighteen months spent in Tibet.

The daughter of a writer, she herself began writing in 1979 as an army war correspondent covering the Sino-Vietnamese border war. After her discharge from the army with the rank of major, she moved to Beijing and published her first novel, *lüxue* (Green Blood, 1985), about her experiences as an adolescent girl soldier. In 1987, the novel won the ten-year prize as Soldier's Favorite Novel, awarded by her publisher, People's Liberation Army Publishing House. Her second novel, *yige nubing de qiaoqiaohua* (Whispers of a Girl Soldier, 1987) deals with the life of a young girl in the People's Liberation Army.

In 1988 Yan Geling earned a bachelor's degree in Chinese literature from Wuhan University. That same year, she was invited to visit the United States under the auspices of the U.S. Information Agency's International Visitors' Program. In 1989, she returned to the United States and studied at Columbia College, Chicago, from which she holds a master of fine arts in fiction writing. In that same year, she became a resident of the United States. She currently lives in Alameda, California.

Her novel *nüxing de caodi* (Female Grasslands, 1989) is the story of a group of girl soldiers among the Tibetan population of the grasslands of remote Qinghai Province. In this novel the author deals in a metafictional form with metaphysical themes. She has since published three more novels, all first published in Taiwan. *Caoxie quangui* (Straw-Sandaled Nobility, 1994) is the story of the decline and fall of a noble family, told from the point of view of their young peasant nursemaid. *Fusang* (Fusang, 1996) is the story of a Chinese prostitute in San Francisco in the 1960s, who eventually marries a white American; the book is currently being translated into English. *Renhuan* (Inner Space, 1998) is the story of the effect of the Cultural Revolution on the friendship of two men.

The author has published a number of collections of short fiction, including *shaonü xiaoyu* (A Girl Called Xiaoyu, 1993), *hai nabian* (Beyond the Ocean, 1994), *daotang he* (The River Flows Upstream, 1995), *fengzheng ge* (Kite Song, 1999), and *baishe* (The White Snake, 1999). Selections from among the stories of these five volumes appear in English translation in *The White Snake and Other Stories* (Aunt Lute Books, San Francisco, 1999).

Yan Geling has also published a collection of essays, *Bohemian Towers* (1999). Her collected works were published in five volumes by Bu Laohu (Cloth Tiger) Publishing, Beijing, October 1998.

Several of the author's works have been made into Chinese-language movies. *Xiuxiu: The Sent-Down Girl* (1997), based on her short story "tianyu" (Celestial Bath), was directed and produced by Joan Chen (Chen Chong). The film recounts the gradual destruction of a girl sent to the countryside during the Cultural Revolution and deals with the relations between Han Chinese and Tibetans. Yan Geling's script won the Golden Horse Award (Taiwan's equivalent of the Oscar) for best script adaptation. In all, the film won a total of seven Golden Horses, including Best Director, Best Actor, Best Actress, Best Picture, Best Music, and Best Original Song. *Xiuxiu* was selected for competition at the Berlin Film Festival, February 1998. It had its U.S. premiere at the San Francisco International Film Festival on April 25, 1998. Yan Geling has written a biography of the film's director: *chen chong qian zhuan* (Joan Chen: The Early Years, 1994).

The movie *Xiaoyu* (Little Yu), based on her story "shaonü xiaoyu" (A Girl Called Xiaoyu), won the prize for Best Picture at the Asia Pacific Film Festival, 1994. The film was directed by Sylvia Chang. Yan Geling's script won the award for Best Script. Like the novel *fusang*, this story deals with the theme of the abnegation of women.

Nothing but Male and Female, based on her short story of the same name, was made into a movie by Yanping Film Company of Taiwan, released in Asia in 1995. The movie tells the story of a girl who falls in love with her fiancé's brother, an invalid.

Yan Geling also wrote the script for *New World*, a twenty-six-episode series for Chinese TV, released in 1995 by China Central Television (Beijing), as well as a twenty-five-episode Voice of America radio series on American life, 1997. She is currently working on *Gold Coast*, a TV series for China Central Television on the lives of Chinese immigrants in the United States in the 1920s and 1930s.

Yangdon

Yangdon (pinyin equivalent, "Yang Zhen") was born to Tibetan parents in Lhasa on February 14, 1963. While still in her teens, she began publishing essays in Chinese in the Lhasa magazine *xizang wenyi* (Tibetan Literature and Arts). After graduation from high school, she entered China's most prestigious institution of higher learning, Beijing University, in the department of Chinese literature, from which she graduated in 1985. Yangdon then returned to Tibet, where she worked, until 1994, as an assistant editor of the periodical *xizang wenxue* (Tibetan Literature). In this magazine, in 1986, she published her first short story, "wanzi de bianyuan" (The Edge of the Hooked Cross), which was awarded a national prize in a competition for new minority writers in 1991. Through the 1980s she continued publishing works of short fiction in various journals, among them "wu xingbie de shen" (A God without Gender), which appeared in *xizang wenxue* in June 1988. This story, an exploration of gender roles in the experiences of a young nun, vividly depicts the beliefs and customs of Tibetan Buddhist monastic culture.

Yangdon expanded this story into her first novel, also entitled *wu xingbie de shen*, published in 1994. The novel expands the story's theme of the dialogue between Tibetan culture and Chinese culture, portrayed in the story in the relationship between the young nun and the Chinese servant. The Chinese press calls it the first novel written by a Tibetan woman. The novel has attracted critical attention in China and has been adapted into a twenty-episode television serial, *Lasa Wangshi* (Old Times in Lhasa).

Throughout the 1990s Yangdon published essays on various topics. In 1994 she returned to Beijing to work at the Chinese Center for Tibetan Studies, where she currently serves as an editor for the China Tibetan Studies Press.

Yangdon is married to Long Dong, a Han writer and editor who worked in Lhasa as assistant general editor of *xizang qingnian bao* (Tibet Youth Daily) and has himself published fiction on Tibet.

About the Translator

Herbert Batt was born in 1945 in Buffalo, New York, where he attended local primary and secondary schools. In 1967 he graduated with a B.S. in mathematics (maxima cum laude) from the University of Notre Dame. In 1975 he received a Ph.D. in English literature from the University of Toronto, specializing in Elizabethan drama.

In the late 1970s and 1980s he organized and managed Project CANOE, a charity that takes young people from the children's aid societies of Toronto on wilderness canoe trips in northern Ontario.

After teaching English at the University of Toronto, in the 1980s and 1990s he taught English for eight years in the People's Republic of China, where he began the study of Chinese literature. He subsequently taught English for eight years in Polish universities.

He began publishing his translations of contemporary Chinese fiction in 1995. His own fiction and poetry have appeared in a variety of journals and anthologies.

Asian Voices

Series Editor: Mark Selden

Tales of Tibet: Sky Burials, Prayer Wheels, and Wind Horses
    edited and translated by Herbert Batt, foreword by Tsering Shakya
Voicing Concerns: Contemporary Chinese Critical Inquiry
    edited by Gloria Davies, conclusion by Geremie Barmé
Comfort Woman: A Filipina's Story of Prostitution and Slavery under the Japanese Military
    by Maria Rosa Henson, introduction by Yuki Tanaka
Growing up Untouchable in India: A Dalit Autobiography
    by Vasant Moon, translated by Gail Omvedt, introduction by Eleanor Zelliot
Rowing the Eternal Sea: The Life of a Minamata Fisherman
    by Keibo Oiwa, narrated by Masato Ogata, translated by Karen Colligan-Taylor
Japan's Past, Japan's Future: One Historian's Odyssey
    by Ienaga Saburo, translated and introduced by Richard H. Minear
Red Is Not the Only Color: Contemporary Chinese Fiction on Love and Sex between Women
    edited by Patricia Sieber
Dear General MacArthur: Letters from the Japanese during the American Occupation
    by Rinjiro Sodei, edited by John Junkerman, foreword by John Dower
Unbroken Spirits: Nineteen Years in South Korea's Gulag
    by Suh Sung, translated by Jean Inglis, foreword by James Palais
Bitter Flowers, Sweet Flowers: East Timor, Indonesia, and the World Community
    edited by Richard Tanter, Mark Selden, and Stephen R. Shalom